Breaking Links

Razia Fasih Ahmad
A portrait by Iqbal Mehdi

To Mary

Razia F Ahmad.

1/13/2007

Breaking Links

RAZIA FASIH AHMAD

Introduction by
Asif Farrukhi

OXFORD
UNIVERSITY PRESS

OXFORD

UNIVERSITY PRESS

Great Clarendon Street, Oxford OX2 6DP

Oxford University Press is a department of the University of Oxford.
It furthers the University's objective of excellence in research, scholarship,
and education by publishing worldwide in

Oxford New York

Auckland Cape Town Dar es Salaam Hong Kong Karachi
Kuala Lumpur Madrid Melbourne Mexico City Nairobi
New Delhi Shanghai Taipei Toronto

with offices in

Argentina Austria Brazil Chile Czech Republic France Greece
Guatemala Hungary Italy Japan South Korea Poland Portugal
Singapore Switzerland Thailand Turkey Ukraine Vietnam

Oxford is a registered trade mark of Oxford University Press
in the UK and in certain other countries

© Oxford University Press 2006

The moral rights of the author have been asserted

First published 2006

ISBN-13: 978-0-19-597895-7
ISBN-10: 0-19-597895-1

Typeset in Goudy Old Style
Printed in Pakistan by
Print Vision, Karachi.
Published by
Ameena Saiyid, Oxford University Press
No. 38, Sector 15, Korangi Industrial Area, PO Box 8214
Karachi-74900, Pakistan.

Dedicated

To the Victims of War all over the world

Contents

	pages
Introduction	ix
List of Characters	xv
Prologue	1
Part One: Chapters 1–32	9

West Pakistan—Past and Present
Concept of National Integration
Friendship and Marriage

| Part Two: Chapters 33–89 | 149 |

Starting a New Life
The Changed Political Climate
Disintegration of Relationships
Broken Links

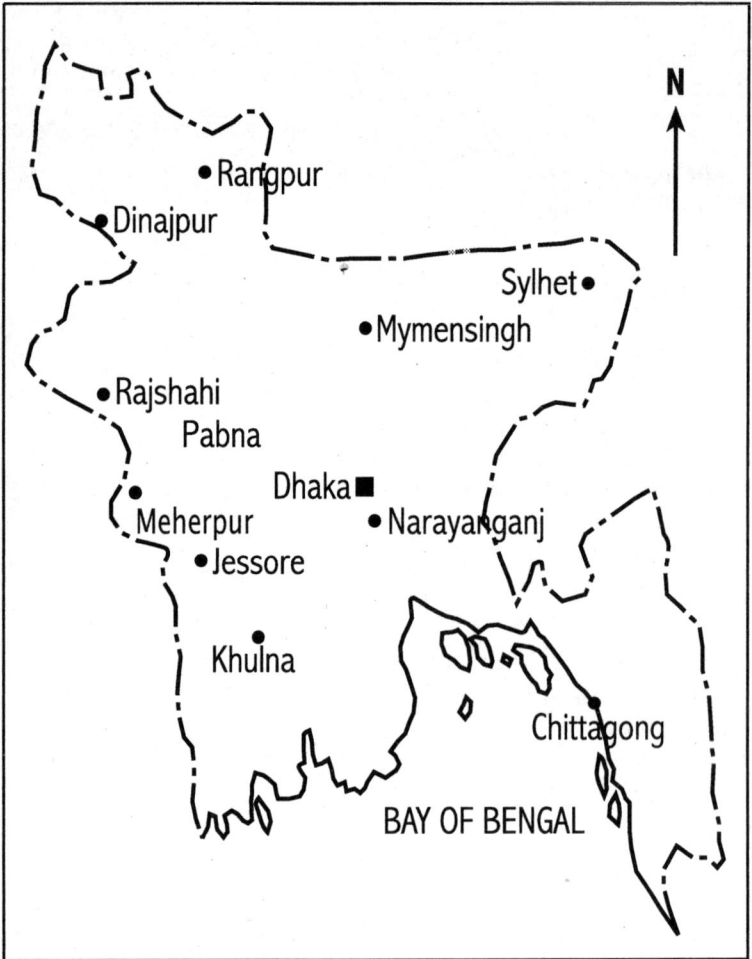

East Pakistan
(Now BANGLADESH)

Introduction

All happy countries are alike. Each unhappy country is unhappy in its own way. This book is set in one such country. We find it in a time of crisis, not unlike the Tolstoyan household with its unforgettable opening lines. There is, however, a difference in degree. Going beyond the taut beginning, we realize that a malignant secret is coming out, far more consequential than domestic squabbling or occasional and regrettable lapses in marital fidelity: for goodness knows how long, one partner has been cheating on the other, and becoming habitual in matters of deceit, things have come to a stage where the relationship has lost whatever affection or trust there once was. Now it's no more than a matter of throwing dust in the eyes of the other as little or nothing is being shared, resources are routinely usurped and instead of being ashamed when found out, the wrong-doing partner plays the jilted lover, weeping over broken links. This unhappy state is Pakistan in and around 1971, the period when the two unequal and distant 'wings', as they were euphemistically termed, of the relatively young nation-state which had been slowly but steadily drifting away from each other, finally came apart with a vengeance, and untold violence. This coming apart is at the centre of this novel by Razia Fasih Ahmad, the veteran Pakistani fiction writer. She has built her story around the looming crisis and the final hour of disintegration and dissolution.

A compelling tale of love gone awry through a grievous sense of 'honour' reaching out across generations, this is a novel dealing with 'History with a capital H'. A basic contextualization of this book within this history may be useful for its non-Pakistani readers, but even within the country, younger readers especially need to be reminded of what ensued, since Pakistan has not effectively addressed nor come to terms with the forces and factors which created an irreconcilable chasm and subsequently, the cataclysmic events terminating in the country's break-up as well as the emergence of Bangladesh as a sovereign state.

Such an assessment is still conspicuous by its absence in the country's curriculum and some textbooks that ascribe to the ever-popular and ubiquitous 'conspiracy' theory. Such self-righteous chest-beating effectively blocks the space for any assessment of what went wrong. Analyzing records of actual transmission from the state-controlled radio and television, Prof. Mehdi Hassan published a study (*Mashriqi Pakistan Ki Alehdigi Aur Zara-e-Ibhlagh*, South Asian Institute, Punjab University, Lahore, June 1977), which described in detail how these state bodies became instruments of short-term propaganda and failed to contribute to the national cause. He also includes a chapter on language and cultural issues, but as far as I know, the ramifications of such discussions have not been analyzed from a literary perspective. Hassan's book was also not as widely discussed as it deserved. A more detailed political analysis is offered in Hassan Zaheer's invaluable '*The Separation of East Pakistan: The Rise and Realization of Bengali Muslim Nationalism*' (OUP, 1994). Zaheer takes a longer view, stating that:

> The organic process of disintegration in modern nation-states arises from the accumulation of perceived grievances and a sense of injustice, repression, and hopelessness; it takes a long time to reach breaking-point.

This long process and the time involved seems to invite a novel. But hardly any novel was forthcoming. As a result of what may be termed a failure of the historical imagination, literary responses from Pakistan about these events have been 'sparse and casual' according to Prof M.U. Memon. This seems surprising when one compares it with the writings that emerged after the Partition of British India in 1947, including the well-known short stories of Manto and the poems of Faiz, as well as Qurratulain Hyder's '*Aag Ka Dariya*' (trans-created by the author into English as '*River of Fire*), among others. In his analytical study of creative writing in Urdu from Pakistan on this issue ('Pakistani Urdu Creative

Writing on National Disintegration: The Case of Bangladesh',
Journal of Asian Studies, vol. XLIII, No. 1, November 1983),
Memon came to the conclusion that:

> Pakistani men of letters, otherwise known for their strident
> espousal of social and political issues at home and abroad, have
> been less than forthcoming on the meaning of and consequences
> of their own national disintegration.

More than four decades after these events and almost two
decades after these words were written, Memon's verdict still rings
true:

> Contrary to the general sense of gloom and loss pervading the
> discussion by Pakistanis of their corporate disaster, the incident
> appears to have touched only a few; fewer still are those for
> whom it has had any deeper emotive significance at all, with
> ramifications in national morality. The country might just as
> well have written off the whole incident.

Perhaps it was this concept of the nation itself that was the
actual political fiction. Writing off—this comes easier to us than
rekindling passions that may not have entirely died down and may
require going against the grain. A few notable exceptions being
the short stories of Intizar Hussain (there are a number of others
in addition to 'Asir' cited by Memon) and Masood Ashar's
collection of stories 'Band Aankhon Par Donon Haath.' Sarwat
Hussein's poem 'Aik Insaan Ki Maut' (The Death of A Man)
strikes a collective note but with a personal conviction missing
from the verse. A noteworthy recent example is Sorayya Khan's
debut English novel 'Noor.' These are exceptions, however, rather
than the norm. In this condition of relative paucity, this remains
one of the few novels from Pakistan to reach out across the
inexpressible void in a serious attempt to address this gap.

Like most Urdu fiction-writers, Razia Fasih Ahmad began her
literary career with short fiction. She shot into prominence with
her novel 'Aabla Pa' which won a literary prize in 1965. Recently

reprinted and adapted for television, this remains her best-known work although she moved on to write an armload of books—novels, long and short stories, travelogues, plays, humour and even some poetry. Out of all her work, my heart goes out to the long story 'Tapti Chaon' (recently reprinted with another story in 'Tabeer') which delineates a remarkable woman against the backdrop of the early days of Pakistan in which relationships and values, the very outlook of people underwent major changes. Razia Fasih Ahmad migrated to the United States in the 1980s and has used this experience as a subject matter in some of her recent writing. Her latest work is 'Zakhm-e-Tanhai', a novel based on the lives of Charlotte and Emily Bronte, with whom she has felt an affinity of sorts.

Her most ambitious work is the novel entitled 'Sadiyon Ki Zanjeer'. A considerable time in the making, this novel resulted from her conscious decision to write about the historical reality of the major crisis that the country had faced. She researched the novel's background and talked to eyewitnesses in Pakistan as well as Bangladesh Sometime back when I had the occasion to write a profile of her as a writer, she spoke about the hard work that went into the making of this novel:

In Bangladesh, I stayed with a Bengali family. I met many people over there and came to know what was actually happening in different parts of the country. I visited the camps. I met people with different ideas including the Mukti Bahini people. I read the newspapers that were not available in Pakistan and read the books that were banned in Pakistan, so I was able to write about actual happenings. People who came from there told me that I have written a correct history of the events.

Strict adherence to facts may have become a limiting factor. 'Literary truth is one thing, historical truth another,' according to Mario Vargas Llosa, the great contemporary Latin American novelist. In his essay, 'The Truth Of Lies', he goes on to add, 'the reconstruction of the past in literature is almost always false in terms of historical objectivity.

Recounting her labour of love on the novel, Razia Fasih Ahmad also told me that she had to revise the novel four or five times and then she also added that she felt that she may have overdone her labour on the novel. Even then, more labour was to follow. The novel is now translated and rendered it into English by the author herself as 'Breaking Links'. In this process she has condensed the 662 pages of the original Urdu text into the present version. The story is pared down to the bare essentials, and while some of the richness in detail may have been lost, the swift narrative seems less laborious and is easier on the reader.

When I first read 'Sadiyon Ki Zanjeer' and reviewed it upon its first publication in 1988, I liked those parts of the novel in which the locale remained in the 'western wing', and included what seemed to me to be the author writing at her best, while the portions set in Bangladesh hung somewhat loose, weakly connected like the country's federal structure. I could not have foreseen then that the first few chapters of the novel, describing the angry husband's act of revenge against his wife, stemming from an outraged sense of honour, would strike a familiar note decades later as 'honour killing'—a phenomenon that has become an everyday occurrence in society today as Pakistan rapidly slides back into a feudal mind-set.

Now that this novel is being published in English, I am sure that it will find many new readers and I hope that it will open a new enquiry and debate on the unfortunate events it depicts. The novel's real value, of course goes beyond any attempt at historical objectivity, as in the words of Mario Vargas Llosa, 'literature recounts the history that the history written by the historians would not know how, or be able, to write...'.

It is in the narrative force and the power of the imagination that there is the final redemption for any novel. And it is for you to decide about this novel too as you turn the page to read on.

Asif Farrukhi

List of Characters

Major Characters

1. Qasim Khan   Ancestor of both Zari and Shams
2. Mukul   Qasim's wife from Bangdesh (Bengal). Shams is her descendant
3. Suzan   Qasim's second wife from the Northern Areas of Pakistan. Zari is her descendant
4. Shams   The main protagonist from East Pakistan
5. Zari   The main protagonist from West Pakistan
6. Shoshi   Daughter of Shams's stepmother from her first husband
7. Nargis   Mutual friend of Zari and Shams
8. Noor   Mutual friend of Zari and Shams
9. Ronjhu   Shams's stepbrother (leader of the Mukti Bahini)
10. Benu   An Urdu-speaking girl sympathetic to East Pakistanis
12. Mr Mirza   Benu's father (a refugee from Bihar, India settled in East Pakistan)
13. Mrs Mirza   Benu's mother (prejudiced against people of East Pakistan)
14. Ilyas   Benu's younger brother
15. Akbar Khan   Zari's father (Zari calls him Daji)
16. Guljan   Zari's mother
17. Omar Khan   Guljan's cousin, Akbar's closest friend (Zari calls him Chachaji)
18. Qudsia   Omar Khan's first love
19. Shahzore Khan   Qudsia's husband
20. Bara Khan   Shahzore Khan's father
21. Nasir Khan   Shahzore Khan and Qudsia's son
22. Aijaz   Nasir Khan's friend
23. John   An English tourist
24. Zeb Quadri   Omar Khan's wife in later years, has two sons from previous marriage

25. Ahsan   Zeb Qadri's son from first husband
26. Sarwat   Ahsan's wife, mother of Shezzy and Neely
27. Adnan   Zeb Qadri's younger son from first husband
28. Sinan   Adnan's son
29. Shezzy   Ahsan's elder daughter
30. Capt. Jawwad   He and Shezzy are joined in Nikah but not
                     married yet
31. Neely   Ahsan's younger daughter, Shezzy's sister
32. Khushal Khan   Zari's poor relative, and her friend from
                     childhood

Minor Characters

1. Major Tajammul   An officer from the Pakistan army
2. Abdul   A taxi driver
3. Suraj   Mirza's young and faithful servant
4. Muneer   Ilyas's friend
5. Kajal   Muneer's neighbour
6. Afzal   Muneer's cousin
7. Chaya   Kajal's sister
8. Misbah-ul-Haq   Ikram's father
9. Puttal   Ikram's sister
10. Melo   Ikram's younger brother
11. Major Zahir   Puttal's fiancé (East Pakistani officer in the
                     Pakistan army)
12. Maulana   A religious learned man from East Pakistan
13. Brig. Qadir   Leader of a section of the Mukti Bahini called
                     Qadir Bahini
14. Sanaullah   Nargis's father
15. Kamal   Nargis's brother
16. Jamal   Nargis's brother
17. Gul Sanobar   Qudsia's maid
18. Gulgoona   Zari's maid
19. Daisy   Shezzy's friend
20. Sajid   Guljan's brother
21. Jannat Bibi   Gulgoona's mother

Others

1. Zaman Khan   Omar's father
2. Mehro   Zaman Khan's sister-in-law (Guljan and Sajid's mother)
3. Aunt   Zari's relative (who takes care of Zari's ancestral home in Abbotabad)
3. Uncle   Aunt's husband
4. Naghma   Neely's friend

Prologue
Qasim Khan

The lake was full of brilliant pink lotus flowers, but the sky was overcast with dark clouds. The boatman rowed skillfully, without disturbing the green umbrella-like leaves that lay spread gracefully across the span of water. One of the queen's companions plucked a huge heart-shaped lotus-leaf, and holding it by the stem, stretched it like an umbrella over her head making her young and lively companions burst into laughter. The laughter rang like tinkling *cowries* from the *Pacheesi* game they played at the palace.

The young queen smiled charmingly. She was only fifteen years old but as graceful as a fresh lotus flower. Her body was as delicate as the lotus stem, her teeth as the purest of white *cowries*.

The boatman rowed the boat casually on the still waters of the lake and then moved towards a deep dark forest where bamboo, coconut, mango, and *jaman* trees were in abundance.

Qasim, a young man who had climbed a tall coconut tree to pick a coconut, viewed this striking scene and was fascinated by the young queen's beauty. All of a sudden Qasim heard a strange voice, very solemn and foreboding. 'The pyre is ready.'

The voice echoed through the coconut and bamboo forest traveling as far as the palace walls. He was stunned. He glanced at the boat, in which the young girls were having fun splashing water on one another. Apparently they had not heard the ominous voice.

Qasim got down from the vantage point preoccupied with what he had heard. He asked his fellow soldiers if they had heard it, but none seemed to have. Anything can happen in this strange country called Bangdesh, Qasim thought.

Qasim had arrived in this part of India as a soldier with Bakhtiar Khilji all the way from Turkey. Khilji's army had captured many provinces in India and then had invaded this eastern province of Bangdesh. There were only seventeen other cavalrymen. These tall, sprightly Turk riders had traveled so fast that they had left the rest of the army behind and had crossed the Talyagarh pass. Mistaken for horse traders they were allowed into the palace without suspicion. Once inside they had drawn their swords, attacked, killed, and created a panic. They had met with no resistance whatsoever. The old King Laxman Singh, who had been eating supper, had jumped out of the rear window of his palace into the river and escaped in a boat to Jagannath. By the time the rest of the army had arrived, the palace had already been captured. The King's soldiers and guards had surrendered. The eighteen soldiers had conquered the Sen capital of Nari.

After that, Bakhtiar Khilji moved on and conquered Dinajpur, in the North, and established a post at Devkot. Qasim was with him there. But when Bakhtiar Khilji went on a military expedition to Tibet, Qasim was unwell and couldn't accompany him. After recovering from his sickness, Qasim set out to wander through the mysterious landscape of this region.

The country was heaven and hell at the same time. It was full of beautiful trees, flowers, fruits and colourful birds, and flowing rivers, streams and lakes. It was also inhabited by elephants, tigers, cheetahs and venomous snakes that roamed everywhere unhindered. Qasim traveled far and wide to capture the soul of this country, galloping on his splendid mare. Fortunately, the weather was extremely pleasant at the time. Since he had very little provisions for the journey, he planned to settle down at one place at times but somehow kept moving on. There was plenty of fish and fruit available for his needs.

Soon, the rainy season began. Dark, threatening clouds rolled ceaselessly overhead and burst into endless showers. Lightning flashed and the clouds thundered. He took shelter in an abandoned hut, but rainwater dripped through countless holes in the ceiling. Outside was one big expanse of water.

When Qasim came out of his hut early the next morning he saw that, struck by a falling tree, his mare had died. The fields were submerged in water. In some places only the tops of the trees could be seen above the water level. The farmers had set out in boats to survey their rice and jute fields. To Qasim it looked like the end of the world, but he was surprised to see that there was no panic among the people. His few belongings were either washed away or soaking wet. Up until now he had viewed this land very differently, and was depressed to see this paradise devastated. But he soon realized that this destruction was taken with stoic resignation by the people. During the rainy season it would often rain continuously for hours, sometimes for days and weeks, and life would go on.

With mosquitoes everywhere, soon Qasim came down with malaria. A family living nearby gave him boiled rice, milk and vegetables twice a day even though their own supplies were scarce. The grandmother, a native of Kamrup, which was known as a centre for black magic, came to treat him. Qasim soon recovered under her care.

Qasim wanted to leave the country, but its soft and sticky soil seemed to cling to his feet and he found it very hard to shake it off. The indigenous fruits were so full of juice and the native language so sweet, that he kept postponing his day of departure.

Then, on an extremely hot day, a snake bit Qasim. The grandmother was called immediately but before she could come to treat him, her granddaughter, Mukul, laid him on golden jute, put her mouth to the bite, sucked the venom from his burning flesh and spat it out. Mukul kept him awake by talking to him and bidding her younger brothers and sisters to beat on drums to make a noise so Qasim would not sleep and he was thus saved.

After that deadly accident, Qasim felt that he was obliged to ask for Mukul's hand in marriage for there was no other way he could repay the family. He also liked her—she was so soft and tender and evidently in love with him. On her wedding day, Mukul wrapped herself in a new *sari* and adorned herself with flowers and seashells. Her tanned skin was very smooth and her eyes sparkled like stars. Her arms were thin and delicate, and her hands tiny, yet those hands toiled all day long.

Qasim started wearing a *lungi*, like the local people, and took to drinking coconut milk direct from the coconut. He learnt their language but the Bengali language he spoke, blended with his native Persian, was as strange as the union of the tall, fair Qasim to tender, dark Mukul.

Grandmother doted on Qasim. She knew that he was a soldier and that it was hard for him to become a farmer like most of the men in that region. He could not stand for hours in knee-deep water in the fields to sow paddy. She thought it would be better for him to learn magic from her and practice medicine. She started instructing him in black magic and medicine like mixing potions with ingredients such as nails of tortoises, blood of crows, teeth of crocodiles, feathers of bats, bile of a black dog and brain of an owl.

Qasim did not believe in any of that humbug. But the local people could never really shake off those age-old superstitions any more than he could forget the cool, dry climate of his country. He still craved the grapes, apples, pears and apricots of his country. He constantly compared them with local fruits. One day, grandmother said to him, 'If you love something, never compare it with anything else.'

She was right. The inhabitants of this region never compared their land with any other. If it was heaven, it was theirs; if it was hell, it was theirs too. The floods and tempests to them were phenomenon as natural as the rising and setting of the sun. But for Qasim the rains and floods were a tragedy that upset him. He had set out with the ambition of rising to the rank of a general in Bakhtiar Khilji's small army. His inner voice kept reminding him that this land was never his destination.

At last, one day, he decided to go back to Turkey. He did not tell anyone of his plans and started the journey as if he were going on the usual tour of the province.

* * *

The day Qasim began his journey was ominous. Just before his departure, Mukul's brother Shaupin sneezed and Grandmother made the mistake of calling him back, to give him his lunch; he had hardly gone a few paces when a snake emerged from the swaying bamboo forest and crossed his path.

Qasim reassured himself that he did not believe in these omens and moved on. When he reached the forest where he had first seen the lake full of lotus flowers and the young queen sailing in the royal yacht with her friends, he recalled that beautiful scene again. To his amazement he again heard those fateful words echoing through the forest 'The pyre is ready'. It came from the bank of the river, filling the entire atmosphere. This time a farmer confirmed that the call was real. The King had died that night and his queen was to die with him on the burning pyre. The fuel for the pyre was collected from the bamboo forest. Dried grass and *sandalwood* were added to the fuel. Pure clarified butter made from cow's milk was poured over the planks. The breeze carried the fragrance of incense throughout the entire region. In the meantime, maids prepared the queen for *sati*. Her hair, dark as storm-clouds, was strewn with pearls. A perfumed ointment mixed with flour and oil, was rubbed on her tender body and lines of *kajal* were drawn across her lotus-like eyes to enhance their beauty.

Qasim climbed a coconut tree to watch the scene. People who surrounded the queen gave her messages to give to their loved ones in Heaven. She blessed them and then sat on the pyre with her husband's head in her lap, and with a roll of drums, the pyre was lit. He recalled that *sati*, an Indian ritual performed in the pre-Vedic period was only symbolic and the widow would lie beside her dead husband for just a moment to declare that she was faithful to him to the end. Then the man who would want to marry her would ask her to get up by taking hold of her hand.

Up in the coconut tree, Qasim waited anxiously to see the lucky person who would come forward to rescue the queen. No one did. As the flames rose higher and were about to lick her splendid long hair, Qasim climbed down from the tree determined to save her. But the royal guards stopped him from going any further and the queen was burnt with the king.

* * *

Qasim Khan continued his journey and after a few months reached North-West India. His plan was to cross the Khyber Pass and enter Afghanistan. He continued his journey towards the mountain ranges of the North, till he came to a place surrounded by high mountains on all sides. At the center was a valley, and below on the top of a low hill, three *chenar* trees stood with their heads joined together. Qasim recognized this to be the place he had dreamed of a few days ago. Convinced that this place was destined for him he built a small hut here and spent his time in prayer and writing. In due course, his name spread far and wide. People from far off regions came across the deep valley to become his devotees, and Qasim came to be respectfully known as *Miyan Sahib.*

He usually sat in a tiny mosque, which he had built with stones, and taught the people how to read and write. One day, four men brought a very sick young girl to him. When *Miyan Sahib* looked at her, he remembered the queen he had seen in Bangdesh, lying on the pyre with her husband, and indeed, there was some resemblance between the two. *Miyan Sahib* put his fingers on her pulse. The girl's companions knew that she had died on the way. *Miyan Sahib* gave her some medicine, prayed to God and sprinkled the clear water of the nearby stream over her face. The girl slowly revived.

The relatives of the girl had nothing to offer to *Miyan Sahib* for his miraculous treatment. *Miyan Sahib* was also unwilling to charge them in return. When the parents insisted upon his accepting a token of gratitude, *Miyan Sahib* asked for the girl's hand in marriage. This was how Souzan Jaan became his wife and how this place where, according to popular belief, he had given the girl a new life, was called *Miyan Dum,* meaning 'Miyan's breath.'

Souzan, dressed in a spotted loose cotton *peshwaz,* did all the hard household chores just as Qasim's first wife Mukul had done. He often thought of asking Souzan whether she was happy with a man twice her age. But in the midst of so much activity he would forget just as he had forgotten about Mukul and the magic land of Bangdesh. Souzan bore him three pretty children. The children addressed their father as *Miyan Sahib* like everybody else.

He taught his children, along with the other children who came from the surrounding villages crossing hills and dales.

The strange thing was that the strange voice he had heard in Bangdesh still echoed in his ears sometimes. He heard that same sound in the stormy night when Souzan died giving birth to their fourth child. Very early in the morning, while he was going down the valley to fetch a mid-wife, a sound rustled through the pine trees that swayed in the wind to say, 'The pyre is ready.' When he made his way back to his cottage with the mid-wife, Souzan, after delivering a boy, had already breathed her last.

This time *Miyan Sahib's* miracle did not work. He arranged her funeral prayer soon after the regular morning prayers and buried her beside his hut. Their newborn also died soon after, and was buried beside his mother.

The people from the mountains took good care of their graves and planted shady trees over them.

* * *

Mukul waited for Qasim. The years passed and Qasim did not return. One day, weeping, she said to her grandmother, 'I'm sure he isn't coming back. He used to tell me that he hears voices calling him from afar. I knew that one day he would leave never to return.'

Grandmother replied, 'Daughter, Qasim was not like us and we were quite different for him. That is why we were attracted to him and he to us. But those foreigners are like birds. They keep moving. We are like lotus flowers that bloom only in deep waters. They do not understand our ways, we don't understand theirs, as a bird would never understand a lotus flower living happily in a lake, and the lotus flower would not want to fly. Our roots are buried deep in our land and this is our destiny.'

Mukul, burying her face in her grandmother's lap, sobbed bitterly. 'Yes, Grandmother. You are right. Those foreigners do like many things about our country, but then there are a lot of things they are not fond of. For us, this land is like our mother, whether she scolds us or caresses us, she will always be our mother. We can never think of deserting her.'

'That's true, my child,' consoled her grandmother, 'but you should have told him that you were carrying his child in your womb. The children are the heaviest chains that bind the parents together. It's hard even for a man to break this chain.'

'Yes, I should have, but I was too naive to know that I was pregnant at the time,' Mukul said.

Her grandma said, 'The soft sticky clay of this country is stuck to his feet and I'll use my magic. He might come back some day.'

'Yes, Grandma,' Mukul said, 'if not him, someone from his successors may visit this country some day, a few centuries later.'

She was right. Zari, who was Miyan Sahib's descendant, came there after many centuries with Shams, who was also his descendant from his first wife Mukul.

PART 1

West Pakistan—Past and Present
Concept of National Integration
Friendship and Marriage

1

When Omar reached Topi, their village in the Hazara district, from Aligarh, his cousin Akbar, came to see him. Akbar was younger than Omar but called him *yar*. Their friendship was ideal. They were sitting outside the big mansion of Omar's father. The servant had just brought two huge glasses of *lassi* for them. The weather was mild. They could hear the murmur of the Indus River, which flowed not very far from the mansion.

Akbar never missed an opportunity to make fun of Omar about Qudsia whom he called Omar's girlfriend.

'I have read those stories about your ancestor, Qasim Khan,' Akbar said. 'And I know that it is in your blood to fall in love with beautiful women. It's not your fault.'

'Yes, you're right.' Omar said laughing.

'So, you are going to marry Qudsia.'

'I don't know. She is only a child.'

'You are not that old either. You're a handsome guy like your ancestor. They say you should catch them young.'

'I think it's too early. Let our country be independent first. Then I'll think about the bond of marriage.

'Why don't you talk to your mother about her? Just let her know that you're interested in her.'

'The problem is that my father and Uncle Hayath are miles apart in their ideas. Father is a disciple of Khan Abdul Gaffar Khan. His sympathies are with the Congress, Uncle and I support the Muslim League. My father is worried that his son is going astray and adopting the ways of uncle.'

'So what, if your father and your uncle don't agree on their political views?'

'There are a few other differences. The foremost is that Uncle Hayath went to Aligarh for his education and married a girl outside his clan. After he got commissioned in the army and started teaching in the Military Academy at Dehra Dun, he adopted the western culture. His wife doesn't wear a veil and his daughter is studying in an English school. In my father's opinion, that's a family disgrace.

'This could be a serious matter.' Akbar said, 'cultural differences are more important for us than political ones.'

'Yes, Uncle Hayath dare not take his unveiled, liberated wife to his village. That is why he is cut off from the entire family. In order to bring him back to the family, Father had suggested that he should marry his younger brother's widow. Uncle Hayath hated the idea. Being in the British Army how can he have a second wife!'

'I know you went to Dehra Dun just before coming to Pakistan? Did you shake hands with Qudsia?' Akbar asked mischievously.

'Yes, I did,' Omar replied cheerfully. 'Listen, this time she looked more beautiful than ever. Every now and then, her image comes to my mind—her elegance, her looks, her clear crystal laugh. Now she moves among the English girls, cycling along the neat and clean roads of Dehra Dun.'

'With all these *questionable* qualifications will she be acceptable to your family?'

'That's what I'm afraid of.' Omar said, 'I'm waiting for the right moment.'

Before Akbar could give any more advice, a servant came with the message that Omar's father wanted to see him immediately. It was not very often that his father wanted to talk to him and hardly ever in urgency. He stood up guessing what his father might want to talk to him about. Akbar left immediately sensing that there was something important going on in the family and Omar went inside the house to his father.

* * *

Omar's father was sitting in a chair in his room with a *hukkah*. Omar said *salam* to him. He answered and motioned him to take a seat.

'What I want to say to you...', Omar's father removed the *hukkah* from his lips and began to talk but started puffing on his *hukkah* again.

Omar sensed that his father's lengthy prelude could mean that there was something disturbing about whatever he wanted to say.

'Yes, Father,' Omar said, as though trying to encourage him.

'This is very important,' Omar's father began, 'but there is no need to be emotional about it.'

Omar became tense. 'It is now a year since your Uncle Meher died. Now we must seriously think about what we can do for his widow and his children.'

Omar thought the problem might be managing their vast business till the children grew up. Maybe his father wanted him to take up that responsibility and give up his studies. He started preparing strong arguments in his defence.

His father sucked deeply at his *hukkah* and said, 'Rahmath Bibi, your aunt, is still young as she was twenty years junior to your uncle. Without a husband it will be very hard for her to manage the property and take care of children. That is why it is your duty,' he hesitated a little, stretched his hand towards the *hukkah* again as if for solace, then withdrew it instantly and said, 'to marry her.'

Omar felt as if the waves of the river Indus had rushed all over him. His head began to spin. Did he hear correctly?

'Marry my aunt?' He asked in a feeble voice.

'It is a tradition in our family. She is no blood relation to you. Besides, we can't allow our brothers' property to go to the winds. I have asked you to marry her because she is young and beautiful. I have already thought about it. She comes from a good family.' He took a puff again and changed his tone of voice.

'Don't say anything to anybody about our conversation. Think it over for a couple of days.' His tone became more and more severe.

'But...' Omar began.

'Now you can go.'

Omar stood up and planting his feet firmly on the ground, spoke with great poise. 'Father, I could never even dream of such a thing. I'd appreciate if you forget that you ever mentioned the subject to me. She is your sister-in-law and my aunt. Taking care of her property and supervising her children is our joint responsibility. We should do that in any case.'

His comments made Omar's father furious. 'That was why I told you not to be emotional about it.' He tried to control his temper. 'I told you that I don't want an answer now.'

His face was still red with anger. 'You don't know the traditions. She was only related to us through Meher. After his death she can leave us and take all that belonged to my brother with her including the acres of land and the children who are our blood. She can re-marry and disgrace our name. She can squander our money and can give it to a stranger. So think about it with a cool head. Now you can go.'

Omar stood up and left with a very sour taste in her mouth. In the back verandah, Omar saw Guljan playing quietly with her dolls. His father's proposal was so bizarre! He, a twenty-year-old, should become Sajid's and Guljan's father? Ridiculous! He would never allow that they call him father instead of brother.

When coming to the new country of Pakistan, and to their ancestral village in the Hazara district, Omar first thought that he would be able to go back to Aligarh after the riots were over, but soon he and everyone else who had been thinking of going back, knew that it would be impossible.

2

Rahmath didn't realize at that time what the effects of her rebellion would be. She came from a wealthy family and thought that she could manage without her husband.

She didn't know that although widows didn't wear collars around their necks like slaves and were not branded, they were expected to be completely obedient to their in-laws. Sajid and Guljan, Rahmath's children, couldn't understand the changes in their lives either. They could not figure out why their eldest Uncle, Zaman showed them so much affection after their father had died. He visited his sister-in-law every day, consoled her and made big plans for the children's future. But long before those plans were put into practice, his attitude towards them suddenly changed. He did not even want to talk to his sister-in-law and treated the children so curtly that they shrunk back from him with fear.

Then, Uncle Zardar started visiting them regularly. He brought gifts for them and took them to parks for picnics. Sajid and Guljan realized that Uncle Zardar also, like uncle Zaman Khan, occasionally whispered something to their mother that made her face turn red in anger. Even Uncle Zardar's favours didn't last long, and gradually, on the pretext of getting her rooms remodeled Rahmath was sent to a dilapidated part of the house. She was never asked to come back. Occasionally, she got messages that her crops were not doing well. They were either destroyed by rain, hailstorms, or frost. Her sugar mills were closing down one by one because of lack of sugarcane production.

She had closed the doors of compassion upon herself by refusing to marry her husband's brothers. She had no friends to whom she could go. There was no way she could knock at the door of justice without a man's help. Getting the cue from the family, the servants started neglecting Rahmath and her children giving them leftovers and insufficient food.

Rahmath wove her dreams about the future of her children especially around her son. She dreamed that Sajid would grow into an educated young man. One day he would demand his share of the property and then all their sufferings would be over. Omar Khan, son of her husband's brother, was the only person on their side. He had often told Sajid's father in the past that he would take him to Aligarh for his education. On such occasions Guljan would ask, 'And what about me, cousin? I want to be educated too.'

Omar knew that her father and uncle would never allow a girl from their family to go to a school, so he would say, 'Don't worry, we'll employ an English governess for you.' Unfortunately, before employing the English governess to teach Guljan, her father died and Omar could not do anything about it. But Omar kept his promise about Sajid. After his uncle's death, when he was going back to Aligarh, Omar said to his father, 'I want to take Sajid with me to Aligarh. If you could send a little more money, we'd manage.'

Omar's father agreed. He had never been to a college or a university. He thought that Omar was taking Sajid to attend to his personal needs. He also thought that separation from Sajid would be a fitting punishment for his mother. Guljan stayed home and was brought up an ignorant, conceited, and arrogant girl like the other girls of her family. The aunts told Guljan that her mother had chosen this life of misery and distress for her children. Believing them, Guljan thought that her mother did not care for her, so she spent less and less time with her mother and more and more time with her aunts and cousins.

3

Qudsia emerged from the long veranda of her bungalow and stretched out in a chair to read a book in the pleasant November breeze of Risalpur. Tiny orange training planes circled the sky. It was only when one of the planes did not get the 'all clear' signal from air control and suddenly shot up into the sky with a scream of protest that Qudsia looked up. She knew that her brother Obaid was among the young cadets flying in one of those planes.

Omar stood at the garden gate watching Qudsia for some time. Suddenly, Qudsia turned and looked in his direction. She rose silently from her chair and came to him. Omar told her that he had been to Swat on a picnic and wanted to pay her family a visit on his way back home. Qudsia received him courteously, escorted him in and announced him to her mother. Omar noticed that she had grown quite tall, still more beautiful, and she behaved like a young lady. He didn't dare offer his hand for a handshake.

Qudsia's studied at the Convent School and Omar was sure that she must be the favorite of the nuns who taught there. The nuns liked beautiful and intelligent girls, and Qudsia was a good student.

That night they were having a Guests' Night in the Officers Mess. Usually, officers' children were not invited to Guests' Nights. They were only invited for Christmas and other special occasions. But this time, because a General from the British Army was visiting Risalpur with his family, it was designated a special night and the children of other officers were also invited. Colonel Hayath invited Omar too.

Obaid, Qudsia's brother, was scheduled to fly that night too. So he came out from his room in his green flying uniform, and bidding good-bye to everybody, was about to leave when Mrs

Hayath called him to her side and stroking his head gently, said loudly 'Fi-amanullah,' meaning 'I entrust you to God.'

* * *

Omar, suitably dressed for the party, came out and sat in one of the chairs on the lawn. They family waited for Qudsia to come out.

The night had begun to dampen with dew. The tall limbs of Eucalyptus trees on the edge of the compound wall swayed in the wind. Slowly the moon rose and the sound of music emerged from the mess.

Qudsia came out wearing an ankle-length black velvet shirt with golden threads. To Omar she looked like a moonbeam glimmering among the dark clouds.

'Come, let's go,' said Colonel Hayath. The Mess was a few paces away. Passing along the small stretch of parade ground, they entered the spacious room through the entrance on Flag Staff Road. A few guests had already arrived. British officers and their wives and smart Pakistani women and men stood in small groups, talking to each other. The women who couldn't speak English and were not accustomed to such gatherings sat on the sofas looking like decorative cushions.

Qudsia and Omar were introduced to the General's children. They instantly made a separate group and vanished into the building. Waiters moved about efficiently with trays of snacks and drinks. Most of the young officers had besieged the bar. After a lengthy session of gossiping, drinking and dancing, dinner was announced. They ate in the oak-paneled room and after dinner, the guests once again separated into smaller groups. A few went out, others stayed behind to smoke cigarettes and cigars and chat. The bridge addicts hid in the card-room behind closed doors. The band started playing soft tunes as the night advanced.

Omar asked Qudsia to show him around the mess. A few other young men who were visiting for the first time accompanied them. Every room was named after the colour of its decor. In the blue room, along with blue carpets and curtains facing the hearth, were two huge vases and a beautiful ivory-engraved screen from China, belonging to the Ming Dynasty. In another room, a lot of heads of Marco Polo sheep hung from the wall with plaques marking the dates on which they were killed. The sounds of the music came in with the breeze from outside.

The wind had become damp and chilly so most of the ladies had gone inside the building. But Mrs Hayath was still sitting out in the open. The telephone rang somewhere in the Mess and intuitively Qudsia felt that there was something wrong.

'Come, let's go out,' Omar urged Qudsia, and for a moment held her little white hand. It was as soft as a flake of cotton flying in the air. Qudsia did not resist. Omar wished to open his heart to her, but felt that it was not the right moment because there were other people there. He couldn't hold her hand for long. He let it go slowly. They had scarcely walked out of the Mess into the garden when they heard an agonizing cry.

The band stopped suddenly. An unnatural silence fell over the hall. Leaving Omar behind, Qudsia ran in. The other guests rushed about through different doors of the Mess. The waiters, trays in hand, also came in.

'What happened?' Qudsia asked.

'A plane has crashed.' she heard somebody say. Her heart skipped a beat. Tearing through the crowd she ran to her mother who was lying unconscious on the sofa. Her face was so pale it seemed as if the last drop of blood had been drained from her body. Obaid's plane had crashed during the night training.

4

It was nearly daybreak when Obaid's coffin was brought in front of the veranda of Colonel Hayath's bungalow. There was a thin fog and everything was moist with last night's dew, as if the trees, the grass and flowers had been crying throughout the night. The birds hidden in the bougainvillea and jasmine over the pillar of the veranda seemed to be weeping too.

The coffin was already sealed. Nobody had the heart to tell them that it was impossible to separate the plane's burnt debris from his charred bones. So they gave them a few lame excuses, and despite Qudisa and her mother's pleas, the lid of the coffin was not opened. Soon the coffin was taken to the graveyard to be buried with full military honours.

Omar had planned this day to declare his love to Qudsia and to give a subtle hint to Uncle Hayath that he wanted to marry his daughter. But time did not favour him. Qudsia and Mrs Hayath were heartbroken. Hayath was silent as a statue. All the brothers and sisters of Colonel Hayath, including Omar's parents, came to offer condolences on Obaid's death and stayed in Risalpur for a few days.

A few days later he asked his mother to make a formal proposal of marriage, but she opposed it tooth and nail. Besides the ideological and cultural differences, she made a shocking revelation that completely confounded him.

'Qudsia is not the innocent virgin you think she is. I am afraid I'll have to tell you something that I didn't want to. Qudsia was kidnapped by the *Sikhs* during the riots in India and her father was able to get to her after three days.'

'Impossible!' Omar said. 'Someone has given you wrong information, Mother. She is the daughter of an army officer and they had been living in a very protected area.'

'You don't know a thing.' His mother said crossly, 'Nobody talks about such things, but these are open secrets. It happened when Qudsia and her mother were not in Dehra Dun but visiting her grandparents. During the riots there, girls were forced out of the houses. Qudsia was among them. When Hayath came to know about it, of course he managed to rescue her but what had happened in the meantime nobody knows and nobody dare ask them.'

Omar treated this news as no more than a rumor. He approached his father. His shrewd father had never liked Hayath and hated the idea of having a modern, fashionable girl as his daughter-in-law. He told Omar that this was not a suitable time for a proposal of marriage when the family was grieving for their only son, and the mother was sick with grief.

Moreover, Qudsia and Omar were both very young and the marriage proposal could easily be postponed for a year or so.

A suit was filed on Sajid's behalf against his Uncle to get his share in his father's property. Omar was on his Aunt Meher's side and Sajid won the case. It was at this time that Akbar was entranced by Guljan's beauty just as Omar was fascinated by Qudsia's charms.

Then, suddenly Omar was sent to England to study. A few months later he got news from home about the death of Qudsia's mother. She could not handle the death of her beloved son. He wrote a letter of condolence to Colonel. Hayath and asked permission to correspond with Qudsia but did not get an answer.

5

At the age of fifteen Qudsia was offered a proposal of marriage from Shahzore Khan. The Mother Superior of her Convent School had opposed the marriage strongly. Qudsia was an exceptionally intelligent girl. Marrying her at such a tender age would ruin her, but Qudsia's father, decided that she should get married to the boy. Qudsia's mother was dead, and he was suffering from lung cancer and wanted to see Qudsia settle down before he was gone.

He personally went to see Shahzore's family and accepted the proposal. He told Qudsia that the family was rich and well established. The boy was educated and handsome. The only drawback he could find was that the family was a little old fashioned, even rustic, but it didn't matter because only some years back his own father was as conservative and old fashioned as anybody else. It was only a matter of time. He had consoled her.

Even then, she had not agreed to the proposal. She had told her cousins that she did not want to get married in the first place, and not to Shahzore Khan in any case. But it was put down to nerves. Qudsia thought of opening her heart to her father, but he was too sick to be bothered. It would break his heart to see his daughter defy him.

So Qudsia married Shahroz Khan. She felt an invisible chain around her neck and felt it tightening more and more everyday. The men made all the decisions and the women were informed of only those which concerned them. Shahzore did not believe in women's liberation. He had married her in the hope that she would gradually come around to his way of thinking.

Qudsia's father had gone to England after her marriage for his treatment. She wanted to go to see him but was not given permission by her husband and father-in-law. Her wish to have a house built in Peshawar for her was denied. Her father had died during his operation.

Omar was in London busy with his studies. But he kept thinking of Qudsia as his future wife. One day he got a letter from his mother announcing Qudsia's marriage. She had written that Qudsia's father was dying and wished her to get married right away. Fortunately, she received a proposal of marriage from Shahzore, a boy from a very rich and respectable family.

Omar felt betrayed, as if his most valued treasure had been given to someone else in his absence. He spent the entire day strolling restlessly on the embankment of the Thames.

He remained sad and depressed for days. After losing her, he was very angry with himself and everybody else. A few days later came the news of his Uncle Hayath's death.

Gradually a light mist overtook the names of Qudsia and Uncle Hayath. Dehra Dun became a city of distant memories. So did Risalpur where, for the last time, Omar had seen Qudsia dressed in black, like a candle melting with grief over her brother's death.

6

When Omar came back from England, memories were revived. He was not happy with his mother and sisters who had no knowledge of how Qudsia was doing.

'We're the only relations she has.' He said. 'How could you be so heartless as never to go to see her or invite her?'

They replied that it was she who never came to see them after her wedding. When Omar insisted they agreed to go with him to visit her.

When they reached the big house on top of the hill close to the river Omar's mother and sisters were escorted to the ladies apartments. Omar was asked to come in the grand drawing room where he talked with Shahzore and the elder Khan. They were served all kind of delicacies with tea while Omar waited to be invited to join the ladies. The call never came. His mother sent word that it was time for them to leave. Omar told Shahzore that he would like to meet Qudsia. He just ignored his request.

Since he was not allowed to meet Qudsia, Omar got extremely upset. Omar's mother told him that Qudsia looked very tired and sad, maybe because of her pregnancy. Qudsia did not get a chance to talk to them in private, because pretending hospitality to her guests, her mother-in-law and sister-in-law never left her alone.

A few days later, Omar went to Qudsia's village alone. He had decided to see Qudsia this time. In his first meeting with Shahzore, Omar had guessed that he was a narrow-minded and obstinate person.

Shahzore also surveyed Omar carefully. He hadn't forgotten the name that his wife had mentioned to him lovingly a few times in the past. Whenever Omar talked about Qudsia, Shahzore either ignored him or pretended to be preoccupied with something else. At last, Omar asked bluntly to see Qudsia. Shahzore replied that he would send word in the ladies' apartments. A few minutes later he also went in there. When he returned, he informed Omar that Qudsia was sick and that she was very sorry for not feeling well enough to see him.

Omar knew that her husband had never asked Qudsia to meet him and had just made up an excuse. A few days later, Omar again tried to meet Qudsia. This time instead of going to her house, he stayed in the rest-house in *Mian-Dum*, where his ancestor Qasim Khan had sprinkled the holy water on a young girl to revive her from a coma.

The spring of crystal clear water was still there, but the *chenar* trees mentioned in the book were not. Maybe the rest-house was constructed at the very place where those *chenar* trees had once stood. Omar had sent for Gul-Sanobar, Qudsia's maidservant and her confidante. The sun was setting behind the mountains splashing its gold and orange colours all over when Gul Sanobar reached the rest house heaving and panting. Omar told her that he wanted to meet Qudsia. It didn't matter to him whether she invited him to her house or came down to meet him here. Gul said she would deliver the message to her mistress and do whatever she decided.

The following night, while Omar waited for Qudsia on the rocky dirt road of the mountains, Gul came alone, very pale and fearful. She handed Omar a note written by Qudsia. She had to leave immediately because those were the orders from her mistress. When he asked about Qudsia she replied that she was all right, but then she sighed and turning back said, 'Please, don't try to meet her again. It could be dangerous for you and for her.'

After she was gone, Omar returned to his room in the rest house, and in the flickering light of a candle tried to read Qudsia's letter. It wasn't a letter. It looked like a strange astrological chart or a map of a lost treasure.

Omar shuddered while he looked at it. There were circles drawn into circles all over the paper. In one circle, the letter 'Q' was written in a flowery hand and all the roads leading to the letter 'Q', were blocked as in a maze. The blocked roads, however, had dragons and snakes ready to strike anybody who tried to reach the letter 'Q'. At some places between the lanes not leading anywhere were written a few words or half sentences. It was hard to discern the meaning of those words. The word 'death' was common among them.

Beneath the diagram was the text:

The treasure hunt should stop now. The map should be sealed in a small box and thrown into the river so that somebody in some future century could rediscover it and hand it over to a museum.

In a corner of the paper Omar instantly recognized Qudsia's signature. The writing, deliberately distorted, was hers, too. In another corner was written: *Blessed are the people who bury their dead.* And in yet another, *Meddling with the dead is blasphemous.*

Why had Qudsia created this puzzle!

The reason could be that if the letter were to be caught no one would know the writer and the addressee—and it could mean that she was extremely angry and disappointed in him—or she was mentally sick.

Omar came back very dejected. There was no way he could contact her again. He knew that the doors of that house were closed for him forever. He never consented to get married though his parents tried as hard as they could. But he was happy for Akbar when he married Guljan, his cousin.

7

The beautiful 15-year-old Guljan, holding her heavy, shocking pink wedding dress, had entered Akbar Manzil, in Abbotabad where Akbar and Omar had decided to settle down. The bridegroom, Akbar, was very happy. He was an upcoming lawyer. She was very dear to him, but she was childish and ignorant, so most of the time he treated her like his books bound in their attractive volumes.

Guljan acted as a silent dutiful wife for a while, but in course of time she began showing her true colors. She was much younger than Akbar and inferior in knowledge, but, she openly defied him, argued and quarrelled with him the way she had seen women of her father's family quarrel with their husbands. Being educated doesn't mean that the husband shouldn't put up with the whims and airs of his wife.

When Guljan became pregnant she began to make a lot of fuss like other rich and illiterate women of her family. Guljan was not willing to accept that bearing a child was something normal, and it was not in Akbar's nature to put up with his wife's fake airs. Akbar wanted the baby to be delivered in a hospital or, at least, by a female doctor instead of a midwife. But Guljan didn't agree.

Guljan left for her parent's house where her mother was willing to put up with her whims, and there were a lot of servants to obey her orders. It was also a custom in her family for girls to have their first babies at their parent's house. So, Akbar's daughter was born at the house of her maternal grandmother. Mothers never breast-fed their babies in her family. A mid-wife was hired for this purpose, and as long as the infant was breast-fed it lived with its maternal grandparents.

When Akbar went to his in-law's village to see his daughter, Omar accompanied him.

Their village, Topi was unique in many ways. It was situated in Frontier Province but the Punjab border was very close. The Hazara District started a few miles away on the other side. Because of the great Indus River it also had the expansiveness and the serenity of the plains and the look of a valley. On each side of the horizon there were mountain ranges. Their fields were on the plains below, where the multi-colored poppies stretched for miles creating an illusion of flying butterflies. On the borders of the fields, stately white poplar trees waved in the wind. There were wide gullies made by the torrential rainwater coming from the mountains during the rainy season. Topi was especially suitable for cultivating tobacco and opium.

They crossed the bridge in their car very slowly. Omar purchased fresh sweets from a confectioner from the small market place of Topi and had them packed in a large box. The two friends went along, laughing and talking until they reached their destination where they were warmly received. The baby was brought to them. They eagerly leaned over the baby girl to have a closer look and saw a beautiful face encircled by thick golden hair. Her light brown eyes seemed to be very intelligent and eloquent.

When Omar saw her he shouted in delight: 'Hey, the *Zar*, pure gold. Absolutely pure.' Since that day, the baby got the name *Zari*. Akbar wanted to take his wife and daughter back to Abbotabad. But the village traditions and the hard journey made it difficult for them to go at that time.

Akbar had to wait more than a month for his wife and daughter to come. As Zari grew older she became very fond of his father and his friend Omar. Although Omar was her mother's cousin, she never called him *mamoon* but *Chacha* as if he was her father's brother. Zari remained the apple of their eyes all their lives.

8

John, a British tourist was sitting at the foot of the hill with a line cast in the azure water of the river. He was fascinated by the cold, transparent water through which colored pebbles could be seen as clearly as if they were seen through glass. The light breeze was tossing the long grass, and the fragile orange and purple poppies.

At a little distance, the maids with their heads covered discreetly by white embroidered *dopattas* were busy filling their vessels with water to carry to Khan's house. Among them, wrapped up just like her maid servants, was Qudsia who, being lady of the house, was not supposed to go out at all except on very special occasions such as a wedding or a death in the family, and that, too, in a covered cart. She had found it impossible to abide by the rules because she was born and raised in quite a different environment. She had read Wordsworth, Shelly and had been very fond of swimming and playing tennis and even ballroom dancing.

As a last resort, she started going out in the disguise of a maidservant.

Qudisa noticed a bearded foreigner sitting at a little distance in a broad trimmed hat writing something occasionally in his diary, which was lying beside him on the grass. Then, as if on a sudden impulse he got up and started towards the women. Qudsia saw him coming with his jeans rolled up to his knees showing his white legs, and looked the other way pretending not to have seen him at all.

He came to the maidservants and started talking to them in Pashtu, which surprised and amused them. He then turned his attention to the woman who sat with her beautiful feet in the water. Weighing his options cautiously he went to her and said,

'Salam Alaikum.'

'Walaikummusalam,' she said in a soft voice, hardly more than a whisper, and drew her *dopatta* up to her forehead, then up to her eyes.

He kept staring at her, and then asked, 'Who are you?'

She hesitated a moment, then answered, 'I am a maid servant at Khan's house.'

'Really!' He seemed amused, 'What do you do?'

'I work there as all these women do.' She said.

'But I have seen you doing nothing all this time while these women were washing clothes and carrying the water to the house.'

'It's my day off.' She said and smiled in spite of herself.

'Come on,' he laughed, 'the servants have no days off here, not even on Eid day. Then he said in English, 'If you are Khan's wife and have come here for an outing, I see no harm in it. Don't be afraid of me. I rather appreciate your ingenuity and am one hundred per cent with you.'

At that moment Qudsia threw all caution to the wind and started talking to him in English. She told him that her position in Khan's house was exactly that of a bird in a cage.

'You are not happy, I presume,' he said.

'Just as much as a caged bird.' She said.

Then they talked some more and when the women announced that the elder Khan was coming that way she hurriedly advanced towards the narrow path to the house.

* * *

John stayed there for ten days. Then he bade the two Khans goodbye the night before leaving because he intended to leave very early in the morning and insisted that nobody should get up so early only because of him.

He had an old two-door, weather-beaten Italian car with a high, oval-shaped rear window like a ventilator in an old building. The back seat and the whole back portion of the car were stuffed and cluttered with hundreds of things from sleeping bags to fishing rods, dangling at all angles. On looking in from outside, one could see no part of the back seat from any of the windows. The car seemed to be old and battered, but its engine was new and very reliable. John drove the car at a high speed, talking at the same time to somebody lying hidden under a heap of clothing in the back seat.

He had no means to know whether the person he was talking to was listening to him at all, because there was not the slightest hint of a response. He still continued his monologue, 'Ah, what a lovely place, a beauty not ruined by modern living. This is the real thing in here.' His voice had such exultation as if the cool breeze he was breathing was intoxicating. 'It's not like the places in Europe and England where hundreds of tourists swarm like bees. The promoters of tourism, who have made it an industry, charge admission fee to every building, so that one gets exasperated and hotel bills are enormous! Here, I was treated like royalty for two weeks and was not charged a single *paisa*. When I insisted on making a payment, the elder Khan got red in the face, "How can you insult us like that?" he said, "Taking money from a guest! We are *zamindars*, meals for guests are ready here every day as a matter of course. People from other villages come and they are always welcome. If you had a mind to pay, you should have stayed in a hotel in a big town. You shouldn't have come here in the first place." My God! What hospitality, what values! But at the same time what atrocities! Man slave to man, and wives treated worse than slaves. If women had to live like that for a single day, in our part of the world, I'm sure they would either commit suicide or kill their husbands.'

He took a deep breath and said, 'Hi there, is anybody at home? Oh, what's the matter? I'm really scared, Qudsi, are you all right?'

'I'm crying.' A faint voice arose from among the pile of clothing in the back seat.

'Oh, I'm so relieved. You are still alive! Now tell me what happened to your sense of freedom? Have you ever seen a bird crying on being set free?'

Suddenly Qudsia started laughing at the idea of a bird crying, then, again, reversed to her weeping.

'Look, I don't have time to stop the car, give you something to drink or wash your face. We still have a long way to go. Just tell me if, by any chance, you want to change your mind. Don't worry about me, just say so, and I'll go back and face the consequences.'

'No, no, for God's sake don't talk like that! If we go back, both of us shall be killed.' Qudsia said in a frightened voice.

'Then, Qudsi, dear, cheer up. We are in this together till death do us part. Have a sip from the flask, forget the past and think of the future.' John speeded up the car concentrating on driving and stopped talking. He realized that it was naïve of him to talk as if there were nothing the matter, as if he was on a date with a girl.

Qudsia tried to think about the future. But she felt as if her mind was full of fog. She was unable to see any future for herself. Every thing was so uncertain; she was not sure of her freedom. Every thing had happened so fast! When she came to know that there was a person who was willing to take a risk freeing her she only thought that it was the chance of a life-time. The big question loomed upon her. 'Now or Never?' For fear of 'never' she had taken a leap into the unknown without thinking whether she would ever land on her feet alive. As much as she wanted to think about the future, her mind unwittingly dragged her to the past.

Qudsia was roused from her memories at day-break by the fragrance of the flowers in the cold morning breeze. She could tell from only a glimpse taken from the junk through the window that they were passing through the old familiar places. She could see Amandra Rest House, a new building constructed in an old fort so high that from the rest house one could see the miles of fertile lands, canals, mountains and zigzagging roads. She had been there many a time with her father. She had played chess with him and his friends and had painted from its balconies the fabulous scenes of sunrise, sunset, and moonlit nights. Very soon they were passing down the Malakand Fort. Qudsia had stayed once in one of the buildings in that fort too. She would never forget the night when the earthquake hit the place. They had rushed out of their bedrooms in the dark because the electricity was disrupted by the quake. No one else stirred at all because of the earthquake. The people there were used to the earthquakes and knew better than to go out of their houses.

'Wake up Qudsi.' She heard somebody whisper in her ear; and when she woke, she felt someone slapping her gently on her cheek. For a few moments, she had no idea where she was and who he was who dared to wake her up in such a rude way. She was almost outraged with anger when, suddenly, the whole thing came to her mind as a shock. It was not a dream!

John was stroking her cheek trying to wake her up, talking at the same time, 'you can't do this to me. It's only the beginning. You have taken such a big step. You can't let things go now. You have to have courage. Otherwise we could both be in danger.'

'Where are we?' Qudsia asked, sitting up in her seat.

'Listen, we are in Risalpur. This is a house of a friend. We cannot continue our journey in this car. I will leave the car here, and my friend will take care of it. We shall travel in his car. I will try to change my appearance, and you will have to change yours. You must wear the outfit of my friend's wife to look like an English woman. Can you do that?'

'I'll do whatever you say.'

'Good girl.'

So she was in good old Risalpur!

She knew the roads, streets, and lanes of the place as the lines in her hands. The roads always seemed bare. How fast she used to ride on her red bicycle along the metalled roads. The *Farash* trees with their low branches, seemed to caress her head like loving hands. The green hedges and the rose bushes along the roads adorned them. Getting out of the car, she cast a look around. The houses were still the same, having big gardens and courtyards that were so large that each house was a hundred yards apart. The place had looked so desolate as if it were a town where dwellers were made to disappear by magic. Staggering, she went inside the house.

After taking a shower, changing into a new set of clothes and having a little breakfast they had started again. 'Qudsi, you told me that you love Wordsworth and I tell you that you would simply fall in love with the Lake District when you see it.' John started talking, 'It is so pleasant by the lakes at all times. The afternoons are so calm and quiet with long shadows of the trees across the grass, turning it into a beautiful hue of pale green. In the evenings the waters are so quiet that you want to hold your breath not to disturb their serenity. I don't think you would ever be able to forget the feeling you get when you see Lake Windermere at night for the first time. Qudsi, please say something.'

'I don't know. My mind is in a haze and I find it impossible to be able to think at all.' With all that confusion, though, Qudsia was surprised how he had presumed she was going to accompany him to England.

'Till now, you have known England by books only through Galsworthy, Virginia Wolf and Forster; but when you see it with your eyes, it is going to be such a novel experience—a bell ringing in your head every time. Well, this is the Parliament Building with Big Ben at its side; this is Marble Arch, and this is the Tower!'

Qudsia smiled in spite of herself. John was not a tall and bearded man at the time, but a boy from a country who was excited at the glamour of the big city and wanted to show everything to his friend.

She dozed off again till they reached Rawalpindi.

As always, Rawalpindi was a little quiet and a little noisy, a little pretty and a little ugly at places, a bit new but lots of old too. There were new buildings, schools and new roads. Yes, changes do come in life. They are more visible in cities. She, Qudsia, was running away with someone though not in the same sense of the word, but that would make no difference for her in-laws. People would only think that she must have been carrying on an affair with somebody and that she found an opportunity to elope with him. The name of the sons of some neighboring *Zamindars* would come up, no doubt.

Her father-in-law, a clever and shrewd person, might suspect that the English tourist might have something to do with her disappearance. The police must have been informed by now and the people from their own estate must have been sent to catch them. What would happen if they were found? She did not like to think beyond that point because there was death, certain and cruel.

She hated to think of death while she was alive. She shook her head in order to do away with the thoughts that disturbed her, and, raising her head a little over the pile of things, looked out. There were villages along the road, and the atmosphere there was as calm and quiet as ever. The monotonous sound of the Persian wheel run by the mundane circling of oxen with bands on their eyes, the usual fluttering of the fowls, and the routine hum-drums of human voices were all mixed in the surroundings. In the midst of all the usual everyday life their car was rolling fast to an unknown destination, a place of which neither she nor her fellow traveller had a clear idea.

Why not go to her mother's relatives in Karachi? They were educated and lived in a big city; they would understand the terrible situation she was in! But what if they don't and secretly inform her husband about her whereabouts? Well, Karachi was still far off and she could decide later. At present they had just reached Lahore, the capital city of the province of the Punjab. She had visited the city with her parents when she was a little girl.

She remembered Lahore as if she had seen it in a dream. She had no idea of time and space, how old she was at that time, which building was situated where, or how far one place was from any other place. But she remembered Lahore was colourful and beautiful though hazy as seen through a mist. One afternoon they had taken her to a big park where they had stayed till dusk, She had seen fireflies glowing up in the trees, twinkling like hundreds of lamps flying down to the grass and then flying back again to the trees.

She wanted to concentrate on the future, but her memories were dragging her back. She had read somewhere that if you could go close to the speed of light you would be able to see the things behind you. Was she going too fast into the future?

John wanted to have lunch in a sidewalk restaurant but Qudsia was too terrified to get out and take the risk of being seen. So, John bought some food, and they ate it by one of the banks of the canal. The breeze coming over the canal and the green fields made her drowsy and she slept in the car again.

She was suddenly awake, feeling very hot. She knew instantly that they were crossing the desert near Multan. The sky was hot and the sand dunes were glistening in the sun. The shadows of the sparse palm trees were lolling like tired animals on the sandy waves. The spiky bushes were looking toward the sky as if begging Heaven for showers. She saw a few caravans of nomads going from one small oasis to another where they would find a mossy pond, the shelter of a few palm trees sprouting from the same root like a finely assorted bouquet, and a patch of grass for their animals to graze from.

The evening sun on the horizon started sinking rapidly. There were red, orange, purple, and grey streaks in the sky. As it set, these stripes of colour gradually mixed with increasing darkness. Soon, it was totally dark, and the darkness magnified the unknown fear in his heart. She still lay in the back seat. Sometimes the approaching light of a car would throw its beams on their car and then it would be dark again.

9

It was almost midnight when she felt that the car had changed its route and advanced on a narrow dirt road. After about a quarter of an hour it came to a halt. Qudsia sat up in her seat and cautiously looked out. She saw a building of a moderate size surrounded by trees with servant quarters at a short distance.

John got out, stretched and went towards the servant quarters. Soon he came back with the caretaker of the rest house, giving him instructions to fix something to eat. He did not hint that there was another person with him. When the man offered to take the bags into the rest house John said, 'No there is no need to take them in as I will leave very early tomorrow morning. Please do something about the food, if nothing is available, omelets and a piece of bread will do, then make the bed and go home. Don't worry about the dishes. I'll put them in the kitchen and you can wash them in the morning.'

Qudsia heard the whole conversation and noticed that John acted as if he were alone. She knew that he was cautious, but his asking for a meal for one person and making one bed made her very uncomfortable. John went in with the man, and Qudsia waited in the car till the caretaker went home. Then very quietly he sneaked her in and led her directly to the bedroom. He brought the omelets, bread and fruit to the bedroom and put it on the table between the two chairs.

'Come on Qudsi, let's eat. I want to go to sleep as soon as possible. I'm dead tired. Today, I can sleep on a scaffold, as the saying in Urdu goes.'

Qudsia went into the bathroom, washed her hands and face and joined him at dinner; but she hardly ate a thing. John finished everything. After dinner John carried the dishes to the kitchen and came back.

'Listen Qudsi,' he said, I know you are scared to death, but
don't be afraid of me. Have faith in me and everything is going
to be all right.' Then he smiled and added,' maybe we have
forcefully occupied countries and established colonies, but we
respect women. I, at least, would consider it below my dignity to
have a woman without her consent. I'm not going to bother you
in any way. Just lock the door and go to sleep I have locked all
the doors from inside.' He smiled to reassure her, 'There are other
rooms in the building and plenty of bedding, so don't worry
about me. I'll knock at your door early in the morning half an
hour before leaving. Be ready and we will leave quietly. This will
be the last leg of our journey. Once we reach Karachi, we'll be
safe.'

'I hope so.' Qudsia said softly.

'Let's hope for the best. Good night.'

He closed the door behind him which Qudsia secured at once.
Then she went to the window and looked out. It was a moonlit
night; very still, even a leaf was not moving. The continuous
sound of the flowing river had become a part of the silent night.
Suddenly she felt a strange courage and strength coming to her
from nowhere; everything had gone well so far. Soon they would
be out of danger and she would be able to decide what she wanted
to do with her life. She was not sleepy at all. She wanted to feel
her newly gained freedom all by herself. Feeling happy and
confident for the first time since she left her house she opened
the door, slid into the hall, and sneaked out of the rest-house.

There was a path, half hidden with bushes and shrubberies.
She took that path and reached the bank of the river. There she
sat on cool, wet sand like a happy and contented child. It was
such a forsaken place! The caretaker of the house must be the
only living soul here for miles, she thought, and he would never
come out of his house at this late hour. She was completely free
to enjoy the moonlit night and her solitude. Then she heard the
rustle of clothes and footsteps on the sand approaching her. She
had her back to that side, so she did not know who it was. Her
blood froze in her veins and she held her breath in faint hope

that it was only her imagination. Then she saw a long shadow falling in front of her and heard John's voice,

'Is that you Qudsi?'

He advanced slowly and coming close, sat beside her.' Are you feeling any better?' he asked.

'Much better,' she answered. 'This is the first time I have started feeling free. I managed even to come out of the house, as I was sure there wouldn't be anyone out here at this hour. This is great, isn't it?'

'Yes it is, and it's going to be better still. Qudsi, I believe that everybody has a right to be free. Nobody can keep you chained like an animal. You are, now, out of reach of your husband and in-laws and can demand justice. The law would be on your side, I know that.' He kept on talking, encouraging her in one way or other while she was thinking all the time, 'Has this all been happening in a dream? 'It could not be real for her to be sitting on the bank of a river at night, and with a stranger, too!

'What is it you particularly want to do, Qudsi?' John suddenly broke her chain of thought.

'To tell you the truth, I only want to get lost, literally, just get lost to the world. Karachi is a big city, and a very crowded one. I want to lose myself, my identity, in the multitude so that nobody knows I ever existed, not even myself.'

'What are you talking about?' John countered. He bent toward her as if to tell her a secret. 'Listen to me, a piece of rock can remain hidden in a drain or in a corner of a street, but do you think a diamond can remain hidden from the eyes of folks?' He smiled and his eyes glistened in the last rays of setting moon.

The truth of what he had just said started sinking in. She was a pretty, young, and educated woman. She might remain obscure in a western five star hotel but not in the average locality of Karachi.

A renewed feeling of helplessness gripped her. John continued, 'Let me suggest something. You go to England and complete your studies. I know you will be happy there. You could wear western dress and speak English and no one would know you are not English. He smiled encouragingly again.

Before Qudsia could reply she heard a faint noise behind her. Then she felt a powerful hand on her shoulder and on her mouth and a heavy sack over her head. She lost all consciousness.

The darkness of that moment when the cloth was thrown over her head and she was carried like a bag on a shoulder turned out to be her fate forever.

* * *

Qudsia was never allowed to leave the house. In the beginning, she kept waiting to be poisoned or shot, but nothing happened except that one night her husband came to her.

'Tell me the truth,' he said, 'did that foreigner sleep with you?'

Qudsia was aghast. She did not know how to phrase her answer. She knew that he would not believe it any way. After a moment she decided to say it as John had put it, 'They may look very immoral to you, but they think it below their dignity to have a woman without her consent.'

She saw her husband's colour change. In extreme rage he shouted like a madman, 'All right, from now on I will never take a woman without her consent.' Then he closed the door behind him and never came back—not for thirty years. She came to know later through Sanober that her life was spared only because she was pregnant before she left. She had heard her mother-in-law saying to her son, 'By killing her, you would kill your child too! It may be a boy, who knows!'

After his son was born, she awaited her death afresh; but the fatal moment had probably passed. She was not shown her son, and her husband never came to see her again. Soon after the birth of her son, all the furniture given by her father was taken out of her room and was replaced by a few very old pieces. To her great anguish, the bookcase with all the books was taken to the guest room. She was still junior Khan's wife, but in name only.

10

It was so dreamlike.

The four friends, all from the department of tourism were staying in Mingora rest house in Swat to find means to promote tourism in the area. After supper, as the four sat inside and talked, they heard the beating of drums and the echo of clapping. They went out to see what was going on. The sight enchanted them.

Behind the distant mountains, the moon was trying to sneak through a sheet of fog. Short triangular tents, illuminated by the light of an occasional glimmering lantern, were scattered like toy houses amidst the trunks and under the branches of the *chenar* trees. Outside the tents, in a small, levelled place the men from the border police were dancing the *khattak* dance. Their white dresses revolving in the moonlight looked like white chrysanthemums waving in the breeze.

'Let's go out and enjoy the dance.' Zari said. They all got down from their balcony and stood closer to the dancing circle. 'I wish I could dance with them,' Aijaz said.

'Go ahead. It isn't a hard dance,' Noor said.

'I don't know how to dance.'

'What about you?' Zari said to Shams. 'I've heard that in East Pakistan, everyone knows how to dance, even the Muslims.'

'Yes, I know how to dance, but I don't know whether they'd welcome me.'

'Of course they would,' Nargis said. 'Why don't you try?'

Shams stepped forward to join the dancers.

Seeing Shams join in their dance circle, the men shouted joyfully to welcome him.

'Whenever I see a dance in the open under the sky, I am reminded of Austria,' Zari said. Zari's musical voice touched Shams's heart while he was dancing.

'Did you have a good time in Austria?' Aijaz asked.

'Yes. The time I spent in Austria was like a dream that has no beginning and no end.

'Is Austria a beautiful country?' Nargis asked.

'Yes, very beautiful. The vast expanse of green grass, the slopes and the neat houses are so attractive.'

'You are right. Nature works like magic,' Nargis said.

'Oh, it's so true,' Zari said and laughed. 'I never thought of it.'

Aijaz was not interested in that kind of talk, but he enjoyed it because Zari was enjoying it. Shams heard the sound of Zari's laughter. He instantly felt that he should go and join his friends. But it did not look proper to leave the dance just yet so he decided to stay till the end.

Gradually, the beating of drums and the sound of footsteps and clapping ceased. The audience clapped and cheered and Shams came back.

The moon had climbed high into the sky. The breeze grew heavy and damp and dew started collecting on the grass. The dancers returned to their tents. The friends started walking towards the river.

'Zari, you must surely have danced in Austria?'

'No, I don't know how to dance. But I enjoyed watching hundreds of people dancing in the open, indifferent to the falling dew and so happy as if they had no problems in their lives.'

'The custom of singing, dancing and enjoying yourself does you good. It's a catharsis for you,' Shams said. 'The reason that we are always mad at one thing or the other is that we have no outlet for our repressed emotions.' Shams said, 'I've heard preachers after Friday prayers who find fault with wearing new dresses and celebrating on Eid days. The result is that people who listen to their speeches become so narrow minded and negative in their attitudes that when they perform the *Hajj*, they focus more on throwing pebbles and shoes at Satan than being a better person.'

'Shams please,' Nargis interrupted him. 'You shouldn't drag religion into your discussions.'

'Why not, Nargis?' Shams suddenly began speaking excitedly. 'We're not allowed to discuss anything. If we talk about language, we are racist—if we talk of religion, we are atheists—if we discuss politics, we are traitors.'

'One shouldn't talk about things that hurt other people's feelings,' Nargis said.

'Why? Are our feelings so fragile that they can't face any difference of opinion? I don't believe in ignoring the issues. You can ignore the serious problems but there is a penalty to be paid. When we don't talk we get in the habit of not thinking. That is the reason we don't produce any philosophers, thinkers, scientists and great leaders among us. Tell me what would be the result if we kept ignoring a disease?'

'Let's go upstairs. It's cool here,' Zari said.

'Let's go,' Shams said and started walking towards the rest-house, but he continued his conversation. 'Everybody knows that there is unrest in East Pakistan, but the leaders are ignoring it. I think they should face it and try to find solutions. Can you close your eyes to tempests, earthquakes and floods?'

'For God's sake, Shams, don't talk about such things, at least not now.' Zari said. 'Enjoy this beautiful sight.'

'Okay, let's enjoy the beautiful sight, but let me say this—people who don't think are not doing any service to their country.'

'Tell us more about Austria,' Aijaz said. 'I was enjoying your description of the place.'

'One thing I liked about Austria was the beautiful pictures that they had painted on the front walls of their houses. Nargis, you must paint the front of your house like this. Maybe neighbors will do the same and you will start a beautiful tradition.'

'I might try that,' Nargis said.

'Now, you are trying to ignore the serious issues I was mentioning, Zari' Shams said, 'we all do this.'

'I told you I don't want to talk about serious problems on this beautiful moonlit night,' Zari said, 'You take life too seriously.'

'I think we should enjoy life as we do good poetry or a nice painting. We shouldn't go out of our way to understand it or find meaning in it,' Aijaz said.

'I object,' Shams lifted his hand but nobody listened to him.

I think that life is like a complicated poem,' Noor said. 'People try to understand it according to their intellect. The poet sitting aloof keeps smiling at their interpretations.'

'That is an insult to life and its Creator,' Nargis said.

'Why are you so cranky tonight, Nargis?' Zari said. 'Our poets have said a lot of outlandish things about life.'

'Yes, such things could be said in the past,' Shams said passionately, 'but nobody dares say such things today. We're afraid of reality, we're afraid of truth. We should admit that we're trying to hide ourselves in the dust like ostriches.'

In the heat of conversation they had forgotten to go up the stairs to their rooms and had kept walking towards the river.

The river Swat was shining in the moonlight at the end of the *chenar* grove, and the crisscross beams of the old wooden bridge gave the scene a picturesque look. Shams came closer to Zari and held her hand. Nargis and Noor started whispering something.

They all stood spellbound for some time till Nargis broke the spell. 'Let's go. It's getting late.'

While returning to the rest-house, Zari said, 'Aijaz, you have a master's degree in English literature and you are so fond of English poetry, you ought to be teaching English literature in a college.'

'I was thinking of working for my PhD. I saw an advertisement for a lecturer's post in a college in Lahore. Should I apply for the position?'

'Sure, don't let this opportunity slip by. You told me that your mother is suffering from asthma. Lahore's dry climate would definitely suit her better than Karachi's damp climate.' Zari spoke so solemnly that Aijaz decided he would apply for the job the next day.

By the time they reached the rest-house, there was perfect stillness in and about the tents. In the moonlit night, the white tents beneath the pentagonal leaves of the maple trees looked like igloos. Zari wanted to enjoy the scene some more, but Shams said, 'Let's go to bed. It is already past midnight. All of you must have heard the maxim: 'Early to bed and early to rise makes a man healthy, wealthy....'

'And dead,' Zari interrupted. They all burst into laughter.

'Good night,' Shams said. They all retired to their respective bedrooms.

11

They had come to Abbotabad only yesterday.

The Pakistan Department of Tourism had decided to prepare a large quantity of brand-new brochures for tourists. It had proposed that a survey of the scenic spots be carried out and guesthouses constructed in suitable locations to promote tourism. This project required a revolutionary approach by enterprising persons who could do their jobs enthusiastically and on their own, without any supervision. Zari had offered her services for the provinces of Hazara and Swat, as she was familiar with every nook and corner of these areas.

Nargis had offered her services as a photographer. She basically belonged to the Bengali school of painting but she had started photography as a hobby. In her new venture, her work had far surpassed the work of even old and experienced photographers. Zari and Nargis had to obtain special permission from their families before taking on the task because women had never been employed for such tasks before.

Zari's uncle in Abbotabad had given Zari permission. Nargis's fiancé Noor, who worked in the same department, had no objection because he was selected for the same job too. Shams, a journalist from East Pakistan, wrote good English, knew Urdu well and had a reputation for being a diligent worker, showing more interest in history and literature than in girls. Aijaz was a new employee and was taken along to learn the job.

The ruling English class could not bear the heat of the plains and developed hill stations to go to during the hot season. These hill stations were now good business for the tourist department. The city of Abbotabad was originally one of those hill stations.

After the last sharp ascent, their wagon had reached Abbotabad and had stopped at its final destination. They had hired a taxi to go to Akbar Manzil, Zari's ancestral home. On the way to Zari's house, the car had passed through the Hazara Bazaar, where they could see men frying *chaplee kababs* in a large pan in front of their shops and baking *tandoori* bread, taking them out from the oven with the help of an iron tong and laying them on sackcloth.

There were piles of garbage everywhere, and certainly, some animal lay dead in the midst of the refuse because there was the stink of rotten flesh. Nargis immediately closed the car's window but Zari did not seem to notice it. At that moment, she was living in the Abbotabad of the past rather than the present.

When Zari saw Akbar Manzil from a distance her eyes filled with tears. She cried out, 'Oh my God!' and hid her golden head under her arm.

As soon as the car stopped, she opened the door, alighted and ran up the long, flat stone stairs. Nargis got down with her camera and followed her. She saw that there were two graves side by side on a platform about halfway up the stairs. Zari threw herself at her father's grave and sobbed hysterically. Nargis was amazed to see her being so sentimental. Knowing she could do nothing to ease her pain, she thought her to be a perfect subject for a picture sitting under the shade of a yellow peach tree, crying. Meanwhile, Shams, Aijaz and the driver carried the luggage to the house. Shams and Aijaz both felt sorry for Zari, but knew that at that moment she needed to be alone.

After the luggage was carried to Akbar Manzil and the taxi driver paid, they all came to the house where the present occupant of the house greeted them.

It didn't take long for the guests to know that the economic condition of the residents was not good. The furniture was old and beautiful—it obviously belonged to Zari's parents, but the cheap sheets that were spread across the beds were barely sufficient to cover them. In the kitchen there was a kerosene stove and a few pots and pans. In the bathroom, a dull, weather-beaten aluminum *samovar* stood in a corner for storing the water, and a soap dish was lying on the wet floor.

Most mismatched with the house were Zari's framed photographs placed in different rooms. The decay of the house had no impact on these beautiful pictures. They looked like fresh flowers in a wilderness.

Zari lead her guests upstairs to show them the Himalayan ranges spreading miles across the horizon, 'That village there is lower Malikpura. That grove is Phagwari Banda. In the local dialect *Phagwari* means fig.' Suddenly she noticed the roof of a side room had caved in.

'When did this roof collapse?' she screamed, turning pale as if she had seen somebody crushed under its debris.

Aunt timidly came forward and said, 'The roof gave way a few days back. I was going to write to you. In fact, I was thinking to get the roof repaired and bear the expenses and then tell you. After all we live here without paying you anything.'

Zari did not listen to what she said. In shock, she ran downstairs and locked herself in her room.

Zari's aunt continued her apologies to the guests. 'It is really difficult for me to look after her property and her things. Zari's mother had prepared costly wedding outfits for her *jahez*. Then there are her mother's own wedding dresses with embroidery so intricate that even the most skillful workmen would be jealous of her work. I have stored a few precious things in the attic, but the rooms downstairs are full of extra furniture, paintings and beddings and I don't know what to do with them.'

'Zari should realize that since she doesn't live here, it's only natural that her things will be destroyed,' Shams said in Bengali so that Aunt did not understand what he was saying.

'But it's also natural to feel sorry for the things being destroyed,' Nargis replied, also in Bengali. Noor and Aijaz just kept quiet.

'I'll go find Zari,' Aunt said, and with tiny little steps went downstairs.

'Zari is doing an injustice to this poor lady. If she leaves the house, bats will inhabit this place,' Shams said.

'But Zari cannot help it.' Nargis again defended her. 'She must have lived here in comfort and luxury, and now she finds the place all in ruins. Maybe we should stay in a hotel with you people.'

'You are most welcome,' Noor said with a happy flash in his eyes, 'but it was Zari's idea to separate us.'

'She didn't trust us men, naturally,' Aijaz said good-humoredly.

'It wasn't that. You know this is Hazara. People will talk when we'll go together for our survey.'

'I had no idea that Zari could be so emotional!' Shams said.

When, after repeated calls, Zari didn't open the door, the three of them were obliged to take tea with her aunt. Her aunt's husband hadn't yet returned from work.

Aunt told them a lot about Zari. 'Zari's father, God's mercy be upon him, was very fond of education. He educated Zari as much as she wanted. She couldn't find a husband in her family and now, as you see, Zari is in government service in Karachi, and here her precious house is falling to pieces.'

There was a knock at the door. Aunt ran and opened the door. A tall and stately person entered. As Zari's Uncle did not bother to shut the door, Shams could still see the two graves. The road here was much lower than the house. There was no other house in the neighborhood. With such privacy the residents were not particular about closing the doors.

'Where is Zari?' Zari's uncle inquired after formal greetings.

'She is in her room, not feeling well after seeing the condition of the house. Go and ask her to come with you.'

Uncle knocked at Zari's door. When Zari opened it and greeted him, Uncle kissed her forehead and embraced her.

'I'm sorry I couldn't come earlier. How are you?'

'I'm fine,' Zari said in a sad tone that Uncle preferred to ignore.

'Come, let's have tea,' Uncle said.

Talking with him, Zari came out, trying to control herself and behave normally.

12

After dinner, the men left for their hotel. Shams couldn't sleep that night, and he didn't even want to go to sleep. He was enjoying a new sensation he had never experienced before. For Shams, it was a night when even sleeplessness was welcome. It urged Shams to discover a new meaning in its charm and the days to come.

He came to the balcony and watched the valley of Abbotabad.

He could see Zari's family graveyard from the balcony, like a circular Greek theater. Lights from the houses scattered on hills looked like stars. As the night advanced, the lights became brighter. He was constantly thinking about Zari. She looked so confident and independent in Karachi but so susceptible and fragile here.

At that moment a very strange thought came into Shams's mind. If Zari and he decided to settle down in Abbotabad, a similar graveyard would become his family graveyard and his women descendants, covering their heads with red and green stoles, would visit it and say, 'Our great-grandfather had come from a far away city called Sylhet, in Bengal. Perhaps, our great-grandmother, who was beautiful like a fairy, had cast a spell on him and had lured him to this place. Fairies have ways of casting spells over humans and Zari seemed to be one.'

Then, he was amazed at his thoughts. What was he thinking! Was he falling in love with Zari? It could not be anything but love, he thought.

Satisfied with the answer, he returned to his room, laid himself down on the bed and went to sleep.

13

That night Zari could not sleep either and finally got out of bed about 4:30 in the morning. Leaning against the wall of Akbar Manzil's second floor, she looked at the shining Great Bear which always fascinated her and then at Yousuf Manzil which, surrounded by trees, was right in front of her. On the veranda of that house, moths circled the lighted bulb as they always did.

Zari had been five or six years old, when Zeb Qadri, a widow, had rented a few rooms in Yousuf Manzil. She had only come to stay for the summer, the *season* as they called it, but had come with all her belongings, including furniture and furnishings. Soon there were all sorts of rumors that she wrote horror stories, and had been wandering among Indian forests, that she had gone to Ceylon to study Buddhism and had studied the Bible from a Christian priest and Hinduism from a Hindu Guru.

She was more mysterious because she did not meet anybody in the neighborhood. Zari was keen to see her. One day she found an opportunity when Gulgoona, her maidservant, was busy conversing with Zeb's maid. She entered the house, and knocked at the door of Zeb's study.

'Who's there?' a voice asked sternly.

'It is me,' Zari said and entered the room.

Zeb scrutinized the audacious girl who was wearing an expensive dress. She had a fair complexion and nice regular teeth. Her golden hair had been cut like a crescent across her forehead and two long golden plaits swung across her shoulders. She was smiling confidently.

'I am Zari,' Zari said, and thought that the frail, pale-looking lady was not intimidating at all. 'I've heard that you write books. I have never seen anyone writing books, though my father and my uncle own a big library.'

'So, what do you want?' Zeb asked her, a little amused.

'Go on writing please. I'll watch you.' Zari tried to sit on a settee, shoving a big leather purse out of the way. 'What's in this bag, Auntie? It's very heavy.' She asked.

Zeb stared at Zari from above her glasses. 'None of your business, girl.' Then she removed her glasses. 'What's your name?'

'Zari Khan.'

'It's a good name.'

'Chachaji gave me this name.'

'So, you like your Chachaji very much?'

'Yes.'

'What is your Chachaji's name?'

'Omar Khan. Auntie, why don't you meet anybody? We're your neighbor—you never visited us.'

'There is a reason for everything, but it is not necessary to tell it to others,' Zeb said. 'By the way, who taught you to ask so many questions?'

'Chachaji. He says, 'Ask questions. By asking questions, one learns.'

'That's not always true.'

'Why, Auntie?' Zari asked innocently raising her head.

'I'll tell you some other day. You better go now.' She adjusted her glasses on her nose.

'Can I come tomorrow?

'If you want to.'

'Can I bring my Chachaji?'

'If you have to. Now run.'

Gulgoona was surprised to see Zari coming happily out of the house.

'Why did you go in? I thought you'd come out crying.'

'Oh no. She even asked me to come tomorrow.'

'Really, this is unbelievable!' Even Zeb's maid was surprised.

'On the way back home, Zari related the details of her interview to Khushal, who awaited her patiently outside Zeb's house. Zari knew Khushal to be a distant relative. They were born on the same day. They were friends and confidantes.

From that day on, Zari and Zeb Qadri also became friends though the difference in their ages was more than thirty years. Wherever Zeb went, she took Zari along. Gulgoona always followed Zari. They took trips to high mountain peaks, low valleys, half-constructed buildings and wildernesses in order to set the locale for Zeb's scary stories. Zeb talked with local people and listened to old superstitious tales with great interest.

When Zari's visits became too frequent, Zeb started keeping her busy with small errands. Zari, who did not do anything at home, ran happily about the house to do Zeb's biddings. She particularly liked to take out dry fruit from Zeb's large box, which she believed to contain a lot of secret treasures. There was a peculiar cool touch to the things in the box and a fragrance came from the box like the breeze in the shade of a large tree. The aromas of old and new dresses, flowers and perfumed potpourri rose from it.

'Auntie, what else is in this box?' One day she asked Zeb.

'A lot. I'll show you someday.' Zeb had a habit of postponing her answers to another day.

'Auntie, don't you have children?' Zari asked.

'Why do you ask?'

'You live with your friend. That's why, I thought....'

'Staying with a friend does not mean that one has no children. Don't presume anything child,' She became serious. 'I have two sons. But they don't stay with me. That's why I stay with a friend. I rent a place in Lahore during the winter and in Murree or Abbotabad during the summer. I take my belongings and make separate arrangements for my meals. Do you have any more questions?'

'Yes. Why do you make separate arrangements?' Zari asked.

'My dear! This "why" and "what" is not going to help you. Come, sit here and copy this writing.'

'Auntie, I don't know much Urdu and my handwriting is very bad.'

'That's why I am asking you to write. It will improve your Urdu as well as your future life. It is not right for girls in our country to question everything, perhaps you don't know that, maybe your father and your uncle don't know that either. Bring them along with you someday.'

Zeb had said this casually. But next day Zari asked her uncle Omar, who had come to visit them for a day or two, to accompany her to Zeb's house. Omar agreed to go with Zari.

'This is my Chachaji,' Zari said rather proudly. Zeb Qadri surveyed him closely. Clad in a pure white *shalwar*, *kameez* and waistcoat, he seemed a graceful man of medium height in his late forties.

He may have been handsome in his youth, she thought.

'Please, sit down,' she said formally. She was thinking that he only came to leave Zari at her house, would excuse himself and leave.

But Omar sat down. After looking around and finding a lot of books written by her he said, 'Have you written all these books on the shelves, Mrs Qadri?'

'Yes.'

'Can you read all the books you have written?' he asked.

'Excuse me,' Zeb got annoyed. 'I'm not a person who enjoys a visitor trying to be familiar with me at first meeting.'

'I am very sorry,' Omar said. 'You're right. I shouldn't have said that. I forgot my manners.'

'I know some people like to be witty to the point of being rude,' Zeb said. 'I don't think I enjoy that.'

'I admit, *Begum* Qadri, that I've been untactful. Can you forgive me this one time?'

'Maybe, but let me tell you that I am not known for my hospitality.'

Zari, who had been enjoying this war of words, put her hand to her mouth and giggled.

'May I ask why you did take the trouble of paying this visit?' Zeb asked. 'It's not customary in our country for men to visit women who are living without male members of the family.'

'First let me tell you that I'm not a very conventional person,' Omar said. 'Then I'll ask you a question before answering your question.'

'What's that?'

'About my visit to you, would you want me to tell the truth or just be courteous?'

Zeb tried to hide her smile He seemed to be a really unconventional person.

'Tell me both,' she said.

'First listen to the courteous answer—I am a great fan of yours and I have read all your books. I've been dying to meet you for a long time!'

'And the truth?'

'Let me warn you, you may not like the truth.'

'Just say it.'

Seeing a trace of a smile on Zeb's lips, Zari was greatly relieved.

'The truth is that Zari is so fascinated by you that I heard her mother say, "If you won't listen to me you won't be allowed to see Zeb Qadri again," and Zari immediately did what she was told. At this moment I thought I would like to see the person who can fascinate a headstrong girl like Zari. Now, that's the truth and the whole truth.'

Zeb eyed him with suspicion. Then she looked at Zari and realized that he was telling the truth. She smiled as if ready to make peace with him. She removed her glasses and placed them on the table, inserted the pen in her notebook, shut it, and pressed the call bell to ask her servant to bring tea and snacks for the guest.

While sipping tea, they talked as if they were old friends.

Omar told her about his studying in the famous Aligarh University and his participation in politics when India got independence and Pakistan came into being.

It was almost dark when he asked to leave. 'I think I should leave before we exhaust all the topics, and don't have anything to discuss next time,' Omar said.

'Please, come again,' Zeb said sincerely. 'I'll appreciate it if an unconventional person would visit a sick lonely unconventional woman.'

Omar returned home with Zari. They were both very happy.

The next day, late in the afternoon, Omar walked in the garden, waiting for Zari to come. As soon as Zari came downstairs to go to Zeb's house, he opened the gate and followed her.

The next day, when Zari had gone to a relative's house with her mother, Omar went alone to Zeb's house, rousing Zari's mother's and grandmother's suspicions.

'What has come over lala? It's indiscreet for a man to visit a woman outside the family, especially when she lives alone,' Zari's mother said.

'What's the harm?' Akbar defended his friend. 'They are not children, and she doesn't live alone. Yousuf and his wife live in the same house.'

'Don't make excuses for him. Everybody knows that she lives in a separate section of the house,' his wife said angrily.

Zeb did not hide the fact that she was ill though she did not disclose the nature of her illness. From the very first day, Zari thought she had looked very thin and frail. By and by, she started staying in bed most of the time. Zari paid her daily visits. Zeb told her interesting stories about many places she had visited. Some of the rumors about her were correct. She had visited the famous temple of Somnath that was invaded seventeen times by Mahmood Ghaznavi. She had gone to a fair in a village named Kullu on a Himalyan slope where she had seen a bull being sacrificed.

One evening, guests had arrived at Akbar Manzil and Omar was summoned there immediately to meet the guests. As they stayed late, Akbar asked Omar to stay there too for the night. 'Why go twenty-five miles at this late hour, why not stay here tonight—or a couple of days, there is nobody waiting for you there,' he said. 'We miss you and Zari has gotten so fond of you!'

Omar accepted the invitation readily. 'Okay, if you insist, I'll stay.'

The next day, late in the afternoon, Omar strolled under the grapevines. As soon as Zari and Gulgoona came downstairs to go to Zeb Qadri's house, he opened the gate and followed them.

Omar was so taken with Zeb Qadri's charm that he could not get out of her spell. Even when Omar went home, he came to visit Zeb Qadri every second or third day.

Zari's mother and grandmother became very suspicious. They asked Zari what Zeb and Omar talked about. If a guest arrived, they immediately sent a servant to call Omar to meet the guest and tried to make Omar return to his home under different pretexts.

Zari felt that Chachaji was not his usual self for some time. If he stayed at their house, she saw him standing against the railing, under the vines, looking towards Yousuf Manzil. Chachaji, who normally looked younger than his age and was always active, looked extremely weary during those days.

Zari knew that Zeb Qadri was ill. Her maid had also told Gulgoona that Dr Yousuf and his wife regularly came to check on her. For a few days she stayed in bed most of the time. She didn't even teach Zari anymore, but Zari went there every day as usual.

Zari's mother believed in the rumors that Zeb Qadri knew magic and thought that was how she had acquired a hold on a sane person like Lala Omar and a carefree girl like Zari.

But now, watching the careworn face of Omar and his slow step, no one dared say anything. At last Akbar knew that though the magic part was wrong, the other suspicions of the two women were not altogether groundless.

One day, when Zeb Qadri was so weak that she found it difficult to breathe, Akbar, at Omar's request, had taken them both in his car to the court, where they both signed the marriage papers. When they came back from the court, and started climbing the narrow path to her house, Zeb became breathless. Omar lifted her and carried her inside the house to her room. Nobody in the town could understand why Omar and Zeb got married at that time and more rumors were started about them.

Zeb died two days after her wedding.

Zari remembered all this as clearly as if it had happened yesterday.

Since Zari had come home from Karachi, she was anxious to meet Omar Chachaji. He was away looking after his lands in the village.

The daylight advanced, first diffused and then glowing. The birds started chirping in the vines. Without a formal announcement, a chorus of countless voices started singing ceaselessly. Zari knew that it was time for Nargis and her to get ready for their trip to Thandiani.

14

When they passed the 'Abbotabad zero mile' milestone. Shams and Noor both noticed that Abbotabad was as lush green as East Pakistan but the trees, plants, and creepers were very different.

'Abbotabad is a beautiful place,' Shams said.

'Yes, it is. I don't know why Zari doesn't like her own town,' Noor said.

'She probably wants to avoid the painful memories of the past,' Shams said. 'Yesterday, Zari's uncle told me that *Akbar Manzil* once was the most beautiful house in the whole town. The garden and its fruits were so special that they were sent as gifts to the English government officers. Passers-by marveled at the beauty of this bungalow. This house was also known for its hospitality as Akbar used to send tea, *sherbet* or fruits to people who just sat down on the small platform beside the garage to rest for a while.

As they reached the house, Noor said, 'Look at the condition of this house now.' Shams raised his eyes. The paint on the walls, doors and windows had faded long ago. The rains had left the walls mossy. The delicate work of lattices was broken at many places. The inscription, *Akbar Manzil,* had lost its glamour and was hard to discern. Once the most beautiful bungalow of the province was like a *caravanserai* of ancient times, dilapidated and abandoned.

'If Zari couldn't take care of the house, why didn't she rent it to a person who could look after her property,' Noor said.

'She is too careless. She let her poor relatives live in the house as a favor, but the problem is that they cannot afford its maintenance.'

They did not go upstairs, but opening the gate on the lower level, walked into a small, overgrown garden. The vines, turning into thick cords, had climbed up to the roof of the building. A few entwined the exquisite pillars of the fences in a wild embrace, cracking them at many places. Innumerable bunches of raw green grapes gaped through the beautiful, ridged, green leaves.

The three lower rooms were filled with wooden beds placed one above the other touching the ceiling and the different sizes of suitcases, and still smaller suitcases sitting on top of them. Old lamps, desks, flowerpots were piled up in the corners. The half-open drawers were stuffed with small objects.

They went into the drawing room, which they had seen yesterday, to wait for Zari and Nargis to come down. The condition of the living room was slightly better than the other rooms. The carpets, sofa, divan and lamp were not as decayed. There were slender and exquisite flower paintings on the walls and a photograph of Zari's handsome parents on the mantelpiece.

After a few minutes a man came to the door. His thin hair was disheveled. His outfit was soiled with stains of oil, and his shoes were dirty. 'You are invited to come upstairs,' he said.

Shams and Noor went upstairs. Zari and Nargis were ready—dressed in brightly colored *shalwar kameez,* and they were busy preparing lunch for their trip. When Shams told them that they had not taken their breakfast at the hotel, they prepared breakfast for them. During the meal they discussed that day's news. Suddenly, hearing a loud excited voice, they looked around.

The man who had come to fetch them was talking in a passionate voice.

'Nothing has harmed President Ayub as much as the celebration of his ten-year rule,' he said, and added, 'To spend a few hundred rupees on repairing your house and spending thousands of rupees celebrating, it doesn't make sense.'

'For God's sake, don't speak so loud. You can be heard outside,' Auntie said.

'Yes, this is not the time to discuss politics,' Uncle added.

'See, what I mean? How everybody is scared of telling the truth or listening to it,' he said. 'All right, if we can't speak inside the houses, we'll go and talk outside in groups. If processions propagating false prosperity of our country are taken out, we will hold meetings to tell people how wrong this propaganda is.'

'Then you will be sure to land in jail,' Uncle said.

'Yes, we'll go to jail. We'll go to the gallows.' He got even more excited.

Zari came from the kitchen and said in her sweet voice, 'Khushal, don't get so disconcerted. Why don't you discuss something with Shams? He'll be more than happy to tell you the grievances of the people of East Pakistan.'

Khushal looked at Zari for a few seconds. Shams noticed something peculiar in the way he looked at her. Then he lowered his eyes and talked no more.

At this point Uncle introduced him to Shams and Noor.

'This is Khushal Khan, an arrogant rebel like his namesake, Khushal Khan Khatak, the famous warrior-poet who fought with Mughal emperors.'

'No, not arrogant, self-respecting,' Khushal corrected him.

But Uncle continued the introduction, 'He used to be a teacher in a school, but now he is jobless and you can guess why.'

He looks more like a laborer than a schoolteacher, Shams thought.

'Are you both from East Pakistan?' Khushal asked them very frankly.

'Yes, we are,' Noor said.

'You speak Urdu well, but the accent clearly exposes the province to which you belong.'

'Why should one hide?' Shams was a little annoyed. 'Everyone should be proud of his place of birth.'

'I didn't mean to displease you,' Khushal said apologetically. 'But to be proud of one's birthplace doesn't mean that one should hate others. I would like to know why the people of East Pakistan don't like us.'

Shams hesitated a little. He looked at Zari who was giving the last touches to her package of lunch. She nodded as if to give him a green signal.

'I wouldn't tell a lie,' Shams said. 'Turning away from the truth doesn't solve the problem. We East Pakistanis think that people from West Pakistan do not try to understand our culture and our customs. Instead we are ridiculed, though we were, and still are, more educated than them. People have now started saying that

just as India has not willingly accepted the partition, the West
Pakistanis haven't accepted the majority of Bengalis in Pakistan.
Otherwise, they would not have hesitated in declaring Bangla as
the second national language along with Urdu. That's not all.
Other provinces have their names, for example, there's Punjab,
Sindh, Frontier, and Balochistan. But our province has no name.
When we try to give it a name, the government sees it as if we are
creating a separate state.'

'So you have started the Bangla Nationalist Movement. Is it
going to be a real danger?' Khushal asked.

'If certain things are not taken care of it might. I know there
is as much poverty here as in the East wing. But when visitors
come to West Pakistan, they are given tours of the neat and clean
suburbs of Karachi and Islamabad. They are shown big factories
in Lahore and Faisalabad. This is bad strategy. They get the wrong
impression of West Pakistan being rich and prosperous while East
Pakistan is getting poorer day by day.'

'Why do you consider the expansion of Dhaka as your right
and the construction of Islamabad as an injustice to you?' Khushal
asked.

'Most people think that we don't need a new capital and that
Islamabad is being built with earnings from our jute. They also
think that our floods and cyclones are not your problem, or a
concern to immigrant Biharis, because they don't live in the
coastal regions where cyclones hit.'

'I beg to differ with you,' Nargis came forward from the
kitchen, drying her hands with a towel, to defend herself. 'You
differentiate between us only because our parents speak Urdu,
though most of the boys and girls of the new generation have
never seen Bihar in our lives, and we consider the cyclones and
floods our problem as much as you do.' Then she said something
to Shams in Bangla.

'So you know Bangla!' Khushal said to Nargis.

My father, who was a magistrate, in the beginning could speak
only one sentence in Bangla. 'Have you committed this crime?'
And often, he would repeat this sentence, pointing a finger at us
jokingly. But now he speaks fluent Bangla.'

'Come, let's go,' Zari interrupted. 'The taxi has been waiting for a long time.'

'Khushal, why don't you go with them? You can help them as you know these areas very well,' Aunt said to Khushal.

'Sorry, I'm going to Peshawar today to listen to the president's phony speech. If you want something from Peshawar, let me know.' He said it to everybody but looked at Zari.

'Come back safely. That's all we want,' Zari said.

They got up to start their day's program.

'He is a very sensitive but excitable man,' Zari told Shams as they got down the stairs. She had a kind of premonition that it would not be good for him to go to that meeting, but she knew that nobody could stop him.

15

Climbing along sharp, twisting bends beneath the shade of pines, Zari, Nargis Shams and Noor had arrived at the 8,000 feet height. The place was beautiful and deserved to be called, *Thandian*, meaning, *cool place*. The far off snow-capped peaks on all sides could be seen clearly from this point and numerous villages spread far and wide in the valley. While they were strolling about, they saw strange pointed stones protruding from the earth as if someone had designed and neatly arranged models of great mountain ranges. Similarly, miniature trees flourished in between those mini-peaks. This natural phenomenon was very surprising.

Nargis got excited, 'Look, the bonsai art of Japan is naturally present here.' She immediately began taking pictures. Noor stayed with her.

Zari walked to the end of the mountain and surveyed the place. The cold, damp air flirted with her golden locks. She could see the valleys of Abbotabad, Mansehra and Kakul draped in green with a delicate white veil of foggy clouds across them. She saw Shams climbing the narrow path coming to her from a different direction singing a Bengali song.

'What are you singing?' Zari asked.

'*Murshidah*, a song representative of our lives and temperament, Zari Begum. You must know that creation and destruction always go together with us East Pakistanis. Let me translate it for you. It is about the rivers of our country.

It fills up one bank
But cuts up another
This is the river's game
He who is rich in the morning
Becomes poor by evening
That is the river's game

'Our temperament is also fluid like the song says. Storms strike the land and the banks are swept away. Cyclones come and the rooftops of our hut houses are gone. But we take it for granted and very soon we forget everything and lead our normal lives. In order to know us, one has to understand the ways of our rivers and the nature of our weather.'

'That's so true,' Zari said. 'To know *us* mountain people you should know about our mountains and the nature of our forests.'

'Yes, I'm here to see your mountains and forests in order to know your nature. I hope you will go to the other wing to see mine.'

Zari looked at him. He was serious. Although she didn't understand the exact meaning of his words, she blushed a little.

Shams repeated the line from the song again.

'This is the river's game.'

Then he started talking about his project. 'This is a very nice place for tourism. What do you think? Should we recommend building a guest house here?'

'I think it's a good idea.'

'Let's go to the post and telegraph office and send a letter and a telegram to Karachi. We would see how much time they take to reach there.'

As they were climbing down to go to the village, Shams said, 'You must come to East Pakistan, Zari. You'll find such natural beauty there and water everywhere. Everything seems to be dancing and singing in the moving waters. It's quite different from here.'

'I'd love to go to East Pakistan,' Zari said.

The sunlight had spread on the distant hills as if the sun had folded the foggy curtain and had taken the entire valley in its loving embrace.

'Can I ask you something?' Shams asked Zari as they walked.

'What?'

'That fellow—Khushal. Is he in love with you?'

'What?' Zari looked at him and laughed. 'Why did you say that?'

'When he looked at you, I could see the emotion in his eyes, the one nobody can hide. Didn't you notice that?'

'No. I didn't. I hadn't looked at his eyes,' Zari said laughing. 'Let me tell you about Khushal and me. Marriage proposals had started coming for me since I was fifteen. My father refused them, saying that he wanted me to get a good education first. One of those days Khushal's mother also came to my mother and asked my hand in marriage for her son, saying that though he was a little eccentric and I was much too smart for him, he desperately wanted to marry me.

'So I'm right. He is in love with you. What did you do about it?'

'Nothing. I didn't know anything about it. My mother told me this incident years later, and Khushal never said a word.'

'Poor man! And now you are pushing another great admirer away.'

'Who's that?'

'Aijaz.'

'Oh no, I'm only trying to help him,' Zari laughed. 'It'll be good for him to be a teacher and for his mother to live in Lahore with him.'

'But the poor boy is only applying for the job because you're taking an interest in his future.'

'I don't know that. Now tell me, have you ever seen that emotion for somebody in your own eyes?'

'I can't say,' Shams smiled. 'I can't look into my own eyes.'

'But did you ever have a similar feeling for somebody?' Zari said.

She was sure that Shams would deny it, but he said, 'Yes, I had once. Her name is Shoshi. When my mother died, my father married again. Shoshi is my stepmother's daughter. We spent quite some time together when I was young. I've not seen her for years now, but I could never understand the relationship we had. While I was a very ambitious little boy, she was an innocent soul, very content, generous and forgiving, but we were great friends, maybe more than friends.'

'So that was your puppy love!' Zari said.

'You could say that,' Shams said and then they were both silent for the rest of the way.

Shams wrote a few lines to his boss about what they were doing there, and explained to him that he was also sending a telegram just to see how much time it would take to reach them. Sometimes, from remote places it took too long for the mail to reach the destination.

When they were coming back, they met Nargis and Noor halfway. Nargis was wringing her hands. Her lips were almost blue. 'For Gods' sake, let's leave. I am frozen.'

'Why aren't you wearing your gloves?'

'I don't have gloves. I live in Karachi, and this is summer for God's sake.'

Noor took Nargis's hands in his own and started rubbing them tenderly to warm them. Zari and Shams smiled.

Maybe I'd like Shams to do the same, Zari thought. But she was wearing her gloves and she could feel that there was some other thing on Shams's mind than her hands. Maybe Shoshi!

They gathered their things, got into their taxi and started towards Abbotabad. The clouds were rolling again and were very close to them. The driver drove the jeep slowly. The jeep picked up speed only after the strong hold of the clouds was loosened.

'It'll be late when we reach Abbotabad. Let's stay at Chachaji's house,' Zari said. 'He'll be very happy to have us. He'll write a note to Uncle that we're staying with him, and we can leave for Mansehra from his house tomorrow.'

'What'll your Chachaji think about us being together so late?'

'Nothing. He has a unique personality. He has full faith in me and I in him.'

'Mutual trust is a wonderful thing,' Shams said.

Zari fell silent. The jeep rolled down the steep road.

16

It was late evening. Sitting on the front veranda, Omar was reading the newspaper. The headlines and news were mostly about the protests and processions in different cities of West Pakistan conducted by lawyers, students, political activists and the public.

Suddenly, he heard the rumbling noise of a jeep, its echo, like thundering clouds, resounded through the mountains. It stopped at his garden gate, and he heard people talking. Then, he noticed a few shadows advancing across the garden towards the house. Two men in jackets and two women wrapped in shawls escorted by the watchman approached him.

Omar rose from his swinging canvas chair. Zari ran up to him laughing and fell into his arms. Omar was delighted to see her. Zari quickly introduced the others to her uncle. He gently stroked Nargis's head and shook hands with Shams and Noor.

'Zari, darling, how have you been? You have come to Abbotabad after ages and you have stopped writing letters to me.'

'Chachaji, I don't have time to write,' Zari said, 'but I always remember you.'

'I know. I, too, remember you all the time. You are going to stay with me tonight, aren't you?'

'Yes, all of us.'

'Good. I want you to make arrangements for your guests and then come and talk to me.' He stroked her hand gently.

'Chachaji, there are so many things to talk about, so many memories. I have been surrounded by conflicting emotions all the way.'

'I know,' Omar said.

Zari showed the guests their rooms and asked the servants to make the necessary arrangements for them. She gave instructions to the cook, asked Chachaji to write a note for her uncle in *Akbar*

Manzil about their staying with him and handed it to the driver. When the driver left, Zari came and sat beside Omar.

'How is Sinan?'

'Bad news! Sinan is in the boarding house of the convent school. I just received a report that he is suffering from blood cancer and must go to Lahore or Karachi for treatment. I am going to write to Ahsan to take care of his brother's son, although I know Sarwat does not really like him.'

'I know she does not want to have anything to do with her husband's stepfather or Adnan's illegitimate child. But if they refuse I will take him to Karachi.'

'It would be a big burden on you.'

'I would do it for you and Zeb Aunty' sake, not for Adnan or Ahsan Bhai.'

'Thank you. You are such an angel. I love you and this is one reason Sarwat does not like you.'

'To tell you the truth, Chachaji, I don't care.'

'Chachaji, do you remember what you had said when I told you that I intended to be a lawyer when I grew up?'

'Sorry, I can't remember much at this age.'

'You had told me that I need not be anything else because you liked me just as I was.'

Omar laughed pleasantly. 'Yes, I knew what you were going to be like. Just as a tiny bud holds the beauty, fragrance and color of a full grown flower, the young girls' budding talents tell what she is going to be like.'

'Did I fulfill your expectations?'

'Yes, you always remind me of Zeb. She had a very impulsive but charismatic personality, like raw gold. People like her don't usually have many friends. That's why, Zari dear, I am always concerned about you.'

'But why? I'm fine. I have many friends.'

'What I want from you is that you look up, but set your feet firm on the ground so that you don't stumble and fall.'

'You still talk in the same old way, Chachaji. I'm not a child now.'

'Listen to what I say. Someday you'll thank me for this.'

When Shams and Nargis came back to the veranda after freshening up, Zari invited them to sit with them.

Omar said good-humouredly, 'You know when Zari was a little girl, I used to say that all children are born free, but a few, like Zari, are more so.'

'Folks,' Zari said, 'my Chachaji is fond of making up theories and relating them to facts.'

'Have my theories ever proved wrong?' Omar said smiling. 'They are proved right ultimately but you people don't give me credit.'

Omar then turned to Shams, 'Tell me about you, Son.'

'My father was first employed with Duncan Brothers,' Shams said, 'in their tea gardens in East Pakistan. Then he joined the government service. He was transferred to West Pakistan and we were moving all the time. I still don't have a permanent home. I feel as if I belong to a race of gypsies and am destined to wander.

'After my mother's death, my father married again and I was sent to a boarding school in Murree. When my father died my stepmother, with her daughter went back to East Pakistan. I don't hear much about them.'

'You don't have a home and feel like a wanderer,' Omar said. 'Zari has a home, but she prefers to be a wanderer with her little tent and a backpack on her shoulders.'

'Chachaji, I have a job in Karachi, that's all.'

'Tell me about yourselves,' he asked Noor and Nargis.

'I'm from East Pakistan and currently working with Shams and Zari,' Noor said.

'My parents migrated from Bihar to East Pakistan in 1947,' Nargis said. 'They live in Chittagong.'

'Let me add something here,' Zari said. 'Noor and Nargis are engaged to be married and leaving soon for Chittagong. Nargis is an artist and has been offered a job in an art school. Noor has requested to be transferred there.'

'You are engaged. My blessings,' Omar said.

'Thank you,' Nargis and Noor chanted.

When the servant announced the dinner, they all stood to go to the dining room.

'Do me a favor, Zari darling,' Omar said. 'When you get up in the morning do come to my room. We've so much to catch up on.'

'Sure, I will,' Zari said.

After dinner, they all bade good night and went to their respective rooms.

17

With curtains drawn, lights switched off, Omar swallowed a sleeping pill with a glass of water but with no result. Zari's arrival had rekindled the fading lights of his memory. Rummaging on the shelf, he pulled out a very old, dust-coated diary, turned the pages and carefully looked into the incidents of one particular year.

That was the year of his meeting with Zeb. It was after his third meeting with Zeb that he had written these words about Zeb in his diary.

'*She is like a beautiful pinecone, which has dried up soon after blossoming, and is more attractive dried than fresh. Every petal is hard but flexible. Its golden color is fabulous and it looks so enchantingly charming whether it is on a tree, lies on the grass, or burns in a bonfire in a wintry moonlit night.*'

He recollected the day when after giving Zari a book to read, Zeb had come and had sat beside him. Her hair was done nicely and she looked younger than before.

'How're you feeling?' he had asked.

'My health had always been very good,' she said. 'Nothing has happened to me over the years, so now I have decided to get a little sick for a change.'

'It's not a very positive decision, I must say,' Omar protested.

Zeb smiled. 'I know. Maybe I'm just lonely and need some attention.'

'Oh, I'm lonely too,' he said cheerfully. 'I used to think that every person has a right to lead his own life, but now I think it's quite hard to live in isolation.

'Why do you think so now?'

'Because now I think that the purpose of life is quite different.'

'What's that?'

'It's continuation of life. Everything in nature struggles for existence and wants to prolong its life through its off spring. It makes the peacock dance to attract a mate, the queen bee to fly high into the sky so that her mate may follow her. Young boys and girls feel an unconscious attraction toward each other. The result is the extension and preservation of life. Once they become parents, their duty is to raise their children so they take charge of the mission of continuing the race.'

'Do you mean to say that parents don't raise their children out of love?'

'Nature makes them do that under the illusion of love and the parents think that they, somehow, continue to live in their future generations.'

'The name and fame of some people remain after them, even if they don't have any children,' Zeb said.

'But there are not many who survive in their own right, Zeb Begum!'

Omar was surprised with the unaffectedness with which he could utter her name.

'But you didn't marry and very wisely stayed away from the snare, didn't you?' Zeb remarked smiling.

'Yes, people like me are exceptions who prove the rule. Ultimately, the people who are exceptions feel that they are like useless tools in Nature's machine.'

Zeb laughed. She was really enjoying the bizarre conversation with the man whom she had met only a few times. 'First you say that nature makes a fool of each one of us, and then you are upset because you did not let nature fool you. Shouldn't you feel like a winner?'

'See, it's like this. Kids love to act in a play. They know that it's only make believe, but the child who is denied a role feels miserable! Doesn't he?'

'But nobody denied you a role. It was your own choice,' Zeb said.

'Sometimes a person insists on choosing a perfect partner. He discovers later that it meant nothing. Everyone has his own part to play. He should play it and make an exit.'

Zeb laughed again.

'Do you write anything?' she asked. 'You talk as if you think a lot about things.'

'Maybe I think about things,' he said, 'but has it ever occurred to you that the ants and the bees that are so sensible don't write poetry or stories! The butterflies that fly so beautifully don't draw or paint!'

'They might.' Zeb smiled a winning smile. 'We don't have the means to know whether they do or not. They might have written volumes about us human beings.'

'Yes, you may be right,' Omar laughed. 'I never thought of that.'

At that time he had wondered whether a chance meeting with someone could change the scenario of one's life too.

That day, after coming back to *Akbar Manzil*, he had paced up and down in the small garden for a long time. It was a moonlit night. He could see a small light shining in Zeb's room.

It was then he had added in his diary the sentence:

I really enjoy conversing with Zeb because she always understands what I say, and after meeting her, I don't feel as lonely as before.

That very night he had decided to marry Zeb if she would accept him.

She did accept him, but it had not been their destiny to live together for more than two days.

Then he remembered Qudsia. It seemed as though Qudsia had come to him in Zeb's disguise.

18

As Zari got into bed, it started raining. It was hard for her to sleep. Memories kept circulating in her mind with the drip, drip sound of the falling rain. Suddenly a big wave of lightning crossed the sky, Nargis woke up, startled, and looked around in panic.

'Zari! What sort of noises are these?'

'Only a thunderstorm, nothing to worry about. These noises shouldn't bother you since you come from the land of cyclones. Just go back to sleep.'

Like a good girl, Nargis obeyed her, curling up into the quilt and covering her ears. Zari stayed awake. She knew that sleep would be hard to come by this night. Gradually the rain stopped and slowly the moon rose from behind a cluster of clouds. Then the rain started again, followed by a hailstorm. The sound of tiny hailstones landing on the corrugated iron sheet roofs resembled another musical sound from childhood—maidservants sitting before tiny hills of grains holding the reed-huskers on their outstretched legs, winnowing the husks.

When that jingling sound ceased, Zari threw her cashmere shawl about her and came out onto the veranda. It was still dark, but the day was about to break.

Zari found somebody sitting in the chair in the veranda. 'Chachaji?' She asked.

'No, it's me,' Shams said.

'What're you doing here?'

'Waiting for you.'

'Waiting for me! How'd you know that I would come out so early?'

'I just knew that you would come out to listen to what I want to say. Don't you believe in telepathy?'

She didn't answer him, 'What do you want to say?' she asked

There was a brief silence. Zari fixed her gaze on him and knew instinctively what he wanted to say.

'Don't you know? Don't you see in my eyes the feeling that cannot be mistaken?' Shams's voice was trembling with emotion.

'It's too dark in here to see your eyes,' Zari tried to joke, but her heart was pounding. Is he going to say, "I love you," is he?'

'I love you,' Shams said softly and Zari felt as if it was her own voice echoing in her ears.

'What?' She had to listen to it again to be sure.

'I love you, Zari. I want to marry you. I want to live with you for the rest of my life. I don't think I can part with you now.'

He stood up and held her hand. His hands were very cold. *He must have been sitting here for hours*, Zari thought.

'I'd like you to talk to my Chachaji—you know the tradition— you have to ask the parents or an elderly person in the family.'

'I'm not sure about that. I know even the most radical people in our country want their children to marry into their clan.'

'Chachaji is not like that.'

'First, I want to be sure about you. You know that I firmly believe in national integration—that all differences between East and West Pakistan can be solved through intermarriages. Don't you think so?'

'I don't know—but I would like to believe that you want to marry me for my sake not for your belief in integration.'

'Oh, Zari, don't get me wrong. I'm head over heels in love with you—and you know that. Say you know it.'

'I know now,' Zari said. She found the darkness helpful in not showing too much of her emotions. That was the way it was supposed to be, the way she was raised to go about these delicate matters of love and marriage.

He pressed her hand. 'I'll gladly talk to your Chachaji if you are willing.'

The day had dawned and it was not as dark now. Zari could hear noises in the kitchen. The servants were preparing breakfast.

'Yes, I am, but I have to go now.' And taking her hand away from his she hurried into the house.

19

She saw the light in Omar's bedroom. She knocked and whispered, 'Chachaji, are you up?'

'Yes, yes, come on in.'

With a gown thrown carelessly over his nightdress, he sat at the writing table scribbling.

'Chachaji, What are you writing?'

'I've always been interested in gardening. Now that I have grown old, I can't tend the plants as much as I want. So, I have turned to pen and paper and trying to grow orchards on paper.'

'Are you writing poetry?'

'No, I'm writing the Saga of Man. Come, sit by me.'

'So you're writing a novel, how fascinating! How long will it take to complete the book?' Zari seated herself on the edge of his bed.

'Man's story is never completed. I found a journal of my ancestors from centuries ago. I thought I'd also write about the life I know and keep on writing until I die.'

'You will not complete the book!' Zari was very disappointed.

'You seem to be more sorry about an unfinished book than your Chachaji's death,' he laughed. 'Listen, the book will be as complete and as incomplete as any man's life. Each man's life is complete in a sense but incomplete in another sense.'

'This book will be about your bizarre philosophy of life, won't it?' Zari laughed.

'Yes, the essence of my life and thought, of your life, of everybody's life...from eternity, the story of every moment, every angle and every age!'

'Then it will be a very strange book,' Zari said, 'Are you trying a new technique?'

'Techniques and such things as the unity of time and place, round and flat characters, story and plot are mere academics.

They keep changing. A book is not great because it has all the ingredients. The great works are created even without them. The beauty of art lies in achieving the goal, be it music, poetry or novel.'

'Then how does one achieve the goal?'

'I'm not sure. The main ingredient is something magical—it has no name. In art you're successful with a pinch of that unnamed ingredient. I call it magic, you can call it whatever you like.'

Omar stood up, opened the curtain, and looked through the window, then continued; 'God created man. He put flesh, skin, bone, heart, mind, this and that but what makes him alive is that pinch of magic, the moving force, and the spirit. When it is gone, the man dies though he still looks whole and complete. Every creation, every art is like that. The artist who puts this pinch of magic in his work becomes immortal. Homer, Michelangelo, Leonardo Da Vinci, and Shakespeare possessed it. Hafiz of Shiraz, Amir Khusro, Mir, and Ghalib had it. The artists and artisans of Ellora, Ajanta and the Taj-Mahal had it—no need to count the names.

'But from where does this grain of magic come?' Zari asked.

'I don't know. Some people may be born with it. Others pull it off through hard work. We only see the result.'

'Chachaji, you still talk in the same old way,' Zari laughed.

'Yes, because I'm the same old fool,' he laughed with her. 'Listen, read my writing—and tell me if I have succeeded so far.'

'How should I know? I am not a critic.'

'Don't be ridiculous! Even a child could tell if a man is alive or dead. The doctors are for writing the post-mortem reports. You'll know.' He handed over the manuscript to Zari.

'Okay, Chachaji, I'll read it. I promise. But right now I want to go to Zeb Auntie's grave.'

'Just go. You don't need my permission for that. She must be waiting for you. You know how much she loved you, perhaps more than she loved her own sons.'

'Yes, Chachaji. This night has reminded me of her. Do you remember there was a similar storm the night she died?'

'How can I forget? It was more severe than tonight's. I was with her. The next day I had come to know that the door of your doghouse had remained open. Filfil had run away and you went out in search of him without telling anybody in the house. It was a very tragic night!'

'Yes, it was. Chachaji, you never told me why you decided to marry Zeb Auntie when she was so sick.'

'She wanted me to take care of her boys and I was in love with her—that's why I married her and you know I never regretted it.'

'Yes, I know that.' Zari wrapped herself in her shawl and went to say *fateha* at Zeb's grave. The whole episode of Zeb's death, every detail came to Omar's mind as he decided to one day write it down.

* * *

Clouds had been gathering since early evening. Thunder and lightning was attacking from all sides. When night fell, still more black clouds rose from the east. Suddenly, there was a strong wind and big raindrops began to fall. The bursts of lightning were oddly sharp and the thunder of the storm echoed through the mountains, magnifying it in intensity and fearfulness.

Omar, preparing to go out, had worn a raincoat and lit a lantern. When Omar rang the doorbell, a servant promptly opened the door and directed him to Zeb's room. Omar sensed that they were expecting him in spite of the weather. Dr Yousuf and his wife Dr Suraiya were both there. Yousuf took Omar's hand and led him into another room.

'This night is critical for her,' he said. 'Anything could happen.'

'Is her condition that serious?' Omar was shocked.

'Yes, I'm afraid so. Her pulse gets very weak at times, but we are watching her closely. Suraiya, you and I need to maintain a constant vigil throughout the night. I'll take the first watch. Suraiya will relieve me. If the night passes peacefully, we'll awake you in the early hours of the morning to watch over her.'

Omar was already awake when Dr Yousuf called him to tell him that it was his turn to look after Zeb. Immediately alert, he sat up in bed, surveyed Zeb's serene face, thanked God for her being alive and then looked out the window. He should have seen a full moon, but all he saw were layers of clouds so thick that not a single beam of moonlight could penetrate them.

After giving him a few instructions, Dr Yousuf retired. Omar drew a chair close to Zeb's bed.

Zeb opened her eyes and asked him in surprise. 'When did you come here?'

'I have been here for some time.'

'Is it early morning?'

'Yes, thank God.' He heaved a sigh of relief. Zeb didn't know that there were thousands of thanks in that one deep sigh.

'I wanted to enjoy the beauty of the full moon one last time,' Zeb said. 'But the night was spoiled by a storm.'

'Yes, it was the night of the full moon. That is beautiful, but the early morning moon of the next night is far more charming.

'Please help me prop up against the pillow.' She looked out of the window. 'What a gorgeous morning! It is sunny in the plains but misty in the valley. The birds are chirping. But the severed limbs of trees and branches show how terrible the storm was last night!'

'Yes it was, but it's all over now.'

'Were you here all night? Was my condition that serious?'

'I wanted to be with you during the storm.'

'Thank you. Go and have a nice sleep in the day so that we could enjoy the setting moon tonight.'

'Zeb, sometimes you act like an excited fifteen-year-old girl!'

'You know what? Sometimes I like to behave like a child with a certain person just to prove to myself that I'm free to feel and do whatever I want to do. Sometimes I feel like a fifteen-year-old. But you wouldn't understand it unless you knew about my past.'

'All I know is that you write mystery and horror stories.'

'To mislead others, like children who try to frighten their elders by putting on masks.'

'Well, you are not supposed to talk so much. Close your eyes and relax or go to sleep.'

'You go first.'

'I'll go after Dr Yousuf or his wife examines you.'

'It is too early. They won't come here for another hour.'

'Then I'll stay with you.'

'Okay. Omar, listen, you still have much to do. You have to live for many more years to see that my sons prosper in life.'

'But what about you?'

'Me! I'm quitting. I entrusted you with all my responsibilities. I'm ready to go.'

'But why do you talk of leaving? We can still lead a long, happy life together.'

'No, I was only waiting for the rescue boat to arrive. You are that boat. Knowing that my children will be saved, I am ready to go with a sense of relief.'

'It's not fair, and I don't want to hear any of this. Just sleep a little more. I'll sit by the window here.' Omar took a chair and sat by the window.

'I want to tell you my story today,' Zeb said. 'Come and sit by me.'

Zeb closed her eyes and started talking in a low voice.

'It's a tale of the most shocking tragedy of the sacred relationship called marriage. My husband suffered from a strange psychological complex. Somehow, he felt that he was not worthy of a woman's love or at least her first love. The story of our companionship is so bitter that poison seems to flow into my veins when I think about it. And mind you, I've been living with that poison for many, many years.

'The most tragic point is that my silence deepened his suspicions of my infidelity. He insisted that I confess to an affair I did not have. For years he went on vexing me to own up to a sin that I had not committed, and he promised that once I confessed, he would forgive me.

'At last, one day I confided in one of my old friends. She was unmarried and inexperienced. She advised me to confess falsely to get out of that hopeless situation. Since I was good at telling stories, she thought I could easily invent a story to satisfy him.

'You know, under pressure, even innocent people prefer to plead guilty. I made up a story of a sin I had not even imagined committing before, hoping that I would be relieved of the pain from then on. And what was his reaction? The man who had assured me that he would never question me again if I disclosed "the truth" once, got my picture published in the local newspaper the very next day with a declaration, *that he disowned me and our children forever–that I cease to be his wife from that day. And the children, well, of course, they never were his.* And with that, he disappeared.

'I don't think anybody can understand the sense of shock and humiliation my children and I suffered.'

Tears streamed down her cheeks and rolled onto her neck.

Wiping her tears, Omar said, 'Now, you have entrusted me with your grief too. If I open my heart, you'll perhaps find as many scars there as in your own heart. I will try to compensate for all your pain as best as I can.'

'I don't think you'll be able to do that for me, but I thank God immensely, that in my last hour he has sent me a man before whom I could bare my heart without a sense of guilt.' She smiled faintly.

'He must have spent the rest of his life in a mental hospital,' Omar said.

'I don't know. But he did one good thing—he didn't disinherit me from his property and money. After his death, I inherited all his money.'

'I know the rest of the story by heart,' Omar said, 'Now will you please do me a favor and rest awhile.'

'Whatever you say.' Zeb languorously closed her eyes.

Omar put his hand slowly on her cheek. Zeb's lips trembled. He put his ear to her lips. She was slowly reciting lines from a poem:

When I first learned how to write
The first name I wrote was yours!

Outside, a large number of birds chirped ceaselessly to greet the gentle morning.

Peace prevailed over her face. Omar ran and awakened Dr Yousuf. He came hurriedly and felt her pulse. He shook his head, indicating that she was gone. Omar looked at Zeb's face and saw that it held the same angelic beauty as the setting moon of the fifteenth night.

20

At breakfast Omar said to Zari, 'You're going to stay with me for a few days. I don't know when you'd decide to come again. I might be dead by that time.'

Seeing Omar in a serious mood, Zari tried to cheer him up. 'Chachaji, I'm not leaving today, and why be so pessimistic. You and I were two very lively and spirited people in the family, weren't we?'

'Yes, people used to laugh at us saying that an uncle has a niece for his best friend.' Then he said to Nargis and Noor, 'The truth is that even when Zari was a child, she understood me better than anybody else.'

'Chachaji, I only pretended,' Zari laughed. 'Your talk is Greek to me even today.'

While Zari was talking, Shams was looking at her with love and admiration in his eyes. Zari was conscious of this, though, she was trying to ignore it.

The sun had risen. The poplar leaves were clapping their hands and the soft cotton flakes had started falling on the lawn. They looked like the hailstones of the night before. Breakfast was announced and they all went to the dining room.

Noor was a reticent person. He noticed that neither Shams nor Zari were discussing today's program. He took out his diary and started telling them what they had planned for the day.

'Zari is going to stay with me today,' Omar said. 'I would like all of you to stay for a few more days, but I will not insist if you want to leave.'

'Yes, I want to spend some time with Chachaji today.' And then she looked at Shams and said, 'Would you mind staying with me. We will survey the area here and leave in the evening.'

Shams turned his large black eyes on Zari. She could see the love, faith and trust in Shams's eyes.

'I'd love to,' Shams said.

Nargis and Noor exchanged glances. They suspected there was more in Zari's words than what she said, but couldn't decide what to say. They kept their eyes on their plates and ate their breakfast.

When Noor and Nargis left, Zari went to her uncle and said, 'Please give me your manuscript, I'll read it. You show Shams around. He wants to talk to you.'

Zari retired to the backyard with Omar's manuscript.

Omar took Shams around Abbotabad and showed him the *Ilyasi Mosque*. Walking through the gray hills across the mosque and sitting by the cold water spring, Shams told Omar that he wanted to marry Zari.

Shams felt that Omar was not surprised. Maybe he had guessed what was coming? Omar told Shams about Zari's parents and her temperament. He also told him about Sinan and that Zari wanted to adopt him not because she had any sympathy for Adnan but because she wanted to help her uncle and because of the fact that he was Zeb's grandson.

'What do you think about it?'

'I don't have any objection. She can do whatever she likes.'

'I'm happy to hear that. It's a great thing to understand somebody fully and have trust in that person, especially in marriage. Zari might look very tough but she is very fragile,' Omar said, 'I value Zari as a treasure. Take care of her. She has no parents, no siblings and not many friends, but I'm sure you'll make her happy. To understand someone completely is a great thing so go ahead and marry her. My prayers will always be with you.'

21

When Zari came back to *Akbar Manzil* the next day, she got a message that Khushal's mother wanted to see her. Zari freshened up and left to see Khushal's mother. Their house was not far from *Akbar Manzil*.

Khushal's mother was very pleased to see Zari.

'Listen, Zari,' she said, 'Since Khushal has returned from Peshawar, he has locked himself in his room. He is not eating anything and refusing to see a doctor. I think you are the only one who can figure out what's going on with him. You are his childhood friend. He cares for you and respects you.'

'Okay, Aunt, I'll go and talk to him,' Zari said, and advanced toward Khushal's room.

The door was shut but not locked. She entered the room, which was very dark. Khushal lay on an old rug, his head rested on an embroidered pillow with a Persian motif of the tree of life. An embroidered, brown, helpless-looking tiger, who seemed to be more like a lamb was suffocating under Khushal's weight. He had a pillow wrapped about his head to evade the ray of light coming from the window. Newspapers from different dates lay scattered on the floor. When Zari's eyes could see a little better, she called him by his name.

He removed the pillow from his face and said, 'So, you have been sent to find out what is wrong with me?'

'Yes. Your mother asked you several times, but she didn't get an straight answer. She is really worried about you.'

'I couldn't tell her. She wouldn't understand, and it's not something that can be explained in a few words.'

'Then tell me. Maybe I can understand,' Zari said, sitting beside him on the rug.

'This is not the story of one single day. This had been going on for months, even for years.'

'I would like to hear it,' Zari said.

'Do you read the newspapers? Listen to the speeches that are broadcast on the first of every month. While all the wheat and sugar is being smuggled to other countries and there is a food shortage here the despot wants to celebrate his ten years of reign as if he was a king. Nobody in the government dare object. When students started protesting, they passed an ordinance that their degrees would be confiscated. They have no right to forfeit the degrees which the students have earned after passing their examinations?'

'I agree,' Zari said.

'After hearing about many incidents of firing on protestors all across the country, I at last decided to shoot the president in that public meeting at Peshawar.'

Zari held her breath. She had heard the news that somebody had tried to shoot the president. 'Was it you who had fired that shot at the president in Peshawar?' she asked horrified.

'Just listen. I told you it's a long story. Yes, I left home with a revolver. On my way, I saw all those buses that were transporting people from different small cities to Peshawar. Some people were being paid money to raise slogans and cheer the president. Anyway, the poor people were excited about a free trip to a big city and a day's holiday.

'Then what?' Zari asked impatiently.

'You know that I have nobody in the world except my mother, and I am not a source of happiness for her. I'm sure that others will take better care of her if I die.'

'Don't talk like that. Just tell me what happened in Peshawar.'

'I'm going to. As Ayub Khan came to the stage to deliver his speech, the hired people shouted welcome slogans. I thought this hoax should stop forever.

'I fished in my pocket for my revolver. At that very moment, a young boy in a linen suit who stood by me fired the shot. The bullet didn't hit Ayub Khan. But it caused a lot of panic and confusion. People fled like sheep do on seeing a jackal in their herd. Many stumbled and were crushed in the stampede. The meeting was disrupted. An overbearing person, perhaps someone from the army, caught the young boy.

'Later, I heard that the gates to the park were closed and people were forced to stay in and listen to the president's speech. The newspaper praised the president for remaining calm and giving his speech before two hundred thousand people. No paper reported that the gates of the park were kept locked and that the guards wouldn't let anybody leave. This is what happens in our country.'

Khushal raised his eyes and looked at Zari.

'Please go on,' Zari said.

'I had gone with the intention of killing the president. I think I am as guilty as that poor young boy Mohammad Hashim, who is a student of the Polytechnic Institute. His parents were very upset and claimed that their son was never involved in any political activities. I feel I should make a confession that it was I who had fired the shot.'

'Are you crazy? Why should you confess when you didn't shoot him?' Zari said, 'And where is that revolver?'

'Ah, the revolver! When I reached for it in my pocket, it wasn't there.'

'Khushal, you are having delusions. You didn't have any revolver at all. Look, don't say a word about this to anybody, and don't do anything foolish like taking the blame.'

'I am telling you I had the revolver in my pocket. Either it got lost or Mohammed Hashim saw it and took it out a few seconds before I searched for it. He was standing very close to me.'

'Don't talk nonsense, please!' Zari said in a firm voice but politely. 'You are inventing things in your mind by piecing newspaper reports together.'

'I'm telling you the truth. I'm not insane. I never tell a lie. I had gone with the intention of killing the president. I wouldn't have missed him like that stupid boy did. Why don't you believe me?'

'Shut up and don't tell this story to others, not even to your mother. Nobody is going to believe you. They'll think you've lost your mind—now let me bring you something to eat.'

'I don't want to eat. I don't have an appetite,' Khushal said.

'We'll have tea together.'

When Khushal didn't object, Zari left to get some tea.

'Can I have tea with snacks for Khushal and myself, Auntie?' She asked Khushal's mother.

'Sure, I'll get it for you presently.' There was gratitude and love in her eyes for Zari, and maybe a little streak of jealousy.

Zari was convinced that the old woman was not entirely wrong after all in thinking that Zari still had an influence over her son. Shams had guessed that too.

Zari brought in two cups of tea and a few biscuits. Khushal was now sitting idly, staring at the newspapers all around him.

'Do you remember Filfil, my little doggie?' Zari asked.

'Yes, I do. I remember everything. The day Zeb Qadri died you were missing all morning. I found Filfil's dead body lying beside the wall of the churchyard. He had remained unchained during that stormy night and had been killed by a jackal. You were lying unconscious near the dog's dead body. I lifted you up in my arms with great difficulty. I am your age,' Khushal smiled.

'I know, we have the same date of birth,' Zari said. 'Heaving and panting at each step I carried you. Uncle Akbar saw me and came down running, took you from my arms and ran home. I remember all this as if it happened only yesterday.'

'After that incident, I was ill for weeks.' Zari said, 'I think it was the result of the two shocks I had suffered. I loved both, Aunt Qadri and Filfil very much.'

'I used to come to read you stories when you were sick and we used to play Snakes and Ladders and Ludo. When you insisted on eating something which was not good for you, I persuaded you not to eat it and promised you never to touch it myself.'

'I remember, after my illness I had become so pale,' Zari said. 'My hair had thinned and I had no energy left. I looked so ugly.'

'No, you never looked ugly,' Khushal said, 'You looked pitiful though when you sat beside Filfils' house looking very melancholy.'

Zari took out a sleeping pill from her purse. 'Take this and sleep for a while. Auntie told me that you don't sleep at all. Your eyes are red from lack of sleep.'

Khushal swallowed the pill and sipped his tea.

Zari placed the cups in the tray and carrying them out, said, 'Be a good boy. Get some sleep. I'll come again.'

'OK, Whatever you say.'

She saw Khushal moving to his bed and pulling a sheet over his head.

She said to his mother, 'He's promised to try and get some sleep. Auntie, he'll be fine. Don't let him go out alone, though.'

Khushal's Mother wanted to ask many questions but thought better of it. Some other time, she decided as Zari wished to leave. It is enough that he has eaten something and is willing to go to sleep.

22

Before going to Lahore for his interview, Aijaz came to see his friend Nasir in Swat Valley. Nasir's village was the most beautiful place he had ever seen, and his house was situated by a river, surrounded by emerald green grass and colorful wild flowers. The range of high mountains overlooked the valley and gave the village an entrapped, but pretty, look.

In the beginning, when Nasir told him strange stories about superstitions, sicknesses and the treatments, Aijaz hardly believed him, but now that he had witnessed so many incredible incidents, he started believing in the tales. He had seen seven demons possessing a girl, seen them exorcised one by one by a Mullah. He had come to understand the psychology of the inhabitants. Being associated with high mountains, a man is bound to become rugged and harsh. Living in a place where tumultuous rivers carved their way, where fierce blizzards rage, human feelings are apt to become reckless. Where the comforts are so rare and nature is man's friend as well as foe, it is not surprising to have complicated feelings. Aijaz had seen a queer mixture of opposites in Nasir, who was an Afridi Pathan.

Nasir's father was the landlord of all the nearby land and also owned a few sugar mills. He was not only rich but the soul and master of every person and thing in his land. He was the king and the commander of his estate. According to his people's custom, he had a separate abode for men and women. Men's quarters along with guest suites were designed and built by highly qualified architects and engineers. They had all the modern facilities, while women lived in old dark buildings made of stone and mud surrounded by a high wall with only one huge gate through which, no man or even a boy over twelve-years-old could pass without permission. It was in that area that the pets and farm animals had their thatched houses.

In the living room there was a bookcase full of books. Aijaz had always been charmed with words. They were like enchanted castles in which hundreds of fairies, genies and demons were living. Old books fascinated him even more.

Most of the books in the bookcase were either English classical novels or collections of English poets. Every book, in a beautiful, round, feminine hand was signed with the name *Qudsia Khanam*. The leaves of the books were getting soft and yellowish as if they had not been exposed to air and light since they were first put in there. The leaves of *Neem* trees, which had been placed in the books to protect them from bookworm had dried and fell from the books like tears from the eyes of a princess imprisoned in a castle. Whenever Aijaz found Nasir reticent, he found solace in those books.

One day Aijaz asked Nasir, 'Who is this Qudsia Khanam? You have been telling me that there is no history of women's education in your family, but this girl seems to be so fond of English Romantic poets!'

'Yes, those kinds of incidents, or you might call them accidents, did occur in my mother's family.' It was clear that he did not want to continue the topic. 'Come, let's go out. You haven't come to my village to read books, have you?'

Aijaz suspected that Nasir was either hostile to or jealous of those books. One day when Aijaz was reading a decayed poetry book, a picture fell from it. The picture was very beautiful. It could be of none other than the owner of those books, Qudsia Khanam. She was much more beautiful than Aijaz had imagined. Aijaz, who was already impressed with Qudsia's handwriting, was mesmerized with her picture. He didn't show it to Nasir because Nasir had not yet told him who Qudsia Khanam was.

23

Aijaz was slowly coming to understand Nasir but there were still a few things about him which seemed odd. Nasir would suddenly get lost in such deep thought as if he were not there at all. Strangely, unlike most boys his age he would not show any interest in girls or talk seriously about marriage.

In his own home, he seldom went to the part of the house where the women lived. One day, Aijaz asked the reason for this and Nasir replied that it was not considered discreet to always be visiting the women's quarters. Besides, though there were lots of cousins, aunts and other womenfolk, not seeing them often created a gap in communication, leaving not a single common subject to talk about.

'What about your mother?' Aijaz had asked. The moment he uttered the last word he realized his mistake and knew what was coming. Nasir had once told him never to ask any questions about his mother.

'Sorry,' Aijaz said apologetically, 'you had asked me not to mention your mother, but it was in the days when we were mere room-mates, Now we are friends and I share with you everything which happens in my family, don't I?'

Nasir kept looking at him with an intent eye but said nothing.

'I think I have a right to know whether your mother is alive or, God forbid, dead...even if she belongs to a family which people regard as humble.'

'Shut up! Don't you say another word,' Nasir shouted, and leapt toward Aijaz as if he were going to strike him. But, suddenly stopped and went out of the room slamming the door behind him.

Aijaz felt resentful and angry. He had said nothing to get him into such a frenzy! He knew that women of inferior status were often taken into the household of the rich landlords. If Nasir was born of such a mother, it was all the more appreciable that the elder Khan treated him as his first born and given him all the privileges of a highborn son. As far as Aijaz was concerned, it did not make any difference whether his mother was a darling daughter of a lord or only a milkmaid. Aijaz felt so bitter that he decided to pack and leave.

When Nasir came into Aijaz's room again he saw him packing.

'What are you doing?' He asked rather curtly.

Aijaz kept quiet knowing that silence would hurt Nasir more than an answer would have.

'All right,' he said, 'go! But never call yourself my friend again or talk of friendship for that matter.' There was something in his voice, which made Aijaz look up. He saw a very wretched person standing there. Nasir's face was drenched as if all blood was drained from his body. His eyes were red as though he had been crying.

'Do you believe in Heaven and Hell?' He asked.

'Yes I do,' Aijaz said, still looking at his face that looked stranger than ever.

'I don't know what concept of Hell you have,' Nasir said solemnly, 'Just imagine your mother to be there in flesh and blood and to remain there till all eternity. Can you do that?' he said staring at Aijaz in a strange way.

Nasir's look more than his words made Aijaz shudder. He had never seen Nasir look or talk like that before. Nasir's face was chalk-white, he was trembling and his hand swelled up with the tight grip he had on the door.

'Thirty years, for thirty years my mother kept burning in this inferno and is still there.' Nasir's hands were trembling and his face was pale with emotion and stress.

'I have not been with her since the day of my birth, although she is only a few paces away from me! Have you ever heard of anything like that before? Tell me, tell me.' Nasir's voice grew fiercer as he demanded an answer from Aijaz, not really conscious of what he was saying.

Aijaz felt helpless. He advanced towards Nasir to console him in some way. Nasir placed his head on his friend's shoulder and broke into tears. He wept like a child in anguish and felt somewhat relieved. Then, he lifted his head from Aijaz's shoulder and looked at his friend, ashamed and puzzled as a child. Before Aijaz could utter a word, Nasir moved toward the window and sat beside it on a chair, drowned in self-meditation.

Aijaz wanted to say something but did not know what to say. Then he remembered a picture he had found in one of the books from the shelf. He went to the bookcase and took out the picture from the book.

'Look at this picture. Have you seen a prettier face?' asked Aijaz.

Nasir gave a disconcerted glance; then suddenly, he snatched the picture from Aijaz and studied it closely.

'How did you get it?' he asked excitedly.

'I found it in one of the old poetry books which bears the name of Qudsia. Do you know anybody by this name?'

'I have never seen my mother or her picture,' said Nasir ignoring his friend's question, 'but this can only be my mother's picture. Oh, what beauty, what grace!' his eyes were filled with tears and he pored over the picture lovingly, rapturously.

'Is her name Qudsia, by any chance?'

'Yes, you silly!' Nasir smiled still looking at the picture.

'Nasir, now I can see a great resemblance between you and her,' Aijaz said.

'Don't be ridiculous,' Nasir said impatiently. The idea of his resembling his mother was almost sacrilegious to him because in his mind his mother had risen above being human—almost divine.

Nasir again plunged into deep thoughts; then he whispered, 'Imagine, what a great risk a foreigner might have taken in helping her, and I, her own flesh and blood, did not lift a finger to free her from this dungeon. Isn't it disgraceful? You could never know how the thought keeps torturing me.'

'I'm sorry, I didn't know anything about that.' Aijaz let the shirt he was folding drop on the bed and sat down. 'You were not in a position to help her while you were just a student, but now you can. You might be able to get a house next to the hospital as other doctors with families have. If you don't get it right away, my mother would be only too glad to take her in until you have your own place.'

Nasir did not answer Aijaz but remained engulfed in his thoughts.

Nasir then went to his room and came back after a few minutes with an old notebook in his hand. 'This is my mother's diary, and I want you to read it. It has not been read by anyone other than me. Remember it's sacred to me, and I expect you never to tell its contents to anybody. If you can promise that to me, I'll let you see it.'

'I promise,' Aijaz said, and held his hand out to take the notebook.

'Then, go ahead and read it.' Nasir handed the notebook to him and left.

This was how Aijaz came to know the story of Nasir's mother's captivity in her own house.

When Nasir came back, he said, looking very concerned, 'Aijaz I've made up my mind!'

'About what?'

'Let's start immediately.' He took Aijaz's hand and dragged him out of the room towards the female suites. His determination knew no bounds. He passed the giant gate as if he had all the authority to do so. Aijaz followed him timidly, unable to defy his friend but afraid in his heart for his friend and himself.

Inside the gate there was a dark, narrow corridor with huge, earthen pots containing corn lined up on both side of the wall. Nasir went through the corridor like a warrior. Stopping at the entrance to the actual building he shouted,

'Sanober, come out.'

A middle-aged woman came out of the house at once, but she looked very unhappy and perplexed.

'I've come to see mother and see her I must, do you understand?' He demanded with an indication to the woman that he meant every word he said. 'Don't just stand there, show me the way.'

The woman trembled as if, suddenly, a wave of cold air had caught her. She kept rubbing her hands together.

'Come, if you must,' she said and led the way.

Nasir followed her and beckoned Aijaz to follow. They passed a labyrinth of rooms and corridors and finally reached a dark room in which a kerosene lamp was burning. With her back to the light a tall woman was taking out something from a cupboard. Hearing the footsteps she turned around to look. They both saw her in amazement. She looked beautiful, tall and fair like a statue in marble. She stood there, looking at Nasir, mute and motionless as if rooted there for years.

'Mother!' Nasir whispered and bowed down a little.

She lifted him up, holding his head in both hands, hugged him and then kissed him on the forehead. Then, as if not believing her eyes she kept staring at him, fearing that he should vanish as so many times before she had experienced this image to be an illusion or a dream.

'Mother, I want to take you to Karachi.' He noticed the terrified look on her face and added, 'Don't be scared. I'm your son and you can go with me. I'll make complete arrangements. We shall cover some distance on horses; it will shorten the journey and arouse no suspicion. Then we shall travel in a car.'

'Son, this is the first time in my life that I've seen you and talked to you, I beg you to say something nice and cheerful to me. Tell me about yourself; what have you been doing all these years?'

Then she saw Aijaz and a streak of fear and distrust gripped her. 'Who is he?' She asked perplexed.

'He is a friend. You can trust him as much as you can trust me. He shall be going with us. Now, you want me to tell you something nice. Is there anything better than what I just told you? I'm going to take you out of this dungeon forever.'

'I'm not going anywhere,' she said firmly.

'You don't mean it?' Nasir said in astonishment.

'Yes, I do,' she said, 'You should realize that he cannot harm me any more than he has already done, but he can make your life miserable. He can disinherit you, deprive you of all you have and can even kill you. He is capable of doing anything.'

'But I don't care, and I don't believe he can harm us once we are out of his jurisdiction.' He foresaw his mother trying to persuade him again and decided to put forward the trump card he had. 'It's not fair, mother!' he said, 'you were willing to go with a foreigner but are reluctant to go with me, your own son.'

'At this, the soft, crumpled face, smiling and crying at the same time, suddenly stiffened. Her hands remained suspended in the air. She clenched her fists and stared at Nasir as if she were in a trance. It was after quite some time that she was able to speak. Tell me,' she said, 'What have they told you about me? The deceitful fiends! I had assented to this life of unthinkable misery because they had promised me not to tell my son anything about my past.'

'They haven't told me anything, Mother. I know everything because I've read your diary.' He took her hand in his and tried to comfort her but she was extremely distressed.

'Where did you find my diary?'

'From among your old books.'

'Where is it now? Did your father read it?'

'No, he didn't, and it's safe with me. Trust me, Mother!'

'Well, I was sure that it was burnt long ago, I'm surprised to hear that it's still there. I don't really remember fully what I wrote in it—it was so long ago, but I remember that I wrote only the absolute truth.'

'You don't have to say that; I believed it while I read it.' He patted her hand to comfort her.

'Did you?' She said, 'Let me tell you one thing, that besides God, you are the only one I cared to know how I felt at the time and what had really happened.'

'Oh, don't worry about the past now, we have a life ahead! Just be prepared tonight. Only take a few things with you. First, we will take the path among the hills. Can you ride a horse?'

'Yes, I can.'

'It's all settled then. I'll come for you just after midnight. Mother, I have found your picture in one of your books, may I keep it?' Nasir seemed to linger on with the conversation because he simply had'nt the heart to leave.

'Why not!' His mother said lovingly, 'who has more right to keep it than you.'

The elderly woman who had ushered them in came to the door. It was already late, She wanted them to leave.

'Goodbye, Mother,' he said, taking hold of Aijaz's hand again and leaving, though not as fast as he had entered the house.

When he came back to the room he was in a state of euphoria. 'I feel as if I had come out from under tons of weight. I'm going to pay, at last, some of the debt I owe to my mother.' He kept saying such things while pacing the room.

Aijaz could understand his excitement—still, he chose to give him a word of warning. 'Mind you, there are still some very hard times ahead.'

'I don't care. Just tell me did you notice how beautiful my mother still is, how graceful and elegant?' Nasir said. 'How can a man destroy such a person for his own vanity? Aren't we men mean and selfish as compared to such women?'

'Yes, I think we are, now what could have happened to the person who tried to free your mother? Did your father have him killed and buried someplace here?'

'I don't think so. It is never easy to get a foreigner killed just like that. He must have gone back home. Now, get some sleep. I'll come back after making arrangements for the journey.'

Soon after Nasir came and explained to Aijaz that they would take two different routes and meet at a certain point. N a s i r would go with his mother while Aijaz would go with a confidant. At the secret rendezvous, they would have a car ready, and from there they would travel together in the car. Nasir left in haste, and Aijaz accompanied the confidant. They went stealthily to the back of the house, rode the horses, and descended the narrow path between the hills. It was a dark night and the horses seemed to know the way. Aijaz had mixed feelings; the fear of being caught and the thrill of adventure. It was not for long that he could entertain these ambivalent emotions because the same man who was accompanying him came close to him, grabbed him, put something close to his nose, and Aijaz blacked out.

When Aijaz came to his senses again, he found himself lying in the back seat of a taxi. How he came to be there he had no idea. It was a bright, sunny day and the rays of the sun were falling directly onto his eyes. He started to recollect the events of the night before.

'Where are you taking me?' He asked the driver. A hefty man sitting beside the driver looked back and said something in his own dialect, not to Aijaz but to the driver. The driver pulled up the taxi at the side of the road. The man got down and came to Aijaz.

'Here's your wallet,' he gave the wallet to Aijaz. 'Count your money and check other things. Your suitcase is in the trunk of the car. The elder Khan wants you to take the taxi as far as Rawalpindi, after that you will be on your own. Take a train and go straight to Karachi. Don't say a word to anybody about the incident and never try to come back to the village. Do you understand?'

'Yes, but where is Nasir Khan?' Aijaz asked.

'I was instructed to tell you this much only,' he said sternly and moved up to the driver.

'You can continue,' he said to the driver. 'I will take a bus from here and go back.'

Evidently he had his orders from the elder Khan, so did the taxi driver because he did not answer any of the questions Aijaz asked.

'Where shall I drop you?' He asked in return.

'Wherever you like,' Aijaz said angrily, 'May the devil take you.' He mumbled grudgingly.

Then, there is no need for me to go to Rawalpindi, you can take the bus from Nowshera,' The driver said.

'It's fine with me,' Aijaz said indignantly.

They did not talk to each other after that. Aijaz was drowned in his nightmarish thoughts. The happenings of the last few days were like a dream, unbelievable and incorrigible. God only knew what had happened to Nasir and his mother. Was it possible that they escaped from the clutches of the elder Khan? It was highly unlikely, but what the elder Khan was going to do with them was something Aijaz could not think of.

There was no discussion between Aijaz and the taxi driver after that. The driver stopped his taxi in the main bazaar of the small town of Nowshera. He took out the suitcase from the car unceremoniously, dropped it on the sidewalk and left without a word. Aijaz felt humiliated but there was nothing he could do about it.

He didn't have to wait long. Within half an hour, he saw a bus at the corner bound for Rawalpindi. He jumped in with his suitcase . As soon as his luggage was taken care of, he bought the ticket and seated himself comfortably. The episode of the previous night became vague and misty, as if it had all happened long, long ago.

Once in Lahore, Aijaz wrote many letters to Nasir but never received an answer.

24

Aijaz reached Lahore by train. He hired a taxi and asked the driver to take him to a decent but not very expensive hotel. The taxi driver brought him to a hotel, and Aijaz asked him to wait because he wanted to deliver Zari's letter to Mr Ahsan as soon as possible. He gave the address to the taxi driver and he drove him to the Cantonment area, which was very clean and quite different from where he was staying. The house was palatial with *Qasr-e-Neelam* engraved on the wall close to the big gate. There was a chair for a guard, but incidentally, nobody was there. The gate was ajar, so, hesitatingly, Aijaz stepped in and waited for somebody to come.

He saw the velvety green lawns stretching from the gate to the porch, and flowers blooming in spite of the cold weather. There was a small winding stream with an arched decorative bridge on one side of the garden. A huge marble terrace, which seemed to dwarf the house, hung above the house. When nobody came to ask him why he was there, he timidly advanced and rang the bell. A teenage servant came to the door immediately.

'Is Mr Ahsan in?' Aijaz asked.

'No,' replied the servant.

'What about Madam?'

'She is not home either.'

'Is anybody home?'

'Only the youngest daughter.'

'Can I speak with her?'

'What business do you have?'

Aijaz got nervous. He did not know how young or old the youngest daughter of the family was! However, he had come with a purpose and he had to do his job.

'Tell her that Aijaz has come with a letter from Madam Zari.'

The boy went in. Presently a fair, plump young girl peered at him from a half-opened door.

'Where have you come from?' She asked solemnly. Aijaz thought perhaps she was trying to imitate her mother's airs.

'I have come from Abbotabad,' Aijaz said. 'I've brought a letter from Zari Khan for Mr Ahsan.'

'Zari Khan gave you a letter addressed to Papa!' The girl's eyes rounded with surprise.

'Yes,' Aijaz said. 'Zari asked me to give it to your Papa by hand. I am not sure who really wrote the letter.'

'You can hand over the letter to me and I can give it to Papa—or you can come again,' she said.

'It would be very difficult for me to come again,' Aijaz said, and after thinking for a few seconds, added, 'I'll give the letter to you but please don't forget to give it to your father. It must be important, because I was asked to deliver it personally. I'll call and ask him whether he got it. Could you please give me your phone number!'

The girl gave him the phone number while carefully studying the address on the cover as if trying to guess the contents of the letter.

'You can call Papa or if you come some other day in the late afternoon—maybe you'll find both Mama and Papa at home,' the girl said.

'All right,' Aijaz said and left. The girl was still looking at the envelope with keen interest.

The next day, instead of thinking about his interview, he decided to go to *Qasr-e-Neelam* and meet the residents. On his way to Ahsan's house, he noticed that the traffic was exceptionally thin. When he signaled a taxi, the driver was reluctant to drive him because a procession of demonstrating students was on their way towards them. The driver agreed to take the risk when Aijaz offered him extra money. The driver did his best to avoid the demonstrators but they were caught up in the procession. So far it was a peaceful procession with police vehicles accompanying them and a lot of policemen half hidden behind the trees. The protestors were shouting the slogans. 'Release Mr Bhutto,' and 'Down with police excesses.'

When the police demanded that the students disperse, they refused to do so and started pelting stones at them. The policemen responded by beating the students with batons and the commotion began.

The taxi driver turned into a side lane, and zigzagging through a maze of streets, finally brought the taxi back onto Mall Road, crossed the Railway Bridge, and reached *Qasr-e-Neelam*. Aijaz gave his name to the guard at the gate, a servant came and escorted him into a sitting room.

After a few minutes, a lady wearing a sleeveless blouse and a costly *sari* wrapped around her enormous figure came in. She must have been pretty in her youth and Aijaz could still see a little resemblance to Zari who had told her that Sarwat, Mrs Ahsan, was related to her.

Sarwat asked him to take a seat. Her voice was a little hoarse.

'How was your journey?' she asked him formally. Her tone revealed that she was not least interested in him or his journey.

'It was fine,' Aijaz replied in the same vein.

'How do you know Zari?' she inquired.

'Zari and I work in the same...'

Aijaz had not yet completed the sentence when a tall, well-dressed man entered the room. Aijaz got up to meet him. They shook hands and introduced themselves to each other.

'Did you get the letter I left yesterday morning?' Aijaz asked.

'Yes, I did. Where have you been since then?'

'I've been at the hotel in the city where I am staying.'

'I've heard that a huge demonstration is being held in the city today, and that there was a *lathi-charge*.'

'Yes, I almost ended up in that procession. The taxi driver somehow managed to get me safely to your house by going into a labyrinth of side roads.'

'Are you on a business trip?'

'I am here for a few days only. I came for an interview.'

'Well, staying in the city is not safe these days,' Ahsan said. 'Since you are here for only a couple of days, why not stay with us?'

Before Aijaz could say anything, Ahsan called one of the servants and said, 'Ask the driver to go to the hotel with Mr Aijaz and bring him back with his luggage.'

Aijaz glanced at Mrs Ahsan. She did not look too pleased with her husband's proposal but did not say anything.

Aijaz wanted to know more about Zari.

As Aijaz rose to go to the hotel, Mr Ahsan said, 'Come back as soon as you can. It's better to be back before dark.'

As Aijaz was proceeding towards the expensive car with the servant, he was sure that there must have been an argument between Mrs and Mr Ahsan about inviting a stranger into their house.

25

When Aijaz woke up the next morning, a servant waited for him to come out and escorted him to the dining room.

All the family members were present at the breakfast table. Sarwat looked at him carefully. Aijaz observed that her mood was a little better than yesterday.

Ahsan introduced Aijaz to his daughters. 'My eldest daughter, Shahzadi, we call her Shezzy. She is studying medicine. And this is Nilofer, but she is called Neely. She is in ninth grade.'

They were all quiet. When the silence became a little too much, Ahsan said, 'Why don't you talk to our guest, Neely! You are such a chitchat.'

Neely blushed a little, tried to think about something to say but obviously could not think of anything appropriate. She abruptly said, 'Do you need anything in your room?'

'No, as a matter of fact, I can prepare a list of things I don't need,' Aijaz said pleasantly.

'Like what?' Neely asked.

'Like the air-conditioner,' Aijaz said.

Neely laughed; Shezzy smiled.

'What should I call you?' was Neely's next question.

'Aijaz Bhai would do. If you think you're older than me, then you can call me Aijaz.'

This time Neely laughed unreservedly.

After breakfast, Ahsan offered to drop him at the college on his way to work but Aijaz declined politely saying that he would prefer to take a taxi.

When he took leave of them, Neely said pleasantly. 'Best of luck!' Ahsan wished him good luck too. Aijaz thanked them both. Sarwat and Shezzy kept quiet.

Aijaz walked the short distance to the road to summon a taxi.

Aijaz enjoyed the beautiful morning. Lahore fascinated him. Compared to Karachi, it was smaller, but it had a character of its own.

It was a pleasant coincidence that when he entered the interview room he saw a professor from Karachi University was one of the interviewers. This chance meeting boosted Aijaz's morale because he knew the professor had a very good opinion of him as a student. He answered all the questions with confidence. Aijaz thought that his chances were great because there were not many candidates for this lecturer's job due to the political situation in the country. When they told him that they would let him know the result very soon he decided to stay in Lahore. But it would not be appropriate for him to stay at Ahsan's house any longer and he must find a place to move to from their house.

Maybe he would pretend to have come across a friend in Lahore who insisted he move in with him. But before going away, he had to find out a few things about Zari.

While returning to *Qasr-e-Neelam*, he came across another procession, which was moving from Tollington Market to the Assembly Hall. As it neared the Assembly hall, policemen prevented the people in the procession from moving toward the building. The students threw stones at the police. The police retaliated with tear-gas and *lathi-charged* them.

When it did not work, they fired directly at the people. Walking briskly on the footpath, Aijaz thought it wise to take shelter somewhere. He entered the zoo, which was very close. He loitered about there thinking that the political conditions were getting so uncertain that the schools, colleges and universities might be closed for a longer period. Now they were open one day and closed the next.

When the protestors dispersed and the suspended traffic resumed, Aijaz came out and walked towards the cantonment. When he reached the Canal Bridge, he rode a bus for the remainder of his journey.

As he entered *Qasr-e-Neelam*, Aijaz heard a lot of female voices chuckling, laughing and talking at the same time as if many radios were tuned in to different stations simultaneously.

At first Aijaz felt a little nervous, but he came to know that it was nothing but a ladies' coffee-party. There were dozens of cars parked outside the house. Some of the drivers were snugly sleeping in the cars while a few sat on the curb talking.

A few moments after Aijaz entered his room, there was a knock at the door.

'Come in,' he said, expecting a servant, but Neely came in

'Were you selected for the position?' she asked as soon as she entered the room.

'Not yet!' He laughed. 'It takes them some time to select a person after the interview.'

'How many days will you stay with us?' she asked making herself comfortable on the velvety sofa.

'As long as you want me to,' he said, just to hear her answer.

She burst into a mild laugh. 'I always like guests. There are so few people in our family and life is so dull and colorless. I get awfully bored.'

Aijaz was amused by her remarks—a girl of her age getting bored with life. Then he seized the opportunity to ask her about Zari. 'Does Zari visit you often?'

He was ready to ask some more questions, when Neely said, 'Never, I haven't seen her in my life.'

'Why? I think she is your mother's cousin and often comes to Lahore.'

'I don't know, I think Mama doesn't like her. She never mentions her name. Papa doesn't either; but I think he doesn't dislike her. What do you think?'

'I don't know. That's why I'm asking you.'

'Yesterday, when I gave the letter to Papa, Mama got very upset. She and Papa kept arguing about something till late at night.'

'Didn't you ask your mother what the argument was about?'

'I did, but Mama didn't tell me anything. She only rebuked me for being so inquisitive and said I shouldn't poke my nose into everything.'

'It's really strange,' Aijaz said. 'Zari's letter makes your Mama upset, but the person who brings the letter is invited to stay as a guest.'

'I think that was what the argument was about. Papa said to Mama that it's our obligation because Gulshan, your sister, had stayed so long with Zari, and then he said something about Sinan—I don't know who he is.'

'I don't know either.'

'Listen,' Neely leaned toward Aijaz. 'Though I haven't met Zari, I like her very much.'

'Well!' Aijaz smiled. 'How come you like her without having met her?'

'I have seen her pictures in Mama's old album,' Neely said. 'She is beautiful. Mama keeps that album hidden in a closet but I take it out sometimes and look at the old pictures. Can I show them to you?'

It was a temptation very hard for Aijaz to pass.

'If your Mama finds out?'

'No, she is playing Mahjong with her friends. She never leaves them.'

'If Shahzadi were to see us with the album?' Aijaz asked.

'Shezzy! She is busy reading in her room as always. She never talks to me. I get so bored.'

'Neely!' Shezzy's voice came from the balcony, 'Are you in there?'

'Yes,' Neely said.

Shezzy came into the room.

'Neely! What are you doing here? Why do you keep bothering people? You shouldn't intrude on guests like this.'

Neely didn't take any notice of her reproach.

'You can see now,' Neely said to Aijaz, 'she neither talks to the guests nor allows me to talk.'

Aijaz just smiled. 'Neely is a lot younger than you, isn't she?' Aijaz asked Shezzy to start a conversation with her.

'Not many years,' Shezzy replied, 'but she likes to behave like a child.'

'Shezzy is not as old in years as she pretends to be,' Neely said.

'Are you coming with me or not?' Shezzy demanded.

'I am,' Neely said, but kept sitting.

'I have a few small gifts for both of you. May I give them to you now?' Aijaz said.

'Not now,' Shezzy said, 'I would like Papa and Mama to see them.'

'Why? Why not now?' Neely asked Shezzy.

'Neely,' Shezzy said, 'come with me right now!' Her tone was very firm.

'Okay, I'm coming.' Then she looked at Aijaz and asked him, 'Are the gifts from you or from Zari?'

'Don't be silly, Neely.' Shezzy checked her again, caught hold of Neely's hand and got her out of the room.

While leaving, Shezzy turned to Aijaz and said, 'Neely doesn't let anybody alone. I hope you don't mind.'

'Not at all,' Aijaz said.

Ten minutes later, there was a gentle knock. Aijaz rose to see who was at the door. Neely stood there with an album in her arms.

'May I come in?' she asked.

'Oh!' Aijaz felt a little alarmed. 'You shouldn't have brought the album right now.'

'It would be hard to get it any other time. Mama is busy with the party now, and Shezzy has dozed off.'

'All right, please leave the album here. You can take it back in ten minutes,' Aijaz said.

'No, I want to see it with you.' She sat on the sofa, placed the album on her lap and opened it.

'Look,' she said triumphantly as if she were going to show a big trophy she had won. Then she leafed through a few more pages. A wave of discomfiture ran across her face. 'Mama has taken out all of Zari's pictures.' She was so disappointed that Aijaz thought she might cry.

'Has she?' Aijaz, though very much disappointed, tried to stay calm. 'Let me see.'

He sat on the other sofa-chair and browsed through the album. The pages of the album were black, the names of people and the years in which the pictures were taken, were neatly written below the pictures in white ink. Most of them were group photos. Aijaz could see that the pictures taken out were the ones which, invariably, had the name of Zari written beneath them.

'I'm as disappointed as you are,' Aijaz said to Neely, 'but there is nothing we can do about it.' Aijaz handed the album to Neely and added, 'Now, I have to write a few important letters.'

'If you are writing to Zari, I'd like to send her a little note. Would you please send my note along with your letter?'

Aijaz did not know what to say. 'Why don't you call her Auntie Zari?' Aijaz tried to distract her.

'Because I haven't met her. I may call her "Auntie" when I meet her. I call Shezzy by her name too.'

'But why do you want to write to Zari?'

'Because I like her,' Neely said with child-like innocence. 'And I want to know why Mama is angry with her?'

'That you should ask your mother.'

'I have asked her so many times, but I don't get the right answer. That's why I want to write to Zari.'

'Okay,' Aijaz said. 'Write your note if you wish to, but if something goes wrong, if your mother comes to know about it, the responsibility will be yours not mine.'

'Sure,' she laughed. 'I am writing to her of my own free will, and I'll also tell Mama about it someday when I'll find her in a good mood.'

She carried the album with her. The moment she stepped out of the room, Aijaz locked his door.

26

'What are you doing this evening?' Ahsan asked Aijaz at lunch.

'Nothing in particular.'

'Why don't you come with me to the golf club,' he said cheerfully. 'Men ought to have some outdoor activity.'

'I will, thank you,' Aijaz said.

'Shezzy, please ask Karamdad to put my golf kit in my car and bring my gym shoes.'

'Yes, Papa,' Shezzy replied obediently.

'How are your studies going at college?' He asked as an afterthought.

'Papa, schools and colleges are not functioning normally because of the strikes and demonstrations, but I'm doing fine.' After a brief pause, she hesitatingly said, 'Papa, I want to go to see Daisy today.'

'Yes, go. By the way what's she doing these days? Where does she live? Her parents have moved to Karachi, haven't they?'

'Yes, Papa, she stays at the YWCA.'

'Why on earth do you want to see Daisy?' Sarwat said angrily. 'It's so dangerous to go out these days. Don't you read the news about shootings?'

'Oh, Mama, you know how the media exaggerates everything. Those shootings happen when there are processions and protests going on.'

'When there is unrest in a city, people try to take advantage of it,' Sarwat said knitting her brows, 'Anything can happen anytime, I won't allow you to go. Besides, I don't like this friend of yours.'

'She is my friend from school, Mama. We've been classmates for years,' Shezzy said.

'She was allowed to study in your school only because Mrs D'souza was the music teacher there. They are not the type....'

'Oh, Sarwat, don't be so class conscious,' Ahsan chuckled to soften his remark a little.

'Mama is always so status-conscious,' Neely said, and blushed as she realized that the remark was too bold for her to say.

'You are becoming a blabber,' Sarwat said, looking sternly at Neely.

Neely decided to sneak off.

'Daisy ought to have gone with her parents,' Sarwat said, 'but, no, she wants to live independently, without anybody's control over her. How can I allow my daughters to mix with those kinds of girls!'

'Look, she is a Christian. Their culture allows a few things that ours doesn't,' Ahsan said. 'That doesn't mean that she is bad. Besides, our Shezzy is too intelligent to be influenced by anybody. I'll give Shezzy a ride and bring her back to you safe and sound. Are you happy now?'

Sarwat was not happy but thought it prudent not to create a scene before Aijaz.

Shezzy called Daisy about her visit and found her waiting at the YWCA gate. She came towards the car and greeted Ahsan in English. Ahsan inquired after her parents. Then Daisy threw a swift glance at Aijaz. He also judged her to be more mature than Shezzy in age and in experience, but he did not have time to make any more judgements as the driver quickly drove the car away.

'Do you and Zari work together?' Ahsan asked Aijaz after leaving Shezzy at the YWCA.

'Yes, we work in the same department,' Aijaz replied.

'What are you folks doing in Abbotabad?'

'We are on a research project.'

'I see. And where does Zari stay in Karachi? In a women's hostel?'

'No, in a house with her old maid-servant. Have you never visited Zari in Karachi?'

'I haven't, but I would certainly like to have her address if you can give it to me.'

'Sure, would you like to write it down?'

'Yes.' Ahsan took out his diary and wrote Zari's address with great precision.

So, that was the reason the guest was asked to accompany the host to his club. But why couldn't he ask for Zari's address at home in his wife's presence! Aijaz had that question in mind but he put another question to Ahsan.

'Was the letter from Zari important?'

'It wasn't from Zari. It was from my stepfather, Omar,' Ahsan answered briefly.

And by this time they reached the club.

The facade of the Officer's Club had lofty pillars and slender, ivory-colored lattices.

They entered into the big hall. Aijaz noticed that the ceiling was very high, and close to the ceiling was a colorful flower border on the wall that indicated that the building was old, but well kept.

There were several sets of sofas and chairs arranged in a way that families and small groups could sit together. Senior government officials, army officers and a few foreigners were playing golf, their caddies following them carrying their golf clubs.

Ahsan showed him the library and then asked, 'Would you like to come with me or would you rather relax here for a while?'

Aijaz chose not to go with him and settled in the library to read the newspapers.

After half an hour Ahsan came back. He held one wrist in his other hand. A little later, a waiter from the club came, knelt and courteously dressed his wrist with a bandage. 'I hurt my wrist,' Ahsan said, 'it's my punishment for neglecting the game for such · a long time. Aijaz said nothing, as he didn't know much about golf. Ahsan then ordered coffee.

Sipping coffee, Ahsan abruptly asked, 'What sort of a girl is Zari?'

Aijaz hesitated a moment then said, 'Surprisingly, I wanted to ask you the same question. I have only known her for a few months, while you are related to her.'

'Oh!' Ahsan laughed. 'I absolutely have no idea. She is related to my wife and we've never met.'

That was the end of their discussion.

* * *

'Shezzy, what's the matter?' Daisy brought Shezzy to her room and asked right away. 'You sounded very worried on the telephone.'

'Yes, I am very upset,' Shezzy replied. 'I got a letter from Jawwad today. He is coming to visit us soon.'

'Jawwad, your fiancé?'

'Unfortunately, he is my husband.' There was a tremor in her voice.

'Oh, I'm sorry, you have told me so many times, but my mind does not accept the fact that you are a married woman although you're still single.'

'I've told you so many times that if the *Nikah* papers have been signed, the marriage is considered valid in every sense of the word, even if the couple has never been together. No woman can get out of it without a divorce.'

'Even if they haven't lived together as husband and wife for a single day—or night. It's hard for me to digest.'

'But it's true.'

'Okay, I understand that,' Daisy said, as if she was ready to go into the depths of the matter. But now, what's the problem?'

'Well, the problem is—listen to me attentively, and for God's sake, don't make fun of me. You are the only person in the world I can tell about the miserable situation I'm in.'

'Then, tell me, before you pass out. I can see you are going to,' Daisy said.

Shezzy began to talk in English so Daisy could understand her better. Somehow, she felt that it was easier to express her situation in a foreign language.

'You know my mother. At first she was fascinated by Jawwad and his family, I was too young and naïve at that time and could not decide for myself and didn't dare oppose mother when Jawwad's family insisted on the *Nikah*. To tell you the truth I was also impressed that Jawwad was so handsome and the family was kind of rich and educated. There was no chance of knowing any more at that time but now my opinion about him has changed considerably. I am still confused and don't want to see him until I make up my mind.'

'Fine, I understand so far. Go ahead.'

'But my mother wants me to go out with him every time he comes. She kind of takes pride in the fact that, unlike other narrow-minded women, she lets her daughter go with her fiancé or bridegroom, or husband, whatever. She thinks there's nothing wrong with it. She sends Neely with us, but what actually happens is so sickening that I'm ashamed to tell.' Shezzy hid her face with her hands.

'What is it?' Daisy suddenly became very serious.

'I'll tell you everything that happened the first time. Three of us went to watch a movie in the club Jawwad was staying in. Neely insisted upon inviting her friend, Naghma also. Naghma is a poor girl and she had never seen a movie in her life. We went to see a comedy, which was filmed at the beaches around the Mediterranean Sea. There were a lot of nude and sexually explicit scenes.

'I told Jawwad that I was not enjoying the movie and didn't want to see any more. He behaved as if he respected my feelings and stood up immediately, but when I asked the girls to come with us, he asked me to let them enjoy the hilarious situations. We'd be back in a few minutes. As his room was not far from the theatre it was a good time to give me a gift he had purchased for me.

I agreed and Jawwad took me to his room in the club.

He handed me a beautiful, hand-carved, wooden box with a pair of beautiful earrings in it. And then he started behaving like the hero of that movie, kissing me and coaxing me to his bed. The more I resisted, the more forceful he became. When I told him that I didn't want to have sex he got very angry.

Shezzy sat silently, with her face pale and white lips trembling as if overwhelmed by a sense of deep exhaustion.

Daisy looked at her for a few moments, then said, 'To tell you the truth, I don't understand your problem. You are husband and wife in every conceivable way. Why then make sex a taboo?'

'After I said "no" and he insisted, I felt so humiliated,' Shezzy said almost tearfully.

'There's no humiliation in love, my dear. You should thank God that he loves you and you love him. My advice is, be brave. You are his wife. Love him and let him love you.'

'But this is very hard for me, Daisy! Had it not been so, I wouldn't have come to you. Maybe you don't understand my problem, but it's real for me.'

'Does that mean that your mother or society would not approve of your having sex with him!'

'Exactly, my mother would kill me if she knew about it, and she would not blame him but me for not taking care of myself.'

'So your mother doesn't understand the dilemma she has put you in, is that it?'

'Exactly.'

'Oh, my God!' Daisy looked up toward the sky. 'Mothers still live in the ivory towers they make for themselves.'

'My Mama does,' Shezzy said.

Daisy thought a moment then said, 'The only way out for you is not to meet him alone again.'

'But Mama insists, saying that the poor fellow comes from Peshawar only to see me.'

'When is he coming again?' Daisy asked.

'Next week. What should I do?'

'Tell your mother everything.'

'This is impossible. I can't do it, Daisy. She'll blame me for everything and I'll feel even worse.' Shezzy was about to cry.

'Then there is only one solution left. I am going to Karachi next week. Let's go together. The change of climate will do you good.'

'How can I? I have no close relations in Karachi where I can stay.'

'I am your friend,' Daisy said. 'My house is not as luxurious as yours but you can stay with me. Look, nothing's impossible. I'll come to your house in a day or two and talk to your parents. I'll put the matter in a way that your mother won't find it hard to accept.'

'If only Mama would give me permission,' Shezzy said, 'but I know she won't.'

'Don't worry, she will. All the schools and colleges are going to close down very soon. You wouldn't be travelling alone so there's hardly any chance of getting lost,' She smiled. 'Cheer up and be firm.'

'I don't know whether this plan is going to work.'

'It will.' Then, Daisy changed the subject saying, 'Now tell me, who was that young guy in your Papa's car?'

'He is a guest.'

'Can he be of any help?' Daisy winked at Shezzy. 'Any chauvinistic streaks?'

'No, not at all. He seems to be infatuated with my aunt.'

'Oh, he's a bore!'

'I suggest you talk to Papa on the telephone first,' Shezzy said, 'I'd give you his office number. If he agrees more than half the battle is won. We'll be three against one.'

'It's settled then,' Daisy said. Then they chit chatted till Ahsan came to take her home.

27

It was an extremely sluggish day. The schools and colleges were closed for an indefinite period.

A big demonstration was scheduled and a complete strike was announced too. There were no buses and taxies running on the road. The students loitered on the deserted streets to ensure that the shops were closed in observance of the strike. They threw stones at the stores that dared open for business, forcing them to pull down their shutters. Occasionally, a car passed by.

Aijaz had gone to a nearby bookstall to buy a newspaper. He wanted to look for a one-bedroom apartment for the rest of his stay. The newspaper stall was closed too. When he came back to *Qasr-e-Neelam*, he felt quite a difference from the previous days. The lawn that had always been clean was now full of fallen leaves. A thick layer of bougainvillea petals floated on the turquoise-blue waters of the canal. There was an eerie silence as if all birds and insects had conspired to leave the locality. He went directly to his room and kept himself busy reading the paper and looking for advertisements for renting houses.

In the afternoon nobody called him for tea, which was quite unusual. When he came down, he found several servants gathered at the main gate looking sad and puzzled. On inquiry he learned that Neely was missing. It was more surprising that she had not informed anyone before leaving the house. That was not done in this house. Sarwat panicked and went around from house to house in the neighborhood in her car. Ahsan called each of Neely's friends to find out if she was with them. The answer was in the negative so far.

Aijaz recalled that only yesterday, Neely had shared a secret with him. She had told him about Naghma, a young friend she met in a park and liked very much. She did not tell anybody about her because she was from a poor family and lived in the servants' quarters of one of the bungalows behind the railway station. Neely knew that her mother would never approve of her friendship with her. Aijaz did not say anything to anybody, and with a vague hope of finding her, set out for Naghma's house behind the railway station.

He cut his way short through St. John's Park. The dry leaves blanketed the narrow paths of the park. After leaving the park, he came to the lanes that ran along a row of bungalows. In front of a large, old house, he saw a group of agitated students talking excitedly. Suspicious passersby stopped for a moment to see what the matter was, and shaking their heads, moved on.

'Why are so many people gathered here?' Aijaz asked a passer-by.

'The son of a maid-servant living here was shot at in a demonstration today. The police is not disclosing if he is dead or alive—if alive, in which hospital, and if dead, where his body is. So the students are really mad.'

The owner of the bungalow came out to appease the students. He tried hard to persuade them to return to their homes, but the students refused to go home and were determined to do something about it. The owner was threatening to call the police if they didn't leave his premises.

Leaving them arguing, Aijaz quietly entered the path going into the bungalow and proceeded to the back of the building towards the servants' quarters. In the back yard, a melancholy cow stood beside her newborn calf. There, in front of the servants' quarters, a few women sat on a bare cot in the open. One of these women, with a very pale face, was wringing her hands and grieving in a monotonous tone. Behind the cot, Neely stood silently near a weeping girl about her age. Neely's eyes were filled with tears as she watched the lamenting woman with sympathy.

Aijaz dared not call Neely, but she saw him. She was about to come to him when Sarwat suddenly appeared on the scene with the owner of the house.

Seeing Neely, Sarwat felt relieved that she was safe, but instantly her sense of relief turned to anger. She grabbed Neely roughly by her arm and almost dragged her up to the car.

'Who was that woman?' one woman asked another after they were gone.

'She was the mother of Naghma's friend, the girl who stood by her.'

'She took her daughter away, but didn't say a word of sympathy to the mother of the boy who was shot.'

'They are rich people. They don't care for poor people like us. Did you see how angry she was?'

Aijaz didn't wait to hear more. He left the premises as quietly as he had entered.

When he reached home, he learned that Sarwat had locked Neely in her bedroom and had retired to her own room. She had declined to talk to anyone.

Unable to free Neely Ahsan had gone to his club for diversion.

Aijaz sat in the lounge waiting for Sarwat to come out of her room so that he could beg her to pardon Neely. But she never came.

When Ahsan came home, he beseeched his wife to forgive Neely but she was adamant. He then came to Aijaz and said, 'Sarwat is terribly angry with Neely and not at all in a mood to listen to anybody. It looks like Neely will have to remain confined in her room for a day or two. Maybe it's good for her. Please have your supper and go to bed. I had my meals at the club.'

Aijaz skipped his meal and went out for a short walk. The autumn trees stripped of their leaves were adding a unique kind of sadness to the night. The moon peeping through the cluster of dark clouds also had an air of sorrow.

When Aijaz returned, he wanted to call out to Neely to comfort her. But there was no way he could do this, so he just went to his room and prayed for her.

In the morning, Ahsan took Aijaz into his confidence and told him that he had managed to get hold of the key to Neely's room and had secretly slipped into it at night. Neely, resting her head on his chest had sobbed, 'Papa, am I really bad? Have I done something very wrong? Naghma is my friend. Her brother was shot—was it improper for me to go to her?'

'I told her that her mother was angry because Neely had kept a secret from her and had gone to her friend's house without telling anybody. When her anger would wear off, she'd forgive her. That quieted her. Then in the morning, before Sarwat woke up, I sneaked in to her room again. Neely was sleeping. I placed a few storybooks and her favorite chocolates near her pillow and left.'

Sarwat sent Neely's breakfast with a servant, but did not go to see her and did not allow anybody else to go to her room. When Aijaz asked permission to visit Neely for a few minutes, Sarwat firmly said, 'No. No one from the family should talk to her for a couple of days, so that she comes to her senses. She is getting far too headstrong.'

Conditions in the country were taking a new turn. The government had imposed Section 144 in every big city but people disregarded it. The police tear-gassed and lathi-charged, but it only resulted in more and more protests. The demonstrations were spreading like wild fire across the country, demanding blood money for the families of the martyrs, for the release of political leaders and for restoration of democracy.

Aijaz stopped at the edge of the road to watch. He could not believe his eyes when, in the second row from the front, he saw Neely walking along with Naghma with a banner in her hand. Aijaz tried to figure out how Neely might have come here. Had Sarwat permitted Neely to join the procession? Impossible. Could Neely have escaped from her room? That didn't seem possible. There was no more time for Aijaz to think.

The police had drawn a line on the road and had warned the people in the procession again and again not to cross the line. If they did, the consequences could be deadly. The protestors were too excited to stop at the line. The big boys tried to form a circle around the girls to provide them a little security and then crossed the line. They were instantly showered with bullets. Aijaz, his eyes burning from the tear gas, rushed into the mob, and holding Neely firmly by the hand, dragged her to the side of the road. It was not safe there either so he pulled her into a side lane and up the stairs to a store where they could watch the procession from behind a pillar. The police was trying to arrest people in the procession, and they were now running about in panic.

There, in a very serious tone as if he had the authority to question her, looking straight into her eyes, Aijaz asked, 'Neely, how did you get into the procession?'

Helpless and angry, her eyes burning with tear gas, Neely's face had turned purplish red. She started crying. 'Why did you pull me out?'

'I'll tell you later,' Aijaz said. He soaked his handkerchief from a nearby tap and handed it to Neely. 'First wipe your eyes and face with this. Then come along with me. We can't stay here.'

Holding Neely's hand again, he walked her to a footpath and proceeded towards the cantonment. They could still hear the shots fired in the air to harass people and the cries of the protesters. Neely was panting for breath. Aijaz made her walk fast still holding her hand till he was convinced that they were out of danger. Aijaz, then, asked her to sit on a small bench at the roadside.

'Now tell me, how did you get out of your room?' The concern and care in his tone did not allow her to challenge his authority.

In a heavy voice, she said, 'I knew that Naghma's family would participate in today's procession and I had promised to be with her.'

Aijaz looked her in the eye. 'I am asking you how you managed to get out of that locked room?'

Neely started crying, shivering from head to foot. Perhaps, for the first time, she had realized the seriousness of what she had done. Without her companions, her borrowed courage had dissipated. Aijaz drew her closer, and in an effort to encourage her, said consolingly, 'Don't cry. Just tell me everything truthfully so that I can think what to do next.'

Neely continued to sob. Gradually, she regained her composure and told Aijaz that, holding on to a branch of the tree close to her window, she had climbed into the tree, jumped down into her neighbor's garden and quietly slipped from his gate. Nobody had seen her. Had they seen her they would not have questioned her because she often visited the neighbors.

From the neighbor's house, Neely directly went to Naghma where all her brothers and sisters, even their parents were ready to join the procession.

'Don't you realize that not a single member from your family was in that procession,' Aijaz said. 'And did it ever occur to you what your parents would think and do if they found you missing from your room?'

'I left a note saying that I had to be with Naghma,' Neely replied

'Ah, you did. I don't think you realized what the consequence of this rash action would be?' Aijaz said bitterly.

'Maybe Mama would keep me locked in my room for a month,' Neely said, still crying.

'You might get a worse punishment. Now think about me. Seeing you with me, they might think that I let you out and accompanied you to join the procession. I'm going to be in big trouble.' Aijaz purposely kept his tone bitter.

'I'll tell mother everything,' Neely said nervously. Aijaz noticed that she was shaking like a leaf does in a strong wind. Aijaz felt sorry for her. He knew that children sometimes do things on impulse and suffer later for it.

'Now, don't be afraid,' Aijaz said politely. 'I'll take you to your neighbor's house. You should go there as you usually go to visit them. I'll go to your house and tell your father that you're there. He will come to fetch you. You must be prepared to face whatever happens after that.'

He got up and started walking. Neely walked with him. There was very little traffic on the road. Aijaz signalled a few cars for a lift, but they ignored him. At long last a person stopped and gave them a ride.

After leaving Neely at the neighbor's house, Aijaz entered *Qasr-e-Neelam*. A servant told him that Ahsan was not at home but Sarwat was, and that Neely was still locked in her room. So far no one knew that Neely had escaped. Sarwat sat reading a letter in the sunroom.

Since no one was aware of Neely's absence, Aijaz thought the best solution to the problem would be if he could, somehow, get the key from Sarwat and have Neely enter her room unnoticed.

'Can you please give me the key to Neely's room for about five minutes?' he requested Sarwat in all humility.

'Why?' Raising her fine, sharp eyebrows, she looked at Aijaz as if to say, 'How dare you!'

'I would like to talk with Neely,' Aijaz said, 'and explain the seriousness of the matter. I think that she will listen to me.'

Sarwat did not say anything but did not give him the key either. Aijaz sensed that Sarwat's anger was fading and that she wanted to compromise with Neely. She thought for a moment, took the key from her purse and said, 'Let's go. I'll open the door for you.'

Aijaz was baffled. What should he do now? Would it be possible for him to act as if he knew nothing about Neely's disappearance when Sarwat would find that she is not in her room?

He followed Sarwat timidly, praying for Neely and himself. Sarwat turned the key in the lock and asked Aijaz to open the door. She held herself back deliberately. As Aijaz opened the door, Neely looked at him stretching her neck from her pillow. What a relief!

It was certain that Neely had climbed back up the same tree she had used for her escape. Relieved, he looked at Neely smiling. She looked very innocent, very sweet and mischievous at the same time.

Pulling up a chair, Aijaz sat beside Neely.

'Now, promise me that you woudn't take part in any meetings or processions.' Neely had seen a glimpse of her mother standing behind the door.

'I promise,' she said.

'And promise that you will never go to your friends' house without your mother's permission.'

'Promise!' Neely replied. Aijaz extended his hand.

'A gentleman's promise, non-reversible,' Aijaz said jokingly.

Neely slowly placed her little hand into Aijaz's hand. 'Yes,' she said laughing cheerfully.

Sarwat watched this dialogue with surprise. There was a glimmer of friendship and understanding in their eyes. Why can't Neely trust me like that? She thought, feeling a little jealous. Then Sarwat entered the room

'Neely has promised that she will not go anywhere without your permission from now on,' Aijaz said.

'Good.' She still held the letter she had been reading. She said to Neely, 'This letter is from your aunt in East Pakistan. She has invited us to East Pakistan because they are thinking of leaving the place for good.' Sarwat read the last sentence from the letter. 'Shezzy and Neely should see East Pakistan. It's a place that is really worth seeing.'

'Mama, let's go to East Pakistan,' Neely begged, as if she were once again the pampered little baby of the family. 'The schools and colleges are already closed indefinitely. This is the best time.'

'There is political unrest there too,' Aijaz said.

'But the daily routine has not yet stopped anywhere,' Sarwat said. Then looking at Aijaz, added, 'Can you imagine that Ahsan agreed to take Shezzy to Karachi in such disturbing times?'

'She would come back immediately if we decide to go to East Pakistan,' Neely said. 'Jawwad Bhai is also going there. We can all go together.'

'No, Jawwad has to go with his regiment,' Sarwat said. 'It will take some time for him to reach there.'

'For the happy occasion of visiting East Pakistan, Neely's punishment is waived, isn't it?' Aijaz said.

Sarwat smiled at Neely lovingly.

Neely threw her arms around her mother and kissed her on the neck.

28

Since childhood, Zari had lived in her family's old village mansion or in a large well-established house in Abbotadad. Karachi had developed very rapidly. Zari detested the emptiness and brashness of the new houses and did not want to live in one of those modern houses where the sound of an alarm clock shocks one awake with the premonition of a frantic day ahead.

It took some searching but Zari found a beautiful, high-domed stone building that housed an art academy in some of the rooms. The other rooms were empty. She rented the vacant part of the house and was very happy. There were a few rooms which Zari never entered, but their presence satisfied the sense of spaciousness that Zari had grown accustomed to. The building had broad, polished wooden staircases, checkerboard tile floors that danced before the eyes presenting a new design from whichever angle one saw it. In front of each room was a veranda. Long branches of fruit trees draped over the building's arched windows. The heavy, rattling dry leaves fell from the almond trees. New sprouting leaves on these trees looked like birds that were getting ready to fly. The big red flowers dropped from the tall *Gul Mohur* trees. On still summer afternoons cooing doves hidden amid the leaves and cuckoos calling from the mango-trees dispelled the feeling of loneliness.

Zeenat Bibi, an old woman, stayed with her as her housekeeper. She was her old maidservant Gulgoona's mother. One evening, when Zari had returned from office and was basking in the sun after eating, Zeenat Bibi brought the day's mail. Zari opened the first envelope. It was a letter from Aijaz. A little note slipped from the letter and rested in her lap. It was from Neely. Reading the letters from Aijaz and Neely, she smiled. They were both like children who, somehow, have great expectations of their elders.

The second letter was from her Chachaji. With the very first sentence of the letter, her heart sank.

Khushal Khan has died. The letter said. *You know that the people in our family holding important government position did not want his name to be involved with any prohibited party meetings or processions for their own sake.*

He died because of the wounds he got at the hands of police but it was not difficult to put the blame for his death on his weak health and his weird and unusual whims. He has been buried in his family graveyard. His mother's condition is pathetic. She is a very proud person like her husband and son, and does not accept help from anyone. She does not want to leave her home. I have decided to look after her meager land in the village so that it yields a satisfactory income for her. It would have been better had I thought of doing that earlier. As so often happens we think of these things after the damage is done.

'Kushal's wallet contained a few rupees, two or three newspaper clippings and a hazy photograph on the back of which is written in pencil 'Khushal', 'Zari' and 'Filfil'.

'I am greatly shocked by his death and I am sure you also will be deeply moved. But, what can we do? It is a national tragedy that sincere people and men of character in our country, not only fail to achieve anything in life, but they are known as good-for-nothing and crazy. Our nation doesn't know how to make use of their sincere enthusiasm and true sentiments. We do not learn anything from their deaths. They lead a purposeless life and die an anonymous death. On the other hand, people who are petty, self-centered and hypocritical are rewarded.

Your Chachaji

29

Shezzy wanted to meet Zari. Along with Daisy she called her from a public telephone. Zari told her that they were welcome. Shezzy and Daisy hired a taxi and went to the Metropole Hotel where Zari's office was located. On meeting her Shezzy felt uncomfortable. Maybe she had made a mistake intruding upon Zari. What on earth made her think that Zari, whom her family never liked, would be courteous to them.

'So, you are Shehzadi?' She said. 'Come here, give me a hug.' Zari rose from her chair and advanced toward her. Shezzy, too, stood up. Zari enfolded her in a loving embrace, and kissed her gently on the cheek. Then she shook hands with Daisy. The informal air in Zari's tone touched both Shezzy and Daisy.

'My friend, Daisy,' Shezzy introduced Daisy to Zari.

'Your name is beautiful,' Zari observed with a smile. 'Daisy is a delicate, sweet, little flower. Have you ever visited England?'

'Oh, no. Not even in my dreams,' Daisy said with her natural frankness.

'In England, there are lots of daisies,' Zari said. 'They are everywhere—in open fields, by the roadside, in people's gardens... Shezzy, where's your luggage?' She abruptly asked.

'I was staying in a hotel with Papa but now I'm staying with Daisy for two days.'

'Oh, I see,' Zari said. She then rang the bell, put a few things in her desk drawer, closed it and got up.

'Lunch time in our office starts at one. Come, let's go.'

When her assistant came into the room, Zari told him, 'Tell Juma Bibi that I've gone out with guests. I'll come back after lunch.'

Shezzy and Daisy wondered where she was taking them. They decided that Zari must be taking them to a hotel. Zari asked about the weather in Lahore and compared it with the warm and pleasant weather in Karachi. Walking along the long corridor, they got into an elevator. A tiny car was parked outside the hotel. Zari asked Shezzy to sit in the back seat and invited Daisy to sit in the passenger's seat. Starting the engine she said,' So, Daisy, where do you live?'

'Are you going to my house?' Daisy asked unbelievingly.

'Yes, why not! Didn't I tell you it's lunchtime? You both will have lunch some place, wouldn't you?'

'Oh, yes, definitely.' Daisy regained her confidence. If she wants to have lunch with us let it be so, she thought. 'Turn to the left on Quaideen before Tariq Road, near Model school....'

'Oh, yes, got it,' Zari said, interrupting her.' Shezzy, tell me about your hobbies, do you sing?'

'No, I don't,' Shezzy replied.

'Dance?' her tone was warm and engaging.

'No,' Shezzy started laughing.

'Thank God, at least you laugh,' Zari said laughing with her.

'Turn to the right,' Daisy guided her, 'then to the left in the next lane.'

After passing through three or four narrow lanes, the car slowed down in one. A group of boys was playing cricket there. They suspended their play to allow the car to pass.

Zari stopped the car in front of the house and Daisy led them in.

'Shezzy, please put your luggage in the car, we've still to have lunch.' Shezzy, surprised, looked at Daisy.

'This isn't fair,' Daisy protested. 'Shezzy came to stay with us.'

'I need Shezzy badly these days,' Zari said.

Shezzy was surprised. Why would Zari need her? 'But...' she started.

'Don't worry, I'll ask permission from your Papa.'

Zari held Shezzy's hand as they went back down to the car. Before getting into the car, Daisy went toward the window on the passenger side and whispered, 'You didn't want to go but you are going. Some day, some one will take you to a tribal area and you won't be able to resist, you poor helpless girl!'

'I'll come back soon,' Shezzy said sincerely. She was sure that her mother would not approve of her staying with Zari.

At night, Shezzy called her mother to tell her that she was staying at Zari's house. Sarwat was very angry and refused to listen to any excuses. She wanted her to leave for Daisy's house immediately. Shezzy for the first time defied her, and told her that she wanted to stay with Zari and would explain everything to her when she returned.

30

Aijaz went to Karachi to collect his belongings for Lahore, then he went straight to Zari's house. Zari's reticent maidservant only said, 'She is at the hospital.'

'Hospital? Which hospital? Is she all right?'

'Jinnah Hospital, room number 36.'

Aijaz thought that Zari must be ill, particularly since she had only replied to one of his many letters. He went straight to the hospital in the same taxi.

While in taxi he visualized Zari lying weak and frail in her bed, her golden hair forming a halo around her pale, sickly face. He would console her and declare her love to that beautiful, sickly girl today. He'd assure her that he'd take care of her all her life.

Aijaz's hands were trembling as he knocked at the door of the hospital room.

'Come in.' It was Zari's voice.

Aijaz pushed the door open. Zari stood in front of the bed, she was as healthy and beautiful as ever. It was someone else who was sick and lay in the bed. Aijaz looked at him. He was a child, nine or ten years old with thick, red, chiseled lips and big brown eyes burning with fever. Aijaz had never seen the boy before. He turned toward Zari.

'My son, Sinan,' Zari said, 'is very ill. That's why I couldn't reply to your letters.'

Aijaz looked at Zari as if he didn't trust his own ears. Did she say 'my son?' She had said it in such a casual way as if everybody knew about her son. She did not seem to notice what a devastating effect this one sentence had on Aijaz.

'Have some sleep, my dear. Just close your eyes.' She moved her long fingers gently over the child's eyelids. The child closed his eyes.

'Sit down Aijaz. How are you? Did you get the job?' Zari asked.

'Yes,' Aijaz said still standing and gazing silently at Sinan's face. The nurse came in and Zari got up to help her. During the blood transfusion Sinan kept saying in agony. 'No, Mummy, please no. It hurts. It hurts a lot!'

Zari pulled her chair closer to the boy's bedside and stared at him.

'Does his father know about his illness?' he asked

'How did you come to think that Sinan has a father?' Zari said irritably.

Aijaz felt utterly in the wrong as if he did not know that every child who comes in this world has a father.

He said good-bye and left quickly.

Aijaz stayed home for two days but on the third day he decided to go and see Zari again. When he reached the hospital the lady at the desk told him that Sinan had been taken to a private clinic. He reached the clinic and entered Sinan's room.

Hearing Aijaz's footsteps, the man sitting on the sofa turned back.

'Ah Aijaz!' the man was Ahsan, 'How are you?'

'I came to see Sinan,' Aijaz said in a firm voice, sending a message that nobody could stop him from visiting Zari or Sinan.

'I too came to see him,' Ahsan said apologetically.

Aijaz could see clearly that the boy resembled Ahsan—same eyes, same lips, and same contour of the face and the same color of hair. The chiseled dry lips of both were exactly alike.

Now Aijaz understood the reason for Ahsan's presence here and why Sinan was moved to this costly clinic and why Zari's name was an abomination to everyone in *Qasr-e-Neelam*!

But no! If Ahsan was Sinan's father there were many questions to be answered yet. The timeless questions—why, how, where and when—continued to hammer at his brain.

It is impossible for three of us to be in the same room at the same time, Aijaz thought. Zari had to be there—maybe Ahsan, too. Then, he ought to leave!

'See you!' He rushed to the door, but passing close to Zari, he involuntarily whispered, 'I don't know why I assumed that Sinan's father was dead.'

'And you can see that sometimes dead fathers can be very beneficial,' Zari said, not lowering her voice, 'The child who had nobody to care for him while he was alive now has the means to die in luxury.'

'You should not have accepted his offer,' Aijaz said.

'I thought about that too. Then I decided, why not let him die in a happy and cheerful room, decorated with flowers and expensive pictures watching TV.'

Zari tried desperately to hold back the tears that threatened to break out. It was a consolation for Aijaz to think that whatever she was saying was for Ahsan's ears and not for him.

'Good-bye,' Aijaz said and left the room.

Zari followed him to the gate of the clinic. When Aijaz looked at her questioningly she said, 'If you go back to Lahore, don't tell Ahsan Bhai's wife that he was here.'

'Ahsan Bhai!' She calls him brother! Aijaz thought bitterly, and Zari had walked all the way to the main gate with him, not to say good-bye to him but to say this sentence!

Aijaz didn't look back. He went to Zari's house to retrieve his belongings from the office. There he saw Shezzy sitting in the veranda. Was this an optical illusion! How could Shezzy be in Zari's house? To test his senses, he walked slowly and stood right in front of Shezzy.

'Aijaz!' Shezzy said in surprise.

'May I ask you the same question?' Aijaz said. 'I was extremely surprised to see your father here. He told me that he came to see Zari's son. Now I find you here.'

Zari had returned from the clinic after spending a very long and exhausting day. She had immediately retired to her room without even having her meals. That evening there was a telephone call from the clinic saying that Sinan's condition was very serious. Shezzy had taken the call and had gone to give the message to Zari. Zari's face had turned pale and instantly she got ready to go to the clinic. When Shezzy timidly asked to go with her, Zari did not object.

When they had reached Sinan's room, the doctor had been present. A nurse had her hand on his pulse. They could see that Sinan was breathing his last. The oxygen was not helping him any more. A young woman sitting close to the head of the bed, watched him steadily, weeping bitterly.

Shezzy noticed that her Papa was also present in the room and was watching the boy with intense sadness. She tiptoed up to him. Holding each other's hands, they watched the boy's innocent soul depart from the world.

Zari held the child's hand until the very end. When the boy looked at her for the last time, Zari leaned over him and kissed him on his forehead. He breathed his last.

One night, after the third-day service of Sinan's death, Zari went into Shezzy's room.

'Look, Shezzy,' Zari said, 'Nothing in the story is my or your parents' secret. Had I been in your mother's place, I'd have told you everything a long ago. It is more harmful than useful to hide such things from children of your age.'

'You're absolutely right,' Shezzy said. 'Some of the suspicions I have are killing me.'

'I know. Let me tell you the truth.' Zari made herself comfortable by sitting close to Shezzy on her bed. 'You saw that woman who sat at the head of Sinan's bed and fainted at his death. She is Sinan's mother. Her name is Gulgoona. She used to be my servant girl.'

Zari continued, 'Perhaps you don't know that your grandmother, Zeb Qadri married Uncle Omar because she wanted to give security to her two sons who were teenagers at that time. When Zeb died, her sons, your father and your uncle Adnan, were studying abroad.

'Ahsan continued his studies in England but Adnan came to Pakistan and Uncle Omar, whom I call Chachaji, got him admitted into the Military Academy at Kakul. Chachaji cared much for him and loved him like his own son. He wanted him to marry me after he completed his training and became a military officer. But he was a flirt and his relationship with Gulgoona was physical.

'When it became known that Gulgoona was pregnant, Chachaji was furious. In the meantime, Ahsan's marriage with Sarwat had been arranged. Chachaji wrote all the details to Ahsan and insisted that Adnan should marry Gulgoona, but Adnan refused and went to Germany.

'Chachaji asked Ahsan and Sarwat to help the poor pregnant girl but they turned a deaf ear to his request, saying that they were not in the least interested in Adnan's illegitimate child. Finally, Chachaji engaged the services of an elderly woman to take Gulgoona to Mansehra to look after her.Gulgoona gave birth to a son whom Chachaji named Sinan. Chachaji raised him with the help of an *ayah*.

'Ahsan and Sarwat stopped visiting Chachaji. They wanted him to have nothing to do with the child.

'There was a time when it was rumored that the child was not Gulgoona's, but mine, that Gulgoona had simply been used as a scapegoat, but that rumor died its own death after a few months.'

Shezzy listened to all this as if dazed. She neither moved nor said a word.

31

A great surprise awaited Shezzy the next day in the form of Jawwad, who, at her Mama's order and two air tickets, had arrived at Zari's house in Karachi. In only a few hours, they had to leave for Lahore.

Shezzy was even more surprised that on seeing Jawwad, she didn't shrink back with fear. Maybe this is the effect of Aunt Zari's company, whose presence gave a person confidence, Shezzy thought.

Jawwad asked Shezzy to hurry up so that they could reach the airport in time.

'Were you not to leave today,' Zari said, 'you would have heard some good news. But that doesn't matter. You'll hear it in Lahore.' Zari embraced Shezzy warmly and walked with them to the gate to bid them good-bye.

Shezzy asked Jawwad about her mother and Neely while they were driving to the airport in a taxi. She was also curious about what Aijaz said about her after reaching Lahore.

'Has Aijaz returned to Lahore yet?' Shezzy asked.

'Are you inquiring about Professor Aijaz?' Jawwad asked sarcastically. 'Your Mama introduced him to me as such, although the poor fellow is only a junior lecturer.'

'I know. Where did you stay in Lahore this time?'

'At your house. I was invited to stay in the guest house of *Qasr-e-Neelam*, because you were not there and the professor has vacated the rooms.'

'Where has he gone?' Shezzy asked.

'He has rented a room somewhere not far from your house.'

At that moment Shezzy noticed that instead of going straight from Star Gate to the airport, the taxi was taking a turn toward the hotel Midway House.

'Where are we going?'

'I have to collect my luggage. I kept it at the hotel.'

'What luggage? You came only today and you're leaving today.'

'It doesn't mean that I can't have any luggage,' Jawwad said. 'We have plenty of time.'

'If there's enough time,' Shezzy said, 'let's go to Daisy's house. I want to give her a gift I purchased for her.'

'No, we don't have that much time. You are so keen to meet everyone except me.'

Shezzy kept quiet. Passing through the open gate of the Hotel Midway, the taxi came to a halt beside the fountains. They got out, and Jawwad called a waiter. As he approached, Jawwad said, pointing to Shezzy's suitcase, 'Take this to my room, number 141.'

'Why take a room for such a short time? Let him take my suitcase to the reception and ask to bring yours down.'

Jawwad looked at her reproachfully. Shezzy avoided his gaze.

'I want to go to my room and place an order for coffee for both of us,' Jawwad said.

'We can have coffee in the dining room. I'll go there and place an order. Come straight over there when you get your luggage.'

Saying that Shezzy headed toward the dining room.

'You are as stubborn as ever!' Jawwad said.

'More,' Shezzy replied confidently and turned to her left. On the way to the dining room she stopped at the reception area and inquired about the morning flight to Lahore. She was told that the morning flight had already left. However, there was another flight in the evening. When Shezzy called the airline, she was told that their seats were booked for the evening flight. Shezzy at once demanded her suitcase from the receptionist. It was not there. Jawwad had taken it with him to his room.

Shezzy debated whether she should press the hotel management to get her suitcase, creating a scene, or leave quietly. She searched her purse, tore a page from her diary and scribbled a note.

Jawwad, I'm not going with you. Leave my suitcase at the reception with the instructions that it should be handed over to me when I demand it. Thanks.

After giving the note to the receptionist at the counter, Shezzy rushed out. She hailed a taxi and went straight to the airport, purchased a ticket for the next day and set off for Daisy's house. She was not worried about traveling alone in a taxi or about not finding Daisy's house.

As soon as she reached Daisy's house, she said, 'Daisy, I've just escaped from a delinquent.'

'Who?' Daisy inquired anxiously.

'Jawwad.'

'Really?' Daisy burst out laughing.

'I'm telling you the truth,' Shezzy said, 'thank God, he doesn't know your address otherwise, he would have come here.'

'Well, nobody unwanted in this locality can come here. If I give the boys a hint they'll scare a person away. Everyone is free to do what he or she likes here. But I couldn't help laughing when you told me that you have just escaped from your husband.'

When Shezzy told her everything, Daisy got really angry.

'This man is a liar and a cheat. There is a right and wrong way to do things. I think this man likes to rape you.'

'Please don't use that word. Someone will hear!'

'You are such a coward. I thought you might have changed a bit.'

'I ran away from him. What else do you expect from me?'

'Very brave of you! Come, make yourself comfortable.'

Daisy brought her to her room and they sat more comfortably there.

'If you don't reach Lahore with Jawwad today, your mother will surely be miserable,' Daisy said.

'I'll call her that I'm not coming with Jawwad tonight. I'll be there tomorrow. It should give her some indication that everything is not okay between us.'

'And what will Jawwad tell your mother!' Daisy said.

'Let him go to hell. I don't care,' Shezzy replied.

'Good. There is a definite change in you. Could you live with a man forever who doesn't respect you?'

'No, I'm thinking the same thing. I would have sought Aunt Zari's opinion on this, but I didn't go to her house because Jawwad knows her address and might go there to find me.'

'Don't seek advice from Aunt Zari. Consult your own heart and trust your judgment. Make a decision and stick with it,' Daisy said.

'I feel I must put it off as long as I can. Let's see what Jawwad tells my parents.'

'Don't wait so long that you find yourself deeper in this mess.'

'I'll think about it,' Shezzy said.

When she reached Lahore, she discovered that Jawwad had gone directly to Peshawar from Karachi and told Sarwat on the telephone that Shezzy did not come with him. Maybe she'll come with her father.

Shezzy learned much from Neely. She realized that not only she, but Neely also, had matured intellectually during the time Aijaz had been staying there. Neely had told her about Naghma's brother getting wounded and her own participation in the procession. She had already recounted the episode to her mother and Sarwat appreciated Aijaz for rescuing her that day.

After arriving from Karachi, she waited for many days, expecting her parents to have a heart-to-heart talk with her, but they did not.

Her mother often used to discuss her marriage in the past, and Shezzy always gave her the same answer, 'Mama, what is the use of talking about something that has finally been settled?'

Now Shezzy wanted to tell her mother that she wanted to put an end to the marriage, but she didn't quite know how.

32

Zari wrote a letter to Omar the next day.

Chachaji,
Shams and I are getting married next Sunday. I wish you could be here at this occasion but it'll be hard for you to manage at such a short notice. It's going to be a very simple ceremony.
We may be leaving for East Pakistan very soon and I hope that you'll come there to visit us.
Yours,
Zari

Aijaz also got a letter from Zari. It said,

Dear Aijaz,
Shams and I believe that there ought to be more and more marriages between people of our two provinces. Now we are setting an example. Shams and I are getting married next Sunday. We sincerely hope that you will come and share our happiness.
We may be leaving for East Pakistan very soon.
Your friend, Zari

* * *

Aijaz was sad at the news at first. Then he realized that he was a little infatuated by Zari and that she had never loved him. Now was the best time to get over her. How fortunate that his best friend, Nasir, was coming that very day. Nasir would stay until after Zari's marriage. They would visit all the historic places in Lahore and have a good time together. If Mrs Ahsan agreed, they would take Shezzy and Neely along with them.

Nasir's train was slightly late. On the way home from the station, they talked about weather and various trivial subjects. Arriving home, Aijaz escorted him into his room.

'Now tell me, what happened to you...and to your mother on that fateful night. I'm so eager to know. I can't wait any longer.'

'It's a long story. Can't you wait till after dinner? Won't you even allow me to refresh myself?'

'You have travelled in an air-conditioned compartment and you look quite fresh to me. Besides, I am dying to hear the story from the horse's mouth'

'Okay, then listen.' Nasir sat in the chair and Aijaz beside him.

'That night, when I told Mother to be ready to come with us, she took a dangerous step. She thought if she went with me, my life would become miserable, my father would disinherit me and would do anything in vindictiveness. She could not turn down my request either. So she left a note with Sanobar for me. It read,

I had been dodging death for thirty years in hope of seeing you. Now I've met you and those moments have been the best in my life. What use is my life now? I want you to believe that your mother had died thirty years ago. Good-bye.

'After writing this note, she set off to commit suicide by jumping into the river. She did not know that she was still being watched. So she did not succeed in her attempt and for the first time in so many years, she was once again face to face with her husband that night. I watched them. You have seen my place and you have seen my mother, try to visualize the scene. The river, the white rocks, and the marble benches all glittered like silver in moonlight. Everything looked like a dream.

'She stood there so dignified and beautiful! After so many years, a husband was looking at his wife, who must have been like a jasmine in her youth, but now looked like a marble statue. She stood tall, straight and fearless.

'Maybe Father's heart melted at seeing her. He advanced toward her with confidence and dignity and said, "Enough, Qudsia, you've been punished enough. I pardon you today."

'Mother kept silent for a while. Then she looked Father in the face and said, "Khan! You must pardon me for one more thing... I told you a lie. That foreigner slept with me that night but not without my consent."

'Then, with measured steps, she disappeared into the ladies' quarters. She didn't know that I had overheard this conversation. However, I am convinced that her confession to her husband was the most bitter revenge. She had suffered for a sin she had never committed, and finally decided that only her confession could totally destroy her husband's ego. And it did.

'My Father, her husband, wanted to meet with her again just to make her say that it was a lie. But she refused to see him again.

'She is still alive, Aijaz, but she has almost stopped eating. She doesn't even talk to me. I can't watch the misery of my parents. I have joined the Army Medical Corps. Six months from now I'll get a commission in the army. Then I'll go and serve as a captain wherever I am posted. With my father's permission, I'll try to take my mother with me. For once, I hope Father will agree, and Mother may concede too.'

Nasir was silent and looked very sad. Aijaz was also depressed by the story.

'I'm sorry that I made you tell the sad story. I shouldn't have done that.'

'It's okay, friend. Talking about sad things lightens the heart. Come, get me a cup of tea, at least.'

'Sure, and then I'll take you to a nice family. I think that they are from the same area your mother is from.'

'Really! I look forward to meeting them,' Nasir said.

Aijaz called Ahsan and asked his permission to bring a friend to visit his family.

Ahsan said that they were both most welcome.

When Neely saw Aijaz, her eyes lit up. She welcomed him very graciously. Aijaz introduced his friend to the parents first, then he introduced Nasir and Shezzy; 'This is my friend, Nasir Khan. He is a doctor and wants to join the Army. Shezzy is a medical student. Obviously, she wants to be a doctor too.'

After some time Ahsan and Sarwat left the young friends to talk and went to their room. Nasir leaned towards Aijaz and whispered, 'Don't you think Shezzy resembles my mother?'

'Yes, I think so,' Aijaz said.

'How was your trip to Karachi? I think it did you good,' Aijaz said to Shezzy.

'Aunt Zari's company suited me well,' Shezzy replied.

For a moment Aijaz felt as if Shezzy had hurt him by mentioning Zari's name, but he recovered quickly. He had promised himself not to be disturbed if somebody mentioned Zari's name.

'You came back without attending Zari's wedding!' Aijaz said trying to steady his quivering voice.

'Aunt Zari's wedding? With whom and when?'

'Zari and Shams are getting married this Sunday. Didn't she tell you?'

'No, she gave me a hint by saying that if I were to stay more, I would have heard some good news. How did you come to know?'

Aijaz paused for a moment then said, 'I received an invitation from her. After their wedding they plan to live in East Pakistan.'

Shezzy said to Neely, 'Would you please ask somebody to bring tea and snacks.'

Aijaz said to Nasir, 'Shezzy and you belong to the same profession, but you haven't yet begun to talk shop.'

'I was just thinking of asking about her studies,' Nasir said teasingly, 'but I know that the students of F. J. College are not studying these days but leading processions and showering rose petals on the participants.'

'It's not true,' Shezzy protested. 'It is the spectators who shower the petals not the students.'

'Do you take part in the processions?' Nasir asked.

'No, I don't.'

'Don't you approve of democracy?' Nasir was provoking her, because he liked the way she protested and blushed before she answered.

'To be interested in democracy is one thing but to be involved in active politics is quite another,' Shezzy said.

Neely came back and told the guests that they were invited to have dinner with the family. Then she sat beside Aijaz.

After dinner Sarwat asked her driver to drop them home.

Getting down from the car and stepping onto the veranda, Nasir heaved a deep sigh.

'What's the matter, friend?'

'I had read somewhere that God created all souls as twins, then dropped them down into the world separately, so that they could search for each other. Seeing Shezzy, I feel as if she is my soul mate.'

Aijaz was appalled. This young man's misfortunes had started well before his birth. The son of a well-to-do landlord had lost all interest in his estate and was perfectly content living in a small studio-apartment as a medical student. The man had never shown an interest in any girl! Now he liked a girl who was already married. He pitied Nasir.

When they settled down in their beds to sleep they were still talking. Aijaz asked Nasir, 'I don't quite understand why you want to join the Army?'

'I don't understand why it bothers you so much.'

'Because I know you to be a sensitive person who shouldn't be interested in wars,' Aijaz said.

'Look, the medical profession has the most to do in a war,' Nasir said, 'don't you know that innocent young boys get wounded or disabled in war, boys who many times have no idea what that particular war is about?'

'That's why I think everyone should be against war,' Aijaz said, 'You should condemn war rather than joining it in any capacity. Nothing is achieved in a war. Thousands on both sides die or are wounded or held prisoners. They are subsequently rewarded with artificial limbs or medals. The dead soldiers are buried in mass graves, sometimes in a foreign land. The two parties carry on with the propaganda of their military superiority for a few more days, but very soon the worthlessness of their claims is thoroughly exposed because nobody wins in a war,'

'No sane person can have faith in a war,' Nasir said in his defense, 'but wars are inevitable like death.'

'I don't think so,' Aijaz said. 'I think a time will come when wars will be abolished as cannibalism and slavery were abolished, and people will call us barbarians for having wars.'

'I wish you were right,' Nasir said. 'People say there always have been, and always will be wars.'

'When slavery and cannibalism were common they must have said the same thing.

'Yes, you may be right. But the kind of future you predict appears rather distant. Right now, every country is busy preparing for war, and wars are being fought in the name of peace. As long as there are wars the doctors would be needed. Isn't that right?'

'Yes it is. By the way I need to tell you that Shezzy is married.' Aijaz covered his face with a sheet and turned towards the wall.

Nasir didn't say a word.

Nobody spoke after that.

* * *

PART 2

Starting a New Life
The Changed Political Climate
Disintegration of Relationships
Broken Links

33

Zari sincerely wanted to start a new life. Why should people think her marriage with Shams was bizarre only because he was from East Pakistan!

Before leaving Abbotabad, her Uncle Omar had given her a copy of the manuscript written by their great-great-great grandfather, Qasim, who had migrated from Turkey to Bangdesh and then had come and settled down in West Pakistan. Zari had brought the manuscript with her to read in the airplane.

It was a chilly, depressing, winter day in Karachi, when Zari and Shams left for East Pakistan. The cold wind that blew from Samarkand and Bokhara across Pakistan and into Karachi was icy.

When Zari cursed the weather, Shams said, 'Don't you worry my dear. The weather in Dhaka will be splendid, even summer-wear will do.'

Zari put on an embroidered *shalwar* and *kameez* and wrapped herself in a woolen shawl, so that if the weather were too hot, she could easily put the shawl aside. Shams would have liked Zari to wear a *sari*, because it was the dress women in East Pakistan wear. Shams did not express his wish because he knew that Zari didn't feel comfortable in a *sari*, especially during traveling.

Zari looked out the window. In pitch darkness, she could only see a green light over the wing of the plane.

'Shams, it's very dark outside. Where are all the stars tonight?' Zari asked half seriously half in jest.

'Maybe, they have gone to enjoy their weekend,' Shams also replied in a lighter vein, then realizing that Zari was rather gloomy, coaxed her tenderly, 'What are you afraid of? Just don't look out if you don't like the darkness.'

Zari pulled the blind over her window and took out the story of Qasim, and read from it. Uncle Omar had written a few notes on the top page, which she read first.

The whole land is a delta in the making. All the cities, towns and villages are located at the center of this delta. How strange! The great river connections spread about a million tons of soil each year before they join the Bay of Bengal. They make the land so fertile that it yields three crops a year. Hundreds of waterways provide transportation. Average rainfall is 88 inches per annum, and the density of population is 922 per square mile. So many people! Floods, storms, and incessant heavy rains devastate large areas.

Everything was so different from her own region! Yes, she had sought a place that was dissimilar from hers. At first she was surprised that her friends were alarmed at her marriage but today she herself felt as if she were traveling from reality to an illusion. Her heart was heavy, and she could not pinpoint the reason.

'Shams, is it possible that we are the descendants of the same Miyan Sahib?'

'Why do you ask?'

'Because the story you told me about your great-great-grandfather is so similar to the story I read about my ancestors.'

'Maybe we are,' Shams said.

'Don't you find it strange that we might be the offspring of the same person though now you are from East Pakistan and I'm from West Pakistan, and culturally we happen to be so different!'

'Don't you find it strange that we are still alike in many ways though there are centuries between us?'

'Yes, you are right,' said Zari, smiling and looking reassuringly at Shams.

'Do you think it strange that Zari Khan is going to East Pakistan as Zari Shams?'

'No,' Zari said, 'My used to say that nature uses the migration of races in the same way it uses the wind for spreading the seeds. People migrate to new places for economic or political reasons but by mixing the blood of different races, the process of growth continues. Maybe as we get more civilized, computers will tell us where to go and why.'

'Yes, Ma'am Zari, your mind's computer might have told you to migrate to East Pakistan,' Shams laughed. 'And I predict that you will fall in love at first sight with my region and will decide to live there for ever after. You will even make a pledge with the region, as Christians do at the time of their weddings, "For better and for worse, in sickness and in health, I will love you and cherish you till death do us part, et cetera, et cetera."'

'But why didn't you make a similar pledge with my city?'

'I did.'

'But you left it right after.'

'Look,' Shams said solemnly, 'leaving things that we are attached to does not mean that our love for them will diminish. Can you really dissociate yourself from people and things you love?'

'No,' Zari said. At that very moment she had been wondering whether inhabiting a new world would dissociate her from her past.

'You look so happy and excited,' Zari said to Shams, 'because you're going back to places you cherish.'

'Maybe. But with a wife like you for a companion, I'm not only excited but proud as well.'

'Really!' Zari smiled. 'With your exaggerated poetic expressions, you could write poetry in Urdu also. Even Urdu scholars would envy your perfect diction, but I'm worried about my Bangla.'

'Don't worry about it. You'll learn it very quickly. The important thing is your sincerity in learning a language and speaking it. When you'll speak Bangla, even if it's not perfect, people will understand that you don't consider them inferior to you, as many other West Pakistanis do. They would know that you want to live among them as their own. That's all that matters.'

'Do you think Shams, they will accept me as one of their own?' Zari asked doubtfully.

'Certainly, they will. You have chosen a person from East Pakistan for your husband, come to his part of the world and speak his language. What else would they want?'

'Shamshu!' Zari asked coaxingly, 'will any of your relations come to receive us at the airport?'

'My half-brother Ronjhu might come. He studies at the Dhaka University. I have written to him. Otherwise people from my office will certainly be there.'

'Okay. That sounds much better. Neither you nor I have any near relations in the world. Maybe we wouldn't be together if we had.'

'What makes you think that? Are you complaining about us being together? You know that I love you and will always love you, no matter what. Don't you believe that?'

'Time alone will tell.'

'Yes, let time decide then and it will tell you that our love would get stronger with time,' Shams said, and patted her hand lovingly.

Zari realized that a new kind of euphoria had taken over Shams as his native land was getting nearer. He unconsciously indulged in the Bangla pronunciation of the words such as *shonder* instead of *sunder* and Shomsh instead of Shams, and the Bangla intonation in his speech became more and more clear.

The plane was landing at Dhaka airport.

'Now, you can look out the window,' said Shams. 'Had it been daytime you would have seen the old swaying Ganges, countless ponds, lakes and grassy plots, but at night—'

Zari removed the window-curtain. She noticed that the moon shone like a gold disk beneath them. She did not hear the last part of Shams's sentence. Zari wonderingly lifted her head to look up. There was a moon there, too!

She was amazed! 'Why do I see two moons?' She almost screamed. 'Am I seeing double?'

Shams laughed. 'Don't you know that this is the land of ponds and rivers? What you first saw was not the moon but its reflection in water.'

'How beautiful!' Zari said. 'It is just as shiny and real as the one in the sky.'

'Yes, it is.' Shams also looked through the window and was delighted to see the two moons exactly alike. 'Because it's Bangladesh, the magical region, remember!'

The plane was turning at an odd angle and everything was a little tilted. The two moons really looked close to each other.

At that time they could see the lights of Dhaka City distinctly.

In some streets, the lights stretched in unending, dazzling rows, in others they looked like colorful scattered jewels.

The plane touched the ground, ran briskly along the path lit by the runway lights, and then taxied slowly towards the airport building. Suddenly, the lights of Dhaka city mellowed Zari's heart. This was the city of her hopes and aspirations. Her eyes became moist with tears!

34

Shams and Zari collected their luggage, went through the customs and were about to leave the airport building when a small boy handed Shams a note. Zari could only see that it was written in Bangla script. Shams read it while Zari looked around. It said, 'Please come and meet me in the restaurant, but come alone. Yours, Ronjhu.'

Shams said to Zari, 'Please wait here. I will be back in a minute.'

Zari wanted to ask Shams where he was going but he, climbing the stairs was gone in an instant.

Shams re-read the note as he reached the top of the stairs. A young boy in his twenties, who had stood beside the window, saw him, advanced towards him and said, 'Shamsul-bhai, *Asalaam Alaikum!*'

They embraced each other, then Shams looked at Ronjhu from head to foot. He was as tall as Shams, but he was much darker. He had typical Bengali eyes, big and very dark, but they also had a mysterious look, a mixture of intellect and shrewdness.

'You're a grown man now,' Shams said pleasantly in Bangla. He felt proud to be able to speak perfect Bangla after so many years.

'A person grows with time, doesn't he?' said Ronjhu, his white teeth flashing. The mysterious luster in his eyes proudly intensified. 'Come, let's have tea.'

'Your sister-in-law is waiting for us downstairs,' Shams said.

'Oh,' the spiciness of his tone suddenly went down, 'so she is my sister-in-law! But you never wrote about her in your letter.' There was more disappointment than complaint in his voice.

'I wanted to surprise you,' Shams said cheerfully.

'Surprise is usually associated with good news,' said Ronjhu curtly. 'Isn't it?'

Shams now noticed that Ronjhu's face wore a sad and troubled look. Maybe he would apologize for what he said, but he didn't.

Then Shams knew that Zari's being a West Pakistani was bothering him!

'I have married her,' Shams said. 'She is my wife and I expect you to respect her.'

'I am sorry,' said Ronjhu without a trace of sorrow or repentance, 'I can't welcome her. I'm afraid you can't stay with me—and I cannot make any arrangements for you to stay some place else.'

'Don't worry about our lodgings,' Shams said angrily, 'I didn't know that you were so prejudiced.'

Shams kept the tone of his voice deliberately sour. He wanted to press his claim as an elder brother and wanted to clear the situation once and for all about Zari.

'You don't know a lot of things that have changed here recently, I suppose,' Ronjhu said. 'You will come to know by and by. A man living thousands of miles from home, living with...non-friendly people, doesn't often know the truth.' Ronjhu's mysterious tone now turned to sarcasm. 'Let me give you a hint. Working in the department of the National Integration Council is no longer a matter of pride here. It's a disgrace!'

'Why?'

'The very concept of national integration is history. You'll be surprised at a lot of things. I know you've been kept in the dark.'

'Whatever the situation, I want to make it clear that if you want to have no relationship with your sister-in-law, you'll have none with me.'

'As you wish. I live in Iqbal Hall, at the university. If you need help...anytime....' Ronjhu didn't complete the sentence.

An unpleasant silence fell between them. There was nothing to be said or done.

Shams decided to go back to Zari. As he turned, he heard Ronjhu say, 'I happened to meet Shaista Apa. She was inquiring about you.' A bell chimed in Shams's mind and his feet wavered a little. So many thoughts and questions came to mind with the

mention of a name. But in the bitterness that filled his heart and
mind by Ronjhu's conduct, he thought it unwise to stop and make
inquiries about Shoshi. Ronjhu shouldn't have mentioned her
name at this moment, he thought and went down the stairs.

Zari stood by her luggage, looking puzzled and a little
worried.

'It was Ronjhu,' Shams told Zari. 'He didn't want to meet you.
I've told him that in that case he cannot have any relationship
with me either.'

Zari was very disturbed. 'Are things gone so far? My husband's
brother does not want to meet me!'

'Don't be upset,' Shams said. 'He is my step-brother and we
were never very close. It's quite possible that he is using you as an
excuse to break off with me.'

'Maybe,' said Zari, but her heart was sinking with the first
disappointment in her Promised Land.

'Let us go out now,' Shams said, and stepped towards the exit.
Zari followed him.

When they came out they met a few people from Shams' office
who came to receive them.

After the formal greetings one of them said, 'It is one of those
days, the whole city has been on strike the whole day because the
Awami League has asked people to go on strike—no buses, no cars,
no traffic at all. The strike was called off towards evening but
we've hoisted black flags on our car just in case somebody stops
us.'

Zari became even more depressed.

35

Though Zari was transferred to the Department of Tourism in East Pakistan she was working passionately for Shams's National Council for Integration. Shams and Zari still believed in the cause and wrote articles for the newspapers, and with each other's help, translated them into Urdu and Bangla. Zari was often asked by Pakistan Television and Radio Pakistan to deliver speeches on the subject of national integration.

But of late, Shams had the feeling that his co-workers and the lecturers at the university looked at him as if he was a character from Rip Wan Winkle, who had just awakened after so many years from a deep sleep. It looked as though they pitied him and hinted that the coins in his pockets had gone out of circulation long ago. It was then that the mystery of Ronjhu's statement at the airport unfolded itself before him. 'You'll come to know a lot more. What does a man sitting thousands of miles away from home know?'

On a number of occasions, Shams had found, lying on his table, brochures and booklets written against the Pakistan Government, in both Bangla and English. These brochures had been distributed in both provinces of Pakistan at different times, blaming the government for different misdeeds—the 1965 war against India, the hundreds of killings during a general strike in protest against the arrest of Sheikh Mujibur Rahman, the Bengali leader.

They cataloged a comparative study of the economic conditions of East and West Pakistan: the glaring disparity in government jobs, particularly in the armed forces, the difference between the prices of commodities in East and West Pakistan. Shams read these publications once in a while. At other times he threw them into the wastepaper basket without reading them.

Shams wanted to talk with his colleagues and staff about the issues, but they seemed to avoid talking with him openly. He was still trying to convince them that they should try to bring the two wings of Pakistan together. He did not know that the younger generation in East Pakistan had lost all interest in national integration.

They had other plans for their province, and their leader Sheikh Mujib, whom they called 'Bondu', meaning friend, was putting forward fourteen points demanding political favors from the government and making them tougher and tougher on public demand.

Whenever Shams contemplated a bold step in this direction, his plan stalled for want of co-operation. In place of the national anthems by Farrukh Ahmed, which could be written in Bangla and Urdu without a change of script, his friends wanted the Integration Council to promote established writers of East Pakistan and publish their work in Bangla, comparable with deluxe editions of Dr Iqbal and Chughtai from West Pakistan. They now wanted to promote the Bangla traditions instead of developing a mutual culture.

They believed that promoting the Urdu language was harming Bangla language and was a waste of time and money that should be avoided in their province and that the department should be eliminated if it cannot fight for Bengalis.

By and by, Shams came to realize that seeds of scorn and hatred against West Pakistan had been sown deep in young minds.

One day he found a placard written in bold letters on his desk which read: *If a boat develops a leak, isn't it wise to go on board a new boat rather than keep repairing the old one risking your luggage and your lives?*

36

'Breakfast is on the table,' Suraj announced in Urdu with his Bengali accent.

'Ask the guests to come for breakfast first...and where is Benu?' asked Mirza.

'She must have gone to the University. She'll never miss a day unless it's doomsday,' Mrs Mirza said crossly.

'Come, let's have breakfast. Call Sarwat, Shezzy and Neely,' Mirza tried to distract his wife from the painful subject of Benu's insolence.

Sarwat, Shezzy and Neely had reached Dhaka a few days before. They had found everything so different here. Even the food on the breakfast table was totally different from the breakfast they used to have in West Pakistan. The table was full of puris, parathas, fish, and vegetable dishes and boiled rice from the previous evening's supper. Sarwat thought that even though her sister didn't like the people of East Pakistan she was adopting their habits. They could never eat rice and fish at breakfast, so they asked for their usual bread, butter, eggs and tea instead.

As Mirza finished his breakfast and was getting ready to go to his office, Mrs Mirza said, 'Give me some money for shopping.'

'But you have your own account in the bank.'

'I need cash.'

'Now you will spoil Sarwat, too!' he said. Then he addressed his sister-in-law. 'Your sister goes out on a shopping spree every morning and comes back late in the afternoon.'

'What else should I do? I don't want to shout in Mahila Parisad meetings making myself hoarse.'

'Why not? The Bengali women always complain that non-Bengalis don't care to become members of their association. They are taking out a procession for women's rights today. Why don't you join them? Take Sarwat and the girls with you.'

'I don't want to. I know how to protect my rights.'

'You have only one right—shopping,' Mirza said teasingly. 'I'll grant that.' He placed a small stack of notes in her hand.

'What is this?' Mrs Mirza said crossly. 'My nieces have come from Lahore. I want to buy gifts for them.'

'Take them for window shopping today. We will buy the gifts later.'

'All right,' Mrs Mirza said haughtily. 'You should know that all shopkeepers in all the supermarkets know me very well. I can purchase things worth thousands without giving them any money. They will charge you later.'

'I know that. For whatever wives do, husbands have to pay,' Mirza chuckled. 'What do you think, Sarwat?'

'Yes, Bhaijan, I think that's the best way for wives to behave. Let their husbands pay for whatever they do.'

'See, how aggressively your sister talks now that her daughters have grown,' Mirza addressed his wife jokingly. 'She was very respectful before.'

'She does that,' Mrs Mirza said, 'because you provoke her. You have made your own children so arrogant! Look at Benu, she never listens to me.'

'She is fine. Go shopping. Enjoy yourself.' Mirza tried to avoid the subject of Benu's behavior again.

He took out another bundle of notes from his wallet and gave it to his wife.

After Mirza left, Mrs Mirza, her sister and nieces left for New Market in another car. All the shopkeepers knew Mrs Mirza very well because of her regular visits. The officers who came from West Pakistan on official visits always carried a long shopping list for their wives and Mrs Mirza was always willing to do the shopping for them. The shopkeepers treated her as a very valued customer.

Panting for breath and dragging her heavy torso along, she went in and sat down in a clothing store. The shopkeeper immediately ordered Coca-Cola for all. Mrs Mirza had a number of *saris* brought out—Kanjeevaram and Rajshahi silk *saris* with flowers embossed in silk. The young sales boys promptly opened them, pleated and wrapped them around their thin waists to show them how beautiful they looked.

Mrs Mirza asked for their price and moved on to the next shop without striking a bargain.

'Don't let them open the *saris* when you don't intend to buy anything,' Sarwat said.

Pressing her hand, Mrs Mirza whispered. 'Just have a look—these people love to exhibit their stuff. They enjoy it.'

Then she said, 'Listen, Sarwat would you rather buy carpets? They are beautiful and cheaper than in West Pakistan!'

'Why are they cheaper here?'

'Things are cheaper here, you know, because these Bengalis demand their share half-and-half in exported goods as in everything else. But there are only a handful of us West Pakistanis who could afford to buy them.'

'I don't understand. Why should they have so much stuff if they can't buy it?'

'You know, it's the passion for equality. They cry to have equality and parity and God knows what else...I don't understand these things. I only know that they don't have the taste and money to buy them.'

'If I buy the carpets how would I carry them to Lahore?'

'That could be arranged, no problem! I receive requests to buy crockery, cutlery, china, carpets, furniture, and even cars. Everything is sent by airplanes or by ships.

'Auntie, if you don't intend to buy anything today why don't you show us around,' Neely said.

'Ah, you want to see Dhaka. OK Let's buy some sweets, delicious *rasgullas* and fruit, and then we'll go sightseeing.'

The car was loaded with dozens of bananas, mangoes and coconuts. Suddenly, they heard the sound of an explosion. Thick, dense fumes of smoke rose from across Dhaka College, and went straight up to merge with the clouds in the sky. The shopkeepers at once began lowering the shutters of their stores. A boy from the store came running to them and said to Mrs Mirza, 'Madam, come into the store. It's risky outside.'

Mrs Mirza looked at her sister. Sarwat had turned pale. She did not know whether to trust a local shopkeeper for their safety. Mrs Mirza was doubtful, too.

'Shaupin!' Mrs Mirza asked the driver, 'Can you take us out from here safely?'

'Yes, I can. Please get in. I'll take a different and safer route.'

The boy from the store frowned, angry at their mistrust. Nobody paid him any attention. They were pre-occupied with getting into the car. The driver turned the car into a smaller lane.

'Take us to Lal Bagh Fort,' Mrs Mirza said.

When they approached Azeempura, they saw a procession of women holding placards written in Bangla. Their faces were grim, determined and impatient, and a glimmer of fire lit their eyes. They were all clad in starched cotton *saris* with their hair done up in simple buns. Elderly women had their heads covered with the palloo of their *saris*, but the young ones did not cover their heads.

'I think we should go home, now. It's not wise to go anywhere else today,' said Sarwat.

'O.K, let's go home, Shaupin,' Mrs Mirza said to the driver.

'Whatever you say, Ma'am,' the driver said.

'Auntie, what is written on those placards?' Neely asked.

'God only knows, child. I can't read Bangla. I can only understand a little bit.'

'You haven't learned the language in so many years, Auntie?' Shezzy asked.

'No, why should I? Everyone spoke Urdu till recently. Even the servants spoke beautiful Urdu. Now, all of a sudden, they want us to talk to them in Bangla.'

'That's only fair. If they learn Urdu, we should learn Bangla,' Shezzi said.

'Now, you are talking like Benu. I don't like it. And I don't approve of their demands either,' Mrs Mirza said sharply.

'Auntie, please don't speak so loud!' Nelly whispered pointing to the driver.

'Oh, I'm not afraid of these good-for-nothing people,' Mrs Mirza said, then shouted at the driver, 'Shaupin, keep the car at a safe distance from the procession.'

'Yes, Ma'am,' the driver said as he turned into another street.

37

Benu Mirza stood silently in the balcony of her house looking at the sky filled with billows of black clouds up to the horizon and feeling the moist breeze on her naked arms. A few old women were dipping themselves in the green waters of a nearby pond. At a little distance three boys swam vigorously.

Benu was trying to listen intently to the conversation in the adjacent room. Her friend Puttal was not with her today. She was with the elders of the house because she, with her parents, had brought her brother Ikram's proposal of marriage for Benu.

Benu recalled the day when Ikram had proposed to her in a strange way. A few scenes rushed past her mind's eye like scenes glimpsed from a moving train. That had been the last day of classes at the university. That was a fun day when students flung mud balls at each other. Benu's mother was dead against these kinds of things. She said that mixing colors with mud and spraying it on each other was a custom taken from the Hindu Holi festival. She also objected that the Bengalis had learned from the Hindus to love the earth and call it their mother, while Muslims never considered the soil sacred as a mother.

Knowing well that her mother wouldn't approve, Benu had gone to the university any way. She had been standing under a banyan tree, watching others playing with mud and having fun when a servant from the Madhu cafetaria brought her a note. In a hand soiled with mud, someone had scribbled a poem by Tagore in Bangla, which meant something like this: *The boy who wears a royal gown and strings of beads around his neck can never have fun, because these things keep him away from the healthy soil and enjoyment.*

A little later she saw Ikram coming towards her.

'Why do you watch us from a distance? Why don't you join us?'

'I don't know. I feel shy!' Beena said.

'You feel ashamed of playing with the soil of the country. Does it make you nauseous? Do you feel like the Biharis that you are too good to be playing in mud?'

Benu was stunned. Didn't Ikram know that she was from a Bihari family? Ikram held her by the hand and drew her close.

Benu, freeing her hand, said quickly, 'Ikram, I want you to know that my parents are not Bengalis.'

Seeing shock and surprise in his eyes, she added, 'But it makes no difference. I am with you people.'

'Are you?' He looked at her, his jet black eyes penetrating into hers. She lowered her eyes. Although they had been meeting in a group for months and Benu knew that Ikram was attracted to her, he had never declared his love.

A bird fluttered in the banyan tree. Ikram, who was still watching her in surprise, composed himself. He leaned down and took a handful of soil. He caught Benu's hand and placed the soil in her palm.

'Now repeat what I say,' he said.

'What's it all about?' Benu asked in amazement.

'It's about what you just said, that you are with us.'

'Yes, I am.'

'Then repeat what I say: I Swear by the soil that I will consider this land as my own. I'll live and die here, and do whatever will be in the best interest of the people of this land.'

'That is how I feel. Do I need to take an oath?'

'There's no harm in saying it, is there?'

'No,' Benu said and repeated the words.

Then he added more words, 'I love Ikramul Haq and promise to marry him.'

'Enough—enough for today. The rest in time,' Benu said and snatched her hand away.

Benu saw that Ikram was very serious. She peeped into her own heart. There was a definite 'yes' there. She loved him and wished to live and die in this country.

'I'm ready to make a pledge but, as you know, our marriage will depend on the consent of my parents. So your parents should come to my house with a proper proposal.'

And now Ikram's parents were here. Benu knew that her mother would oppose the proposal tooth and nail. She could never imagine a relationship with a Bengali family. She distrusted all Bengalis and had developed a special dislike for the people of the Chittagong region, where Ikram's father lived in a village.

Detecting a cloudy expression on his wife's face, Mirza quickly intervened and asked for a few days time before giving an answer.

No sooner had the guests departed than Mrs Mirza started sobbing hysterically. The thoughts that had spun in her mind a few moments earlier came coming in torrents, 'These... uncivilized...rustics,' she wailed, 'how dare they ask for my daughter's hand.' She started recounting the details to her younger sister. 'The women go out veiled, holding umbrellas, while the men shout warnings to other men to keep away from them. These women don't even have the decency to wear blouses with their *saris* and cover themselves only with the *palloo* of their *sari*. They take baths in ponds in front of their homes, where young boys catch fish at the same time and fetch water for drinking from the same ponds. Would I denounce my daughter to live among these untouchables?'

At first Mirza was amused by her remarks, but realizing that she was going too far, he got angry. 'Enough, enough,' he said. 'You don't know what you're saying. You are describing the poor villagers there. Is the living standard of the poor in Bihar or West Pakistan the same as yours? I don't think there's any difference between you and Ikram's mother.'

Benu listened to all this, standing silently on the balcony. If she tried to intervene, the situation could get worse. This is but the first torrent of a flood. Let it pass, she thought.

After seeing Shezzy and Neely's fair complexion, glittering as jewels, her mother has reached the conclusion that the climate of East Pakistan had conspired to turn Benu's complexion dark brown. Otherwise, she, too, would have been like her cousins.

Now she would definitely start thinking about going to West Pakistan, since having a fair complexion was really a big deal for her.

38

Benu returned early from the university. Nobody was at home except the servants. She asked Suraj where they had gone. Suraj told her that the guests had gone shopping with her mother and that Ilyas was in his school.

'Anything to eat?' she asked, sitting on a circular cane chair and stretching her feet on a stool in front of her.

'Lunch is ready,' Suraj said.

'I have to have lunch with the guests otherwise my mother will kill me.'

'Would you like to have some pineapple then?'

'Pineapple! It is not the season. Where did you get it?'

'A visitor from Sylhet brought it as a gift.'

'All right, I would love to eat it,' said Benu.

She picked up a copy of the *Pakistan Observer* and turned its pages. Suraj cut slices of pineapple, sprinkled pepper and salt on them and brought them to her. 'Benu Apa! Can I take my English lessons now?' Suraj asked in Bangla.

'Yes, sure. Let's sit on the veranda.'

That was her favorite place. This was where, sitting on a low wooden *takht*, she practiced playing the *sitar*.

From here she could see the coconut and palm trees in the garden waving gently in the breeze. Nearby, lotus flowers floated on the surface of the pond.

Benu removed the pins from the knot of her hair and shook her head, letting her long, dark hair flow freely. Suraj brought his book, sat beside her on the *sheetal pati* and opened the book. Benu taught him a lesson from Ilyas's old book and asked him to do an exercise from the workbook.

Watching Suraj write the English words attentively, she thought about how people migrate from one place to another. Suraj had come here after Sandeep Island was hit by a fearful cyclone. Very few persons had survived the cyclones and the floods on the island that year.

Benu remembered her mother saying scornfully that these people don't give importance to death because they are like insects. They are born and die in great numbers, like insects. Nature is cruel to them so they avenge themselves upon others.

When her mother said things like that, Benu always tried to restrain her.

Suraj looked very pensive.

'What are you thinking, Suraj?' Benu said.

'Apa, the West Pakistani soldiers who have come here, shoot the big fish from our pond with their guns and take them away.'

'Of our pond?'

'I mean from ponds of all the villages. They also catch their goats, sheep and poultry and devour them.'

'Are you sure? This could be one of many rumors I hear about them,' Benu said harshly. 'Why don't you do another exercise?' In her heart she was troubled. She wondered why she felt guilty if someone spoke ill of the Pakistani soldiers?

At last the car arrived with Mrs Mirza and the guests. Mrs Mirza lost her temper when she found Benu teaching Suraj.

'Go and set the table, Suraj,' she said. 'Everybody here is turning into a scholar or a politician to shout in favor of six or eleven points.'

When Suraj was gone with his books, Benu said in a calm voice, 'There is no harm in being politically conscious, Mother.'

'All this killing and head splitting is perfectly reasonable for you, isn't it?' her mother retorted.

'Did you go sightseeing?' Benu asked Shezzy to change the topic.

'Yes, we did, but there was some tension in the city. We'd like to go some other day with you.'

'Sure, why not!' Benu said. 'Let's go and have lunch.'

39

Misbahul Haq had invited Mr Mirza and his family to visit his native village. Mr Mirza and Sarwat succeeded in persuading Mrs Mirza to visit the Haqs' ancestral home.

Misbah's village, Rowzan, was at a little distance from Chittagong.

Sarwat had said to her sister, 'If Benu wants to marry Ikram, let her lest you repent like me, later.'

'What is the matter? Is Shezzy not happy with her marriage?'

'No, she isn't. I don't want to hide anything from you. Both seem equally unhappy but they don't tell us why. There seems to be a cold war going on between them. Jawwad has stopped writing or visiting us. Shezzy doesn't open her heart to anybody. I don't know how we can resolve this matter. Don't make the same mistake I made. Ikram is from a rich educated family, and our aim should be the girl's happiness.'

'Yes, that's right, but my heart, somehow, has an aversion to the idea. These women in their cotton *saris* don't look like educated ladies to me. Even the maidservants of our households dress better than these women. I know they are stingy.'

'You have been living here for several years. Don't you know that this is their way of living?' Sarwat said.

'Yes, it is,' Mrs Mirza said. 'That's what I think too, there's such a big difference between their culture and ours.'

'Your daughter has grown up in East Pakistan. She likes their culture and likes Ikram,' Sarwat said. 'The people are sincere and the boy is very handsome.'

'Is she any less handsome?' Mrs Mirza asked teasingly and a new thought dawned on her. Benu has a dark complexion like the Bengalis. The West Pakistanis always prefer fair girls. It'll be hard to get a suitable boy there. It's not such a bad match. She decided.

'Sleep on it, Apa,' Sarwat said. 'We will discuss it in the morning.'

Neely got up very early in the morning. She stood at the window, surveying the surrounding landscape. She was enjoying, the palms bending low in the strong breeze as if bowing in salutation and then standing up straight again. It had been raining all night. The land and water had become one. Tall trees had fallen into the water. The huts, like children bathing in a pond, stood drenched and dripping. Some huts could be identified only by their rooftops, on which chicken and crows perched. Neither the road, nor the lake, nor the river, could be distinguished because there was a vast stretch of water as far as the eye could see. Water gushed down the hills like a waterfall. Only houses built on top of the hills could be seen.

Ilyas saw her standing alone in the veranda and came to her.

'I've never seen so much water in my life,' she said.

'You'll be amazed how soon all the water will flow away because it's a hilly place. Chittagong will emerge clean and tidy, as before. But in the villages water stagnates for days and diseases like malaria and cholera spread.'

'All this is because our villages suffer from poverty,' said Neely, philosophically. 'I have once read that according to a great philosopher there is so much wealth and so much work that if it's distributed equally among the people of the world nobody would be without work and nobody would starve. And all would enjoy their leisure too!'

'Why talk of the world. Is there not enough wealth in Pakistan? People say that there are palatial houses in Karachi and Islamabad, the new capital looks like Paris.'

'So, you, too, are jealous of the West Pakistanis!' Neely said seriously.

Misbah, who was used to getting up early, came out and heard their conversation. When the children saw him approach, they greeted him. He returned their greetings saying, 'Can you tell me, my girl, where is the lake and where is the land?'

Neely looked intently. Green and purple creepers still floated on the water. Sea gulls and other birds dived at them and emerged to fly away with something dangling from their beaks. She knew that the treetops and the roofs of the cottages represented the land. When Neely told him that, he was immensely pleased.

They joined the hosts and guests at the breakfast table. A long line of Bengali servants offered the dishes very respectfully. If, for some reason, they presented a dish with the left hand, they held their left elbow with their right hand, so as not to appear uncivil.

It was not a breakfast but a sumptuous meal of *penta bhat* and fish, *lochi prathas*, *bhujia*, *halwa*, *kheer* and fruit.

After the meal they proceeded to the ancestral village enjoying the rough ride. Along the way they saw hills covered with a variety of plants, villages surrounded by clusters of trees. Here and there they witnessed small boats anchored in tiny ponds with children spreading their nets to catch fish. They heard the melody of a song, accompanied with a harmonium, coming from one direction. There was a fair going on in a nearby village. On either side of the road, vendors sold vegetables, fruits, eggs and poultry from their movable markets.

The village house was small, but beautiful. The garden had hundreds of trees, all trying to recover from the assault of the previous night's rains.

In the backyard, maidservants, wrapped in dark purple, blue and green *saris*, were busy washing utensils, fetching water and cleaning fish.

Mrs Mirza had opposed the idea of bringing Benu along. A girl never visits her prospective father-in-law's house was her maxim. But Mirza insisted that they should give Benu an opportunity to see their way of living.

Ikram and Benu looked so happy together. Zahir, Puttal's fiancé, asked about Jawwad, but Shezzy, avoiding the question, started talking of the unrest in East Pakistan. She knew that young men in East Pakistan were ever ready to speak on this topic.

'I belong to the Pakistani Armed Forces. I should not speak as a Bengali, but I feel that the military officers of West Pakistan who come here treat the local people just like the Englishmen treated the Indians. In the beginning, the Indians thought that everything English was good. In the same way we too thought that the West Pakistanis were superior to us. In order to impress others, we spoke in Urdu, rather than in Bangla. The conflict started when we realized that they considered themselves superior to us without a valid reason. If we wear a *lungi*, or eat in stainless steel plates, it does not mean that we are barbaric or uncivilized. The bottom line is that the people here are not going to bear those airs any longer. That's why the gulf between the two peoples has been widening.' He joined his hands together, and then set them apart.

They enjoyed sipping tea mingled with raindrops along with their snacks while the elderly persons at home talked about them.

'After Benu's marriage, you can happily return to West Pakistan,' Misbah said. 'But you can get a good price for your business and residence now.'

'It hurts me when somebody like you talks to us about leaving, Haq Saheb,' Mirza said. 'We had already burnt our boats when we came here. Tell me, how can I set up a business in West Pakistan at this age? I have almost forgotten Urdu. I feel extremely uncomfortable in *shalwar* and *kameez*. Ask Sarwat. I always dress like you in a *lungi* and vest at home.'

'We don't want you to go,' Misbah said, 'but the truth is....'

'What is the truth? Please, do tell us!'

'I personally think that Mujibur Rahman has now turned into a cyclone. When a cyclone has to come, it comes, it's better to leave while you can and come back after the cyclone has spent its force and conditions improve.'

They had a very nice evening and a heavy meal as usual. They went to sleep early that night because everybody felt tired.

The next day guests felt a strange tension in the house. There were mysterious whispers among the family members though everyone tried to look composed. When Zahir took Ikram to a separate room and talked with him for quite some time, Benu was certain that her mother must have been its cause.

Melu, Ikram's brother, had received a letter from Dhaka telling them that his father's sister who studied at the Barisal Medical

College, had married her classmate, a West Pakistani, and that they were both staying at a friend's house after the wedding.

Ikram didn't want to break this news to his father without first confirming it. He informed the guests that he had to go to Barisal on an urgent errand but they could stay in the house during his absence.

Mirza apologized for not being able to stay on any longer. He had to attend to an art show arranged by his niece in Chittagong.

40

There was still time for the guest of honor to arrive for the inauguration of the art exhibition, so Nargis took Shams and Zari to see the masterpieces of the Bengali school in another room.

'The Bengali school is a pleasant blend of the Mughal miniature, Japanese drawing, Ajanta frescoes and modern European art,' Nargis told them. Zari and Shams liked K.N. Majumdar's painting 'Raas Leela' very much in which women with braided hair, wearing swaying petticoats and *saris* were painted in soft flowing colors.

M.R. Deb's painting, 'Honey of the Lotus', in ethereal background colors depicted a beautiful girl wearing a petticoat and an *odhni*, her bosom's naked beauty comparable to the paintings of Ajanta. She had a tiny earthen jar in her hand. Banerjee's 'Evening' showed Radha's eternal wait for Krishna on a riverbank in the golden twilight of an evening.

'How much have you learned from these masters?' Shams asked.

'I am greatly impressed with all of them, but I had a new idea. The whole beauty of Bengal can be seen in its waters. So my paintings are mostly shadows and reflections. I make the images and reflections of East Pakistan more conspicuous rather than the actual things.'

After the exhibition was opened all the guests scattered looking at Nargis' paintings. Zari and Shams noticed how beautifully she had painted the reflections of the mausoleum's arches; the conical temples; the Buddhist Pagodas; the vibrating, tranquil images of buildings and trees; the chaos of violent winds and devastation done by cyclones on seashore and on waters. The waves of the sea always contributed to the beauty of the landscape. A few landscapes were like shadows in sunshine and reflections in the moonlight. They had no colors; but the combination of black and white, light and shade gave them a depth and novelty making them more meaningful.

'Shoshi!' Shams heard somebody say. He glanced through the crowd. Yes, there she was. Suddenly, time stood still for Shams. The people in the hall ceased to exist. There was only a figure, a presence as in N.R.Deb's 'Honey of the Lotus,' and the emotion of Banerjee's 'Evening,' in which time had been transformed into a feeling of eternal, infinite anticipation!

Shoshi was taking a tour of the hall with her husband and two children. Shams stood still and studied a painting. He waited for Shoshi to notice him and call him 'Shomsh' in her old sweet voice.

He turned to look again. Shoshi with her family was leaving the hall. Did he have the heart to not talk to her? To lose her again for an indefinite period? No! Leaving Zari behind he followed them outside.

Under the *Krishnachoora* tree, amidst green leaves and orange flowers, while a dove chirped its afternoon song, Shams greeted Shoshi. She was sweet and gentle and nice as always. She did not let her feelings show, if she had any for him after so many years, and introduced him to her husband and children in a natural way. He watched the calm face and remembered the face from the past, as he knew it—smiling, laughing and crying.

When Shoshi left with her family, he went back to the exhibition hall. He was quiet for the rest of the evening. Zari respected his silence and did not probe him.

That night they stayed with Noor and Nargis, sat up late talking and dozing till the melodious rhythm of the waters of the Buriganga lulled them to sleep.

Next day they all returned to Dhaka.

41

The political situation in the country was still uncertain. Newspaper headlines were still reporting disturbances all across the country. The government and its laws were, lately, totally ineffective. Every department, every section of society was busy holding a meeting or arranging a procession over one grievance or another in both wings. Even beggars conducted a procession in East Pakistan with their exorbitant demands.

This situation continued till 19 March 1969. Then the people in the army realized that it could not go on like this forever. They would have to stop this. The commander-in-chief, General Yahya Khan, summoned General Muzaffaruddin from East Pakistan to Rawalpindi. A top-secret meeting of the army was held, and it was decided that on 25 March martial law would be imposed. A headline on 22 March reported new Governor Yousuf Haroon's statement: 'My first task will be to hold free and fair elections.'

The 23 March headline cited Field Marshall Ayub Khan's statement: 'People must come forward to safeguard the ideology of Pakistan.'

The very same day, the Governor of East Pakistan took the Oath of Office. These were only fake dramas enacted for the benefit of the public.

The real drama that unfolded behind closed doors was altogether different:

On 24 March, General Yahya Khan, Major General Rao Farman Ali, Altaf Gauhar and Fida Hasan sat in conference with Field Marshall Ayub Khan at the Presidential Palace.

Ayub Khan was visibly worried. He suspected that something was going on behind his back, but he was ready to play the game. After a few moments' pause, he said, 'I think there is no way out except by imposing martial law. This martial law must be immediate and strict. Every section of the public and every party should know that we mean it.' General Yahya Khan threw a meaningful glance at Rao Farman Ali. The word 'we' was questionable.

The old man was still under the illusion that he was going to be the chief martial law administrator.

'Let us finalize the details,' Field Marshall Ayub Khan said again.

'Sir,' Yahya Khan said in gruff low voice, trying to keep it down, 'this martial law will be imposed by the army,' meaning that Ayub Khan, after being elected, was a civilian president.

Shocked, Ayub Khan looked at General Yahya Khan, and knew immediately what he meant. A dark shadow passed across Ayub Khan's ruddy face. He remained mute for a few moments, perhaps trying to control his emotions or searching for the right words.

Finally, attempting to make his voice appear normal, he said, 'I understand. I'm ready to resign.'

A speech written previously was given to him to be recorded. He complied.

After recording the speech, it was handed to another general to be taken to Karachi, from where it was to be broadcast under the supervision of a third general. In the meantime, General Yahya Khan's speech was also recorded.

On 25 March, while protestors wearing garlands of flowers sat under the tents on their hunger strike, General Yahya's speech declaring the immediate imposition of martial law was telecast on TV and broadcast on radio. A total ban was imposed on meetings and processions. Section 144 was enforced all across the country.

42

May 5th, 1970—Puttal's friend, Mukul, was announcing the day's programs on the radio—Rabindra *sangeet*, Nazrul *Geeti*, *Amar Desh*, *kabita path*.

Benu, tanpura in hand, sitting on the *takht*, was singing a *khayal* from the *Des Raaga*. Shezzy, sitting beside Benu, watched the movement of her well-shaped fingers on the tanpura, and admired her eyes. The shades of purple, blue, gray and green in Benu's eyes fascinated Shezzy and sometimes she was afraid of their depths. Her eyes glittered from some unknown source like the reflections of lights from ships anchored miles away.

Benu ended her practice session. Just then she heard a Rabindra *sangeet* from the radio and remembered that Tagore's birthday celebrations were to begin in three days.

'You must attend the Tagore birthday celebrations, Shezzy,' Benu said. 'You should wear a *sari* that day. You'll look exactly like Zari Shamsur Rahman,' Benu laughed. Her white teeth radiated against her dark complexion.

'Will Mama and Auntie allow me to go?'

'Why not! I'll get permission, don't worry about it,' Benu said combing her long black hair. Such an air of self-confidence shook Shezzy as if something within her was going to break. Why couldn't she have that kind of self-reliance!

'Benu, tell me what do people say about Aunt Zari?' Shezzy asked.

'She frequently attends the political meetings with Shams. Some people appreciate that, some don't.'

'Have you ever met her?'

'No, but someday, I hope to visit her with Ikram. Ikram is Shams's friend and he likes Zari.'

'Mama doesn't like her at all,' Shezzy said, 'maybe your mother doesn't like her either.'

'So what? They have lived their lives. Now, it's our turn to live ours the way we like. Come, let's go for a walk up to Ramana Park.'

'At this late hour?' Shezzy said.

'There's no time-schedule for a walk. Besides, it's not late. I'll tell Mother, that's all.'

Benu and Shezzy walked to the park, which was not far from their house, and sat on a bench near the lake. Benu started singing one of her favorite songs. 'I'm going to sing this song in just a few days in the Tagore's dance drama "*Chitrangada*", with Puttal, my best friend,' Benu informed Shezzy.

She then closed her eyes to enjoy Benu's song without distraction.

Bang! Suddenly they heard the sound of an explosion from across the Topekhana road. Benu kept singing. Shezzy was scared and stood up immediately. 'Did you hear that?' She said.

Benu continuing with her song stood up slowly. 'Let's go home,' Shezzy said terrified. It was dark and Shezzy was not used to hanging around like this at night. Seeing her so afraid Benu hired a rickshaw in front of Kripa Sidhi to take them home.

There was a commotion at home. They learned that a bomb had exploded at the Council of National Integration building while Ilyas was there in the library.

'You must have been very frightened,' Neely said in great excitement. 'Please tell me all about it.'

'I wasn't afraid at all,' Ilyas said, feeling like a medieval knight. 'I was reading in the library with my friend Muneer when we saw three boys storm into the hall. They stood at the door and said something very authoritatively in Bangla. I was at some distance from the boys, so I didn't hear exactly what they said. I only saw that people ran out quickly leaving their books and newspapers behind. I asked Muneer what was the matter.

Muneer looked at me. 'Didn't you hear what they said? They told everybody to leave the library at once because they are going to blow it up.'

'As we were leaving the library, one of the boys caught Muneer by the collar, and said in Bangla. "I know your father is the

chairman of the Union Council. Stop coming here, otherwise—"
He left the sentence unfinished.

'By that time the library was deserted. As they raised the
cocktail bombs that they held in their hands, we ran out of the
library. Then we heard the explosion.'

'Was Shams there at that time?' asked Benu.

'No, the offices were closed.'

'Thank God that they gave notice. What would have happened
if they had thrown the bombs without notice?' Shezzy said.

Mirza, hearing the details of the incident became furious and
started roaring like a lion. 'What point do these people make by
doing such things?'

Ilyas and Benu had never seen their father in such a temper
before. Mrs Mirza was so afraid that she couldn't say a word.

'They were simply expressing their frustration with the council,'
Benu said trying to ease the tension. 'That's why they asked the
people to leave.'

Mirza became angrier by Benu's explanation.

'Is this the way to express one's frustration...with bombs and
blasts?'

'All other methods have failed, Father. Haven't they?' said Benu
calmly.

'You better keep quiet,' Mrs Mirza rebuked Benu. 'You should
never justify or try to support those bullies!' Benu, humiliated by
her mother's remark in front of Ilyas and Neely, quietly retired to
her room.

Neely and Ilyas went out to sit on the veranda stairs.

'Didn't anybody try catching the boys who attacked the
building?' Neely asked.

'No. The people were watching the scene as if it was a display
of fireworks. We stood outside the Press Club expecting police to
arrive and make arrests. But nobody came. Those three boys had
already disappeared on their scooters.'

'Did the blasts do a lot of damage?' Neely asked.

'I don't know but lots of books and furniture must have been
burnt.'

Then they were both silent for some time.

'Are you afraid, Neely?' Ilyas asked.

'Yes,' Neely said.

'But this is happening in West Pakistan too.'

'No, the agitation here seems to be very intense. Mama would like to leave early because she's afraid too.'

'My mother also talks about leaving East Pakistan for good but father doesn't like the idea.'

'If you come to Pakistan stay with us at Lahore.'

'It all depends on Mother and Father but I'll certainly like to come to Lahore.'

'It's getting late, let's go inside,' Neely said and they both went to their respective rooms.

43

Zari was very upset when she returned from a meeting Shams had asked her to attend.

'Shams, I see that the poison of hatred has already spread too far. I'm convinced now that the bombs and the demonstrations are not just aimed at the government, but the people of West Pakistan and Biharis are their actual targets.'

Shams did not know the extent of her bitterness. He looked at her and said casually, 'Why didn't you wear a *sari* for this meeting?'

Zari was furious. 'My wearing a *sari* cannot hide the fact that I am a West Pakistani. Shams dear, don't you know that my height, my features, and color of my hair give me away.'

'You don't have to hide the truth that you are from West Pakistan,' Shams said. 'They want you to respect their sentiments. While in Rome, do as Romans do.'

'What about my sentiments? Don't I have any feelings? I am now convinced that whatever I do, I'll never be accepted by you people.'

'You people!' Shams said in surprise, 'Does this include me too?'

'Yes, of course. The first thing you asked me was about my dress, wasn't it? Now, Do I have to explain that I was so late from my job that I had to rush with whatever I was wearing? But nobody appreciated the fact that I did attend the meeting.'

'You are very disturbed.'

'Yes, because now I feel that trying for integration is like making sand castles against the storming sea-waves.'

'Don't say that, tell me did anyone say anything bad to you?'

'A woman openly insulted me. When I asked her how long it was since the meeting started, she immediately turned her back on me, and addressing another woman sitting beside her, said loudly that *shalwar kamiz* should be banned in East Pakistan.'

'Look, this might be because the dresses you wear seem to be very costly to women here. I've told you not to wear silk and expensive jewelry here. I personally think that jewelry is not something to be proud of for a woman. It's a symbol of oppression.'

'Why, women in every country wear jewelry.'

'In the old days women, who were nothing more than men's possessions, were ornamented just as people decorate their cattle today. The young daughter-in-law was supposed to always wear jewelry, including anklets, so the mother-in-law could track the young girl's every movement by the sound of her bangles and anklets.'

'Marvelous!' Zari laughed. 'You can make theories just like Omar . Now let me tell you something. In 1857, at the time of the Indian Revolt, the Mughal princesses fled from Delhi's Red Fort in panic. They did not have any money, but they were wearing a lot of costly jewelry at the time. Those jewelry pieces sustained them for years.'

'It proves my point,' Shams said. 'That was the time when intelligent mothers thought that women should always have some jewelry on them day and night. They made it a symbol of being a woman and made men culturally bound not to borrow or sell their wives' jewelry even in the worst of circumstances.'

'You may be right here,' Zari said. 'Think about the insecure wife who was never supposed to have any money, and who was in danger of being thrown out of her house in a fit of anger by her husband at any time of the day or night. She would have at least something to support her.'

'I agree, but the question is, why do educated girls like you, who have their own bank accounts, still have a passion for jewelry.'

'Maybe because in our part of the world a woman is as insecure today as her predecessors were a hundred and fifty years ago, whether she is educated or not.'

'But the women in East Pakistan are not so fond of jewelry. It means that they don't feel that insecure.'

'Must you always support the women of your region against me?'

'Do I always do that? I don't know. Maybe I do.' Shams became serious. 'Let me tell you that the first time in my life I ever hit a young man in West Pakistan was when he remarked that prostitution is very common in East Pakistan, and one could get a woman for one rupee there. Many people from West Pakistan went to spend their weekends in East Pakistan only for that purpose.

'Such women exist in every part of the world,' Zari said. 'Why should you feel so offended if somebody talks about the women here?'

'I am offended because I know who's responsible for the extreme poverty, the real reason behind the girls' selling their bodies? Surely the girls don't deserve our condemnation. My sympathies are with the women, not with those who buy them.'

'Mine too.' Zari was about to cry. 'Let's not argue about it. I am depressed because I cannot have a sense of belonging here when everyone around me makes me feel an outsider.'

'You are suffering from persecution mania, Zari.'

'Look, you accuse me again!' Zari said.

'No, Darling! I don't and I won't in future, I promise.' Shams hugged her and continued in a sentimental manner, 'Haven't we agreed always to support each other and always be together.'

'I didn't violate the agreement,' Zari said.

'Neither did I! Now, I want to tell you something important. I am quitting the National Council for Integration and joining the faculty at Dhaka University.'

'So, you don't like the integration work any more, is that it?' Zari cornered him again.

'I don't think I can do my work there. I'll have more freedom at the University. I'll be able to write for the newspapers. We'll live with enlightened people there I'll get accommodation there too.'

'It's fine with me,' Zari said.

'Wait a minute; I almost forgot that there is a function at the press club tonight. We've got to attend it. You are going to wear a *sari*.'

'Is this a command?'

'Just a humble request.'

'OK, I'll wear a *sari*, then,' she reconciled.

For the evening's function, Zari wore a beautiful *sari*, tied her hair into a simple knot with a fresh-flower ring around it and put a big colored *bindi* on her forehead.

'Do you know how pretty you look?' Shams said escorting her into the building, 'I've seen many people turning around to have a second look at you.'

'I know why they were looking at me,' Zari said. 'They were looking at me not with admiration but with aversion.' She found the proof inside the building when people looked at her sarcastically. Not a single person complimented her on how she looked.

At night she wrote a letter to to please come to see her. Omar replied promptly that he would.

44

Benu helped Shezzy dress in a cream-colored Rajshahi silk *sari* with a red border and with a matching red blouse. She tied her hair into a bun and placed a multi-colored *bindi* on her forehead.

As they were leaving for the Tagore birthday celebrations, Neely stood gazing at Shezzy in wonder. 'You look gorgeous!' Neely said. 'Benu, please, don't forget to take Shezzy's picture,' she added.

'Come, let's go.' Benu took Shezzy by the hand and they left.

'Do they like Tagore so much over here? I thought he was a Hindu poet,' Neely said to Ilyas.

'So what! we love him. He was the greatest Bangla poet. Every house has his books and pictures. And the radio is broadcasting his songs today even though he has been banned on radio and television.'

'Why is he banned on radio and television?' Neely asked.

'I don't know. But I have read about his life and I like him very much. We are celebrating his 109th birthday today.'

'Yes, I too have read his stories in English,' Neely said.

'I want to visit his village again and see the room where he sat to write his poems,' Ilyas said.

'So, you've seen it already! Is it close?'

'Oh, no. It's very far—in Kushtia. The name of his residence is "Kothi Bari". There is a huge garden with a lot of trees. How he must have enjoyed living in such a house! His elders used to stage plays behind closed doors where children were not allowed.'

'Not even your Thakur—the greatest poet!'

'He was not allowed either,' Ilyas laughed. 'But he was only a kid then.'

'How nice! Why didn't Benu take us with her? I want to see what a dance-drama is like.'

They both sat quietly on the stairs in the dark for some time. Ilyas, lost in thought, watched Neely's face and her radiant eyes. Then he said, 'Come, let's go inside.'

When Benu and Shezzy came back they were extremely happy. The play had been a great success. Benu and her friends Puttal and Mukul had all impressed the audience.

Shezzy was so happy to see the great Bengali celebrities in person.

Dr Shaeedullah looked so cute in his loose pyjama and *sherwani*.

Kavi Jaseemuddin had great sleepy eyes behind the thick glasses. She particularly liked the way he laughed with his hand thrust in the pockets of his unbuttoned coat while talking to people, sometimes in English, sometimes in Bangla, and occasionally, in broken Urdu. He swayed when he walked, and his unfastened coat swung with him.

45

The next month, Captain Jawwad arrived in Dhaka. Sarwat gave him her sister's address and urged him to visit her family. Captain Jawwad did not visit them for months. Then, seeing that the other army officers were visiting local citizens, he decided to make a social call at Mirza's house.

Mrs Mirza received him like a traditional mother-in-law because he was her sister's son-in-law. She prepared a variety of dishes for him and treated him as a special guest as the tradition demanded. Mirza's attitude was neutral. Benu and Ilyas, however, were never very enthusiastic about his visits. Despite that, Capt. Jawwad paid regular visits and often warned Mrs Mirza against Benu's friends whose activities, in his opinion, were very suspicious.

Benu did not want Jawwad to come to their house. She asked her mother to tell him not to visit them, but her mother got angry, 'Why not? He is your brother-in-law.'

'But my friends ask insultingly, "Who is this West Pakistani army officer who visits your house regularly."'

'Can't you explain that to your friends? You know very well that your so-called leaders also married in Bihari families and you also know how much Subhan cares for her mother-in-law, and Shaukat's mother-in-law stays with him in the same house.'

'They have real relationships. They have regard and affection for each other. But I don't know why this captain comes here, maybe to spy on me.'

'Don't be ridiculous! He comes here because Sarwat wants him to, and it's only proper.'

Jawwad came that very day. Benu was practicing *raga madhwanti* on the *sitar*, when Captain Jawwad tiptoed in and stood in front of her. Benu tried to ignore him.

He, in turn, said, 'You are associating with the wrong kind of people, Benu. You're playing with fire, don't do it otherwise a time might come when even I won't be able to help you.'

Benu got furious. 'Keep your sympathies to yourself—we do not need your protection.' Benu stopped playing and looked at him angrily.

'Think it over,' he said calmly, surveying the *shapla* flowers outside through the lattice of the veranda. 'Conditions are not good at all. People are making friends with army officers these days, and you are kicking Lakshmi, the goddess of good fortune, out of your house.'

'Don't be so arrogant,' Benu said. 'This military dictatorship of yours is going to last only for a few more days.'

'You know that saying such things to an army officer amounts to treason.' Jawwad turned back to look at her in anger.

'Why? The elections are over. The government will have to be returned to the people. If saying this is treason, let me be arrested.'

'It's quite possible that your name is already on the list,' Jawwad replied, stroking his starched pants with his stick.

'Your name may be on the list made by some others,' Benu retorted, and turned to the *sitar* again.

'We know that the bombs that explode every now and then are made in colleges and universities. If, someday, you were to be caught red-handed, even the loyalties of your parents wouldn't help.'

Benu released her hand from the strings, gently laid the *sitar* on the *takht* and said,

'The new residents of the house at the corner, where the jeeps of army officers are often parked, who are they loyal to?'

'They are artists. They invite us to listen to their singing and we go,' Jawwad said. 'After all, we are human too.'

'Say men instead of humans! But do men, especially army people only want to have a good time?'

'You can just as well say the same of these girls from your locality,' Jawwad answered, trying to smile.

'They are not the girls from our locality. They do not even belong to the city. I don't know from where they have suddenly emerged! Maybe they are not from this country. Now, it is my turn to warn you—they might be spies.' Benu's eyes sparkled with hues of different colors.

'How can you say that they are not from this country?' Jawwad drew close to her.

'The same way you can guess, by appearances, people from different regions in West Pakistan.'

'But these girls don't do you any harm, do they?'

'They might do some to you. Sometimes, these personal matters become very dangerous. The debauchery of the great people of your region is, after all, their personal matter. But look how it has ruined the country.'

'You are exceeding your limits.' Jawwad became serious.

'I haven't said anything new. Even a child knows it.' Benu began peering out through the lattice to give him a hint that she was bored by the conversation.

'These are all rumors spread only to defame the West Pakistanis and the army. I am sorry to say even my own relatives are involved in this rumor-mongering.'

'Then keep your distance from such relatives. We, ourselves, are afraid that because of your visits, people may think that our family also is....' Benu suddenly stopped.

'Why did you stop? Did you want to use the word traitor?'

'Maybe.'

'You might be extremely naïve, Benu. People want the army officers to visit them so that the bullies are kept in check. Your family might need us in future.'

'OK. Let's make a truce. We'll call you when we need your help.'

'I have a feeling that you listen to all the rumors against us very attentively. Why are you so suspicious about us? Have you ever considered how soldiers spend their days and nights on the frontiers, in the open? How they get killed, trying to protect citizens from the ravages of war? Or how they live while in training? Were you to spend a week like that, you'd die.'

'There is nothing extraordinary about it. Lead the life of our peasants for a couple of days. Standing in knee-deep water day and night, their skin peels off, and mosquitoes attack them from all sides. Every now and then, their cottages are blown away by cyclones; the floods wash their children away and their animals die. Those who had nothing to live for to begin with, resign themselves to the will of God. They start struggling again, straining every nerve, only to be crushed under a tree or to succumb to death for lack of medication.'

'Are we to blame for all this?' Jawwad asked bitterly.

'Yes, very much so. More than a hundred thousand died in the last floods. The whole world offered help and poured out supplies, but nothing reached those people. Everything disappeared on the way.'

'All this is mere propaganda. The aid was distributed through foreign agencies and the intention was to tarnish the image of Pakistan. Tell me what people like you did for them? Was it only lip service or did you do something concrete? You, who live in such a big mansion and own two cars. Your prospective in-laws own many acres of land. Why don't they distribute it among the poor?'

'So, the news of my in-laws' lands has reached you too!' Benu said sarcastically. 'Listen, Mr Jawwad, we have had three agricultural reforms here, and unlike the West Pakistanis, nobody here owns hundreds of acres of land.'

'You talk of the West Pakistanis as if you have been living in East Pakistan for generations.'

Mrs Mirza entered at that moment.

'What are you talking about?' she asked.

'Please ask your daughter—she thinks that people forming secret organizations and entering into secret pacts with other countries are her friends. I am telling you, Auntie, that her friends, Puttal, Mukul, and Pawal, all belong to those organizations.'

'You have no right to speak against my friends,' Benu protested.

'But I have a right to warn Auntie to keep an eye on her children and their activities, especially now that the so-called "Martyr's Day" is coming.'

'Please don't put my mother against me. I have enough problems here even without you.' Saying this, Benu left quickly.

'Auntie, don't you know that after Awami Leagues meetings and processions, these people come out in groups and burn down the houses they had marked earlier. I am telling you sincerely that you should keep Benu away from them otherwise, your whole family might be harmed.'

'God forbid!' Mrs Mirza said. 'She is going to get married soon and then we will be leaving for West Pakistan.'

'But why must you think of leaving?' Jawwad said proudly. 'We have come here to protect you.' Watching Benu coming back to the room, he pointed to her and repeated the phrase, 'to protect you.'

'Not me,' Benu said.

'You don't know, Jawwad,' Mrs Mirza said, 'You have come from entirely different surroundings. You don't understand this place. We've been living here for thirty years. We know the direction in which the wind is blowing. In one black cloud we can read the signs of an approaching storm.'

'We don't know about any approaching storms, but we do know that if they don't behave we'll chasten these black pygmies.'

'Listen, I tell you once again. Don't talk of fighting and killing. These people are very simple and straightforward. They look weak, but they are spirited. Once they are excited, they aren't afraid of anything.'

'Not even of tanks and guns?' Jawwad laughed.

'Not even of tanks and guns!' Benu, who stood looking out the window, said.

'You be quiet!' Mrs Mirza admonished her.

'Let's see what happens. Let me now take leave of you, Auntie.'

'Come on, have a meal with us.'

'No, thanks. I'm not hungry. Goodbye—'

As Jawwad came out, he saw Suraj and Ilyas standing at the door talking and laughing. He, somehow felt as if they were laughing at him.

'You there, go and ask the driver to bring the jeep here,' Jawwad ordered Suraj.

The jeep was parked but a few paces away.

Suraj made a scornful face and went, but he didn't say anything to the driver. Noticing Jawwad standing at the door, the driver drove the jeep up to him.

46

The 21st of February was declared Martyrs Day. A minute past midnight of the 20th, millions of placards were raised at the same time and shouts of *Joi Bangla* hit the skies.

Noor and Shams were attending a public meeting at the Press Club. Nargis was with Zari at her home. They had not asked their wives to accompany them today. Zari felt hurt. tried to console her. 'Zari, do you remember Zeb Quadri?'

'Yes, , I do. How about you?'

'How can I forget her! Sometimes, I remember her words, sometimes, her charm. She was an extraordinary woman.'

', people talk of the union of opposites. Is it possible?'

'In my opinion, no,' Omar said. 'If they are really opposite to each other, they will never unite. If darkness were the opposite of light, it wouldn't blend with it? If white color dissolves into black, it isn't really its opposite.'

'I don't know,' Zari said. Maybe Shams and I are not really opposites, she thought.

'It's very late. Let's go to sleep now.' Saying this, Omar retired to his room. Zari asked Nargis to sleep in her room.

At the press club, after fiery speeches against the Pakistan Government, the best singers of radio and television entertained the crowds with their songs.

Then Shams came on to the dais and announced that his friend, a rising poet, would present his poem especially written for this day. Noor came to the dais and looked around. He said, 'The moon of the month of Moharram (mourning) will rise soon. My poem is certainly appropriate to this solemn month.'

Then he recited his poem, entitled 'Lotus.'

The poem was a direct hit against the Biharis whom they called opportunists and was an instant success. The applause and echo of clapping seemed to reach up to the skies. A boy came forward to garland Noor. A few others presented him with bouquets of flowers.

Then the entire crowd set off for Shaheed Minar and Azeempura Cemetery. The street was decorated with posters and portraits with wreaths laid on them all the way. It was *Phagun*, the month of flowers and showers, but most of the posters were like the explosives wrapped in beautiful papers. The posters showed men with breaking fetters and angry figures with torches in hand.

A sea of students and citizens was on the move. On their way to the Shaheed Minar, people picked flowers from the nursery of the Ramana Green to offer at the martyrs' graves. Millions of barefoot people holding flowers in their hands marched in that direction. Everyone wanted to be as close as possible to the martyrs' graves, where Sheikh Mujibur Rahman waited with elected members of the assembly. He was the leader of all these people. A wreath of flowers was offered to him on behalf of the Press Club and another on behalf of the Union of Journalists.

When Sheikh Mujib began his speech, the audience, hundreds of thousands, listened in pin-drop silence—even the birds perched in trees seemed to be holding their breath to listen to him.

'We had shed much blood in 1952, and if necessary, we will not hesitate to shed more. We will never compromise on our demands. We will stick to our fourteen points—nothing less. I appeal to turn each and every Bengali house into a fort in order to repel the attack of the conspirators.'

Nargis and Zari sat at home, waiting for their husbands to return.

In the early hours of the morning, Noor and Shams returned. They were both in a very blissful mood. Inadvertently, Shams was humming stanzas from Noor's poem 'Lotus', which had been more successful than they had expected. 'Noor has turned into a celebrity tonight!' he declared cheerfully.

47

Then came the night of 6 March, which was a historic night in Sheikh Mujib's life. People came in large numbers bringing packets of sweets to celebrate a veiled yet joyful occasion. A cool breeze blew from the man-made lake in front of the house.

While entering the house, Ronjhu saw a round bronze plate on which a map of Bangladesh was etched with six stars symbolizing six points. Lights from cars fell on the plate at diverse angles and the various parts of the map glittered suddenly, and just as suddenly the map sank into total darkness as the cars passed.

The prominent leaders of the Students' League, who were present, were pressuring Sheikh Mujib to declare independence. They thought this to be the right moment since instructions from Sheikh Mujib were being published in the newspapers every day and were obeyed to the letter. The National Anthem and the national flag of an independent Bangladesh had been agreed upon. Why, then, delay the declaration? The debate was on when Sheikh Mujib's secretary came to inform him that important military officials waited in the living room to meet with him.

The immediate reaction was that the officers were here to arrest him. But later, it was known that they had brought a message from General Yahya Khan, the president of Pakistan. Reacting nervously to the news that had appeared in a section of the foreign press that the Sheikh would declare the new constitution of Bangladesh on 7 March, the president of Pakistan had requested Sheikh Mujib not to take impulsive action as he himself was to visit Dhaka shortly and he had a plan that would satisfy the people of East Pakistan more than the fourteen point formula.

After the military officers departed, the debate began again. It was decided that the student bodies would take Sheikh Mujib's proposed March 7 speech for review, discuss it and then come back to talk with him. The student leaders returned to Iqbal Hall for consultations. Sheikh Mujib asked his nephew, Sheikh Sufi, to stay with him.

Sheikh Mujib now realized that he was surrounded on both sides. The student members of the Awami League wanted him to declare independence immediately and President Yahya was forbidding him to do so. Standing on the veranda, he watched the checkered chess tiles change their shapes from moment to moment. Then he went, sat down in his library and read the draft of his proposed speech one more time.

Now, he thought of a new strategy: He should neither announce the formation of Bangladesh, nor hint at it. But he would keep the tone of his speech as firm and threatening as possible. This could work.

Then he added to his speech: *The door is open for negotiations with the West Pakistanis and the path of resistance is open for our people. If there is no agreement, we can't do anything, but there is still time. If one shot is fired during this period, or our people are subjected to oppression, then we'll turn every house into a fort. Be ready to face the enemy with whatever weapons you have. And, to the government, I shall say, 'No more spraying of bullets. You can't suppress seventy million people. We have shed our blood once. We are prepared to shed more.*

Then he would play another trump card to enliven the masses and give them something to chant:

Remember, the present struggle is for liberation. The present struggle is for independence. Joi Bangla.

He felt better. These last sentences could easily be interpreted as the Declaration of Independence.

He retired upstairs to his bedroom. The historic day of March 7th was about to break over the peaceful landscape surrounding the lake.

There were noises coming from outside. A few university students were busy planting the national flag of Bangladesh on top of his residence. They were still raising slogans, when the US ambassador, Mr Farland, came to meet Sheikh Mujib.

After splashing his face with water and dressing in a white pyjama, white shirt and a waistcoat, he went downstairs to meet him. Striding across the dining room, he entered the drawing room with a smile that belied his stress. Farland beamed a typical American smile, greeted him, shook hands and sat down. He talked briefly and unemotionally, but made it clear that, if a Declaration of Independence were made that day, the US government would not support it.

And with that same nuetral American smile, which he displayed on occasions of joy as well as sorrow, he shook hands again and left.

The boys who had planted the Bangladesh flag had also left. Once again, Sheikh Mujib watched the game of the checkered tiles, making different patterns like the political moves of the day.

He didn't quite know what the rising sun had in store for him. Years ago, an astrologer, after studying his palm, had told him that he would see many ups and downs in his life. He would touch Himalayan heights as well as steep rough slopes. Would this day bring a Himalayan ascent or a steep slope for him? He wondered.

Returning from Iqbal Hall, Ronjhu with his colleagues saw Farland's car speed past them.

'These big players from the great nations have their own games to play,' Ronjhu said scornfully.

Once again, they met in Sheikh Mujib's library. Mujib showed the student leaders the slightly modified version of his speech. The students insisted on adding the ten points of non-cooperation to the speech.

'We must now raise our own army, sir,' said Ronjhu. 'If you agree, sir, I could go to Chittagong and talk with Colonel Usmani about this matter.'

'I think Usmani has already begun the work. You can go and talk to him if you want.'

Ronjhu with his friends bid him good-bye.

After their departure, Sheikh Mujib stood silently under the shadow of the flag—a field of green with a red circle and the map of Bangladesh etched upon it. A shiver ran down his spine. The morning breeze that blew from the lake had suddenly turned very cold. He rushed indoors immediately.

48

One day, Benu was forced to reconcile with Jawwad. On 1 March, a cricket match was being played at the stadium. Ilyas and his friend, Muneer, were watching the game when news of the postponement of the National Assembly spread among the spectators. There was a lot of anger and hurt among Bengalis and everybody tried to come out of the stadium at the same time to demonstrate and show their anger. There was a stampede in the stadium and then there were riots all over the city.

Ilyas and Muneer came running from the stadium to seek shelter at Muneer's house, because his house was closer than Ilyas's. Muneer's father was not home at that time. The two boys sat in the house like two scared mice, afraid of the cat in pursuit of them. They knew that a procession was heading their way, chanting slogans like mad. The people in the procession were carrying long, thick bamboo and iron rods. Muneer, terrified, called a relative, a junior commissioned officer to help them.

'We can't help you son,' he said. 'The army has been ordered to remain passive.' He was so disappointed in those orders that he was brutally bitter. 'Run away from that house or be prepared to become a sacrificial goat. It's your choice. You have no idea how badly we are being treated. The public hurls abuses at us, they wave their shoes at us and spit in our faces from balconies. We are under orders not to retaliate because they say the situation might get worse if the army intervenes.' The phone coughed and then was silent.

The sound of chanting slogans drew near. Muneer peered out through the crescents of glass above the door. A few people stood under a telephone pole, and a boy already up on the pole, was busy cutting the telephone wire.

'*What use is this phone when no one can help us*'! Muneer thought bitterly.

He bolted the doors from within and took Ilyas to the back door. He glanced at the narrow back lane. There stood Kajal, their Bengali neighbor's son, holding a lock in his hand. Kajal came to them and softly said, 'Go into our house. I'll lock your door, and tell them that your family left long ago. Go, hurry.'

Ilyas and Muneer were thus sheltered in Kajal's house.

As soon as Kajal's father saw them, he told his daughter, Chaya, to hide them in the store. They followed her into the store, which had an iron door. Light and air entered it only through a small ventilator in the wall near the low ceiling.

Chaya looked at them with sympathy but did not say anything. She left them there, came out, shut the door gently, locked it and left them.

All day long, relatives, friends and acquaintances came to meet Kajal's father to discuss politics. They sat on a low, wooden *takht* and talked. 'Do you know that the assembly session has been postponed? We've been telling you all along that Yahya and Bhutto have entered into a secret deal. This session will never be held. Banga Bondu had told them that if there is any postponement they should immediately announce new dates. But they are not listening to him.'

'You may be right, but the people of Taher Bagh and Thiteri Bazar are innocent. They haven't done anything wrong, so we shouldn't punish them,' Kajal's father said.

'But we want to take revenge. If we cannot reach the leader, we will avenge the followers.'

Until nightfall, Ilyas and Muneer sat crouching in the damp, stifling store. Late at night when visitors ceased coming to the house, Chaya unlocked the storeroom and came in with supper. Chaya chatted while they ate. A little later, Kajal joined them.

'I've tried hard to contact your family, Ilyas, but couldn't reach anybody. I'll continue trying.' He had also brought news of the army opening fire at Farm Gate, which resulted in many deaths. Local citizens had launched attacks at many places in the city on Bihari colonies. The residents of Isfahani colony had fled to other areas. Many had sought shelter in the cantonment and hundreds of others had lined up at the airport to leave East Pakistan.

The next day, there was curfew in the city. Sheikh Mujib strongly condemned the army for shooting at peaceful crowds. He defied the curfew and announced instead a program as leader of his party, the Awami League, to hold a strike from 6 am to 2 pm every day from 3 March through 6 March.

The following day, the public violated the curfew. Government House was ransacked and the army shot at the crowd. Kajal brought the news that there were eight bodies at Iqbal Hall and five more were seen lying in Paltan Maidan. There was a constant stream of wounded being brought to different city hospitals. The government agencies, as well as Sheikh Mujib, appealed for blood donations.

Finally, Kajal was successful in informing Mirza about Ilyas being safely sheltered in their house. Mirza couldn't drive there in the situation existing in the city, so he asked Jawwad to take him there in his jeep.

At 11 pm, an army jeep drove up to Kajal's house. Mirza alighted quickly, picked up Ilyas and got back into the jeep. Soldiers with guns in their hands flanked him and Ilyas on both sides. Captain Jawwad sat beside the driver. After passing through the narrow winding lanes of Dhaka City, the jeep entered the beautiful Ramana park area. Empty streets looked broader there. The towering/ shade trees by the roadside were drowned in darkness. Military trucks, slightly hidden from public view, were stationed at every corner. Occasionally, some solitary vehicle sped by.

Hearing the throbbing of a jeep at the door, Benu ran out without stopping to put her shoes on. She greeted Ilyas, embraced him joyfully and then turned to Jawwad. Combing her hair with her fingers in her usual style, she said. 'Thank you, Jawwad Bhai!'

'You're welcome,' Jawwad said, gazing into her deep eyes, which were dazzling bright with tears.

That night, Benu prepared coffee for Jawwad. She didn't argue with him even when he suggested that they move to the Cantonment area till life in the city returned to normal. And

when he took leave, in spite of a light drizzle, she went out to bid
him goodnight.

The street was deserted. The night was bathed in showers. The
trees stood silent in the moist air. While bidding good-bye,
Jawwad looked at her in a strange way. She shuddered though she
was unable to read the meaning of his look.

49

The National Day was celebrated in East Pakistan on March 3 under the chairmanship of Noor Alam Siddique and a large public meeting was held at the Paltan Maidan. After returning from the meeting, Puttal, Ikram and Melo talked quietly among themselves. Like a youth passing through the experience of falling in love for the first time, Melo was intensely passionate, and yet a little frightened about the matter of independence.

Today, for the first time the national anthem of Bangladesh was sung. Melo repeated the words of the anthem, quietly, in the same tune: *My golden land, I love you.*

The national flag of Bangladesh was also presented for public view—a purple sun above the green earth with the map of Bangladesh in between.

'Do you know what Banga Bondu has declared? "As long as power is not transferred to the people's representatives, no taxes will be paid,"' Melo said happily.

Ikram tried to restrain him.

'*The People,*' a hard-line nationalist newspaper, was secretly read at home. '*The Pakistan Observer*' was meant solely for Misbah, who was very surprised that it only carried news about the Awami League, giving front-page coverage to Sheikh Mujib's instructions.

'I congratulate the people on their observing a total strike. I hereby order that all government, as well as non-government institutions, where employees have not been paid their salaries, will work from 2:30 to 4:30 p.m. to facilitate disbursement of salaries. The banks shall function during these hours. All transactions shall be carried out through the two banks of East Bengal. Do not let a paisa be transferred to West Pakistan. The letters and telegrams to foreign countries shall be sent via Manila and London.'

Misbah was puzzled when he read the news. He didn't quite understand what all that was about. Ikram explained to him that since the army had returned to the barracks, a strike was being observed every day on Sheikh Mujib's instructions and banks and other commercial organizations and factories were working under his orders. The Pakistan government was not doing anything for the time being, thinking that a solution may be found only after a dialogue between Sheikh Mujib and leaders of West Pakistan.

What Ikram did not tell his father was that the situation had gone to extremes, so much so that four student-leaders had now been elevated to the ranks of the caliphs. In Nazrul Islam's poem the names of the four caliphs of Islam were replaced with those of Suraj, Rab, Quddus, and Noor Alam.

At the same time, there were incidents of shooting in Sylhet, Jessore, Komela, Tongi, Raj Shahi and Chittagong and curfew was enforced in many places.

50

After Ilyas left, Muneer was alone in the store with the dampness, darkness and loneliness. At times, he felt as if his heart was saturated with the dampness of the store. He should twist his heart and hang it on the line to dry it in the sun and air.

Chaya, like a draught of fresh air, occasionally sneaked into the store. Her visits were restricted only to serving food and taking out the dirty dishes. He did not have the courage to ask her to stay a little more or open his heart to her. One day, rummaging through old books, she found an Urdu magazine and brought it for Muneer. He wanted to read it, but the light that came through the ventilator was very dim and it hurt his eyes.

At last he decided to return home and informed Kajal about his decision. Kajal told him that his father hadn't yet returned. Kajal had pushed a note through the door, urging him to contact them immediately when he came back, but so far they hadn't heard from him.

Even then, Muneer was determined to go home that night. So, at nightfall Kajal escorted him to his house. He arrived safely, but he had scarcely mounted two steps toward the door when he staggered.

There had been reports of the effigies of the West Pakistani leaders being burnt. Was this an effigy? Muneer leaned forward to look closer. His blood curdled at what he saw. It was his father, Zafar Ahmed, lying on the ground like a dry goat-gut. His body was drained of the last drop of blood and then it had been thrown in front of his house. His blood might have been donated to the party who had murdered him. There were rumors that they were doing it.

Muneer broke down and dropped to the ground. A cool drizzle sprayed his father's dead body. His head rolled to one side and he fainted.

Kajal, like a puppet, stood against the door.

51

Nargis and Noor had decided to go to London for the time being when their house was attacked by the Mukti Bahini in Chittagong and Noor was able to save his wife with great difficulty. Shams was driving them to Dhaka airport. The city, which always seemed to be overpopulated and bustling with activity, was now very quiet. The army was deployed at all sensitive points, tactfully hidden from the public.

The Awami League had erected bamboo barriers on the way to the airport. For a very long time, the non-Bengalis had been threatened that they would have to leave the country with nothing but the clothes on their backs. Their goods, their savings and the proceeds from the property they had sold for a song would have to be left behind. And that was exactly what was happening. The volunteers of the Awami League were conducting a thorough check at these barriers and dealing with the people leaving the country the way they fancied. That was why Shams, a Bengali, whom the volunteers also knew as Ranjho's brother had to take his friends to the airport.

Shams slowed down at the barrier at Farm Gate, and leaned out to show his face and to see what was going on. A woman wearing a long white *burqa* was sitting in a cycle rickshaw. A Pathan, who stood by, was being interrogated. They lifted the barrier when they saw Shams and Noor. Passing through the barrier Shams looked in the rear-view mirror. Zari, Noor, and Nargis also watched from their seats. One of the men at the barrier thrust his hand forward to grab the necklace of the woman in the *burqa*.

The Pathan roared, 'Don't you touch my wife!'

At this sudden outburst they began to beat him. The woman in the rickshaw screamed. Watching the people in the car, the rickshaw driver quickly started his rickshaw and pulled it beside the car. Nargis opened the door of the car instantly and dragged the woman inside. The Pathan continued raving. The people who surrounded him laughed at his words and gestures. Nargis and Zari tried to calm the hysterical woman who continued crying. Shams knew what was going to happen to that Pathan. He drove away.

'All this shouldn't be allowed,' Noor said with anguish. 'Somebody should tell Sheikh Mujib about these things.'

'Do you think the leaders don't know what's happening?' Nargis said.

'Do you think that all this is being done with their approval, Shams?' Noor asked.

'It's not that,' Shams said. 'The people think that in a revolution bloodshed is inevitable. The leaders, at this point, are only concerned about the success of the revolution.'

'So, you validate such crimes, Shams Bhai?' Nargis asked.

'No, but when one section of a nation suppresses the other, the suppressed ones are sure to revolt against their exploiters. In an uprising, innocent people get killed. It has happened in every revolution.'

'But why do they provoke people to kill innocent citizens,' Nargis asked angrily.

'Yes, their remarks do instigate people,' Noor said.

'I agree,' Shams said. 'They shouldn't do it but you cannot control everyone when there are so many people involved. But I do regret your leaving us at such a time. What will people say when they'll come to know that the author of that great poem "Lotus" has fled away!'

'For God's sake, Shams Bhai,' Nargis said, 'be reasonable. My family was almost massacred in Isfahani Colony in Chittagong. Now, when I've got admission in Slade School in England, isn't it the best chance to get out of an unstable situation?'

'Does that mean that you are, in no way, concerned with our future, our aspirations? I've been telling Zari what the Bengalis think of West Pakistanis that this province was only a picnic spot for them. They liked its flora and fauna. Since the chances of having picnics are gone they don't need to stay?'

'What's gotten into you, Shams Bhai, you never talked so bitterly?' Nargis said.

'But now I will. How long shall I not speak the truth?'

'Zari, why don't you explain to your husband that we are leaving because our lives are in danger?' Nargis shook Zari, who had been sitting motionless.

'How can I?' Zari spoke almost in tears. 'Don't you know that I'm the cause of this bitterness? This poor man's friends and relatives hate his wife, can you blame him for his behavior?'

'Zari, please, shut up!' Shams burst out.

'Listen, Shams Bhai, come to stay with us for a few days,' said Nargis. 'Zari will have a nice break.'

'Never,' Shams said. 'Not now. Zari is free to go and stay with you. But leave my province and me alone.'

'See how he has detached himself from me,' Zari said.

Suddenly the woman in the *burqa* started wailing again, 'They'll kill my husband, they are going to kill him.'

'No, they wouldn't. I'll send my husband back to save him,' Zari said and started talking to her in Hindko to distract her. Zari found that the couple lived in the Hazara district and told the woman that she, too, was from Abbotabad. The woman felt a connection and was greatly calmed.

When they reached the airport they saw long lines at ticket counters that extended beyond the main building and went upto the road.

Some people had sold their houses and other possessions at minimal prices and a few had exchanged their new cars for air tickets, and they were practically living at the airport, waiting for their turn to get a flight. The Pakistan International Airline's Bengali staff was on strike. They said that the company's airplanes coming from West Pakistan were carrying arms and ammunition. Pakistan air force employees with non-Bengali volunteers were running the flights. Noor and Nargis already had their tickets. At Zari's request Shams went back to the Farm Gate to save the Pathan.

Shams knew quite well that he would not find the Pathan alive. He did not even see his body. Somebody pointed out to his eyes, which were pulled out from the sockets with a bayonet and lay in a drain staring at the sky. It was so hard to look at them. Shams covered his own eyes with his hands.

The woman was expecting Shams to come back with her husband. When Shams returned without him she started crying again. Shams consoled her with the lie that her husband has been wounded and got admitted into a military hospital at the barracks. He would be flown back to Pakistan as soon as he gets well. But the woman refused to leave for West Pakistan without her husband. Zari, speaking her language, with great difficulty convinced her to leave. Shams told her another lie that it was her husband's express desire that she should go back to her village.

By a lucky coincidence, an acquaintance of Shams and Zari was among the passengers leaving for Rawalpindi. Shams asked them to take care of the woman during the flight, and if possible, escort her to her village.

52

Jawwad had, at last, succeeded in convincing Mirza and his wife to leave their house temporarily and move to the safe Cantonment area. He had rented an apartment for them, which was but a short distance from his own room. Benu had told Zari that instead of going with her parents she would like to stay with them. Zari and Shams had agreed to take her in the afternoon. Benu had stayed behind saying that she wanted to store certain precious things and pictures in a safe place.

Benu, going to her bedroom with an armload of pictures and a costly flower vase, saw Captain Jawwad enter the house. She drew back in shock. She was alone in the house and he knew it.

Jawwad didn't know anything about the arrangement between Benu and Zari. Jawwad had been led to believe that she would move into the new house by evening.

'I was passing by and I thought I could take you to your new house with me,' Jawwad said.

'But I haven't yet finished my work.'

'Go ahead, finish it,' Jawwad said. 'I'm going for a little errand. I'll be back.'

As soon as he left, Benu dumped all the things she was carrying on a nearby table and rang Zari telling her about Jawwad.

'I don't want to be here when he comes back. Please come to take me as soon as possible.'

'OK, we'll be there as soon as Shams comes home from the office. Don't panic. Just be careful and be ready to come with us,' Zari said.

Putting down the receiver Benu speeded up her work. She just locked all the pieces in one cupboard in the bedroom.

Then she started getting ready to go with Zari and Shams. Dressed in her blouse and petticoat, she was holding a *sari* in her hand to wrap it around when she felt somebody push her bedroom door open.

'Who's there?' she shouted.

Without replying, Jawwad entered the room.

Instinctively, Benu covered her breasts with the sari. Her orange lips, freshly roughed with lipstick, trembled like tiny tulip petals that quiver gently in the early morning breeze. On her face was a halo of deep, dark clouds and in her eyes—a depth that Jawwad had never seen before. He staggered before he recovered his balance. Benu felt his hot breath on her ears.

'I love you, Benu,' he whispered. 'Your beauty has fascinated me, bitten me. I have come to know what the Bengali magic is all about—the magic of brown skin and a full figure...'

Benu drew back in horror, giving a violent push to his advancing hands. 'Jawwad Bhai, please!' There was anger as well as sorrow in her tone. Her eyes burned with rage and repugnance.

'I know, you dislike me,' Jawwad continued. His tone was mild and appealing. 'But I have fallen madly in love with you. I can't help it.'

Benu understood that he had come to avenge her for all her outbursts against West Pakistan, the army, and himself.

Most of the neighboring houses had been vacated. There was no mutual trust among the neighbors. All the servants had left, and there was nobody in the house. How could she have been so negligent as not to lock the entrance door!

'Jawwad Bhai...' Trying to compose herself, Benu kept her tone gentle and persuasive. 'I don't dislike you but I do love Ikram. You shouldn't say such things to me. Think of Shezzy. She is my cousin.'

'In love, a man isn't able to think of anything else. It's simply beyond me.'

Jawwad had often watched Bengali girls moving about in a blouse and petticoat or in sleeveless short dresses. But he had never imagined that he would see Benu like this...her tanned, voluptuous body like he had seen in Bengali paintings. The thrill of getting an inaccessible thing took hold of his senses like a strong, stimulating wine.

He felt that he was really in love with this captivating face—this soft and supple body—and he was certain that it would be impossible for him to live without having it.

Realizing what he intended to do, Benu tried to slip through the door, but Jawwad held her delicate waist and whirled her towards him. Benu started shrieking fitfully, but Jawwad bolted the door, and pressing her mouth with one hand, pushed her toward the bed with the other. Then he tried to kiss her.

There was a knock at the door followed by an intense rapping.

'Who's there?' Jawwad asked.

Finding his grip loosen about her, Benu wriggled out of his grasp and stood in the corner with her partly wrapped *sari* still in her shivering hands.

'I'm Major Khalid,' Khalid said in a commanding voice. 'Open the door or we'll break it.'

Jawwad stood up dismayed and frightened. Could he face his superior army officer in the condition he was in?

Benu hid her face in both hands and wept convulsively. Jawwad tried to calm himself and tried to make himself presentable.

At another knock Jawwad had to unlock the door.

Zari rushed in, took Benu's arm and led her into another room. Benu was shivering all over. It was only a lucky coincidence that Major Khalid had accompanied Zari and Shams. It was obviously easier for him to handle the situation.

'People like you disgrace the army, Captain,' Major Khalid said. He removed Jawwad's revolver from its pouch.

Benu's crying and Zari's consoling words could be faintly heard from across the room.

53

It was 23 March, Republic Day. While in West Pakistan it was celebrated as a holiday, with a Pakistani flag waving on every building, in East Pakistan, instead of Pakistan's flags, the green and red flags of Bangladesh waved in the pleasant March breeze. The black flags as a protest against Republic Day were also raised on top of many buildings. Young boys were singing and dancing in the streets and shouting '*Joi Bangla.*'

The Pakistani flag, however, could be seen hoisted at the Martial Law Headquarters, Government House, army barracks and a handful of houses in Mirpur and Mohammedpur. The newspapers had published supplements with maps and advertisements with full-page flags of Bangladesh as if Bangladesh was already in existence.

It was also Benu and Ikram's wedding day. Benu had wanted to wear a black sari for her wedding because it coincided with the Demonstration Day and also because of what had happened to her a few days before. However, her in-laws insisted that she should look like a proper bride.

The house was splendidly decorated for the arrival of the new bride.

They made all the arrangements for the wedding feast possible under the circumstances. Not many guests were invited to the wedding, but all close friends and relations were there. Benu left Zari's residence for her new home. She was wearing a red *sari* and donned a costly, laced dupatta of real brocade. She was wearing gold jewelry as well as ornaments made of flowers. Supported by Puttal on one side and Ikram on the other, she entered her new home slowly. Puttal's friends were singing the wedding song, *Haryala Banna*, which Amir Khusro had composed centuries before.

The Maulana performed the Nikah.

The Maulana was a Bengali teacher. At one time he had held an important position in the government at Faridpur. After the wedding when the guests were having dinner, a guest asked, 'Maulana, what is going to happen? Do you know that today pictures of the Quaid-e-Azam were being torn down from the offices and Pakistani flags were being burnt and the advertisements say *Joi Bangla* as if Bangladesh has already been created?'

'Yes, I know,' Maulana said. 'But these advertisements come from businesses, and their aim is to make the people in power happy. They are all worshippers of the rising sun. When the other side wins they tilt in its favor. But we have to remember that Sheikh Mujib hasn't made a Declaration of Independence yet.'

'Everybody knows that Pakistan was formed by the indisputable support of the Bengalis. Why do they want to go against it now?' Another guest asked.

'Because Bengalis think that first the Hindus crushed them, then the English suppressed them. They were in the majority when Pakistan was made, and it was their right to rule the country. West Pakistanis didn't give them that right.'

'Whatever you say, Maulana, but whatever is happening here might have serious consequences.'

'Yes, they should find a political solution. Otherwise there'll be blood shed in every village and town,' Maulana said, lowering his eyes as he leaned over his plate of *biryani*. His words made everybody shrink as if it had thundered all of a sudden on a cloudless day or a storm had invaded in the month of phagun.

Everybody was silent for a few moments.

They could hear the children still singing in the streets, 'I love you, my golden country.'

54

It was midnight. Zari heard someone talking. She got up and found Omar and the Maulana engaged in conversation. This moonlit night of March 25 had made her restless. Shams had left for Chittagong the previous day. Before leaving, he had asked the Maulana to stay with Zari and Omar until his return.

The scales were tilting towards the Awami League now, and the people who were called 'Urdu Speaking' had to be very careful.

Zari leaned out of the window. The night was perfectly still, but Zari felt uneasy, as if something were about to happen. From across the city she could hear mysterious noises. The breeze blowing from the barracks brought a strange smell similar to gunpowder or was it all her imagination? Should she ask the Maulana? People said he could even tell about the future events.

Since Omar had started learning Bangla from the Maulana, they had acquired a habit of chatting for hours. In spite of differences of opinion, their friendship was genuine. Very often they talked on metaphysical matters and rarely agreed on anything. Omar insisted upon talking to him in his imperfect Bangla. He had also started wearing checkered *lungi* and *banian* at home like any other Bengali.

Zari slowly walked towards them. As she approached, she heard Omar talking.

The sudden explosions of cannon fire shook the house to its foundation. Then they could hear the ceaseless boom of cannons and gunfire from the direction where the University hostels were located.

Omar went out to see what was happening. The Maulana followed him. Other occupants from the neighborhood also came.

'I think the shots are coming from the British Council Library,' the Maulana said.

'I think that too. Did you know that the library is now being used as Army Headquarters, since 5 March when the local citizens had set fire to it,' somebody informed them.

'This seems to be an army action.'

'This is terrible!' the Maulana said. 'So many innocent lives will be lost. There should have been a political solution.'

Then they all went back to their homes. The Maulana and Omar came back inside and silently listened to the horrible noises that continued the whole night.

At that time the army stationed at the library was shelling the hostels, Iqbal Hall and Jagannath Hall of Dhaka University. The old, red, soft bricks of the Jagannath Hall were falling apart. The rusted water pipe had been dislodged from the wall, and water from the overhead tank gushed forth to the ground. Some of the boys living on the second floor ran towards the stairs. Others chose to swing down to the ground from the branches of trees outside their rooms. All ran helter-skelter into the dark. Dense clouds of smoke rose from every direction and blackened the moonlit night.

Those who were lucky were able to run into the nearby fields and find shelter there. Those, whom death didn't give a chance, lay on their beds, on the floor, on the thresholds, across windows and on the verandas smoldering.

Some of them might have launched an unsuccessful counter-attack. A message received at the Martial Law Headquarters said, 'We are facing stiff resistance.' But two hours later, the army gained total control of the area.

After that the army targeted East Pakistan Rifles in the Peel Khana area behind the Azeempura Cemetery and the police headquarters in Roger Bagh. The office of The People newspaper and copies of its 23 March issue, which had published the Bangladesh map across many columns with the caption, 'The martyrs' blood has given birth to a new flag today,' were now burning incessantly.

The narrow lane of Sukharipatti in Dhaka was under intense fire. The residents of Sukharipatti had been experts in carving icons for centuries. The huts along the railway line were also on fire. The residents of those cottages, carrying their children in their arms, ran to the fields and ponds where the coconut trees quietly embraced the bamboo trees, seeking shelter. The Kacha Bazar was also in ashes.

The men and women crawled like insects hiding themselves on the various embankments of the old Ganges. They hid in the fields around the Kamlapur railway station. When it was safe they moved in the direction of Tej Gaon and to the roads and paths leading out of Dhaka and to the border of India. They knew that the Pakistan army meant business this time and it was not safe for them to stay in the city.

Zari was terrified. If this were an army action, it would be the same in Chittagong. Similar explosions must be rocking the earth there. Flames of fire must be going up and clouds of smoke must be tarnishing the spotless moonlight of superb green and luxuriant Chittagong. God, please keep Shams safe. Zari was praying in her heart again and again.

'This is horrible!' Maulana said. Then he sat silently, gazing towards the ceiling.

It was not dawn yet, but there was a little hazy light all over. 'Has anybody heard the *azan* for the morning prayers?' the Maulana asked.

'No, the call of the Muezzin hasn't come yet,' said Omar. 'And I don't think anybody will go to the mosque for the *azan* today.'

'Alas! This is the first time in hundreds of years that the *azan* for the morning prayers has not been called from any of the seven hundred mosques in Dhaka. Wait, let me first run to a nearby mosque to give the *azan*.' Saying this, the Maulana hastened out of the house.

'Don't go out. It's not safe,' Omar said. 'Why are you risking your life?'

'Life and death are in God's hands, Omar Bhai.' Walking briskly with small quick steps, he crossed the lawn and disappeared around the corner.

When the Maulana returned, after giving *azan* and saying his prayers in a nearby mosque, they started talking again about politics. Zari was not in the mood to listen. Her mind was preoccupied with thoughts of Shams.

She knew she could not sleep at this hour. Nobody could. She went to the kitchen and tried to keep herself busy. She could still hear the conversation between Omar and the Maulana in between her own thoughts.

'Come Maulana, come Chachaji, breakfast is ready.' Zari stood at the door of the kitchen calling them.

They both turned to look at Zari in surprise. They felt as if it was Doom's Day. The mountains were being shredded and flying like puffs of cotton, the sun stood at a yard's height and an angel was calling them to come and have breakfast.

55

On the bank of the beautiful, man-made lake of Dhan Mandi, the trees stood still with heads bowed. The bridge with wooden crosses all along the sides and a solitary small room at the centre looked mysterious, and surreal. But all of a sudden people living near Sheikh Mujib's residence heard the gunshots. The Commandos had entered Sheikh Mujib's residence and had arrested him. The Commando officers came out with Sheikh Mujib wearing his usual white shirt and a typical Bengali pyjama. His servants were also arrested and they were all taken in a military jeep to the army headquarters.

Sheikh Mujib's son Kamal, somehow escaped, and running across the lanes, shouted to his neighbors, 'Father has been arrested.'

A few soldiers began removing the brass map of Bangladesh from the main gate of Sheikh Mujib's residence. The flowers in their beds seemed to be gazing helplessly at the sky where there were dense clouds of smoke.

General Tikka Khan's headquarters on Jinnah Avenue was under construction, but he was in there. The jeep carrying Sheikh Mujib stopped in front of the building. Sheikh's white shirt shone in the silvery moonlight.

'Hello, hello.' A Major of 57 Brigade was on the wireless in the jeep. 'The big bird is in the cage, sir. The others are not in their nests. Over.'

'Well done!'

'Shall we bring the big bird to you, sir?' One of the staff officers asked General Tikka Khan.

'No, I don't want to see his face,' General Tikka Khan said contemptuously.

* * *

The army action and Mujib's arrest and charging him for treason made the East Pakistanis react more brutally. After the army action East Pakistan passed through a turbulent period, but the government announced that normality had finally returned. Those who had sought refuge in India were finally coming back. All the schools, colleges, offices, banks and factories were functioning normally. In short, as per the rules of procedure in the army:

'Everything okay?'

'Yes, Sir.'

But obviously everything was not okay.

The protestors now openly demanded an independent country—Bangladesh, and tried to gain world sympathy by highlighting the atrocities committed by the Pakistan army in their region.

56

Puttal picked up the newspaper from the ground. No newspapers had been published for the past two days. This paper was dated 28 March. It carried President Yahya Khan's broadcast to the nation in which he had branded Sheikh Mujib a traitor and declared that he would not go unpunished.

Zulfiqar Ali Bhutto, the People's Party leader had also said, 'Thank God, Pakistan has been saved.'

Suraj, opening the door, walked up to Puttal and said, 'Puttal Apa, Benu Apa is waiting for you at the breakfast table.'

'All right,' Puttal said, and came in. Suraj had just brought two glasses of *bel* juice.

'Where is Melo?' Puttal asked.

'Melo Bhai...' Suraj seemed reluctant to answer. 'I don't know, he is not in the house,' Suraj hesitatingly said.

Puttal was alarmed. 'Where has he gone? It's curfew time, no time to go out.'

'Don't know. He was here a while ago. When I brought a glass of sherbet for him, he was gone.'

'Wait, I'll go out and see.' Puttal ran out quickly. She was very concerned. Ikram who had left the previous day on an errand had not yet returned. Benu, his bride, and Puttal, his sister, spent the night wiping the corners of their eyes with the hems of their *saris*. They could only speculate: He may be with Ronjhu or at Sheikh Mujib's residence in Dhan Mandi. But what they were afraid of was too awful to think about.

'Suraj, swear by my head and tell me where Melo went. I know you too well. I can tell that you're hiding something from me. You have to tell me,' Benu said.

'Benu Apa, when I climbed up the building to take out the Bangla flag, I saw Melo Bhai standing in the attic, peering out through the window. I stood silently behind him. We had erected

barriers on the roads during the night, you know. We saw a jeep
of Pakistan army drive up and stop at one of the barriers. A water
carrier, bearing a leather water bag was crossing the road at the
time. Seeing the army in the jeep, he panicked. He flung his bag
and lay down on the ground.

'A soldier walked toward him, poked him with his boot and
shot him dead. The water bag burst open, and the water mingled
with the man's blood flowed along the street. Melo Bhai got so
angry that he started madly punching the wall in the attic. Then
he turned and looked at me. His eyes were bloodshot. He said,
"By God, I will go and join the Mukti Bahini this minute, and
come back to fight them. We have to have our independent
country at all costs." With these words he immediately left the
house.'

'Why didn't you tell us this before?'

'I never thought he would really go away. I thought he was only
releasing his frustration and would come back after a few
minutes.'

'Don't you know Suraj, that there is a twenty-four hour curfew
in the city? The army is everywhere and there are orders to shoot
on-sight. You know that was the reason that waterman panicked,
and they shot him because he was not supposed be out.'

'Melo bhai must have gone to a neighbor's house. Maybe he is
with the Choudhry's.'

'Call and find out,' Benu said.

'The telephones are all dead since last night.'

'Oh!' Benu lowered her head to her knees feeling desperate.
'Where is Father?'

'Saheb is in his library. He has been there all night.'

'And Mother?'

'I saw her saying her morning prayers. She must have retired
to her room after that.'

'Go and ask her if she needs anything.'

The chirping of birds came from the garden. It is such a
pleasant morning of March, but how dreadful!' Benu thought.

'Benu Apa, the fleeing people on the streets say that the Biharis
are killing Bengalis with the help of the army.'

'Don't listen to them. That might not be true,' Benu said and walked out toward the garden to look for Puttal. Benu found Puttal crying bitterly at the gate. Benu didn't say a word but embraced her lovingly, and they both cried.

57

For three days Zari kept going to the front door expecting to see Shams coming home but returned disappointed. She also kept peering out from her bedroom window to see what was happening in the neighborhood, but saw nobody there. The grass had grown tall and was untrimmed between the neighbor's house and theirs.

Omar and Maulana were as anxious about Shams's safety as Zari. Every now and then they also went to the door with an excuse. The twenty-four hour curfew was now relaxed for an hour in the morning and for one hour at dusk. Nobody dared go out even then. In the inner lanes of the university, a solitary figure would emerge from a house, and walking briskly, would disappear into another house.

The darkness of the night had started coming down. The fragrance of jasmine and *raat ki rani* sometimes found its way through the window, reviving an old memory in Zari's mind. Occasionally, a military truck sped by crushing the silence of the surroundings.

Suddenly there was a loud knock at the door. The strategy of living in the house had kept changing with the political situation. After the army action, Omar had given his room to the Maulana and slept in the living room where Urdu books had replaced the Bangla books, and it was Omar who answered every knock at the door now. As soon as he opened the door, two young men and a girl entered the room and bolted the door from within.

'Where is Shams bhai?' one of them asked in urgency.

'Shams is out of town. Please be seated. I'll call Zari,' Omar replied.

When Omar went to call Zari, the older man of the two said to the Maulana, 'I want you to wed my brother and the girl here.

They're going to cross the border to India, and don't have much time.'

Zari recognized them though Omar had not. 'Ikram, Melo, why are you here?' Zari said in surprise.

'Zari Apa, we are crossing the border to India,' Melo said. 'When I went to visit my would be in-laws, Renu's father said, "Take her along with you. She'll be safer with you, but marry her before you go." I brought her here so that Maulana could perform our *Nikah*. Ikram Bhai has also come with me, lest you think she has eloped with me,' Melo smiled.

'This is no time for jokes,' Ikram said. 'He is telling the truth. They have to go. Maulana, please hurry.'

'Have you taken your supper? Have you any provisions with you?' Zari asked.

'We don't have anything—only a few clothes in a bag. That's all,' Melo said, gently stroking the thin bag slung across his shoulder.

After the evening prayer, the Maulana was sitting in his *lungi* and *banian*, one leg folded over the other. He took his saffron-colored shirt from the chair, put it on and adjusted his cap.

'How can you go out at night? The night curfew will begin shortly,' Zari said.

'This isn't West Pakistan, Zari Apa,' Melo said cuttingly. 'We can go clear to the border by entering one house and coming out through another. Hundreds have already reached the border this way—don't worry about us.'

'In order to survive sometimes one has to play hide-and-seek with death, Zari,' said Ikram. 'Do you know what's happening here? They are searching each and every house. I hope Shams isn't here, is he?'

'No, do you know where he is! Could you tell me, please?' Zari clenched the fists of her white hands in despair.

'Wherever he is, he must be safe. I can assure you. Everyone is frightened and being careful. I'm sure he must be in hiding. He'll come back in a day or two.

'I'm ready,' the Maulana said.

Zari guided them all to Omar's room to be on the safe side and shut the door. As the Maulana recited the verses of the *nikah* from the Holy Qoran, Zari read the faces of those present. Getting married in an emergency and heading towards an unknown destination was very emotional for everybody. Bride and groom looked extremely resolute and solemn. Ikram had tears in his eyes. Omar and the Maulana were sorry about the circumstances they were marrying in, and Zari herself was sad and confused. As there were no forms available at the time, Maulana wrote the draft of the marriage himself. The bride and groom signed it, and then Omar and Ikram signed the paper as witnesses.

Zari offered sweets after the ceremony as a token of celebration and then she served dinner. They all insisted that the visitors stay in the house for the night. It was risky to travel at night. Zari offered her own room to the bride and groom. Ikram was lodged with the Maulana. Zari sat with Omar in the living room and they talked about past days in Abbotabad.

Zari lay on the sofa for a while. It was still dark when she woke up. Omar was fast asleep. She tiptoed to her room. The door was open but nobody was inside.

'All of them left during the night,' the Maulana told her. 'I pleaded with them, but they didn't listen to me. They said, "Thousands are crossing the border and entering India hiding in fields and forests under the cover of night. We can't wait till dawn."'

'Is Ikram also accompanying them?' Zari asked.

'No, he is not going with them. I think he's gone back to his house,' the Maulana said as he left for the mosque to say his early morning prayers.

Zari went into her bedroom. She at once spotted the map of Bangladesh drawn on the mirror of her dresser with an eyebrow pencil. With a bold hand in red lipstick somebody had written, '*Joi Bangla*—victory to Bangladesh!'

Zari's heart sank. Questions overwhelmed her. 'Where do I stand in this conflict? Which people do I belong to? Am I among friends or foes? What is my objective, Pakistan or Bangladesh? Even Omar Chachaji and the Maulana don't tell me what is the right course. If Bangladesh is right, then Pakistan is wrong. I am a traitor in any case. Have I committed treason by sheltering those three people who were against Pakistan under my roof? Did they leave so early because they didn't trust me? Whom should I turn to for the answers? Where is Shams? He shouldn't have left me like this in midstream!'

Zari emptied an entire bottle of nail polish remover on the mirror, and vigorously, with a towel, started erasing the writing.

58

Bengali and Bihari families had lived in harmony for years. Like most other people Sanaullah, Nargis's father, thought that if he stayed neutral in the conflict between East and West Pakistan, nobody would harm him or his family. But it wasn't true. They were constantly being tested to determine whether they were sympathetic to the interests of the Bengalis or not.

The cargo ship 'Swat,' was docked at the Chittagong harbor. The Bengalis had refused to unload the ship because they suspected the ship was loaded with arms and ammunition to be used against them.

The army had requisitioned non-Bengali volunteers for the purpose. By and by, the message was sent to Sanaullah that he and his sons should help in unloading the ship. One of his sons, Jamal, was a staunch Pakistani, but Kamal had different ideas. Sanaullah did not want to endanger the lives of his children, so he kept ignoring the messages. One night he locked his sons in the room they were sharing. Then he locked the main gate from outside, which faced the road, and re-entered the house from a side entrance to give the impression that the family was no longer there. The people who had moved to other localities had locked up their houses.

Jamal and Kamal were not at all happy being locked in a room. Their mother had to face their fury.

'Why have we been imprisoned here like convicts?' They would ask.

'You don't realize the seriousness of the situation,' Mrs Sanaullah would say. 'We have to do this.'

'The situation demands,' Jamal would say, 'that we do whatever we can to help Pakistan. Otherwise, how could we face our people?'

'Our people!' Kamal would say sarcastically. 'You live in East Pakistan, boy, you should think of saving the province that provides you bread and butter. Otherwise, the people in this region will never forgive you.'

'Mother, tell Father to keep the rifles safe,' Kamal said to his mother one night.

'What rifles?'

'The ones the Bengalis gave us to fight the army with. They had distributed weapons to everyone in the locality. They gave us two.'

'You shouldn't have taken them,' Mrs Sanaullah said.

'How could I refuse? I cooperated with them in every way, but I still think they suspect Father....'

'Suspect him of what?' Mrs Sanaullah said angrily.

'Of being a Pakistani agent,' Kamal answered, tauntingly. And before his mother could answer he said, 'Don't you know, Mother, that it's a crime to be a Pakistani?'

'You are right,' Sanaullah said. 'I don't know what to do with them. At times I want to keep them for our own safety, but then I think of handing them over to the army or giving them to someone else.'

'Why don't you give them to Mr Michael, our Christian neighbor. I don't think anyone would search him.'

'Good idea. I'll hand them over to him tonight.'

After sunset Sanaullah took the rifles and the box of cartridges to his neighbor.

'Would you please take them for me? I don't want to keep them,' he said to Michael.

'But you should have a weapon for your own safety.'

'No, it's risky to possess arms without a license. I'm sure that they won't search your house, but if you don't want to keep them, I'll take them back.'

'Don't misunderstand me, Sanaullah, I'm only thinking of your safety. I would like you to move into our house. It will be safer. Nobody would know. We don't even have a servant.'

'Thank you, Michael. I'll never forget your offer. It's not easy to offer help in times such as these. I would certainly like to move my sons to your house.'

'Do so.'

Soon after midnight, Sanaullah moved his sons to Michael's house though they protested a lot.

The next morning there was a ceaseless knock at his door. Sanaullah looked out through the eyehole in the door. A truck was parked on the road outside. A few young men from the locality stood by it. Disregarding his wife's disapproval Sanaullah went out from the side entrance.

'What do you want?'

'We need to unload the truck and store the cartons in the house behind yours,' one of the boys said. 'The back lane is narrow and the truck cannot go into it, so we need to take the cartons through your house.'

Sanaullah guessed that the truck was loaded with weapons and they were testing him to see whether he would cooperate with them.

'All right,' he said, after a moment's pause. 'I'll open the front door.'

'Where are Jamal and Kamal? Ask them to help us,' another boy said.

'I don't know where they are,' Sanaullah said. 'I've been worried about them too. They have been away for several days now.'

His wife had just shut herself up in the bathroom. Sanaullah stood silently on the veranda while the boys carried the cartons through his house to the other house in the back. When the truck was empty, they locked the door of the house containing arms and immunition, thanked Sanaullah and left.

'Thank God our sons were not in the house,' Mrs Sanaullah said. 'They were looking into different rooms on one pretext or another.'

Early, the next morning, when Mrs Sanaullah was in the kitchen and Sanaullah was reading an old magazine, there was a knock at the door.

'Who's there?' Sanaullah asked without getting up.

Holding her hands on her chest, Mrs Sanaullah went and stood still on the veranda. Sanaullah got up and rather unwillingly, opened the door. A group of strangers were waiting outside.

'We've learned that your sons are helping the army and that they have unlicensed weapons.'

'It's not true. They aren't here anymore. Maybe they are with my sister who is married into the Pather Ghata family,' he added tactfully to tell them the name of a well known Bengali family.

'We want to search your house.'

'All right, do come in, but only two of you. The rest can wait outside.'

They hesitated for a moment then sent two men to carry out a search inside the house.

'Which one is your sons' room, and where are they?' one of the men asked.

They did not seem to care for the information given by Sanaullah that his sister had married into a well-known Bengali family. They thoroughly searched the house and when they did not find any weapons and were convinced that the sons were not there anymore, they left.

Mrs Sanaullah came out of the bathroom trembling. 'Maybe they gave the rifles to the boys in the first place with the intention of accusing them for having illegal weapons later.'

'I don't know! I don't know what's happening here. Last night, I went to Rahman's house. He had always been such a good neighbor. We used to play chess for hours, but yesterday he was getting restless while talking to me for just a few minutes. He advised me to leave the house and go some place else. I said, "Why do you say so? You also belong to the Muslim League. You believe in having one Pakistan." He said, "Try to understand me. Logic and ideology don't work in times like these. I am a born Bengali. I speak their language and I live like they do. That's all the masses want to know. Just think about it." Saying this he closed the door behind me.'

'Then let's go to Meraj and Shoshi's house.'

'Go wherever you want to, but I'll stay here,' Sanaullah said.

'You are not acting upon your neighbors' advice.'

'Yes, because I'm not a coward.'

'I'll send Kamal to see whether Meraj and Shoshi are home and if they will take us,' Mrs Sanaullah said.

'The boys are not reliable. The moment they will come out, they'll want to join their friends.'

'Then you go with Kamal, please,' Mrs Sanaullah pleaded.

'All right. I might come back home once you are safe with Shoshi,' He said.

59

Shams was in Shoshi's house in Chittagong. He was a little worried about Zari but knew that being with Omar and the Maulana would be very beneficial to her.

Shams was in his bedroom.

Shoshi was in her room with her husband. Her husband was very worried at the time because the Pakistan army was searching houses to find people who were against them and had arms. He had migrated from India illegally and the army was taking in the illegal immigrants as insurgents. Many people had been living in this part of Pakistan illegally for years. They used to cross the border to go to India and come back as they wished, never thinking that one day it was going to be a matter of life and death.

Knock at the door. Yet another knock!

'Who's there?' Coming out of his room, Shams headed for the door, but Shoshi stopped him.

'For God's sake Shams, don't open the door. You go and hide somewhere. Whoever is here, I'll talk to him. I know they'll ask for Meraj—so why tell them you're here. Just hide please—please! Go up that ladder and hide in that small attic.'

'Where is Meraj?' he asked.

'He has already stepped down to the neighbor's house, and must have gone some place to hide. Do as I tell you.' She pointed to the ladder. Shams obeyed her and climbed up the ladder.

'Close the door and be patient,' she said.

He closed the door. It was not a room but a small, dark den in which he could hardly sit comfortably. He heard the sound of the ladder being removed. Shoshi might have put the ladder beneath the wooden seat or flung it outside the window.

The knock at the door was getting fierce.

Shoshi opened the door. There was an officer, a Subedar and a few soldiers. They came in immediately.

'Some one fired a shot from here. Who was that?' The officer said.

Shoshi was terrified but trying to keep her voice calm, she said, 'We have no weapons here and I don't even know how to hold a gun.'

'Maybe someone hiding here fired a shot. Search the house thoroughly,' the officer ordered the Subedar.

The Subedar and the soldiers went into other rooms. Shoshi was afraid that they might find Shams. She tried to put on a brave face and told them that there was nobody in the house at the time but she. The officer went into the living room asking Shoshi to come with him and pushing one of the sofas a little to the side, made room for himself to sit. He then asked, 'Why do you kept the sofas joined together in the middle of the room?'

'Because I hear gunshots all the time, so my husband, my daughter and I sleep on the floor surrounded by the sofas.'

He looked around and asked, 'Where is your husband and your daughter?'

'My husband has gone down to fetch water from the pump. You must have seen him there.'

'No, we haven't seen anybody outside,' he said, then got up and walked around the sofas.

Laila, Shoshi's little doll-like daughter, was sitting terrified behind a sofa. He gently stroked her with his stick and said, 'Come out, come over here.'

Hesitatingly, she got up and came out.

'Where is her father from and what does he do?' The officer asked.

'He is from Sargodha in West Pakistan.' Shoshi told him the lie she had practiced so many times in her mind. He owns a small business. I'm from Calcutta. My grandfather migrated from Kashmir.'

The officer smiled and looked searchingly at her face. She certainly did not look like a Kashmiri.

'Why is it so dark in here? Is there no power in your house?' he asked.

'There is no power or water. We light a lantern at night and fetch water from the pump down the street.'

'What about the rations?' he asked.

'I bought rations just a few days ago.'

'Good,' he said. 'Tell your husband to meet me at the Martial Law Headquarters tomorrow morning.'

At that point the Subedar came to report that nobody was hiding in the house.

'OK. We are leaving now. Keep the door locked.' Then he said to the Subedar. 'Wait downstairs for me.' The Subedar with the soldiers left immediately.

But the officer stayed back. When all others were gone, he paused for a moment then said. 'I'll try to get power and water restored to your house.'

Shoshi kept quiet.

'Don't forget to send your husband to the Headquarters,' he said.

It had been a long time that Shams was crouching in that den. The footsteps and the noises had ceased. He opened the shutter just a little bit to look. There was no one there, but the contents of the cupboard in the room were scattered all over the floor. Thank God, they hadn't noticed the den where he was hiding. He tried hard to listen, but there was complete silence, which frightened him even more. He decided to climb down and see what was going on.

He removed the junk to make more room, tried to clear the cobwebs from his head and hands and cautiously jumped to the floor.

Where was Shoshi? Had they taken her with them?

The thought sliced through his heart like a sharp, pointed knife. He ran around like mad and finally found Shoshi sitting on the ground against the closed door of the drawing room, sobbing with her hand pressed to her mouth. Without saying a word Shams seated himself beside her, and putting his hands around her knees, started crying too.

Seeing them both weeping, Laila came from behind the sofa where she had hidden herself again, and started crying.

'Who was here? What happened? Tell me!' Shams beseeched Shoshi.

Shoshi said nothing but started crying without restraint. Finally, Shams gathered Shoshi in his arms and seated her on the sofa. 'Where is Meraj now?' he asked.

'I don't know. He was the first to see the jeep even before they came to the house. Tip-toeing up to the roof, he jumped down into the neighboring house. Maybe the neighbors hid him or he just ran away!'

What a coward! Shams thought in anger. Fleeing to save his life, leaving his wife and child behind! Suddenly, he realized that he, too, had been sitting hiding in a safe place leaving Shoshi and her daughter to the mercy of intruders!

'What happened? Who were they? Tell me please,' he asked again.

'The army. They said that someone had fired a shot from our house. They wanted to search the house.'

'How many of them?'

'An officer, a non commissioned officer and a few soldiers.'

Shoshi held her daughter in her lap. She kept kissing her hair and sometimes hugged her lovingly. Shams gazed at her with love and sadness as Shoshi narrated the whole incident in a slow, gentle tone. The prevailing darkness and the cluttered surroundings were enhancing the sorrow in his heart.

It's all right,' Shams said, 'but now we have no choice, we must leave this place tonight—no matter what. That fellow will come again. I think we should leave for Dhaka as soon as possible.'

'Isn't it more dangerous to go out of the house in these conditions?'

'Yes, But we have no choice. I know some people there whose names can guarantee our safety. Zari is one. There are a few more. But living here can be very risky for you.'

'I know, but what about my husband!'

'If he doesn't turn up by tomorrow morning, I'm afraid we'll have to leave without him,' Shams said.

'Maybe they know that Meraj is still an Indian citizen. Many people know about it,' Shoshi said. 'And he is really afraid because his parents and many relations are still in India.'

'Whatever, it's decided that we are leaving for Dhaka tomorrow.'

But Shoshi didn't want to go without her husband so they left the house and waited for Meraj at his parent's house. Shoshi was sure that he would either come or send a message.

Finally Shams decided to visit the Mukti Bahini Quarters, which was a rest house in front of Masca Hotel, to see if they knew anything about Meraj.

Once he had stayed at the rest house with Zari, and they had dined at Masca Hotel. It was a pleasant and spacious rest house, but now it lay deserted. As Shams pushed the door open and entered a room, his shoes squeezed through something thick and sticky.

He leaned down to look at it and was taken aback. He was standing ankle-deep in human blood. A Mukti Bahini officer was sitting behind a table in the middle of the room and questioning two men who stood before him. The room was dark. The smell of blood was nauseating. Shams wanted to run away. But leaving the place suddenly could prove risky. Moreover, the thick blood had already arrested his movements.

Nobody paid any attention to him. The officer was speaking to the person who stood in front of him with an air of arrogance.

'Shut up. Nobody wants to hear your lecture,' the Mukti Bahini officer thundered. Waving his pistol in the air threateningly, he said, 'What do you want now. Be brief.'

'I wish to die, holding the Quran in my hands,' the man said.

'Sorry, we don't have that book here.' Saying this the man fired the shot.

By then Shams knew that the person was no other than Sanaullah, Nargis's father. Shams stretched his hand out to stop him. 'I know him and his family. They are good people,' Shams said in a faltering voice.

Not one but three bullets pierced Sanaullah's heart, and he fell face downward.

'He is the father-in-law of the renowned poet, Noor...You must have read his famous poem, 'The Lotus', Shams said.

'But who the hell are you?' the officer demanded.

'I am Ronjhu's brother, Shamsur Rahman.'

'Oh, well,' his tone softened. 'Please be seated. What can I do for you?'

'Leave these people alone. I know them. They are simple citizens, not miscreants,' Shams said.

'One of them has died already, the old bastard! He had the nerve to hoist the Pakistani flag on his car. When our boys objected to it, he said, "Is it written somewhere that hoisting the Pakistani flag is forbidden?"'

'Yes, he was eccentric,' Shams said.

'I release the other one on your intervention.' He pointed to a person to let Kamal go.

'My brother-in-law, Abu Zafar Merajuddin, hasn't returned home for three days,' Shams said. 'We are worried. We want to know where he is and if he is safe.'

'Give me his name and address. We'll try to trace him, but it's hard to trace anybody in these circumstances as you can realize.'

Shams gave the details about Meraj and stood up. He was sad and felt drained. His shoes were sticky with blood, and he was grieving for Sanaullah in his heart. Nargis had asked him to take care of her parents and siblings in her absence.

Kamal hid himself behind a tree and waited for Shams to come out. When he saw Shams coming out of the rest house, he accompanied him. Shams could not hug or comfort him there. He just held his hand and took him to his car. Kamal's hand was as cold as death.

'I repeatedly told father not to take such risks,' Kamal said sobbingly, 'but he never listened to me.'

'I know,' Shams said. 'But he was a brave man. There's no doubt about it.'

60

After the death of Muneer's father, his uncle moved from Mirpur and rented a house across from Muneer.

The scales of power had tilted again. This time Chaya ran into Muneer's house in alarm to seek refuge because some Pakistani soldiers had taken her father and Kajol away for questioning. Chaya knew that this was perhaps the end for them. While Chaya was talking to Muneer there was a knock on the door. Muneer's mother quickly asked Chaya to hide under the *takht* that had a traditional ruffled cover on it. Muneer's cousin Afzal came in. Somehow he knew Chaya was in the house and after issuing veiled threats to Muneer's mother he left, promising to come back with soldiers.

A light drizzle fell through the nearby window. Muneer shivered, remembering his father's lifeless body bathed in a similar light rain.

Chaya lifted the edge of the ruffle and came out from beneath the *takht*.

Folding her hands she entreated. 'Let me go. He will certainly come back with the men in black clothes. Let me go, please.'

'But who are the men in black clothes?' Muneer's mother asked.

'They are called Rangers. They are very big and tall with big moustaches. They don't know anything about Bengalis,' Chaya said. 'They don't even know that Bengalis are Muslims like them. They think that all Bengalis are *kafirs*, and they have been sent to fight the *kafirs* and infidels.'

'Is it so?'

'Yes. I've heard that too,' Muneer said. 'The are looting the houses and abducting the girls. They are so ignorant that if they see someone saying his prayers or find a copy of the Holy Quran in a Bengali house, they are surprised. They think that Tagore must be a Muslim because he had a beard, so they leave his pictures and destroy Iqbal's because he is clean-shaven. People are more terrified of them than the army.'

'These could all be rumors Chaya, don't worry and stay with us.' Muneer's mother tried to calm her. 'Tell me if we let you go where would you go?'

'I don't know. I'll seek shelter somewhere.'

Muneer looked at her with a sad face.

'No,' Muneer's mother said. 'How can I turn a poor defenseless young girl out on the streets. You must stay with us. I'll tell Afzal's father to punish Afzal for his rudeness. You should know that Afzal's father has gone in search of your father and Kajol.'

'Would they kill my father?' Chaya asked, trembling with fear.

'No. They have no reason. We'll tell them how your family protected and sheltered Muneer in your house for days.'

'Chaya, please, go and hide upstairs. It is safe there,' Muneer urged her.

'No, thanks. I'll feel lonely and scared there. I'm fine here.'

Chaya crouched beneath the *takht* again. Muneer fetched a sheet and a pillow and handed it to her. He did not go out of the house all day.

When Afzal's father returned in the evening, he assured them that Chaya's father and Kajol would be released soon after the interrogation. He said Chaya should not stay in this house because the people from the neighborhood had seen her here. She should go to some safe place.

After much consultation they decided that she ought to stay in the same storeroom of her own house, where Muneer had once hidden. They would lock the storeroom from outside as before. This wouldn't raise any suspicions among the neighbors because they already knew that there was nobody in the house. Chaya, afraid of being alone, was indecisive, but there was no choice. They decided that Muneer and his mother would take care of her meals and also provide dry rations and a jug of water in case they couldn't bring her meals for some reason.

There was only one ventilator in the room. It opened toward the half-built staircase outside. Even that was partially blocked with bricks and rocks so that no one from the outside would suspect a presence within. A cot was casually placed against the storeroom door and old and worn out clothes were hung upon the cot haphazardly. Rusty tins and old pots were put in front of the cot in such a way that a stranger who might step in would not suspect a door behind the junk.

Chaya took a kitchen knife and a sickle with her. Using the pillows and bolsters as dummies, she would certainly practice fighting against the enemy.

The day after Chaya left Muneer's house, Afzal's younger sister came into the house very early in the morning. She started looking at the corners and behind the doors, then suddenly lifted the hem of the ruffle and looked beneath the *takht*.

'What are you looking for?' Muneer's mother asked her.

'My cat. Maybe it is hiding here.'

'There's no cat in this house. Do you hear?' Muneer's mother said angrily. 'Tell him, who has sent you that the "cat" has been sent to another city.'

'Would you like me to put this sheet and pillow on the *takht* and the plate in the kitchen?' the girl asked.

'Yes,' Muneer's mother said nervously.

Before leaving, the girl put the sheet and the pillow on the *takht*, while Muneer's mother watched her closely, then carried the stainless steel plate to the kitchen. It was the plate from which Chaya had eaten her supper the previous night.

61

Night had set in when Shams came home with Shoshi and Laila. Zari heaved a sigh of relief when she saw Shams.

'This is Shoshi,' he said. 'Her husband is an Indian citizen, so he has gone into hiding. I've fetched his wife and daughter. He will come here as soon as he can and they will cross over to the other side of the border. The problem is their son is staying with Shoshi's sister in Pabna and Shoshi doesn't want to leave without him. So they will travel to Pabna first and go to India from there.'

'Why should they go to India? Wouldn't it be better if they found shelter in Chittagong or Dhaka?' Zari said.

'Meraj wants to cross the border. He says he is afraid the army will keep asking for him.'

Zari's hadn't had have any servant for months. Shoshi helped Zari cook and serve the meals. The two women talked in mixed Urdu and Bangla. Shams watched them from a distance...Zari looked like a cypress tree, deep-rooted, strong and balanced. Shoshi was like a long, swaying rose-bush that shook under the weight of a small sparrow. She walked bare-footed in the house. When she went from the kitchen to the dining room, Shams felt as if a puff of air had passed across the room.

The next day, Shams went to see Major Khalid.

'Khalid, you are my friend. If you want to help me, find this man.' Shams handed him a piece of paper with Meraj's name and address on it. 'This is very important—I know very well that his name is in the army's search list because he currently holds Indian citizenship. But I assure you that he is not an insurgent. I personally guarantee that he won't indulge in any act of vandalism against the army. If he does you can hold me responsible for his crime and arrest me in his place.'

'All right, don't be so emotional. I'll try.'

'Don't just try. Please find him. I know, this won't be difficult for you.'

'I can't promise anything.'

'But I want a promise—a soldier's promise, Khalid.'

'OK. A soldier's promise. If this man is alive and innocent, he will come back to you.'

'What do you really do to the people you arrest?'

'We record his statement, then investigate. There are three categories, black, gray and white. If a person is proved to be white, he is released immediately. Gray persons are in detention and held under watch. The black ones are imprisoned.'

'Are they kept in jails, or lined up on the bank of a river and shot?'

'Maybe they do that in remote villages, but in big cities, unless the crime is serious, they are put into prisons.'

'I have no right to tell you, but as a friend, I would like to say that these large scale detentions and the plan of cleansing the villages will prove counter-productive.'

Two days later, Shams got news that Meraj would be waiting in a hut in Sunargaon in the afternoon. A person would wait at the bus stop and would guide Shoshi and her daughter to the hut. That person would be a Bengali. Even then, as a precaution, Shams decided to send the Maulana with them.

'Maulana, I trust you, more than anyone else. Whatever Meraj and Shoshi decide, wherever they wish to go, you must accompany them. This is my wish. You'll be doing me a great favor.'

While taking leave, Shoshi's head bumped against the door. His mother used to say that it was a bad omen if someone's head bumped against the door before leaving.

'These are all Hindu superstitions,' his father would say. 'We don't believe in them. Muslims came to break the idols of superstitions not to make them.'

Shoshi knelt to touch Shams's feet. Shams patted her on the shoulder, his large eyes filled with tears. Then she knelt at Zari's feet. Zari embraced her. Shams looked gratefully at Zari. He quietly handed the Maulana a pouch filled with money.

62

Three days had passed, but Chaya's father and brother Kajol had not yet come back. Chaya was a patient girl, but the mental stress was too much for her. Muneer wished to lift the dark gloom off her face but didn't know how.

Afzal's mother had come to visit them the night before and had chatted with Muneer's mother till late at night. Muneer waited anxiously for her to leave. Chaya must be hungry and she needed some fresh air too.

When it became obvious that she did not intend to leave soon, Muneer's mother whispered to Muneer to take Chaya's supper to her. Muneer hastily picked up the supper with some fruit, checked that the street was clear, crossed it and entered Chaya's house.

He distinctly saw signs of disorder and knew that something had happened there. Muneer's heart sank. He rushed to the store and found the door open. He looked around and went into the room quickly. Chaya used to keep the lighted lantern hidden behind the door with its wick very low. Muneer raised the wick to see clearly. He saw Chaya lying on the ground. He could not decide whether she was dead or alive. He saw Afzal there too. Maybe the beast would brag about his victory over Chaya now.

No. He was lying wounded. The sickle Chaya had brought with her from the kitchen had done its job.

Muneer's mind seemed paralyzed. He neither thought of seeking a doctor's help nor running back to report to his mother. He sat motionless and prayed that Chaya was only unconscious. He did not even notice when Afzal opened his eyes, surveyed the scene, and dragging his wounded body crept noiselessly out of the room.

The sound of shutting the door brought Muneer to his senses. He then knew that Afzal had gotten out and had locked the store from outside.

When Chaya regained consciousness she did not know where she lay. It was absolutely dark. She felt as if she was going round and round like a light feather, descending to the bottom of a well. She finally reached the bottom that did not contain water but thick sticky blood.

She heard somebody praying and crying. It was Muneer's voice. Where was he? Was she dead and Muneer was wailing beside her grave?

Gradually, with her eyes able to see in darkness, she saw that she was still in her storeroom. Somebody was sitting by her side.

'Chaya, It's me, Muneer. Afzal has escaped and has locked the door from outside.'

'How suffocating! Am I going to die? There is no air here!' Chaya said.

'Wait. I'll try to open the ventilator.'

As he said that, the lantern flickered and went off. It had sucked all the oil.

Groping in the dark Muneer managed to push an empty box toward the ventilator, climbed it and pushed back the iron grill to open it.

Gradually, the ventilator opened just a little bit. Muneer leaned over Chaya. She had fainted again.

Muneer rapped, knocked, tapped the door while shouting for help till he almost lost his voice but nobody came.

He rested for a while and cried again and again. At last his uncle heard him when he went out to look for him. The cry 'help us out' brought him to Chaya's house. He was surprised to see that the storeroom was locked from the outside and the cry for help was coming from within. He broke the lock and got Chaya and Muneer out.

Chaya was terrified but quiet. Now Muneer was crying, 'For God's sake, get us out. I'm suffocating.'

The doctor examined them both and gave them sedatives to sooth their nerves. He advised their relatives to let them sleep comfortably as long as they could.

63

The first week of April was about to end. But Shoshi still hadn't reached her destination. They had to break their journey whenever they sensed danger. Sometimes even the crew would ask them to leave the launch and hide some place.

When they reached Pabna they found Shoshi's sister's house empty. A neighbor informed them that she had left with the family for her in-law's house in Tangel. Crossing the river Jamuna and arriving in Tangel, Shoshi discovered that her sister and her family were not there either. Nobody knew where her sister, her son or her in-laws had gone. Shoshi was exhausted. The Maulana never gave his opinion.

Throughout the journey, Laila kept asking, 'When will they kill us? When shall we die?'

Crossing the angry waters of the Brahmaputra, Shoshi reached her birthplace. Her aging Grandfather felt as if two angels of mercy had visited him in the person of Shoshi and Laila.

'Shoshi, I have helped you to reach safety,' the Maulana said. 'The Assam border is not far from here. A message can easily reach here from Calcutta. I'll take leave from you now. Please write a letter to Shams saying that you have arrived safely.'

'When are they going to kill us, Mother?' Laila repeated her question.

'Nobody is going to kill us, dear. We are going to live, my love,' Shoshi said and squeezed her daughter to her bosom.

64

The border village of Meherpur in the Kushtia district was named Mujibnagar on 10 April 1971. The establishment of an independent Bangladesh state was announced from there. Members of the new government took an oath of office. This government-in-exile exercised its authority from Fort William in Calcutta, India.

Major Rahman had made a Declaration of Independence even before that on 26 March, after the day of army action from an unknown transmission station near Chittagong.

But now, to make this government and the struggle for independence legal, all points were meticulously considered.

All legal and administrative affairs were entrusted to the newly appointed president, Sheikh Mujib. He was the chief of the armed forces. He had the authority to choose the prime minister and the council of ministers. He was given the power to levy taxes, incur expenses and hold a constituent assembly. If, for any reason, Sheikh Mujib could not perform the duties of this post, the vice-president would hold the post of the president in his place.

The legal statute of this Declaration of Independence maintained that in the National Assembly, convened by General Yahya Khan on 3 March, the Bengali majority had declared independence. The next day, they issued a statement saying that there was a precedent for this kind of declaration in the United States of America where Thomas Jefferson and others had declared independence from Britain.

One purpose of this government was to sway the world's public opinion in favor of Bangladesh. To promote their cause, propaganda literature was prepared in Calcatta and was sent abroad. The Independent Bangladesh Radio in Calcutta told the world why Bangladesh should be independent. It also waged a psychological war, spreading all sorts of rumors in East Pakistan to inspire the Mukti Jodha and invited young people to join the Mukti Bahini. In order to win over the Urdu speakers, it broadcast an hour-long program in Urdu.

The Mukti Bahini fought the war on behalf of this government, with the support of the East Pakistan Rifles, the East Bengal Regiment, the Police and the Indian Border Forces.

After the Declaration of Independence, in their opinion, they had obtained the legal right to wage war and kill any person who opposed Bangladesh.

65

Five days after this declaration started the month of *Baisakh*, the first month of the Bangla calendar. The first day of *Baisakh* was a Bengali festival. On that day old account books were closed and new ones opened. In some places the Baisakhi Fair ran for ten days. Young girls went on picnics, wearing cream-colored saris, with red borders and matching red blouses. Strolling in parks they looked like *bir bhutties*, the scarlet, velvety insects on the green grass.

All shops remained open on the first day of *Baisakh*. The shopkeepers treated each other with curds and sweets. Most of the shopkeepers believed that if Lakshmi, the goddess of wealth, was happy with them on this day, they would have prosperity throughout the year.

They organized fairs in every town and village to lend color and to entertain the people. As some variation of this belief was common to most religions, even those who had no faith in this celebration treated it with respect.

But this year, the first day of *Baisakh* was not celebrated. There were no fairs, no gatherings and no songs. Normally, it rained on this day, but this year there was no rain, though blood has been showered at many places.

The Maulana had seen a lot of celebrations on this day but had never even imagined the cruelties he saw this time that singed and scorched his soul. Wherever he went, people told him the tales of horror:

'Dada, my wife's stomach was ripped open, in the eighth month of her pregnancy. Calling the baby a serpent, they killed him first and then also the innocent mother.' One person told him.

Another one said, 'Uncle, 23,000 residents, the entire population of Shantahar, was eliminated. Those who ran to seek shelter at the railway station and hid themselves there didn't get drinking water for weeks. They were asked to go back home, and when they did, the Bengalis fell upon them like wolves. You can imagine how many must have died in six days. It is hard to tell everything that happened in those days.'

Yet another stated. 'I know it for certain that in Sylhet, the man who drives a non-Bengali to the slaughterhouse gets a reward of Rs.100.00 and the one who brings a Mohajir gets Rs. 80.00.'

Yet another wailed, 'Maulana, by God, I'm telling you the truth. My grandsons were butchered piece-by-piece before my eyes.'

The girls who were kidnapped were told that they were being raped so that they would bear the children of their enemies. Flags and maps of Bangladesh were engraved on their bodies with bayonets. There were flags emerging from mothers' open wombs.

Every Bihari male from nine to ninety was to be killed. People weak and in agony with hunger and thirst drank water from dirty drains and ate grass. The wounded drank blood in cupped hands from small pools around them and, quietly closing their eyes, died.

Mass murders, mass rapes, and mass graves—who was responsible for these? How could they be validated? The inner voices in the Maulana's heart made his life unbearable.

On the night of 17 April, wailing and cries shook Shankipara. The Maulana felt as if, along with the strong wind and the first rains of the month of *Baisakh*, drops of blood were falling from the sky. The tales of horror he heard each day ripped apart his heart. At night, when along with strong winds and rains, the ghostly noises deafened his ears he dreamt that people were accusing him of all these crimes.

The deputy commissioner and the superintendent of police listened to the howling of the suffering, sitting in their jeeps, and said nothing. The Maulana tried to pacify the irate crowds, beseeching them not to massacre innocent people.

The young and angry Bengalis were threatening the Maulana. 'You are a Bengali. Why do you take their side? They are not innocent. They are informers. Their sons have joined Al-Badr, Al-Shams, and are allies to the Pakistan army. They give signals to airplanes. They are our enemies.'

'What about their women and children?'

There was silence for a moment. Then a responsible person, just to end the argument, said, 'Let us make a deal, Maulana. If you can take the women and children into the mosques, we won't harm them.'

Some called the Maulana an agent of the Army. One man from the crowd ran to kill him, but another, who happened to know the Maulana, stopped him, saying, 'He is an old man. Leave him alone. How many women and children can he save after all?'

The Maulana was running against time. He went about knocking at the doors. 'Open the door,' he said in Bangla. Then, realizing his mistake, he said in Urdu, 'Please, open the door. I have come to save you.'

'First show us that you don't carry a weapon.'

The Maulana raised his empty hands. The door was opened and as he went inside, the owner apologized, 'We can trust nobody these days. My nephew has arrived from Chittagong. He says the *Imams* of the mosques there tricked the Biharis into opening their doors and then they were killed. One of the *Imams* has declared that anyone who killed a Bihari would get the *sawab* equivalent to a pilgrimage to Mecca. He himself had killed two Biharis, he proudly told the people.'

'Please move out quickly. This isn't the time to talk. Come, let's go to the mosque.'

In the dark, all of them left for the mosque, but Nargis's younger brother Kamal preferred to stay at home.

Kamal had come from Chittagong to take his aunt to West Pakistan. 'I'm a volunteer working for the Biharis. They are sure to kill me if they see me. Lock the door from the outside.'

Throughout the night, the Maulana evacuated people from their houses and accompanied them to the mosque.

Early in the morning he knocked at a door and overheard a tremulous voice from within, 'God, I prayed for a little comfort, respectability and honor. I was deprived of that. Now my honor and life are both in danger. It was You who had blessed us with these daughters. For fear of losing honor, I submit my life and the lives of my children to your care. My Lord, bear witness to it and absolve me of my sins.'

Maulana kept knocking at the door and calling out to open it, but no one did. He heard six shots. The father had shot his six daughters, and then he had shot himself. Then there was utter silence.

Time, like a body hanging from a noose, stood suspended in darkness. The Maulana rubbed his forehead on the threshold and wept bitterly. 'God, I'd taken the world for your shadow. I knew the shadow because of the light, and the light because of the shadow. But now I'm totally confused.'

The next day, the Maulana was nowhere to be seen. The deputy commissioner ordered a search for him. The people who sought shelter in the mosque also looked for him. The story of his courage spread far and wide. Inspired by his deeds, an *Imam* from the border village of Halwaghat, risking his own life, saved hundreds of non-Bengalis and gave them shelter in his mosque.

66

A twenty-three-year-old boy studying for his bachelor's degree in economics, civics and Islamic studies was leading 23,000 Bengalis who were fighting a war against the Pakistan Army. Qadir had created a sensation in the region. His section of the Mukti Bahini was given the name of Qadir Bahini in his honor and he was given the title of 'Tiger'.

Zahir had defected from Pakistan, gone to India and then came to Bangladesh to join Qadir.

'I've heard in Calcutta that you have demolished hundreds of bridges from Tangel to Dhaka, one at every six miles,' Zahir said to Qadir while they were sitting hidden in a mango grove close to their temporary headquarters. 'I decided there and then that I would like to work with you.'

'Thank you,' Qadir said.

'The paper also said that you were responsible for sinking innumerable boats and that you had taken many prisoners of war. I saw your picture and said here's my man.'

'I also captured a three-story steamer in Matikata, which contained a thousand tons of gun-powder,' Qadir said proudly. 'It took ten hours for my men to unload the steamer and re-load the gunpowder into ninety-nine boats.'

'Wow. You really deserve your title of "Tiger".'

'Now, tell me what else did you see in India?' Qadir asked.

'The big shots of the Bangladesh government are having a good time at Fort William in Calcutta,' Zahir said sarcastically. 'They are well fed and safe from any danger. They broadcast the free Bangladesh program from the secure studios of Calcutta Radio, dream of getting key positions in Bangladesh in the days to come and are squandering the country's hard-earned money.'

'We'll see who gets the important positions in Bangladesh!' Qadir said.

'Exactly, we are risking our lives. We stay awake at night. We should fight for our rights,' Zahir said.

'Yes, but it's not the right time yet. We have to keep working together,' Qadir said.

'Right now, Ziaur Rahman's "Z Bahini", Khalid Asharaf's "K-Force", Shafiullah's "S-Force", your "Qadir Bahini", and Mujib Bahini, all these are working separately, aren't they?' Zahir asked.

'Yes, but with the same intentions. You know Major Najm,' Qadir said. 'He was a captain in the Pakistan Army. Now he has a regular company of a hundred men and has trained seven thousand villagers. Guerilla activities are going on in all the nineteen districts. They create panic. Once people are terrified, our work becomes easier.'

'The Indian defense minister, in an interview with the *Financial Times*, reported that ten thousand soldiers from the Pakistan Army have been killed at the hands of the Bengali guerillas,' Zahir said.

'That might be true, tell me what's happening at the political level in the world. I don't get much news here,' Qadir said.

'The military action of the Pakistan army was certainly damaging for us, but it united all Bengalis and our cause gained sympathy all over the world. People sitting in Calcutta, at least did one good of propagating against Pakistan and gaining the world's support in the name of independence.'

'That's great,' said Qadir.

'India's propaganda about Pakistan's mistreatment of Bengalis and their need for liberty is doing wonders in collecting funds abroad. Dr Triguna Sen has established a Bangladesh Friends' Society that has collected both money and weapons. Emergency hospitals and nursing homes have been opened with the money.

'India and Russia have signed a pact. India will supply arms to Bangladesh and Russia will restock India's arms.'

'Great news! What about Pakistan's friends?' Qadir asked.

'I believe that it's all lip-service. America has not signed any new pact with Pakistan. According to the old pact, it will help Pakistan only if a communist country directly attacks her. The

Americans love the words "democracy" and "independence." We have told them that the Bengalis are being suppressed in Pakistan and we want freedom. India has earned a reputation for a good democracy whereas poor Pakistan is notorious for its martial law.'

'What about China?'

'I think that China is busy developing herself and not ready to go into any war. Russia has also warned her not to do that. India will attack in December when China would not be able to help because of the snow on the mountains.

'My concern is whether a war won with the support of another country will be good for us. Some people are suspicious of the pacts between India and us. They think that those pacts may be harmful to Bangladesh. As the proverb in Bangla goes...cutting the pokhar to invite the crocodile. I think every country must fight its own war.'

'You may be right, but we cannot win against an army by guerilla warfare only. It'll take years and the whole country will be ruined,' Qadir said. 'Come, let me show you pictures of my achievements.'

They rose from under the tree and went to the Qadir's small camp, which had a narrow cot and a small stool. There were two big nails on the wall on which his clothes were hanging. He took out his briefcase from under his bed and showed the pictures taken by an officer. Zahir looked at them with awe.

Then he said, 'Qadir, I've brought a gift for you from Mujibnagar. Let me give it to you.' He went to his little camp and handed Qadir a copy of the Declaration of Independence of Bangladesh.

'Thank you,' Qadir said. 'It's a great gift.'

The Declaration was lengthy, but Qadir glanced through it quickly.

It stated categorically that the Declaration of Independence would come into effect from 26 March 1971, when Sheikh first declared it.

'This is all right,' Qadir said. 'But let me say this, 'Nothing succeeds like success.' The real victory belongs to the victor. If we are victorious, then the Declaration of Independence may not be necessary. If, God forbid, we don't succeed, this same document will be a proof of our crime and we'll have to pay for it with our heads. So we have to succeed.'

'I agree,' Zahir said. 'I sincerely believe that when books about the independence of Bangladesh are published, your name will be on top of the list in gold letters, Brigadier Qadir, Castro of Tungel.'

'Thank you. Thank you, my friend,' Qadir smiled cheerfully and patted Zahir on the shoulder. 'But history is untrustworthy too. Sometimes, the names of those who really work are replaced by the names of those who have done nothing.'

Zahir looked around and whispered, 'Even the walls, it is said, have ears. There are no walls here but maybe the mango trees have ears too. You know what some people say about our leader? That he shouldn't have surrendered himself to the Pakistan Army. He didn't try to cross the border like you did, and he didn't try to escape from Pakistan like I did. If he had, he would have been leading our movement here instead of being in a West Pakistan prison.'

'What are you saying?' Qadir was surprised. 'Are you talking against our Bango Bondu?'

'There are people who say such things.'

'Don't listen to them. Look at some more pictures.'

Seeing the pictures of demolished bridges, Zahir said, 'I'm happy that I will get a chance to work with you, and let me tell you a secret. My fiancée Puttal and I have decided not to marry until Bangladesh is liberated' Zahir said haughtily.

'We need people like you, Major,' Qadir said. 'We are proud of you.'

67

After his father's death Jamal convinced his mother that he should do something to save Pakistan and weaken the people who killed his father. The small towns and villages where the army had no control were death wells for Biharis. He went to Dinajpur with a medical relief team. Countless corpses lay on the bank of the river Kanchan turning its white sand red with blood. Human skulls lay about, and the beasts already over-fed, sauntered close to them indifferently. The pain on the faces of the dead bodies and the questions raised in their eyes pierced Jamal's heart.

Most of the houses were deserted. The residue of burnt papers were scattered everywhere. Jamal felt that if he didn't do something immediately, his heart would burst or he would become raving mad. What should he do? What could he do for these departed souls?

Jamal, too, had watched persons die and was now trying to transfer the anguish of their looks to his drawings. Suddenly he heard the sound of footsteps.

'Who is it? Who's there?' someone shouted in clear Urdu.

'A volunteer.' Jamal thought that some member of the relief committee from the hospital must have come looking for him.

'Joi Bangla!' Somebody shouted, flung the door open, and fired a shot. He had seen people dying with each of their legs tied to two jeeps going in opposite directions. People hanging upside down from a tree like a goat-skin peeled off like a goat's with a butcher's knife and body cut into pieces to feast vultures and crows. A unborn baby lay secure in the darkness of his mother's womb was dragged out of his velvety darkness and raised aloft on the point of a spear and, with the same spear, his mother was bled to death, drop-by-drop.

A young, beautiful virgin, was shot dead by her father. She was grateful for that! The humiliation of the human body that she had witnessed, the depravity of human nature had intensified her longing for death and she was greatly relieved and grateful at the time of her death. Lots of railway employees were thrown like fuel into a burning boiler. And his father was shot dead because he had Pakistan's flag taped on his car.

Death was in pursuit like a ferocious dog. More painful than death was the mental agony of fleeing from it, the bite of its sharp, pointed teeth on one's body and the fearfulness of its red-hot eyes and blood-dripping tongue so close—so close!

He heard somebody sobbing. His brother Kamal was there with another person.

'So it was you who shot me? It was my fate to be killed by my brother—and you are helping them even after they killed our father?' His voice became feebler and feebler then it droned in silence. He died.

'Forgive me brother—I thought that to be with them was our only chance for survival.' Kamal covered his eyes with both hands in intense anguish and kept sobbing.

68

'Where does Puttal go every day?' One day Misbah asked his wife.

'To a neighboring house.'

'Why? What's going on there? When I look out of my library window, I often see boys and girls gathered there.'

'I think they chat and prepare programs for radio and television. What else is there to do? Colleges and universities are closed.'

'Better ask Puttal.'

When Puttal came back, Mrs Haq asked her.

'We're doing relief work, Mother,' Puttal said. 'You don't know that in a house in Someshwari, there are a lot of girls whose families have refused to take them back because...you know why! And there are others who are so ashamed of themselves that they just don't want to go home.'

Benu, who heard that, was very grieved.

'Puttal, take me there,' Benu said. 'I, too, would like to do something for them.'

'No, they wouldn't appreciate it. Those girls are extremely sensitive. They say, "We are not showpieces to be stared at." I go there to meet one of my dearest friends, whose parents do not even know where she is!'

'Mukul?' Benu blurted out without thinking. But immediately, she bit her tongue and shut her mouth. Reading the paleness in Puttal's face, Benu instinctively knew that she had guessed right.

'Yes, you are right. Her fiancé had been searching for her like mad. She made me promise that I wouldn't tell her fiancé about her whereabouts—rather try to convince him that she had been killed. I lied to him, saying that she had gone to India with Melo and Renu. Mukul was among many girls who had been taken to the hospital after the...the next morning from the Art Institute.'

'How sad!' Benu's eyes moistened.

'At first, Mukul had had strange fits. She would begin talking as if she were addressing someone present there. Sometimes it was her fiancé, sometimes her brother or sister. Her eyes would be open and she would laugh and cry and use those gestures that are typically hers. A stranger would think that she was acting. But we knew she wasn't.

'Sometimes she raised very sensitive questions. I think, Benu, there is, in each one of us, a thinking person hiding deep down who doesn't get an opportunity to come out into the open. She wouldn't remember what she had said or done, later. She would ask us in surprise, how come she was moved from one place to another, and how her head came to rest on a pillow, while when she lay down she didn't have it.

'Whenever she had a fit in my presence, the other girls would leave immediately. They knew I was her confidante. One day, sobbing hysterically, she described the horrible rape without knowing what she was saying. She suddenly said. "The bud opens by itself. You know that Mukul means bud. If you try to open it by force, it won't blossom, it will break, wither and die." Then she wept so bitterly that my eyes flooded with tears too. I don't have the heart to tell her how, in her fits, she scratches and lets bleed her wounds.'

'This is terrible!' Benu said.

'What do you think, Benu? Should I tell her fiancé about her?'

Benu thought for a few seconds, then said, 'Wait for a few more days. Let her overcome her grief, then we'll ask Ikram to talk to him.'

'Do you think she will agree to go back to him?' Puttal asked.

'If her fiancé asks her sincerely and compassionately, she should. I think at this time she is not sure about his love. She is afraid he might reject her as many others did.'

'Why do they do it? Don't they know that it's not the girl's fault, she has been a victim of violence?'

'They know it, but it's society's pressure and the way they have been brought up,' Benu said. 'It's the most shameful thing for a man to accept a girl who is not a virgin.'

'I don't think this is true love,' Puttal said.

'It happens, Puttal, you've just told us that there are girls who were not accepted by their own families. Isn't it terrible that their parents and siblings condemn these innocent girls for life?'

'Yes, it is. If such a thing were to happen to me, I would ask Zahir if he would still want to marry me? If he would have refused, I would slap his face and tell him to go to hell because I don't want that kind of love.'

'Puttal, don't say such terrible things,' Benu said. 'Man is a mysterious creature, and you just don't know how one will react in a certain situation. Only pray to God that He keeps us safe.'

'Now you are talking like an elder sister-in-law.'

'I am simply telling you that the world is a strange place. Whatever happens to one might just as well happen to another. Just be thankful that it did not happen to you.'

69

The government needed to give an impression that everything was fine in the East wing, and it insisted that all schools, colleges and universities take the final examinations as scheduled earlier. The students knew secretly that they would boycott the examinations as instructed by the Awami League leaders.

Ilyas had gone to take his high school examination. A few students first complained that the questions were hard and out of their curriculum. They talked in whispers among themselves and left the hall. Seeing them leave, a few others followed. Ilyas had no idea about the plan. He thought that they were leaving because they were unprepared and couldn't answer the questions. Ilyas was among a few boys who stayed in the examination hall. But next time when he raised his head from his answering book he saw that he was the only one left in the hall.

'Shall I also hand in my paper?' He asked the Bengali invigilator innocently. 'I haven't completed it yet, but I can.'

'You just want to pass the examination. You don't care if everyone else fails,' the invigilator said sarcastically.

Taking a cue from him, Ilyas handed him his unfinished answer book and came out. Outside, the boys and girls, standing in groups, were raising slogans against the government and the school system. By and by in groups of three or four, they started for their homes, talking loudly. Ilyas advanced toward the gate alone. He had no close friends. His mother had strictly forbidden him to make Bengali friends.

As he came out of the school gate, he saw Suraj standing there.

'How come you are here, Suraj?' Ilyas asked.

'I was passing by. I saw students coming out of the examination hall before time. So I waited for you.'

'The test wasn't that hard for me. But since everyone had walked out, I figured I might as well,' he said as they both started walking towards home.

'Didn't the supervisor try to detain the students?'

'No, I feel he wanted the students to boycott.'

'Ilyas Bhai,' Suraj said, 'now I think that had I studied regularly, I would have been in tenth grade like you.'

'You should continue taking lessons from Benu Apa and then take the High School examination in two or three years,' Ilyas said.

Leaving the school area, they came up to the road. The mango and *kathal* trees along the road cast thick shadows over their path. Kites soared in the blue sky. It was a bright afternoon.

'I'll write to you from Karachi to know about your progress in studies,' Ilyas said.

So, you are leaving?' Suraj asked.

'Yes, remember, it was you who told Amma that the servants were talking about dividing the household articles among themselves. She is extremely frightened since then.'

'Yes, Ilyas Bhai, I told the truth. They were saying that they wouldn't allow outsiders to touch the belongings. In fact, they were talking of dividing even the rooms and the cars. Shaupin said that he would take the master's big car and leave the smaller one for me.'

'Then what did you say?'

'I kept quiet. If I had said anything, they would have known that I wouldn't keep their secret.'

'You acted wisely,' Ilyas said.

'There's still time,' Suraj said. 'Amma wouldn't be expecting you so soon. Why don't you come with me to see Benu Apa.'

'Good idea,' Ilyas said. 'Let's go to her.'

When they reached Chhaya Beethi, they saw that Puttal and Benu were busy preparing for the Tagore birthday celebrations.

Last year, he had promised Neely to send her a birthday greeting card each year on 5 May. Benu asked him to spend some more time with her, but Ilyas left with Suraj to purchase a beautiful greeting card from the New Market. He selected a card with Haveldar's painting 'After the Rain'. It had the painting of a beautiful peacock perched on a tree, its long tail reaching down the end of the card and beyond. Neely's eyes are as oval and deep blue as the oval eyes on the peacock feathers, Ilyas thought.

Walking back, Suraj asked him again, 'Will you really leave, Ilyas Bhai?'

'I don't want to go, but I'll have to. Amma was only waiting for me to take my exams. She will be very disappointed when she'll come to know about the postponement of the exams.'

'I'll miss you so much,' Suraj said.

'I'll miss you too.'

Suddenly, Suraj realized that someone stood hidden behind a tree on the riverbank. He was aiming a rifle at Ilyas.

'Ilyas Bhai, look out...' Suraj tried to warn Ilyas.

Ilyas hardly had time to look when a bullet hit him in the chest. He fell to the ground. The passersby tried to look for the killer but did not come forward to help the victim. The shooter disappeared in seconds. With the help of a rickshaw driver, Suraj pulled Ilyas into the rickshaw and brought him home.

By the time he reached home, Ilyas was dead.

Ilyas's death left many questions for his family and friends. Who had murdered the innocent boy and why? He had no connections with any political party whatsoever.

Suraj held the blood-soaked greeting card in his hand and sobbed bitterly.

Mirza sat motionless. Many people visited Mirza at his residence. They were all quiet as if there was nothing to say to him. Mrs Mirza fainted a number of times. Benu had locked herself in a room and refused to come out. Zari and Shams, with Ikram's help, made arrangements for Ilyas's funeral. As the dead body was being taken to the graveyard, Mrs Mirza lay unconscious. Mirza sat motionless as before in his chair, and Benu, after a last look at her brother's dead body, once again shut herself in her room.

As the funeral procession moved along, the bokuli tree shed some of its white blossoms on the shroud. Suraj followed the procession, crying and muttering, 'If only that bullet had pierced my heart.'

Ikram knocked at Benu's door again and again. When she opened it she clung to Ikram and wept bitterly. 'They killed my innocent brother because of me. They wanted to punish me because I married you.'

Ikram took her into his arms and said, 'Courage, my love. I don't really know whom they want to kill and why.'

The next day, Benu found the greeting card Ilyas had purchased for Neely. Ilyas' bloody thumbprints were on the beautiful dark blue ovals of the peacock's long tail. Benu sent the card smeared with blood to Neely with the news of Ilyas's death.

After Ilyas's *Chehlum*, Mirza left for West Pakistan with his wife. Mirza, who had always been opposed to the idea of going back to Pakistan, was now totally heartbroken and disillusioned. He had migrated to East Pakistan in 1949 with Benu in his arms. Ilyas was born in East Pakistan. He had never lived in West Pakistan, but he was considered a West Pakistani and he was going there without taking anything with him...anything at all.

He had gifted his business to his son-in-law, Ikram. He was very skeptical about settling down in West Pakistan the way he had done in East Pakistan. He knew in his heart of hearts that it was going to be exteremly difficult for him since the sap of life had dried up in him and his zest for living was gone.

70

In November 1971, after lunch, Maj. Tajammul was playing cards with a few of his officer friends in a military camp in Kaliganj. Col. Musharaff was sipping his second cup of tea and trying to shake off a fever that he had had since last night.

The duty officer reported that there was a phone call from the Divisional Headquarters. It could be an important message. Col. Musharaff rose to receive it. The call was very important. They had an order to march towards Ghareebpur that very night to re-capture the area occupied by the enemy.

A shiver of excitement ran down Maj. Tajammul's spine. At last he had heard the 'good news'. The young soldiers and officers, who had never experienced war, thought war very enticing, even romantic, because they were enlisted in the army at the age when they were full of energy and buoyancy with vague aspirations and dying to do something very exciting. At such a time they were being trained to destroy some unknown army. They waited to meet the enemy with enthusiasm. It was their sole purpose for being in the army and they waited to face it longingly. Now that they were presented with a real enemy, they took pride in fulfilling the task they were trained for.

'You aren't feeling well, sir,' he said to his colonel. 'Would you like me to lead the attack?'

'Yes, why not?' the colonel said. 'You go as a force commander, we have to start at 9.00 p.m. Two companies will move forward. Dildar and Jawwad, keep your companies ready.'

'Okay, sir.' Dildar and Jawwad left their playing cards on the table, and went excitedly to prepare their companies for the move.

The soldiers began preparations with zest. They filled their knapsacks with dry rations, water bottles with fresh water and checked their first-aid kits. After the preparations, there was an inspection, first at the level of platoon, then at the level of the company.

While evening games were played as usual and supper was taken at the appointed hour, the fascination of war continued to hold sway over everybody's mind. The soldiers were asked to fall in line at 9.00 p.m. Col. Mushraff gave a brief speech, uplifting the soldiers' morale even higher, instructing them to obey their immediate officers and expressing full confidence in their abilities. Finally, Maj. Tajammul was told that he would receive orders to attack directly from the brigade commander at his next camp.

The soldiers traveled in trucks to reach the area where they were supposed to stay for the night. It was a thick forest. Everyone carried his haversack on his back, cap on his head, and rifle in his hand. Palm, coconut and bamboo trees abounded at the bank of the pond where they decided to stay. Their arrival had made the birds in the trees very restless, and they could hear various disturbed noises from trees and bushes. The soldiers were supposed to rest with their uniforms on, so they just lay down with their backs against tree trunks.

A few slept. Some narrated stories to their companions to pass the time. Some just stayed quiet with their own thoughts.

Capt. Jawwad pulled out a wallet from his pocket and tried to see something in the faint light of the moon.

'Whose picture is this?' Maj. Tajammul cheerfully asked.

'Wife's and beloved's, sir,' Capt. Jawwad said heaving a sigh.

'Is this one person or two?' Maj. Tajammul laughed.

'The picture is one, but there are two girls, sir,' Capt. Jawwad replied.

'You are lucky to have both in one picture,' he laughed. 'Otherwise you could be in trouble.'

Capt. Jawwad did not respond. He suddenly felt depressed without any known reason. He put the picture back in his wallet, closed his eyes and pretended to be asleep.

It was one o'clock in the morning, when the lights of a jeep were seen among the trees. This was the brigade commander's jeep. He had arrived to give the operation order. The attack was to begin at 6:00 in the morning.

It was a beautiful morning. Early birds chirped among the trees; the frogs in the ponds were croaking again. The darkness and light were engaged in a long farewell kiss.

According to intelligence, the enemy possessed one company, and six or seven tanks. It would not be hard to defeat them with two companies and a tank squadron.

Making quick preparations, the soldiers were ready to go to the next forming-up position. They marched in a single file. They looked like moving trees because of the leafy branches tangled in their helmets for camouflage. The tanks were camouflaged with hay.

After a little while, they met a guide with a flag, who sent one company to the right, and another company to the left. A little further, they came across two more guides, who gave them the signal to advance. They formed a rectangle. On the start line, the platoon commanders were ready with their platoons.

A little behind stood the company commander, and in the middle of the rectangle, the force commander, Maj. Tajammul, was stationed with his battery commander and other members of his staff.

At six in the morning they launched the attack. Immediately, artillery and machine-gun fire began showering from the other side. The Pakistan army continued to advance, taking advantage of the trees. The enemy had to retreat from Ghareebpur.

At that time, Maj. Tajammul saw through his telescope a great number of soldiers with black caps on. At first sight, they looked like soldiers of the Pakistan Frontier Corps, but on close inspection, he found that they were troops of the Assam Rifles, from the Indian Army.

When Brigade Headquarters was contacted about the huge enemy force they had just detected, they were still ordered to advance as far as they could. In compliance with the order, knowing the danger they were in, they continued to move. They had hardly gone three hundred yards when they felt as if the gates of hell were let loose. Men fell left and right, dying. There was no escape. Going further was sure death. Maj. Tajammul saw his own orderly Hazrath Gul, with many others fall.

He ran to his faithful orderly and found him dead. He promised himself to take his body along with him, whenever he could go back, and give him a decent burial. They were not allowed to leave but were asked to dig-in there. They dug trenches to sit in. Maj. Tajammul asked his men to bury his orderly in one of the trenches, and then they worked hard to make bunkers covered with long betel nut and palm leaves. Maj. Tajammul could feel that Jawwad was getting very jittery, and the doctor was taking some pills to calm his nerves. He was feeling sorry for soldiers who had died before he could reach them. He had taken care of many wounded soldiers, who were taken to empty buildings, waiting for trucks to carry them to the field hospital, which were obviously taking too long to reach them.

'We, officers, have a very great responsibility,' Maj. Tajammul said to Jawwad. 'You must have seen the bridges with signboards indicating what maximum weight they could bear. The maximum weight hardly ever gets passed over them. We officers and men are now like those bridges on which the maximum weight is being carried. We have to know that and bear it patiently.'

'I'm not sure whether the people who are giving orders understand the situation we're in,' Jawwad said.

'I don't know that, but I know that this is the time when we need utmost mental equilibrium and an intense feeling of responsibility.'

'I've learned one lesson—that war is no game,' Jawwad said.

'Me too, it's the most serious thing one can face in life, and that's why its demands are so great.'

71

Zahir was landing with a parachute in a wind blowing at twelve knots per hour, from a height of 1200 feet. He remembered what he had once told Puttal, that he would come down straight to her in his parachute wherever she might be. He smiled in midair and looked about. Parachutes of his companions were everywhere, some looming below him and a few above him. The local residents, in their checkered *tahbunds* and in *banians*, surveyed them with admiration. Weapons had been dropped from the air before. The people took them out of the boxes and collected them.

As the paratroopers landed and alighted from treetops and from the roofs of buildings, the people immediately carried them on their shoulders. Zahir landed in a pond, and emerged, shaking off water from his body. The Bengalis greeted him in awe, shook hands with him, and each one of them invited him for lunch at his house. Zahir politely declined. Lunch, with rice and lintel dishes was brought from the homes of the villagers for all paratroopers.

The paratroopers assembled at one place under the guidance of local residents. The counting took place and attendance was taken. The task of the paratroopers was to seize the bridge and the ferry station and then to join the combined force of the Indian brigade and the Qadir Bahini, which had been advancing towards Dhaka with utmost speed.

72

On her way home from the hospital, Zari was thinking that this was a most turbulent time for her child to be born. The doctor had told her that she should expect her baby to be born any day.

As she entered her living room, she saw a framed picture hanging on the wall, a young man, with long hair, and an overgrown beard. He had dark glasses over his eyes and a scarf around his neck. He looked like a runaway convict trying to hide his real identity.

Zari had never seen this man before. As far as she knew, the man wasn't a celebrity either.

'Who is this?' Zari asked Shams.

'Oh, he is my brother, Ronjhu.'

Zari looked at the photograph again. 'Where did you get this picture?'

'He sent it to me.'

'You told me that you wouldn't have anything to do with him if he didn't accept me as your wife.'

'I don't even know where he is,' Shams said and picked up the newspaper to read.

'Then, why did he send his picture to you?'

'What's the harm? After all, he is my brother.'

'Shams, don't talk to me strangely, I don't like it.'

Shams looked at her but did not say anything.

Zari surveyed the room. 'Have you removed the Quaid-e-Azam's picture?'

'Yes,' Shams said briefly.

'Why?' Zari came and stood beside him.

'If I tell you that I have given it to be set in a new frame what would you say?' Shams asked.

'I wouldn't believe you. These are not the days when you need to have a new frame for a picture.'

'If you know that, then why do you ask me embarrassing questions? Ronjhu cares for me. He wants me to have his picture because it's not the Pakistan army this time, but people from the Mukti Bahini who are doing house to house search, looking for weapons and people against Bangladesh.'

'So, the Tigers and Leopards of the Mukti Bahini will guarantee our safety from now on,' Zari said contemptuously. She knew that Qadir of the Mukti Bahini was called 'The Tiger of Tangel'.

'Try to think rationally. In the circumstances, his name is a guarantee for our safety. People should know that he is your brother-in-law.'

It looked as if Zari was going to cry. 'So, now you will put garlands on the picture of that bloody man who is killing thousands of innocent people.'

Omar had been listening to this conversation intently, but didn't intervene.

'Zari,' Shams said, 'there's no use getting emotional. We have to be cautious. You better be prepared to declare that this man is your husband's brother and you're proud of him.'

'I don't understand.'

'Because you don't know what is really happening. You insist on listening to Radio Pakistan only, and you are under an illusion.

'Why don't you tell me?'

'If you have the courage to hear the truth, I can tell you.'

'Tell me.'

'The truth is that the Pakistan Army is losing the war. Each and every passing moment is bringing them closer to doom. The Indian Army has been advancing with a three-pronged attack on Dhaka. There are only fifteen hundred soldiers in this city, and they cannot defend the city.

'Oh, no!' Zari put her hand on her mouth, trying to smother her scream. She wanted to cry on his shoulder, but she kept looking at him, without blinking, as if asking, how come you are saying all this so calmly! What happened to your claims of integration? You, too, have changed Shams. She turned her face away.

Shams felt extremely sorry for Zari. He should have prepared her earlier for this calamity. After all, he loved her and she was going to have his child. It was already hard for her to move about and do the household chores. What a great shock he had given her in this condition!

He advanced towards Zari. 'Don't get upset, my love?' he whispered. 'We can't control what's happening, but you and I are going to be together...always...forever.' He leaned over Zari and removed her hands from her face.

Zari looked at him. 'Shams, don't deceive yourself any further. I can see it...you feel victorious...and now I am really disillusioned.'

'That's not true. Let's hope for the best. Come, tell me what the doctor has said.'

'He has said, any day, any time,' Zari said briefly.

'Good,' Shams said calmly, though he was also worried about Zari giving birth to a child in these uncertain and dangerous times. 'I've talked with Ikram and Benu. Benu has agreed to go with you to the hospital. She'll be good company.' He went towards the door.

'Are you going out?' Zari asked.

'Yes.'

'Where?'

Shams remained silent for a moment and then said, 'I'll tell you when I come back. In the meantime, you can chat with Chachaji.' With these words he quickly left closing the door behind him.

After Shams had gone, Zari started crying. Omar approached her and put his hand on her shoulder.

'Tell me, Chachaji, what's happening?' She turned to Omar. 'Who's telling the truth? The newspapers and radio tell one thing and the people here say differently.'

'Conditions aren't good, my dear. Hope is giving way to despair.'

'But how did it all happen?' Zari asked.

'The Pakistan government has been hiding things from the public,' Omar said. 'They were hoping that conditions might change. Not only the public, but the soldiers, intellectuals, politicians and military officers, even the commander of the Eastern Command, General Niazi were kept in the dark. They were hoping that help was just about to arrive from friends, meaning China and the United States and even when that hope was gone, they kept it secret to gain more time for the representative of Pakistan to seek a cease-fire mandate from the United Nations. They also kept the people of West Pakistan under the illusion that if East Pakistan could bear the brunt of war for a few more days, the Pakistan army would capture Kashmir.'

'But how could this happen?' Zari insisted. 'We were told that the "truth" always wins. Were we wrong to insist on having one Pakistan?'

Zari wiped her tears and started peeling the gourd for cooking.

'Zari, is there anything else on your mind?'

'Yes, Chachaji.'

'What's that?'

'Shams is thinking of moving you to another place,' Zari said. 'He feels that you might not be safe here. As you know he often stays out and I'll feel awful without you. I love your company.'

'I'll talk to Shams. I would like to stay too, but if he insists, I'll have to go. He understands the situation more than we do, and we must trust him.'

'I'll be anxious about you. I know it's hard for you to stay confined in one place. You would certainly take the risk to go out.'

'No. I promise I'll do whatever Shams wants me to. Only I must know about your safety.'

'If only the Maulana were here!' Zari said.

'Yes, his presence would have been very comforting. I also wish he were here!' Chachaji said.

When Shams came back, he told them that he had made arrangements for Omar to hide in a vacant house. He could take care of Zari as his wife, but he could not guarantee Omar's safety.

It was arranged that Omar would be supplied with some dry food. Suraj, Benu's servant whom everybody trusted, would bring everything he needed from time to time. The time to leave the house was still to be decided.

Omar was silent. He, who had always been engaged in the search for absolute truth, was unable to answer Zari's question. The Pakistanis claimed that it was a crusade to save Pakistan. India's Muslim clergy, in language dipped in celestial waters, was making speeches over the radio telling their Muslim population and the Pakistan army that this was not a holy war, a Jihad. The people of Bangladesh want independence, and it's their right to have it.

73

Omar was confined in the upper story of a building and he insisted upon calling it 'imprisonment.' The door was locked from the outside. At night, Suraj brought meals for him and after serving him disappeared into the night. During the day Omar, either read a book, wrote his novel or read from newspapers brought by Suraj. At night, for want of light, he would lie in bed, thinking or simply remembering the past.

Suraj had just left with the supper tray. Omar locking the door noticed that the road was washed with rain, looking very clean and black. The shadows of trees and telephone poles were reflected perfectly on the still wet road.

After fifteen minutes he again heard the same knock at the door. Who could be there? Omar was puzzled. Is somebody trying to copy Suraj's knocking style? Omar peeped through a chink in the door. It wasn't one but two shadows outside. When the knock was repeated, Omar softly asked, 'Who's there?'

'I'm Suraj. The Maulana has come to see you.' Omar opened the door immediately. The Maulana came in and said to Suraj, 'You better go. I'll stay here for the night.'

When they settled down, Omar said, 'Maulana, we were anxious about you. Where had you been all these days?'

'I was wandering about,' Maulana said, sitting down on the low wooden bed. 'Omar! I have witnessed so many horrible things that it's hard to describe them.'

'Tell me,' Omar said.

'I've seen the massacre of so many innocent people that I cannot tell it all in a lifetime.'

'Maulana, did you come across any good people?'

'Yes, thank God there are people like Suraj, who visits you daily, risking his own life. There are people who have sheltered their friends, but I've met people on both sides who confessed to me that they had either killed innocent people, or caused them to be killed, and their conscience was now troubling them.'

'Maulana, I still say that the universe might be billions of years old, but mankind is, nevertheless, still in its infancy. It hasn't been intellectually developed yet, and doesn't know right from wrong.'

'I don't know,' Maulana said. 'It might be a blessing in disguise that God has kept so many things hidden from us, especially the future.'

'Do you believe that ignorance is bliss?'

'No, It's good not knowing what's in store for us in future. At least we can hope for the best.'

'Maulana, It's good that you decided to stay here tonight. There's plenty of room—beds and everything.'

'You know that I never seek comfort for myself. I'll leave with Suraj when he comes tomorrow.'

'Have you met Shams and Zari?'

'Not yet. I'll go there tomorrow.'

'I would like you to stay with them for Zari's sake. She is extremely nervous and upset about what's happening, especially in her condition.'

'I know. I'll be with her. Don't worry.'

Maulana went to wash his face and hands to say his prayers. He never missed his prayers even when he was travelling or when he was sick.

74

It was the morning of 3 December at 2:30 a.m., people were suddenly awakened by a terrific bomb explosion. That could mean an Indian attack! In a few minutes, the confirmation came over the BBC Radio that the war between India and Pakistan had started.

Sitting in their trenches, Major Tajammul and his companions could not enjoy the announcement of a full-scale war as they might have done before. They had already gone through the horrible experience in November.

Maj. Tajammul was still in the same area in December where he had dug in a month ago.

Days passed. It was 4 a.m. on 6 December, the third day of war. An area of 150 square kilometers in front them was still occupied by the Indian army. Several times they had tried to break the fortification of the Pakistan army, but had been unsuccessful so far.

But this time it was very severe. The Indian attack began at exactly four o'clock in the morning. The Indian infantry was huge. The movement of the trucks suggested that the assault was planned, involving at least a tank regiment. Maj. Tajammul's commanding officer Col. Musharraf had arrived too, and everybody was alert, but the shelling was so intense that it was difficult for soldiers to come out of the trenches.

At about ten o'clock, Col. Musharraf received a phone call from Capt. Jawwad from the forward company, saying that the enemy tanks were moving very fast, and it was impossible to stop them in any way. They were still ordered to stay in their trenches.

When Maj. Tajammul, through his telescope, saw the tanks moving to the right, heading towards Jessore, he was horrified.

He knew that the entire platoon was going to be run over and buried alive.

Maj. Tajammul rubbed his eyes, his palms moistening with tears. He felt as if he could see Capt. Jawwad sitting in a trench, holding his rifle, one knee closer to the chin, taking aim, and the tank burying him alive, in the same position. Maybe it is better for a soldier to die in his uniform, rifle in hand, emblems on his shoulders, his helmet, belt, haversack and water bottle intact, and buried with everything, including the picture of his wife and beloved.

At last, when the higher authorities came to know the real situation and realized that two companies could not fight such a huge army, they received the orders of retreat.

They were surrounded on three sides and had only one way open, with a lake two and a half miles long on that side. They had to cross the lake. They advanced in the lakes with their weapons and haversacks entangling and disentangling in the weeds in the lake. The water at some places was up to their heads so that the taller soldiers had to carry the shorter ones. It was getting harder and harder to walk with their weapons and the haversacks, and the soldiers started throwing them in the lake.

They crossed the lake in one-and-a-half hours. It was getting late and night was approaching. Maj. Tajammul had seen many scenes of retreating armies in the movies and had been much impressed by how it looked, soldiers tired and listless, perspiring, with coatings of dust on their faces, and the paste of mud over their heavy boots and uniforms. But now he could see and feel the difference between reality and the artificiality of the scenes. The smartest actors could not imitate the expressions his men had on their faces. He had heard soldiers break into hollow and soulless bursts of laughter, as if strong winds were shrieking like witches in an attempt to pass through broken crevices of ruins. He had seen his soldiers throwing away their torn boots and putting on the shoes taken from the dead companions without any feeling.

Before reaching Jessore, they were diverted to Khulna, which was forty miles from there. They were told that India's Madras

Regiment had captured Jessore. Pakistan's Brigade headquarters had left Jessore in haste, destroying their ammunition, maps and files.

Now, they had to walk even further. The mustard fields looked like green carpets spread everywhere with patterns of yellow flowers on them. Unfortunately, they were not in a position to take a rest and enjoy the scenery. Whenever the enemy aircraft bombarded them, they took shelter in drains by the roadside, and then started to walk again. At about 10.45 p.m., the trucks finally arrived to take them to Khulna. By that time every soldier was so exhausted that he could hardly remember his name. They just staggered into the trucks and lay there like sacks of hay.

75

The night had just begun. Shams had gone to visit a neighbor, and Zari was in the house alone. The doorbell rang. Zari went up to the door and asked, 'Who's there?'

'I am Meraj, Shams's brother-in-law.'

Zari opened the door instantly and held his hand with an air of informality, though she had never seen Meraj before.

'You!' Tears welled up in her eyes. 'Thank God, you are safe,' she said, in a choked voice. 'How have you been?' Meraj was taken by surprise. He had never expected that Zari, who was related neither to Shoshi nor to him, could be so happy to see him.

'Come, please come in. I'll call Shams. He's gone to see a neighbor for a minute.' Her voice was so soft and reassuring. She called the neighbor, but the telephone at the other end was busy.

'Please be seated. I'll go and call him.' Swinging her bulging body a little bit, she went out.

Shams came at once and embraced Meraj. They talked for a long time. Meraj narrated details of where he had lived in India. He knew well that the political ring was now changing. He had accompanied a group of foreign reporters who were coming to Dhaka.

'It wouldn't be advisable for you to go to Sylhet right now,' Shams said. 'You'll have to wait for a few days. However, I've got news of Shoshi and your daughter. They're well and are with their grandfather. Your son is still with his aunt. They are all doing fine.'

When Zari left to cook the dinner, Shams asked Meraj, 'Tell me if the Bangladesh government-in-exile has any idea about the difficulties they'd face here.'

'Yes they have. They would have to rehabilitate millions of refugees that had crossed the borders to India. The damage to the

crops might lead to a famine. The condition of railways, bridges
and roads are very poor because the army and the Mukti Bahini
both tried to destroy them. Moreover, nobody has the real
experience to govern, and the hardest thing would be to fulfill all
those promises which they have made to the masses.'

'Yes,' Shams said. 'In addition to these, there are ideological
conflicts among various Bahinis. There are some elements in the
Mukti Bahini who are not pro-Indian. The men who come in
power will also have to deal with them.'

'Let us see what happens,' Meraj said.

After supper they all went to bed. Shams lay awake till late at
night. Soon after, he woke up startled. He felt as if his body was
on fire and a strange voice was echoing in his ears, as if someone
had just said, 'The pyre is ready.' He got up and looked around
in a daze.

'What happened?' Zari was awake too.

'Nothing,' Shams said. 'I feel very hot in here. I'll go out for a
few minutes.' Saying this, Shams went out.

'Hot, in December!' Zari, who was sleeping in her petticoat and
blouse, wrapped her *sari* in haste and ran out after him. Shams
was sitting on a broken tree. A few roots of the tree were still
intact in the ground, but the rest were out in the open. This tree
was neither dead nor alive. Zari came up to Shams and put her
hand to his forehead. She had guessed right. He had very high
fever.

'For God's sake come inside. You may develop pneumonia. It's
cold and dewy here,' Zari pleaded with him, but he kept sitting
there as if he didn't understand what she was saying. When he
didn't move, even after repeated requests, Zari sat beside him. The
telephone bell kept ringing in the house, but they both ignored
it. Nobody would call them so late. It could be a wrong
number.

At last, Meraj got up to receive the phone. 'Hello,' he said.

'Is Shams Bhai there? Ronjhu speaking. It's bad news. Who's
this?' Ronjhu's voice was disturbed and low as if coming from the
depth of a well.

'What's the matter? I'm Meraj.'

'Who? I didn't get your name...but never mind. Whoever you are, tell Shams bhai that our sister Shoshi has suffered serious burns...don't interrupt...just listen. I had arrived the previous night, and was staying with her in the same *baasha*...Maybe they were following me or it could be an accident. When we smelt smoke we all rushed out but Shoshi Apa, who was sleeping alone in a small back room couldn't make it earlier. In seconds, the flames engulfed the house.'

'I'm Meraj. How is she and how is Laila?' Meraj asked.

'What did you say? Oh, you're Meraj Bhai...I'm so sorry to give you this news. I never knew you were there. But listen, Shoshi Apa got burnt severely. You should come here as soon as possible. I can't stay here at this time because the war is now in its final stages. Pray for our success, and try to reach here, because grandfather and the little daughter can't take care of Shoshi Apa. This is the most difficult time for all of us...Good-bye.'

As Zari, somehow supporting Shams, came into the house, she noticed Meraj sitting by the telephone, holding his head in his hands. In the dim light coming through a room, Meraj looked like an apparition to her. His shadow on the wall, larger than life, was looming like an inert giant.

'Shams is running high temperature,' she said to Meraj and ushered Shams into their room.

When Zari came back to call the doctor who was also Shams's friend, Meraj was not there. He must have gone back to his room, Zari thought.

The doctor couldn't come to examine Shams at this late hour during curfew. Zari gave him the names of all the medicines she had at home, and the doctor prescribed some from among them.

'Nothing to worry about,' the doctor said. 'He will get well soon. It is only the stress of these awful days, but the victory is close. *Joi Bangla!*'

'Shut up,' Zari wanted to say to him, but putting down the receiver she tiptoed and peeped into Meraj's room. He was not there. Then she found the main door unlocked and knew that he was gone.

She came back to Shams.

He, in delirium, was reciting a poem by his namesake.

> In the mournful music of the night the glow-worms dance
> With tinkling anklets around their tiny feet
> And in this world
> I walk alone, in cold winter nights
> For a while, sleep overpowers me
> My door chain remains unfastened
> Someday, the lions might tear me to pieces
> Or my cold dead body, float in a city gutter
> Unknown apparitions lick their tongues
> In the shadow of my door

After taking his medicine, Shams, still mumbling, went into a stupor. Zari did not tell him that Meraj had left, and that her labour pains had just begun.

76

On 14 December 1971, there was a sudden blast. The Indian air force had attacked the Government House in Dhaka and the left portion of the building was hit. The governor, along with his ministers and secretaries, ran out towards the trenches. The debris of the roof fell over the big fish tank and the flower vase, smashing them to pieces. The fish, the flowers, and the little buds fell over the debris.

The secretary to the governor, covered with dust and smoke, ran about looking for the governor. His shoes crushed the beautiful buds and the writhing goldfish as he walked over them.

Watching others rush out, the secretary also ran towards the governor's bunker. There was another air raid and the people ran out to shelters. The entire building emptied in a few minutes. The telephones kept ringing ceaselessly in some of the offices like the cries of anguished hearts, which nobody cared to listen.

'Should I move my family to the Intercontinental Hotel today or tomorrow?' The Governor asked the United Nations' representative, John Kelly.

Gavin Young, the correspondent of the *Sunday Observer*, London, leaned forward to listen closely to their conversation.

'Right now, sir....' John Kelly's sentence was interrupted by another air attack. Yet another heap of mortar and dust fell from the Governor House.

The governor took out a piece of paper from his briefcase and a pen from his pocket. He wrote his resignation and that of his council of ministers. He handed them to Mr Kelly to send to the president of Pakistan.

Then, he went into the adjoining bathroom, performed his ablutions, covered his head with a handkerchief, and stood silently in a corner of the bunker to offer his prayers.

Gavin Young looked out through the door of the bunker. The debris from the third attack was still slowly falling down on the ground. The trenches were crowded with civilians working in the Governor House. Those who did not find a place in the trenches were seeking shelter under the trees. Between two attacks, some of them had courageously come out of the trenches and had run to the Intercontinental Hotel, which was declared a neutral zone. Almost all the foreign correspondents were staying in that hotel.

Towards evening, when the air attacks had stopped, all those people who held high positions in the Governor House and made the most important decisions regarding the fate of the nation, came to the Hotel International depressed, crestfallen and looking wretched.

They entered the hotel building sluggishly, with bowed heads like somnambulists. The cameras clicked as usual. They were used to posing for the cameras, but this time, when their faces were coated with soot and dust, their hair disheveled, and faces showing the fear of death written on them, this exposure was a torment. They did not move from the range of the cameras only because they did not have enough energy left to do so.

77

Tajammul had decided not to lay down arms, and had sneaked out from his camp, leaving his company. On 16th December, when orders to surrender were received, he had continued to fight, so much so, that the Brigade Headquarter reprimanded him for his disobedience.

When the Indian soldiers had appeared on the scene, waving white flags and from the Pakistan side white shirts tied to rifles were being waved, Tajammul had quietly slipped away from his regiment.

Even after his bitter experiences of war, his faith in humanity was not shaken. Maybe somebody would give him shelter. If he were destined to die, he would like to die a free man.

He headed for Barisal and found a desolate church there. He was not unfamiliar with this region, but he had not seen this church before. The rain had made fissures in the walls and the paint on doors and windows had been worn off. The decorative, carved, semi-circled petals in brass, and big brass nails on the main door had been blackened by rain and sun.

Tajammul circled the church. It seemed as if all the doors were locked from the inside. It meant that somebody was inside, though there were no signs of life inside or outside the church. Tajammul decided to force open the main door.

As he pushed the door forcefully, the hinges gave way. The rusty door-chain peeped like a veiled woman from inside through the gap. Holding the revolver in his right hand, he lifted the thick chain and jerked it with his left hand. The clink from the heavy rusty chain rose like a moan, and resting against the side of the door became silent.

Entering, Tajammul inspected the church carefully. It was very spacious. The inner condition of the church now was no better than outside. The brown leather covering of the benches had now been turned gray. There were lots of white and gray rings of pigeon droppings on the ground. The tables were coated with dust, and the floor was cold and lifeless like a corpse. The last rays of the sun, sneaking through the broken colored glasses, were about to depart.

Tajammul looked around once again. Birds had built nests in the windows. In the alcoves of the wall, the space meant for the icon of Mary was empty. Jesus' dust-coated torso was sitting in one of the niches but its head was missing.

There seemed to be nobody there, but there should be someone who had bolted the doors from inside. Tajammul with his revolver ready, began advancing cautiously. Passing by the pulpit, he entered the back room. That too, was empty. Old religious pamphlets, coated with dust, were lying about in the room.

Even the last rays of light had disappeared by now. Tajammul pulled out a search light from his haversack, and lighting it went to the end of the building. There he saw a few footprints on the floor. These prints led him to a long table in the back.

Approaching the table, he focused the light on it. He noticed someone lying under a white sheet. So, here he is the caretaker of the church, sleeping peacefully! Tajammul thought. How come that this person had not seen or heard him? Maybe seeing his rifle he hid himself under the sheet. Tajammul pulled the sheet off with a jerk and looked at the person in the circular light of the searchlight. The scene was like a surrealist painting by Salvador Dali. There was a headless body lying there and in place of the head there was a head carved from stone. It was the head of the statue of Jesus.

Tajammul stood sad and depressed. He looked intently at the somber face with large eyes and long tresses. Who had the audacity to subject him to this appalling joke! He had no clue why there was no living soul in the church while all the doors were bolted from inside. Tajammul ate from the dry rations in his haversack, drank water from the bottle, and spent the night in company of the moon that floated noiselessly behind the church windows.

He got up very early in the morning, took off his uniform leaving his vest on, spread it on the dead body. Then wrapped the sheet taken off from the headless body as a *tahbund* around his waist and came out of the church to continue his journey. He knew a little Bengali and relied on his training as a soldier to survive.

78

Life was perhaps at war with Zari. During the climax of war, along with the waves of air raid sirens, she started having the contractions...the labour pains.

Shams and Benu brought her to the hospital. Her mind was preoccupied with the war. The hospital buildings were immersed in darkness because of blackouts. The sky occasionally glowed with the bombings and from the burning buildings. The darkness, the hustle bustle of the hospital was increasing the intensity of her pains. When the last pain hit her, she felt as if with the baby coming out her own life was going out of her too.

But then she knew that it was all over, and she had given birth to a baby boy. The baby was immediately taken away from her. The nurse told her that he was taken to the nursery, and they'd bring him to her later.

Zari still felt that explosions were hitting her heart and hurting her soul. The looks of the nurses and midwives made Zari feel that she was to blame for what was happening. She was a party to all these sufferings, not as one of the oppressed, but as an oppressor, because she was from West Pakistan.

She was also worried about her son who was not brought to her even after she had moved to a private room.

Shams had gone back to his home to come later. Zari expected him to stay in the hospital during her ordeal, but Benu said he had nothing to do here and wanted to go home to bring some fresh soup and fruit for her.

Zari waited for Shams anxiously, but when he came, she closed her eyes and lay in bed, pretending to be asleep. As Shams went and stood by the window, thinking her to be asleep, her heart began to fill with anguish. Why didn't he hug and kiss her? Why didn't he love her as he did in the early days of their marriage? Why didn't he say, embracing her, as he used to say before, 'Don't

worry the sun of our love will always shine beause Shams is yours
for ever.'

At last, Shams came back from the window and sat in a chair,
looking anxiously at his watch. Zari opened her eyes.

'How are you?' he asked.

'Fine. Did you see the baby?'

'Yes.'

'Why don't they bring him to me?'

'Because he is weak. He has been put in an incubator. The
nurse will bring him to you when he gains a little more weight.'

'Does he look very small?'

'Yes.'

'How is he to look at?'

'Just like you.'

Zari felt uncomfortable with the way Shams was talking. She
felt like shaking him and asking him. *Why don't you look happy if
he looks like me? Why are you clipping words when talking about your
son?* But she kept silent. She did not have much strength left in
her to fight. *She was sure he did not love her anymore. She could cry
and shout as much as she liked but the birds of love and affection that
had flown away would not come back.* Her heart kept sobbing, but
putting on a brave face she tried to look calm. She had never given
up before and she would hold up as long as possible.

With slow steps, Shams came to her, pressed her hand gently,
kissed her lightly and said, 'You know the curfew relaxation time
is soon going to be over. I must leave now, good-bye.'

Quietly, he went out of the room.

79

The next day, when Benu reached the hospital to visit Zari, the nurse in the hospital said to her, 'Please try to talk to Zari, she is very upset.'

'What's the matter?' Benu asked.

'The baby has died,' the nurse replied.

'How?' Benu asked in surprise.

'The baby had a defective heart when he was born. His father knew that, but he didn't tell his wife.'

Benu went to Zari. She was looking like a maniac staring at the ceiling with her hair dishevelled. There were no tears in her eyes, but it seemed as if she has been crying for hours. As soon as she saw Benu, Zari said loudly, 'They have killed my baby, I know that they killed my child, because he looked like me.'

'No, Zari Apa,' Benu said. 'The nurse has just told me that he was sick when he was born. They tried to save him but unfortunately couldn't. Shams Bhai knows all about it.'

'He was not sick, I was going to the doctor for regular checkup. She never mentioned anything. I know he was born healthy. They can fool Shams but they can't fool me.'

'Please control yourself. I'll talk to the doctor and tell you all about it. I'll show you the reports. Just wait for me for a couple of minutes.'

'No, don't go, Benu. These people are going to kill all of us. They didn't spare my little baby. They'll kill me and they'll kill you.'

'Please don't talk like that,' Benu whispered to her. 'Everybody knows me here as a Bengali.'

'But the moment they'll come to know about you, they'll murder you, the way they have murdered my son.' Zari began to cry, holding her face in her hands.

'For God's sake, come to your senses, Zari Apa. Don't talk like this to Shams Bhai. He's already very sad. He'll be greatly hurt. Everybody is troubled these days, you know.'

'I don't think so,' Zari said, clutching her blanket in her hands. 'Don't you see that they are murdering mercilessly? Go around the hospital and see what is happening here. Labour rooms are overcrowded with lovely young girls who were raped nine months before. These girls want to end their shameful lives and the lives of their babies.'

Benu threw her arms around Zari's neck and began to cry. 'I know. Zari Apa, Why do such things happen to us women? Why do women have to pay the heaviest price of wars and revolutions?'

'Because we are not taught to hit back, that's why. We are only taught to take the beating.' Zari's voice was hoarse and quite changed from her normal voice. She was extremely angry. 'I say if all the women of the world decide not to give birth to a child unless all deadly weapons were destroyed, and peace restored, wouldn't men come to their senses? But who's going to teach them such wisdom, and make them realize their strength?'

'Hold on, Zari Apa. I'll come back in a minute!' Benu said. 'I'll ask the doctor to release you from hospital. We can take care of you much better in our house. But remember, in my husband's family every generation has its own ideology. Ikram's parents are loyal to the Muslim League, and staunch supporters of Pakistan but Ikram, his younger brother, and his wife think otherwise.'

'I will not go with you,' Zari replied firmly.

Benu thought it better not to argue with her and to talk to the doctor first. The doctor was not in her office. She was making her rounds.

There was commotion everywhere, a stream of patients was pouring into the emergency ward. The wounded were constantly being brought in on stretchers. Everybody was in a hurry to get things done before curfew time started.

At last Benu found the doctor and asked her if she would allow Zari to go with her.

'She's emotionally disturbed,' the doctor said, 'and is on medication. I can't allow her to go with you in her condition.'

Benu tried to convince the doctor that Zari would have more comfort and peace of mind in her house, but the doctor was determined and told her that nobody could leave the hospital in the evening. The next morning, the senior doctor would examine her to decide if she could be discharged.

Benu returned to Zari's room in despair. Zari wasn't there. Benu heard the sound of water coming from the bathroom. Wouldn't it be better if she could stay with Zari tonight? She kept thinking about different options, suddenly she realized that Zari was taking too much time in the bathroom. The sound of water falling uninterrupted still could be heard. Benu pushed the bathroom door open. Zari wasn't there. She immediately opened the cupboards and shelves. There was nothing there. Zari had left with all her stuff.

Benu informed the nurse. People were sent in all directions to look for Zari, but she was not found. Benu called Shams at home but nobody answered the phone.

When a rickshaw brought in a patient, Benu engaged it to go to Zari's home in the hope of finding her there.

Zari's house was locked and nobody was there. Benu had no choice but to go home.

80

When Capt. Jawwad's mother opened the registered letter from the Army Headquarters, and read that her son had been killed in action, the tragedy that shook the foundations of her family.

The only darling boy, the sweetheart of the family, had lost his life on an alien land and they did not get even his body to bury.

Everyone pitied the beautiful young widow Shezzy, who had never entered Jawwad's house as his wife, because the final wedding ceremony had not taken place.

Sarwat wished Shezzy to go to their in-laws's house for mourning in a white outfit befitting a widow. Shezzy, refused to oblige her mother.

'Don't you realize that Jawwad is out of your life forever,' her mother said. 'Can't you do this last favor for his family and yours?'

'No, mother, please,' Shezzy said. 'I can't act as if I have lost somebody very dear to me. You know that he had never been in my life as he should have been. Please try to understand me this once.'

Her mother was not capable of understanding her, and was quite disappointed in her. Ahsan was on his daughter's side so she couldn't do anything except to use her own talent at acting and telling Shezzy's in-laws that Shezzy was in a state of shock, a doctor was attending to her and she was totally incapable of coming to their house and attending the funeral.

81

Zari remained in a kind of stupor the whole night and the following day. During this time, whenever she woke up, an extreme desire to close her eyes and go back to sleep drowned her in a state of half consciousness. Zari did not know that she had been given strong sedatives to enable her to sleep well and recover her energy again.

The explosions of the aerial attacks interrupted her restless sleep, and when she tried to figure out where she was, she was drowned into deep sleep again. Sometimes, she saw two kindly faces in her room, those of John and the doctor. Once, during a short interval between her sleep, Zari heard John telling the doctor, 'Gen. Manik Shaw has given the last ultimatum. The grace time for surrender is from five this evening to nine tomorrow morning. There won't be any bombardment during this period on their part, and after the expiry of this time, if they don't surrender, he has threatened to destroy all the cantonements and military camps of the Pakistan Army.'

Zari found it hard to distinguish whether she had really heard those words or whether they were part of the complicated dreams she had been dreaming during her sleep.

Late at night, she was suddenly awake, feeling very hungry. Groping in the dark, she lighted the candle kept on the bedside table and got up to look in the refrigerator. It contained milk, water, and fruit. Zari ate some fruit, drank a cup of milk and said to herself, 'I'm not sick. I'm only physically and mentally fatigued.'

To test her strength, she rose from her bed again and walked up to the window. She lifted the curtain and looked out. It was very dark outside. In this darkness, suddenly there was a flash, and she saw the transparent lights of small particles like fireworks, forming into a circle around the racecourse. The trees on the edges of the ground shone with an angelic beauty, and then were dimmed. She didn't know who was doing this, but she thought that it could be a signal. Blowing the candle out, she lay in the bed, making herself part of the darkness, which surrounded her and which she felt within her.

In the morning Zari's mind was perfectly clear. At first she heard an air raid siren, then the telephone started ringing.

She lifted the receiver. Without telling his name, someone said to her, 'The Pakistan Army is going to surrender today. Come to the Jasmine Room. All the guests are going to get instructions about staying in the hotel.'

To hell with you, Zari wanted to say, but she knew that to be mad at her caller was just not right.

'The doctor has advised me to take complete rest,' Zari said. 'I'd be obliged if you could give me instructions on telephone.'

'OK, I'll be brief,' the caller said. 'This hotel will continue to be a neutral zone, but no one will be granted political asylum. Sooner or later, everyone will have to leave, either as a prisoner of the Indian Government, or under custody of the Bangladesh Government. Now this hotel may also be targeted by the mob. So please don't go out of the hotel at anytime. You'll be safer inside the building. You can get a form from the Red Cross office in the hotel to inform your family about your welfare.'

Zari remained in her room. When she came to know that the lecture in the Jasmine Room was over, Zari went down to meet John. Fortunately, she found him alone in one of the offices.

'If you can't protect those who have sought refuge here,' Zari said, 'and you are going to hand them over as prisoners to one party or the other, then I wouldn't like to stay here. I'll try to save myself from being arrested as long as possible.'

'I will advise you to stay,' he said. 'Local people and the Mukti Bahini are still after non-Bengalis and there are differences among various factions of the Mukti Bahini too. So, it might be dangerous, very dangerous, to go and live outside in any place. There are lots of people like you here.'

'I don't care. I am not going to get arrested. Why should I?'

'Try to understand. You wouldn't be able to live in a filthy refugee camp, and there is a grave risk in there too. The camps are being raided and set on fire continuously. Let me tell you one thing...the Indian soldiers have no personal grudge with the civilians. They have been instructed not to harass any local or non-local people. You'll be safe with them because the Independence forces are still after West Pakistanis.'

'Mr Kelly, either promise to get me out safely from here or just leave me alone.'

'Try to understand my position. How can I take anyone out from the Hotel? It's just impossible.'

'I don't think I can expect help from helpless people! Anyway, thanks for your advice.'

'Listen, my dear, you are still weak. I assure you that it's the safest place, I beg you to return to your room and take rest. I'm very busy. The draft of surrender might be prepared in this hotel, and I wish to be there to ensure that nobody's rights are violated.'

'Okay, I'll go to my room.'

'Good girl,' John smiled with genuine affection. As she was going towards the elevator, she heard somebody say to John, 'General Arora's Chief of Staff, Maj. Gen. Jacob has arrived with the surrender papers. We have to compare our draft with theirs.'

Zari stood there as if glued to the carpet.

'So far, there's news of Gen. Arora, Air Marshall Diwan, and Vice-Admiral Krishnan coming for the surrender,' the same man said.

Zari went to her room directly. She put a few clothes and other essential things in a smaller bag, which could be slung across the shoulder. She covered her dead child's clothes with a white *dupatta*, as if laying him in a shroud. Pushing the large carry-on bag aside, she stood by the window to see what was happening outside.

She could see the crowd gathered around the Dhaka Radio Station and could hear them shouting *'Joi Bangla'* with great euphoria. It was from this same radio station that she had broadcast talks of integration.

The Pakistani flag had been removed from the building. One Bangladeshi devotee had torn it to pieces, and holding its shreds between his thumb and a finger, had set fire to it and scattered the ashes in the air. Zari saw a Bangladeshi flag hoisted in its place within minutes.

Throwing herself on her bed, Zari hid her face in her hands and sobbed bitterly. *Was this a nightmare?* She kept asking herself, though she knew the answer, which was too painful to be accepted.

Is there any way of getting out? Zari looked down from the window again, and noticed that the crowd was moving towards the hotel, holding different kinds of weapons and crying that it was the Day of Judgment for the governor, the cabinet, the secretary, the industrialists and others staying there. *Have all these people been hypnotized?* She wondered. *How can plain and simple men, who once led humble and innocent lives, kill their companions and neighbors, and rape their daughters? How can people see their husbands and wives, with whom they had shared their beds, slaughtered before their very eyes? They have certainly been brainwashed,* she decided.

The pro-Pakistan people who were staying in the hotel were afraid. Would members of the United Nations and the hotel manager who were talking with the crowd and the volunteers of Mukti Bahini be able to save them?

As the discussions were going on, a jeep arrived with a few senior Indian Army Officers. They talked to the bloodthirsty crowd diplomatically, assuring them that it was their responsibility to put all these people to account, and that nobody would be spared. At their intervention and reassurance, the crowd dispersed, firing shots in the air.

The telephone rang. Zari lifted the receiver. Someone from the reception desk said, 'A relation of yours is waiting for you in the lounge.'

'Chachaji,' Zari's heart said, leaping with joy. How she yearned to put her head on his chest and cry. Hanging her bag across her shoulders, she ran down. It took her some time to recognize the person who had been waiting for her. In a very tight, faded pants and a printed shirt, with his head smeared with coconut oil, Abdul, the taxi driver was her visitor.

'I just came to see that you're all right,' Abdul said.

'Look,' Zari said impatiently, 'we're going to be handed over to the Indian Army as prisoners. I hate this. Take me to your house or leave me in a refugee camp. I don't want to stay here.'

'OK, let me take you to my home,' Abdul said, 'and see what happens. We are more than ten people in a small house. I don't know whether you'll be able to stay there, but we can try.'

Zari and Abdul left the hotel as stealthily as they could. Although Zari was not wearing any fine outfit or makeup, still she was as distinguished from poor Biharis as from Bengalis.

Her arrival into No. 11 Mirpur was no less than a spectacle for its residents. The word of a lady's arrival spread very fast. All the women, girls and boys had swarmed in front of the small two-room house to get a glimpse of Zari. Abdul had already told Zari that in each household there were an average of eight to ten people.

Taking his mother to a corner, Abdul told her that Zari had no place to go and wanted to stay with them for a few days, till she could find a better place.

Her mother didn't object. As Zari entered the house, she saw that an empty saucepan was burning on a crackling fire, and flies were buzzing on the flour in a flour-kneading bowl, because the girls who were attending to these tasks had run to see Zari.

A heap of black silk lay on the veranda, where a few boys were at work preparing braids to sell. They, too, had taken a brief break from their work to see the 'lady'. There lay on a cot, a consumptive old man with a close-cropped beard, coughing continuously. Abdul's mother, bickering and chasing the boys and girls away, had been able to escort Zari into the room.

They both sat on a mat. Abdul's mother had a typical Bihari accent. She insisted that Zari have her lunch separately. She was offered fried fish, to go with long green salad leaves, pruned cucumber sauce, and goat's milk in a glass covered with a lid. Zari knew that everybody could not be so lucky to have that many dishes, but she could not say anything because she knew that they wouldn't listen to her. To feed the guest even if they had to go hungry was one tradition these poor people were never willing to forego.

Zari knew for certain that, during the curfew that had been continuing for weeks, this family could not have a lot of provisions, but she was still being treated as a special guest.

82

Before leaving for the hospital, Zari had torn her letters and other papers and had thrown them into the basket. Now that basket lay upside down, and the big and small shredded pieces of the poem, *The Lotus,* which Shams had given Zari to translate into Urdu, and Omar's letters, and the articles she had written in which the word 'Integration' came over and over again were all lying trashed.

Shams felt as if similar pieces of trashed papers were stuffed in his brain and he was unable to think clearly.

At last, he heard the telephone, which had been ringing for several minutes. With slow steps, like one walking in his sleep, he went to lift the receiver. And at that moment, his mind, giving him a hopeful jolt, like an electric shock, said, *maybe...Zari!* But it wasn't Zari. It was Ronjhu. '*Joi Bangla,* bhai,' his voice was ringing with delight as he congratulated Shams. Shams felt as if Ronjhu wanted to hug him and enjoy this moment with laughter and mirth. 'Are you listening? There will be a surrender of arms at the Race Course grounds this evening. Do come, please. This is going to be a great historical event.'

But Shams's was dispirited. He only said, 'Ronjhu, my son is dead, and Zari has left me.'

'I'm sorry,' Ronjhu said. 'Where has she gone?'

'Don't know...she isn't at the hospital. She didn't come home. Benu, Puttal...nobody knows where she is.'

Shams could hear the shouts of 'Joi Bangla' and reports of gunshots outside.

'Wait,' Ronjhu said, 'stay home. I'll send my men to find Zari. They will know. They know who is where.'

'Look, if something happens to Zari, I...'

'Nothing will happen to her. They all know she is my sister-in-law.'

Shams could feel the pride in Ronjhu's voice. He took pride in being a pure Bengali and the leader of the masses. He didn't know that he had had a Turk as his great-great-grandfather centuries ago. He wasn't a pure Bengali after all.

'Shams bhai, I'm very busy today,' Ronjhu said. 'People are coming to put garlands around my neck and congratulate me. But I'll try to find Zari only because you care for her.'

'Thanks. But do you hear the shots?' Shams said. 'We got our Bangladesh. Why all these killings now?'

'Patience, bhai, patience! This is the cost of independence. Stay home. I'll ring you again.'

The phone was disconnected. Shams put down the receiver and looked out of the window. The crowd, shouting slogans, was surging ahead on the road. Even small boys, who might never have handled an air gun, were holding rifles in their hands. Most of them were firing shots in the air, dancing like mad.

Only last night he had been reciting the last stanza of a poem by Nazrul Islam, titled 'Ruddy Goose'.

On the deep dark shore of this pain
A love-lorn ruddy goose keeps searching
For his estranged mate
Who calls out to him piercingly

He often used to recited this poem due to the myth associated with the bird that said its male and female live together all day, but separate at night. And then, the female calls out to her mate at the first sign of dawn.

He, too, was anxious to hear from Zari's. But she didn't call. His mate, perhaps, had left him forever!

83

At about three in the afternoon, there was a rumble of heavy trucks on the Mirpur Road. The children went out to watch and came back shouting, 'There are Indian trucks in which soldiers are shouting, you people are independent now...you got your Bangladesh.'

'Be quiet, you idiots, you should be ashamed to say these ominous words?' the old consumptive man rebuked the children.

Zari was surprised that these people still did not know that the Pakistan Army was soon going to surrender! They were still listening to West Pakistan radio, and were being told that the Pakistan Army was advancing on all fronts.

'Grandfather, trucks full of Indian soldiers are going towards Dhaka and the soldiers are saying....'

'Shut up. Don't say another word,' the old man said. 'Let them babble. Come and sit inside, all of you.' All the children huddled together on the veranda at his command.

The local Bengalis attacked Mirpur No. 6 in the evening. The atmosphere rang with cries of '*Allah-o-Akbar*' and '*Joi Bangla*'. The family in Abdul's house was very afraid. They could be attacked too. Abdul had gone out. All others were sitting behind closed doors, fortifying themselves. Men and young boys were holding rifles ready to fight, while women and girls were sitting in dark corners praying.

When it started getting dark, and there was a brief respite from shooting and screaming, Abdul entered the house. His face was very pale. Everybody started questioning him.

By and by he told them that he had gone to his fiancée's house in Mirpur No.6. His fiancée's parents had been killed. One of his Bengali friends had, somehow, succeeded in rescuing his fiancée. She was now living in his friend's house in Sauvergaon.

Foregoing his supper, Abdul lay silent on a mat. His brothers and sisters probed him relentlessly about the news of the surrender till he could hold it no longer. 'Yes, It's true. I've seen the tragic ceremony held in the Race Course Ground with my own eyes.'

'Tell us about it.' They all whispered.

'At first General Niazi signed the papers then he took out the revolver from his pocket and gave it to General Arora. As he turned away, someone from among the crowd hurled his shoe at him. Local people lifted Gen. Arora over their shoulders. The Bengali public threw garlands around the necks of the bearded Sikh soldiers, and hugged them. The caps of Gurkha soldiers were decorated with flowers, and petals of marigold flowers were scattered over their heads.'

Abdul was silent as his voice choked with grief. Resting their chins on their knees, the girls and Zari shed tears, and small children looked sorrowfully at all of them.

At eight in the evening, the whole family gathered to hear the news from Radio Pakistan. They heard no news of the surrender. Everybody was puzzled and looked at Abdul skeptically. Was he telling the truth about the surrender? Radio Pakistan had just declared that the army was going to fight to the last man.

'The truth is that in Dhaka not a single shot has been fired by a military man,' Abdul said.

'Is rioting still going on in other parts of the city?' Abdul's mother asked.

'Yes, attacks were launched in Nawab Gunj, Dhan Mandi, Naya Palton, T&T colony, Mohammedpur and some other places. Young Bengali boys, who till yesterday were not allowed to go out of their houses unaccompanied, are attacking Bihari houses, mugging the residents at gunpoint, snatching the keys of their cars and driving them without drivers' licenses.

At night, there was a meeting arranged among the men and boys of the neighbouring houses. They gave instructions to the women about what to do if their houses were raided. When Zari asked what was happening, Abdul's sister told her that they had gone to help those who were being attacked, and a few men and boys were left to guard the neighborhood.

'We don't have a chance of being attacked tonight, my brother has told me, but if we are attacked, my brother has also directed me what to do.'

'What?' Zari asked.

'My brother is an electrician. He has taught me how to cut the live electric wire that comes from across the street to our courtyard. I'll hold the live wire in my hand. A woman will hold me and all other women will hold each other, so that we'll all be electrocuted.'

Zari felt a shock as if she were electrocuted at that moment. All other women were calmly praying.

'How can you say that so coolly?' Zari said.

'We have no choice. Our brothers made the plans long ago, and we have accepted that since that time.'

Although it was never very cold in Dhaka, it was rather a chilly December night. The quilts and blankets in the house were old and insufficient. A lantern, with its wick lowered, was kept behind the door. Stray gunshots were heard all night. The old man kept coughing, the children kept making a trip to the toilet and the women kept awake, praying for their own safety and for the safe return of their male relatives.

The night passed without any incident. The men and the young boys returned home in the morning. Abdul's sister, confiding in Zari, told her that Abdul, after taking his breakfast, intended to go to see his fiancée.

Zari went to Abdul. 'I have now decided to go to the relief camp of Mohammedpur. I could look after the sick and the wounded there. I had never imagined that living in Mirpur could be this dangerous.'

'The Mohammedpur area isn't safe either,' Abdul said, 'but if you want to go, I can take you there.'

'Yes, I would like to stay in a camp,' Zari said.

She wore a white *sari* and decorated her forehead with a red *bindi* like a Bengali woman. She thanked all the members of the family and said farewell to each one of them. After covering her head fully with the *sari*, she got into Abdul's taxi to go to the camp where Biharis, pushed out of their houses, had taken asylum.

84

At first a refugee camp was opened in Mohammedpur School. Later, it was shifted to the bamboo slums of the same locality. This camp consisted of small rooms made of bamboo and mat, in an irregular circle. These were divided into still smaller rooms, depending upon the requirement of the families, till they had become indivisible. The rooms were very dark without any windows or ventilators. There was no free flow of air or cross ventilation. The mat walls and supports had already turned black due to heavy rains.

The drains coming out of these slums, passed before each house and went around the whole compound. They were always filled with dirty water and filth.

The circular holes used for sewerage always overflowed. In the narrow alleys between two huts women dressed in colored *saris*, cleaned their utensils with dust and talked of migrating to Pakistan. There was no proper kitchen in the house so the narrow entrance was used as one. A lot of T.B patients from different provinces had arrived in these camps, and were quietly spreading their disease among fellow residents.

The small children suffered from rickets due to malnutrition. These poor children walked along these alleys with large hungry eyes, swollen bellies and shrivelled hands. Diarrhea was very common. Zari lived in one of the hospital rooms and helped the inmates of the Mohammedpur camp as much as she could. Refugees of the camp, and those outside, called her Sister Zarina. This was the name she had given them. In the beginning, the inmates of the camp viewed her with suspicion, thinking that a foreign lady reporter had come in a white *sari*, to gather news material and enjoy their misfortunes, but gradually, they came to know that she was as homeless as they were. She wouldn't talk of her sorrows but miseries are revealed in one's gait, in manners and in gestures. She was a good listener and the patients lying in their beds in the camp, and in the hospital, narrated their tales of woe to her voluntarily.

In those days, even dogs, cats and vultures were nauseating. Corpses rotted among the reeds. As cranes and sea birds swooped down to catch fish, human fingers stuck in their beaks. People stumbled on human skulls while walking. Crows, vultures, ants and dust seemed kindlier and more considerate, as they obliterated the bodies violated by their own kind.

There was a nine-year-old girl in the hospital who was very reserved and reticent. One day Zari asked the girl, 'What's your name?'

'Siddiqa,' the girl replied.

'Are you alone?'

'Yes,' she remained silent for some time and then said, 'Uncle has killed all members of my family.'

'Your own uncle?' Zari asked.

'No, he was a neighbour but we called him uncle. He was my father's friend. One day, he came to our house, and said to my mother. "Sister, let me have a cup of tea." My mother prepared tea and put it on the table. He picked up a cup and started sipping it. In the meantime, other people who were strangers to us came and joined him.

'Then suddenly he addressed us, "Now, all of you form one single line."

"Don't indulge in such a cruel joke, friend." Father said to him.

'Uncle poked his bayonet in father's chest, and thundered, "I'm not your friend. Stand in a line," he shouted angrily.

'Father, and the rest of us stood in a line. A few men took my mother and sisters away. Father and my brother were shot dead.

'When I began to cry, Uncle took me to another room. He tried to appease me, gave me a toffee. Then he said, "These clothes are not good enough for you, I'll get you a new dress." The girl was silent and spoke no more. Zari waited for her to resume but the pause grew longer.

'Well, what happened, then? Tell me.' Zari said kindly.

'Then, I don't know. I had kept my eyes shut,' the girl said and turned around.

Zari put her hand to her mouth and sobbed for this little girl who was still calling her rapist *uncle*.

85

A person from the camp had informed Zari that there was a visitor to see her. Thinking that it could only be Abdul she went outside, crossed the huts and reached the entrance door. The visitor stood outside the camp door. The light of the street lamp fell on him passing through the cluster of trees. Zari didn't remember seeing the visitor before.

'I'm Ronjhu,' he said in English. In a flash, Zari's mind went back to the picture in the drawing room, but this man didn't have a beard, nor did he have long hair.

'We were searching for you everywhere,' he said. 'I came to know that a lady of your description was seen in this camp. I informed Shams bhai,' Ronjhu said, weighing each and every word. 'He asked me to go and meet you and bring you home...only if you want to.'

'Why were you looking for me?' Zari asked.

'For your safety, what else?' Ronjhu replied.

Zari felt so disappointed. She wanted to hear that Shams was miserable without her, that he was dying to meet her but he gave the message that she could come home only if she wanted to.

'No thanks,' she said, 'I am perfectly safe in the camp. Anything else?' she asked coldly.

'Let me tell you the truth. The future of the inmates of the camps is very uncertain,' Ronjhu said. 'Nobody knows whether they'll ever be able to go to Pakistan. They might have to stay here for months. We can arrange for your safe journey if you want.'

'On what terms?' she enquired.

'There's no condition. A man will go with you. You'll be safe in all places. We know you are weak. A nice place has been reserved for your comfort in Nepal. You can stay there as long as you wish. After that, through the Pakistan embassy in Kathmandu, you can either go to your friend Nargis, in London, or directly to Pakistan.'

'I have no money,' Zari replied.

'It can be arranged. You have only to give a letter of authority to someone for the money that is in your bank account and we'll take care of all your expenses.'

Zari felt a shiver run down her spine. She wrapped her *sari* tight around her.

'Is this the message from Shams?' Zari kept her tone firm.

'Yes, you can say that.' Bending down, Ronjhu began cleaning the mud from his boot.

'What if I don't do it?' Zari asked him.

Ronjhu stood straight, as if to talk face-to-face. 'Think it over. The government will confiscate your money in any case. Take it as a price for sending you safe and sound to Pakistan, or as the last good deed you would be doing for your husband.'

Ronjhu tried to read the expression on her face in the semi-darkness. Then, he said casually, 'Would you like to meet Shams bhai and consult him?'

'Why should I consult him about leaving him when he has already decided.' Zari couldn't see Ronjhu's smile and didn't hear the deep sigh of relief.

'How did you come to this place? Were you not afraid of entering this camp area?' Zari asked.

'Nobody knows me here. I am one of those who work from behind the scenes. Still, I have come fully prepared,' Ronjhu said. He then continued, 'Be ready, the same time tomorrow. The person who will go with you is a trusted man. He'll receive good payment for his job. Please keep the letter of authority ready and any other letters you want to send to friends and acquaintances here.'

'Can I take a person of my choice with me?' Zari asked him.

'Who, for example?'

'Chachaji, my uncle.'

'He is already in custody of the Indian army and is taken to one of the prison camps in India.'

'Ah, what sad news!' Zari said.

'It was good for him. He will be safe there. The prisoners will be sent home sooner or later, especially the civilians. He had left a message for you and Shams that he had decided to hand himself over to the Indian Army because he could see no other way to go back to his country.'

'He left a message for me? It means he didn't know that I was missing.'

'I think he was kept in the dark.'

'That was good,' Zari said.

'What about Suraj, Ikram's servant, or Abdul, a taxi driver, who brought me here from the Intercontinental Hotel, can any of them go with me?'

'Ikram's servant can't be entrusted with this job without informing him, I'll try to search for Abdul, if he is found, he can be sent with you.'

Zari thought for a moment. 'Abdul goes to Hotel Intercontinental daily. The newspaper correspondents there know him well.'

'Well, sister, till tomorrow, good-bye.' Smiling surreptitiously, Ronjhu walked away. By helping Zari, Ronjhu had saved his brother from Zari for the rest of his life. After Ronjhu left, Zari went back into her room again and kept thinking. God knows what more trials awaited her. Could these people be trusted? Siddiqa was sleeping wrapped in a torn sheet. Her dried thin face, pathetic eyes were closed. She would never have faith in any relationship. And who would she trust?

A few pages were fluttering in the strong wind. Holding them to the light of the lamp, she tried to read. It was one of Ghalibs' letters from an Urdu book that described the conditions in Delhi in 1857, when the Indians rebelled against the British.

> Mutiny by the black, an uproar of the white, a mischief of the demolition of houses, a calamity of an epidemic, a disaster of a famine, and now this rain sums up everything. Dust rises in the Lal Kuwan locality, with not a soul in view. Once it had been a crowded village. If the residents of the place have escaped the bullets, God only knows, where they have gone!

Zari gathered and read the torn pieces. There wasn't any difference between the conditions of 1857 and 1971.
The letter continued.

An army unit of 500 soldiers invaded the city, repeatedly. First, the army of the rebels, in which the credibility of the citizens was lost; the second army was of the Khakis, in which life and property, chastity, land and the signs of life, were all annihilated. The third one was of famine, in which thousands died of starvation. The fourth one was of cholera, which accounted for the wellfed, the fifth was of fever, in which endurance and strength were gone, it hasn't left the city yet. The feudal lords, pensioners, rich and artisans, none was spared.

I'm afraid of giving details. Except foodgrains and cow-dung cakes, there's nothing, which hasn't been taxed.

Ask me, what sorrow is: distress of death, of separation, of daily bread, and of honor.

Zari took up pen and paper and began writing,

Ask me what sorrow is, Benu! When I read the newspaper, I feel as if it is about another world, in some other language, unintelligible to me. People are demanding that the supporters of Pakistan be tried like the Nazis were tried, after the Second World War. On 10 January, Sheikh Mujib, the father of Bangladesh, reached Dhaka, and went straight to the Race Course ground. All the newspapers ran the headlines, 'Bangladesh smiles. Today, we salute the conquerors, and remember the martyrs.

'Who are the conquerors and who are the martyrs? Benu dear, the idea you had accepted from the very first day, I haven't, till now. In such a situation, tell me, what justification is there for me to stay here. I haven't yet learned to live with hate. Shams is now a worshipper of the new order, so we have parted ways. My greetings to Ikram.

Your's
Zari

She also wrote a letter of authority in Shams name, and a few more lines for him.
Then she went to bed thinking about was and what her chachaji and what was in store for her in the future.

86

Switching on his bed lamp, Shams was trying to read the newspaper. The paper, which once was the 'Pakistan Observer,' became 'The Observer' on 18 December 1971, and then changed its name to 'Bangladesh Observer' from 23 December 1971.

Zari was not there beside him, but all her things were in their places. Her exquisite *saris* and *shalwar* suits hung nicely in the cupboard, and her shoes, purses, jewelry and perfumes were arranged in drawers. Each night, as she came out from the bathroom in her nightgown, a typical fragrance used to diffuse in the room. For the past many nights, Shams was missing that fragrance.

He had become lonely, as he had never been before.

The door bell rang and Shams found Ronjhu at the door unexpectedly. He confessed that he had made arrangements to send Zari out of Bangladesh, because she didn't want to live with Shams any more. And at that time, the lives of both Zari and Shams were in danger. They had worked for national integration and were being accused of supporting Pakistan and having close contacts with its army.

'I don't think your intentions were so honorable,' Shams said sarcastically.

'Speak gently,' Ronjhu said. 'We have to make sacrifices for our freedom. This is what happens in a revolution. People die and get separated. This had happened during the French and the Russian revolutions.'

'But I'll never forgive you for what you have done to me.'

'I've only saved your life,' Ronjhu said angrily. 'We know that you're trying to contact Pakistani authorities through other countries, even today.'

'How do you know?'

'You know how I know. Didn't you try to send letters to your wife through different means?' Ronjhu said.

'Yes, I did this because I cannot send a letter direct to her. She's my wife. I'm not conspiring with the Government of Pakistan. Does this mean that those letters have been seized and haven't reached Zari?'

'I don't know that.' Ronjhu said calmly.

'You should be ashamed of yourself. How long is this going to go on?'

'I don't know.' Ronjhu said abruptly, 'Let me take leave now. I had come only to hand you the letter I was entrusted with.'

Ronjhu handed an envelope to Shams. 'Remember, I have saved your life. I didn't know that I would be held responsible for this generosity. Good-bye.' Banging the door, he walked out of the room.

Shams turned the envelope over a number of times. It had neither the sender's name and address nor the date. There was only his address in Zari's hand on the envelope. Shams opened the envelope and started reading. It was neither a letter nor a message, but was perhaps a questionnaire from all women to all men of all times.

> What do you men want from us women? At times you want us to be like water that takes the shape of the vessel in which it is poured. At times you wish us to turn into steel, not yielding to others, but dissolve like salt in water whenever you want us to. You desire us to look beautiful and dazzle your eyes at your wish. You would like us to be strong, but at the same time be soft like silk, to be squeezed in your hand. You want her to say 'yes' to your demands, be a slave to your commands, change with you when you change your ideology, live at your pleasure, and die at your mercy. Think! Even God doesn't demand so much from man. He keeps you alive as long as He wants to and brings death to you when He wishes. It is easier to die one's own death, than to die at someone else's command.

Shams read the letter again and again and then put it under his pillow before going to sleep.

87

Leaving Zari and Abdul at the Nepal Border, the Indian agent had gone back. Zari was now like the princess whom a demon had imprisoned between the mountains in the beautiful Pokhar valley.

In the evening, she would sit with her face towards the long, green shadowed lake. In the evenings, the water of the lake would gradually turn black, like the skin of a snake. The mountains behind the lake, which looked enchanting during the day, would become grim and appalling at night. The barking of dogs and howling of jackals would make the night fearful. Then, the moon would climb up from behind the mountains, and everything would be bathed in its light and look heavenly.

In the morning, when the sun rose on the snow-clad peak of Annapurna, it would look as if snow was on fire.

Zari was living in a house standing on strong bamboos and made of beautiful mats. In front of the house, there was a latticed balcony made from bamboo sticks, on which clothes were hung to dry. The cattle chewed its fodder in a corner in front of the house, the turkeys strutted with swollen bellies, and hens pecked at the rubbish. The only means of transport for the local chieftain was a huge black elephant that walked on the paths among the trees, like a drunkard, shaking his big ears like fans.

As long as Zari stayed here, she slept on the ground like them and ate the same food they ate, mostly dairy stuff, vegetables and fruit. She also separated cottonseed from cotton, like them, but she could never bring herself to wear the type of clothes they wore. The women and girls wrapped themselves in a single piece of cloth, which was wound around their chest and waist. On the back it had a space to comfortably fit a small child.

It was amazing for Zari to know that this village, though far more picturesque than Topi, had the same qualities her ancestral village had: the snow-clad peaks, hills fully covered with trees, and in their shade, green deep lakes and level plains at the same time. The mud houses with husked roofs, and two storied red brick houses hidden behind the bamboo and orange groves were somewhat similar too.

When she felt comfortable with the people there she let Abdul go. She stayed there for about a month and at last, with the help of the chieftain was able to get a seat in a plane for Pakistan. She flew to Rawalpindi and from there, came to Abbotabad in a bus to her own Akbar Manzil

Once in Abbotabad Zari often went to the family graveyard.

Today, Zari came there with two envelopes in her hand; one was from Nargis and the other one most probably from Shams. It bore stamps from many different countries. She stood at the head of Khushal Khan's grave. Rain had fallen during the night. The fresh red and green colors of the pieces of cloth tied to the graves of the elders and on branches of trees looked fresh and elegant after drying. The tall cypresses had grown taller during these years. Once Shams had made a promise to the inmates of these graves that he would love Zari and cherish her till death do them part.

Shams's letter might as well have come from some other planet, and might give quite a contradictory message. Zari didn't have the courage to open the envelope, nor did she have the nerve to tear it up without opening it.

If it were his letter, it would be the first letter since she had left East Pakistan, which was now Bangladesh. She was guessing about the writing inside. He might have written, *since there had been no trace of you and Meraj, for the sake of her daughter, Laila, I've married Shoshi.*

She ought to open the letter. She would decide, but as she was about to do so, something within her would say, 'No, not yet, please.'

She decided to open both letters at the same time. One might give her strength to endure the other one!

She was fearless once, made major decisions without consulting others, but now she felt weak and vulnerable. It's fine, she told herself—at times, even fearless and courageous people can feel weak and frightened.

88

'There she is.' Shezzy was the first to see Zari.

Zari looked at the approaching group. Aijaz had put his hand around Neely as she walked cautiously on the narrow path. Obviously, she was pregnant. Shezzy and Nasir followed them. They were both doctors, so Aijaz and Neely must be feeling very safe in their company.

Zari was overjoyed to see them coming.

'This is such a pleasant surprise,' she said as she advanced to meet them. She embraced Shezzy and kissed her. In the meantime, as Neely came close to her, Zari glanced affectionately at her protruding belly and said, 'My favorite niece,' and embraced and caressed her.

Aijaz watched Zari's affection to his wife with mixed feelings, a little sorrow, but a lot of joy and satisfaction. 'When did you arrive? Where are you staying? With Omar Chachaji?'

'Yes,' Nasir said.

'All of you will be my guests tonight. My house might not be in perfect condition, but I assure you that you wouldn't be uncomfortable there. I have many rooms, lots of comforters and hand-made quilts that ought to be used. Besides, I have a good cook. Won't you stay with me?'

'Sure, Aunt Zari, we will,' Neely said.

Shezzy thought that there is no need to say yes to her because when Zari suggests something, it is as good as settled.

But just then, Nasir said, 'We'll stay with you on one condition.'

'What's that?' Zari asked.

'You'll go with us to my village to meet my mother. We are all going there tomorrow.'

'I accept your condition,' Zari said laughingly. 'I can't find the words to express how happy I am to see you all.'

'Same here,' Everybody said.

'Today I understand Chachaji's philosophy,' Zari said. 'He used to say, "Life flows like a river. Generations come and go. One generation gives so much to the next, that its contribution can't be properly assessed."' Zari stood a little higher than the others and they all stood facing her. Neely suddenly thought that when the apostles in the past delivered their sermons standing on such natural platforms, the scene would have been similar to this one.

Then she said, 'Let's go into the house.' She took the lead and they all followed.

First, they offered prayers at her parents' graves, under the shade of trees laden with yellow plums. Then they all entered into Akbar Manzil.

Most of the rooms were locked. Zari escorted them into her bedroom. But first, she hid the sealed envelope under a stack of books. The room was decorated tastefully. The framed embroidery done by her mother was now hanging in her room.

They talked about their past most of the time...how Aijaz had fallen in love with little Neely and how Nasir and Shezzy had to hide their love till Jawwad was dead. After Jawwad's death, it would be only natural for them to unite. The happiest thing was that Zari approved of this marriage though she was not very comfortable with Neely's. Neely was too young for Aijaz, but by and by she came around when she saw the love and devotion between the two.

Zari avoided talking about her recent past, and nobody else touched the subject, knowing well that it would be too painful for her.

89

Next day the whole party left for Nasir's village. After everybody was greeted by Qudsia and settled in the veranda, Nasir went to her and said, 'Mother, I've just seen a person sitting on a rock at the bank of the river. He wants to talk to you.'

'Me, why?' Qudsia was surprised.

'I don't know. Perhaps he knows you.'

'Who is he? How does he know me? You ought to have asked him.'

'But he seems to be a good man. He is a stranger to me. He might not be to you. There is no harm in talking to him.'

'Why should I? You should have asked him what business he had with me.'

'He is a gentleman. Mother, you should not be a coward. Face the realities of life, please go and see him.' Then, he said laughing. 'I'll be watching from here. If he misbehaves with you, I'll jump right there to help you.'

'You naughty boy!' Qudsia said lovingly. 'I was thinking that he might harm you through me.'

'Mother, I've told you so many times not to worry about me, nobody can harm me through you. I want you to be absolutely free from all fears and inhibitions. Do whatever you wish to do, go wherever you want to go. You are not confined anymore, and nobody is going to judge you. I promise you that. Go, and talk with that man.'

Qudsia threw a white silk stole over the *duppatta*, and slowly began to walk down the stone steps. Nasir had built these steps at the place where once there had only been only a steep slope.

Qudsia walked down the steps carefully.

The stranger sat with his face toward the river.

Who could he be, An old servant, a friend of her late husband or a distant relative? When she reached the last few steps, the stranger turned and gazed at her. Qudsia strained her mind to recollect his face.

'*Assalam-o-alaikum*, my name is Omar Khan.'

Oh! Qudsia felt as if the steps were slipping from under her feet. She sat down then and there. Omar slowly walked up to her. He did not wait for Qudsia to speak.

He looked at her, sat on a step below her and started talking.

He told her how many times he had tried to see her. He told her about his marriage with Zeb Quadri in such a casual way as if he had been meeting with Qudsia every day. The waves were dancing around the jutting out rocks as if trying to move them but the rocks stood firm, their roots being deep in the earth.

'Tell me, how did you bear the brunt of loneliness for such a long time?' Omar asked.

'My English teacher, Sister Patricia, wanted us to keep a diary as an exercise in writing. I used to write the diary during those lonely nights in my past life and felt as if I were reliving it. You can say that I gathered the pearls of recollection during the day and strung them together at night.'

'Did you write about me?'

'Not much. I thought you didn't care for me. I wrote about major and minor incidents of my childhood. I also wrote something about you and my brother who had died in a crash. I wrote about my wedding and the incident when I tried to escape from my husband's prison. And I also wrote about things like how each and every blade of grass on our lawn withered each winter and how they revived and flourished each spring. How daffodils grew in a circle at the center of our lawn and how the gardener tied and gently folded green, onion-like stalks before the end of the season. How all the plants sprouted again each spring, once again forming that perfect circle and how their white flowers stooped to view each other with their yellow eyes—things like that.'

'It would be a very interesting diary to read.'

'Yes, for those who enjoy that kind of stuff—like I wrote about the fog spreading over the lawn in winter, reaching up to the veranda, engulfing everything, and about the dewdrops lying on the grass like tiny pebbles along the avenues. You may not believe it, but even today, I feel I can bend down and touch them and that I can pick those bunches of *Amaltas* hanging down from the trees in our garden, reaching to the ground.'

'Go on, tell me some more.'

'Each year, very early in the morning, we used to get ready to go to the passing-out parade of the Air Force cadets. The whole of Risalpur came out in colorful dress. The planes stood behind the lines of the parading cadets, while the pleasant, cool morning breeze brushed across our faces.

'The whole town gazing at the sky presented a wonderful sight. Thereafter, a tea party was arranged at the Mess, and the cadets came to meet their parents and tried to talk to us girls.'

'I am enjoying your stories now as you are telling them. Anything else?'

'There were thousands of things. To probe your mind daily, to write your thoughts down, it was very helpful—almost therapeutic. I wrote about birds, about butterflies and about our pets.'

'Qudsia, listen!' Omar said leaning forward a little. 'We couldn't share our lives, but can't we share each other's writings? I am writing a novel based upon my thoughts, and recollection. After the 1971 war I was captured and was kept in a prison camp in India. I've seen strange aspects of human life there, and also studied the behavior of those animals that came into our camp. You read my novel and let me read your diary.'

'Yes, I would like to share it with you but I don't know whether you'd enjoy reading about the daily routine of my home life: the scenes in the garden about the squirrels chasing each other and the butterflies hovering over the tall hollyhocks and swinging around honey-suckle plants. Do you know that the sound of the ball hitting the tennis court wall where I practiced, still rings in my ears!'

'I can imagine how lonely you must be all those years.'

'Yes, there was no one to talk to. I felt as if I had lost the power of speech. Now, I feel that I have become very talkative.'

'I wish you would talk to me more about those nice and pleasant things.' He stood up, gazed at the river, then turned his eyes toward the house. 'Everything is the same as it used to be... the same river, the same rocks and the same terrace. How many times I came here in hope of meeting you and was sadly disappointed.' Omar said.

'I had once made a pattern of pop art,' Qudsia said. 'On my painting, I had glued memorabilia like Papa's coat buttons, Mummy's earrings, a piece from the shirt I wore on the night of Obaid's plane crash and a few strands of your hair I found stuck to the brush the last time you came to see us.'

'Oh,' Omar said. 'I still remember your beautiful black shirt with golden threads woven into the fabric.'

'How strange that you remembered the shirt but forgot its wearer.'

'No, I didn't forget you,' Omar said sadly, 'but we'll talk of painful things some other day, such as love and separation.'

'Do you think love is painful?'

'Love is a consuming passion, a loser's game. The wisest and the most practical person, if he is in love, loses all sense of his gain. When I heard the news of your marriage, I was completely lost for days and the strange thing was that I came to know for sure then that I was really in love with you.'

'There is no point in talking about those days now,' Qudsia said. 'I must go now. Nasir didn't tell me who wanted to see me.'

'I know. He promised me not to tell you. I wanted to surprise you. Even at this age, surprises feel wonderful, don't they?'

'Yes they do.'

'I was also afraid that you might refuse to see me. That would have been very disappointing.'

'May be, maybe not,' Qudsia said briefly. 'May I go now?'

'You may. I'll be there presently.'

After Qudsia left, Omar stood for a while gazing at the river. *Love, like time and space, is inevitable and immortal, but at the same time it's evasive too. Like life and time, it belongs to all and yet it belongs to none,* he thought.

Zari took out one of the envelopes from her purse and opened it. It was the letter from Nargis. Nargis had written to Zari from

London. Conditions in Bangladesh were uncertain, so they had decided to settle down in London. They had invited Zari and Shams to London to settle down there.

They had sent photographs of their son. Dressed in thick woolen sweaters that looked like loose quilted coats, he was sitting in his pram with snow all around. Zari could only think of one thing at the time: wasn't it a tragedy that people who had created a new country with such passion now wanted to stay away from it!

Some time in the future these children, or their children's children, would certainly go to Bangladesh, Zari thought, looking at the pictures of Nagis's son.

Then somehow, she found the courage to open the second envelope. It was the letter from Shams. He had written a very emotional letter. He was desperate without her. He wanted to be with her at any cost. He had suggested that they could live in Pakistan, in Bangladesh, in England or in the United states, wherever Zari wanted to live.

Yes, she wanted to be with him too. But she was from Pakistan, Shams would be an alien in Pakistan, while she would be an alien in Bangladesh and they would both be aliens in any other country, although they were both descendents of same *Miyan Sahib* who had come to India with Bakhtiar Khilji, centuries ago.

THE END